ROBERT SILVERBERG and KAREN HABER

SCIENCE FICTION
THE BEST OF 2002

ROBERT SILVERBERG's many novels include *The Alien Years*; the most recent volume in the Majipoor Cycle, *The King of Dreams*; the bestselling Lord Valentine trilogy; and the classics *Dying Inside* and *A Time of Changes*. *Sailing to Byzantium*, a collection of some of his award-winning novellas, was published by ibooks in 2000. *Science Fiction 101—Robert Silverberg's Worlds of Wonder*, an examination of the novellas that inspired him as a young writer, was published in March 2001, followed by *Cronos*, a collection of three time-travel pieces published in August 2001. He has been nominated for the Nebula and Hugo awards more times than any other writer; he is a five-time winner of the Nebula and a four-time winner of the Hugo.

KAREN HABER is the acclaimed editor of the Hugo Award-nominated *Meditations on Middle Earth*, and the forthcoming *Explorations of The Matrix*. She also created the bestselling *The Mutant Season* series of novels, of which she co-authored the first volume with her husband, Robert Silverberg. She is a respected journalist and an accomplished fiction writer. Her short fiction has ap-peared in *The Maga...* *...n, Full Spectrum 2*, and

FANTASY AND SCIENCE FICTION
published by ibooks, inc.:

Science Fiction: The Best of 2001
Fantasy: The Best of 2001
Robert Silverberg & Karen Haber, Editors

The Ultimate Cyberpunk
Pat Cadigan, Editor

The Ultimate Halloween
Marvin Kaye, Editor

SCIENCE FICTION
THE BEST OF 2002

ROBERT SILVERBERG
and KAREN HABER
Editors

ibooks
new york
www.ibooks.net

DISTRIBUTED BY SIMON & SCHUSTER, INC.

Contents

CONTENTS

INTRODUCTION

This is the second in an annual series of anthologies intended to bring together in one convenient volume the best science-fiction stories of the year. It is one of three such anthologies now being published, and, like the other two, it reflects the tastes and prejudices of editors who have had decades of experience in reading and writing science fiction. That these three anthologies have such widely differing contents is a tribute not only to the ability of experts to disagree but also to the wealth of fine shorter material being produced today in the science-fiction world.

Such annual anthologies are a long-standing tradition in science fiction. The first of all the Year's Best Science Fiction anthologies appeared in the summer of 1949. It was edited by Everett F. Bleiler and T.E. Dikty, a pair of scholarly science-fiction readers with long experience in the field, and it was called, not entirely appropriately (since it drew entirely on material published in 1948), *The Best Science Fiction Stories: 1949*.

Science fiction then was a very small entity indeed—a handful of garish-looking magazines with names like *Planet Stories* and *Thrilling Wonder Stories*, a dozen or so books a year produced by semi-professional publishing houses run by old-time s-f fans, and the very occasional short story by the likes of Robert A. Heinlein in *The Satur-*

day Evening Post or some other well-known slick magazine. So esoteric a species of reading-matter was it that Bleiler and Dikty found it necessary to provide their book, which was issued by the relatively minor mainstream publishing house of Frederick Fell, Inc., with two separate introductory essays explaining the nature and history of science fiction to uninitiated readers.

In those days science fiction was at its best in the short lengths, and the editors of *The Best Science Fiction: 1949* had plenty of splendid material to offer. There were two stories by Ray Bradbury, both later incorporated in *The Martian Chronicles*, and Wilmar Shiras's fine superchild story "In Hiding," and an excellent early Poul Anderson story, and one by Isaac Asimov, and half a dozen others, all of which would be received enthusiastically by modern readers. The book did fairly well, by the modest sales standards of its era, and the Bleiler-Dikty series of annual anthologies continued for another decade or so.

Toward the end of its era the Bleiler-Dikty collection was joined by a very different sort of Best of the Year anthology edited by Judith Merril, whose sophisticated literary tastes led her to go far beyond the s-f magazines, offering stories by such outsiders to the field as Jorge Luis Borges, Jack Finney, Donald Barthelme, and John Steinbeck cheek-by-jowl with the more familiar offerings of Asimov, Theodore Sturgeon, Robert Sheckley, and Clifford D. Simak. The Merril anthology, inaugurated in 1956, also lasted about a decade; and by then science fiction had become big business, with new magazines founded, shows like *Star Trek* appearing on network television, dozens and then hundreds of novels published every year. Since the 1960s no year has gone by without its Best of the Year col-

INTRODUCTION

lection, and sometimes two or three simultaneously. Such distinguished science-fiction writers as Frederik Pohl, Harry Harrison, Brian Aldiss, and Lester del Rey took their turns at compiling annual anthologies, along with veteran book editors like Donald A. Wollheim and Terry Carr.

In modern times the definitive Year's Best Anthology has been the series of encyclopedic collections edited by Gardner Dozois since 1984. Its eighteen mammoth volumes so far provide a definitive account of the genre in the past two decades. More recently a second annual compilation has arrived, edited by an equally keen observer of the science-fiction scene, David A. Hartwell. And if there is room in the field for two sets of opinions about the year's outstanding work, perhaps there is room for a third. And so, herewith, yet another Year's Best Science Fiction anthology, in which a long-time writer/editor and his writer/editor wife have gathered a group of the science-fiction stories of 2002 that gave them the greatest reading pleasure.

—Robert Silverberg
—Karen Haber

Tourist

by Charles Stross

Spring-Heeled Jack runs blind, blue fumes crackling from his heels: his right hand, outstretched for balance, clutches a mark's stolen memories. His victim is just sitting up on the hard stones of the pavement, wondering what's happened; maybe he looks after the fleeing youth, but the tourist crowds block the view and in any case he has no hope of catching the mugger. Hit-and-run amnesia is what the polis call it, but to Spring-Heeled Jack it's just more loot to buy fuel for his Russian army-surplus motorised combat boots.

The victim of the mugging sits on the cobblestones clutching his aching temples. *What happened?* he wonders. The universe is a brightly coloured blur of fast-moving shapes augmented by deafening noises. His glasses are rebooting continuously: they panic every eight hundred milliseconds, whenever they realise that they're alone on his personal area network without the comforting support of a memory hub to tell them where to send his incoming sensory feed. Two of his mobile phones are bickering moronically, disputing ownership of his grid bandwidth.

A tall blonde clutching an electric chainsaw sheathed in pink bubble-wrap leans over him curiously: "you alright?" she asks.

1

"I—" he shakes his head, which hurts. "Who am I?" His medical monitor is alarmed because his blood pressure has fallen: his pulse is racing, and a host of other biometrics suggest that he's going into shock.

"I think you need an ambulance," the woman announces. She mutters at her lapel: "phone, call an ambulance." She waves a finger vaguely at the victim then wanders off, chainsaw clutched under one arm, as if embarrassed at the idea of involving herself: typical southern *eacutemigreacute* behaviour in the Athens of the North. The man shakes his head again, eyes closed, as a flock of girls on powered blades skid around him in a elaborate loops. A siren begins to warble, over the bridge to the north.

Who am I? wonders the man on the pavement. "I'm Manfred," he says with a sense of stunned wonder. He looks up at the bronze statue of a man on a horse that looms above the crowds on this busy street corner. Someone has plastered a Hello Cthulhu! holo on the plaque that names its rider: languid fluffy pink tentacles wave at him in an attack of *kawai*. "I'm Manfred—Manfred. My memory. What's happened to my memory?" Elderly Malaysian tourists point at him from the open top deck of a passing tour bus. He suddenly burns with a sense of horrified urgency. *I was going somewhere*, he recalls. *What was I doing?* It was amazingly important, he thinks, but he can't remember what exactly it was. He was going to see someone about—it's on the tip of his tongue—

Welcome to the eve of the third decade: a time of chaos.

Most of the thinking power on the planet is now manufactured rather than born; there are ten microprocessors for every human being, and the number is doubling every

2

fourteen months. Population growth in the developing world has stalled, the birth rate dropping below replacement level: in the wired nations, more forward-looking politicians are looking for ways to enfranchise their nascent AI base.

Space exploration is still stalled on the cusp of the second recession of the century. The Malaysian government has announced the goal of placing an Imam on Mars within ten years, but nobody else cares enough to try.

The Space Settlers Society is still trying to interest DisneyCorp in the media rights to their latest L5 colony plan, unaware that there's already a colony out there and it isn't human: first-generation uploads, Californian spiny lobsters in wobbly symbiosis with elderly expert systems, thrive aboard an asteroid mining project established by the Franklin Trust. (The lobsters had needed sanctuary, away from a planet overflowing with future-shocked primates. In return for Franklin beaming a copy of their state vector out over the deep space tracking network, they agreed to run his cometary Von Neumann factory.)

Two years ago JPL, the ESA, and the uploaded lobster colony on comet Kruschev-7 picked up an apparently artificial signal from outside the solar system; most people don't know, and of those who do, even fewer care. After all, if NASA can't even put a man on the moon . . .

Portrait of a wasted youth:

Jack is seventeen years and eleven months old. He has never met his father; he was unplanned, and Pa managed to kill himself in a building site accident before the Child Support could garnish his income for the upbringing. His mother raised him in a two bedroom association flat in Hawick. She worked in a call centre when he was young, but business dried up: humans aren't needed on the end of a phone any more. Now she works in a drop-in business shop, stacking shelves for virtual fly-by-nights that come and go like tourists in the Festival season—but humans aren't in demand for shelf stacking either, these days.

His mother sent Jack to a local religious school, where he was regularly excluded and effectively ran wild from the age of twelve. By thirteen, he was wearing a parole cuff for shoplifting: by fourteen he'd broken his collarbone in a car crash while joyriding and the dour presbyterian sheriff sent him to the Wee Frees, who completed the destruction of his educational prospects with high principles and an illicit tawse.

Today he's a graduate of the hard school of avoiding public surveillance cameras, with distinctions in steganographic alibi construction. Mostly this entails high-density crime—if you're going to mug someone, do so where there are so many by-standers that they can't pin the blame on you. But the Polis expert systems are catching up with him: if he keeps it up at this rate, in another four months they'll have a positive statistical correlation that will convince even a jury of his peers that he's guilty as fuck—and then he'll go down to Saughton for four years.

But Jack doesn't understand the meaning of a Gaussian distribution or the significance of a chi-squared test, and the future still looks bright to him as he pulls on the chunky spectacles he ripped off the tourist gawking at the statue on North Bridge. And after a moment, when they begin whispering into his ears in stereo and showing him pictures of the tourist's vision, it looks even brighter.

"Gotta make a deal, gotta close a deal," whisper the glasses. "Get a runner, liberate the potential." Weird graphs in lurid colours are filling up his peripheral vision, like the hallucinations of a drugged marketroid.

"Who the fuck are ye?" asks Jack, intrigued by the bright lights and icons.

"I am you, you are we, got a deal to close," murmur the glasses. "Dow Jones down fifteen points, Federated Confidence up three, incoming briefing on causal decoupling of social control of skirt hem lengths, shaving pattern of beards, and emergence of multidrug antibiotic resistance in gram negative bacilli: accept?"

"Ah can tak it," Jack mumbles, and a torrent of images crashes down on his eyeballs and jackhammers its way in through his ears like the superego of a disembodied giant. Which is actually what he's stolen: the glasses and waist pouch he grabbed from the tourist are stuffed with enough hardware to run the entire internet, circa the turn of the millennium. They've got bandwidth coming out the wazoo, distributed engines running a bazillion inscrutable search tasks, and a whole slew of high-level agents that collectively form a large chunk of the society of mind that is their owner's personality. Their owner is an agalmic entrepreneur, a posthuman genius locii of the net who catalyses value wherever he goes, leaving money trees growing in his footprints. This man doesn't believe in zero-sum games, in a loser for every winner. And Jack has stolen his memories. There are microcams built into the frame of the glasses, pickups in the ear-pieces; everything is spooled into the holographic cache in the belt pack, before being distributed for remote storage. At four months per terabyte, memory storage is cheap: what makes this bunch so unusual is that their owner—Manfred—has cross-indexed them with his agents.

In a very real sense, the glasses *are* Manfred, regardless of the identity of the soft machine with its eyeballs behind the lenses. And it is a very puzzled Manfred picks himself up and, with a curious vacancy in his head—except for a hesitant request for information about accessories for Russian army boots—dusts himself off, and heads for his meeting on the other side of town.

"Something, he is not there, something is *wrong*," says the woman. She raises her mirrorshades and rubs her left eye, visibly worried. With crew-cut hair, and wearing a black trouser suit with narrow lapels, she looks like a G-man from a 1960's conspiracy movie.

Gianni nods and leans back, regarding her from behind his desk. "Manfred are prone to fits of do his own thing with telling nobody in advance," he points out. "Do you have concrete reason to suspect something is wrong?" Despite his words he looks slightly worried. Manfred is a core team member; losing him at this point could be more than embarrassing. Besides, he's a friend—for posthuman values of friendship.

The office translator is good, but it can't provide realtime lip-synch morphing between French and Italian: Annette has to make an effort to listen to his words because the shape of his mouth is all wrong, like a badly-dubbed video. And the desk switches from black ash to rosewood abruptly, halfway across its expanse, and the air currents are all wrong. "His answerphone, it is very good: like Manfred, it does not lie convincingly."

"But it doesn't pass the Turing test. Yet."

"*Non.*" A smile flashes across her face, rapidly replaced by worry lines. "Where can he be? You are relying on him and I—"

The minister prods at the highly polished rosewood

desktop; the woodgrain slips, sliding into a strangely different conformation, generating random dot stereoisograms—messages for his eyes only. "You will find him in Scotland," he says after a moment. "That was on his Outlook. I find it harder to trace his exact whereabouts—the privacy safeguards—but if you, as next of kin by common law, travel in person . . ."

"I go."

The woman in black stands up, surprising a vacuum cleaner that skulks behind her desk. "Au revoir!"

"Ciao."

As she vacates her office the minister flickers off behind her, leaving the far wall the dull grey of a cold display panel. Outside, she's cut off from the shared groupspace that she, and Gianni, and the rest of the team, have established. Gianni is in Rome; she's in Paris, Markus is in Dusseldorf, and Eva's in Wrocklaw. There are others, trapped in digital cells scattered halfway across an elderly continent: but as long as they don't try to shake hands they're free to shout across the office at each other. Their confidences and dirty jokes tunnel through multiple layers of anonymized communication: Gianni can swing the best facilities, and it's a good thing too. He's making his break out of regional politics and into European national affairs: their job—his election team—is to get him a seat on the Confederacy Comission, as Representative for Intelligence Oversight, and push the boundaries of post-humanitarian action outward, into deep space and deeper time. Which makes their casual working conversation profoundly interesting to certain people: the walls have ears, and not all the brains attached to them are human.

Annette is more worried than she's letting on to Gianni. It's unlike Manfred to be out of contact for long: even odder for his receptionist to stonewall her, given that her apartment is the nearest thing to a home he's had for the past couple of years. But something smells fishy. He sneaked out last night, saying it would be an overnight trip, and now he's not answering. *Could it be his ex-wife?* she wonders: but no, there's been no word from the obsessive bitch for months, other than the sarcastic cards she despatches every year without fail, timed to arrive on the birthday of the daughter Manfred has never met. *The music mafia? A letter bomb from the Copyright Enforcement Front?* But no, his medical monitor would have been screaming its head off if anything like that had happened. She's organised things so that he's safe from the intellectual property thieves, lent him the guiding hand he needs. She gets a a warm sense of accomplishment whenever she considers how complementary their abilities are: how much of a mess he was in before he met her for the second time, eyes meeting across a microsat launcher in an abandoned supermarket outside London. But that's exactly why she's worried now. The watchdog hasn't barked . . .

Annette takes a taxi to Charles de Gaulle, uses her parliamentary carte to bump an executive class seat on the next A320 to Turnhouse, Edinburgh's airport. The plane is climbing out over la Manche before it hits her: what if the Franklin Collective isn't as harmless as he thinks?

The hospital emergency suite has a waiting room with green plastic bucket seats and subtractive volume renderings by pre-teens stuck to the walls like surreal Lego sculptures. It's deeply silent, the available bandwidth all sequestrated for medical monitors—there are children crying, periodic sirens wailing as ambulances draw up, and people chattering all around him, but to Manfred it's like being at the bottom of a deep blue pool of quiet. He feels stoned, except there's no euphoria with this drug. Corridor-corner vendors hawk kebab-spitted pigeons next to the chained and rusted voluntary service booth; video cameras watch the blue bivvy bags of the chronic cases lined up next to the nursing station. Alone in his own head, Manfred is frightened and confused.

"I can't check you in 'less you sign the confidentiality agreement," says the triage nurse, pushing an antique clipboard at Manfred's face. Service in the NHS is still free, but steps have been taken to reduce the incidence of scandals: "sign the nondisclosure clause here and here, or the house officer won't see you."

Manfred stares blearily up at the nurse's nose, which is red and slightly inflamed from a nosocomial infection. His phones are bickering again, and he can't remember why; they don't normally behave like this, something must be missing, but thinking about it is hard. "Why am I here?" he asks for the third time.

"Sign it." A pen is thrust into his hand. He focusses on the page, jerks upright as deeply canalized reflexes kick in.

"This is theft of human rights! It says here that the party of the second part is enjoined from disclosing information relating to the operations management triage procedures and processes of the said healthgiving institution, that's you, to any third party—that's the public media—on pain of forfeiture of health benefits pursuant to section two of the Health Service Reform Act. I can't sign this! You could reposess my left kidney if I post on the net about how long I've been in hospital!"

"So don't sign, then." The nurse shrugs, hitches up his sari, and walks away: "enjoy your wait!"

Manfred pulls out his backup phone and stares at its megapixel display. "Something *wrong* here." The keypad beeps as he laboriously inputs opcodes. This gets him into an X.25 PAD, and he has a vague, disturbing memory that hints about where he can go from here—mostly into the long-since decommissioned bowels of NHSNet—but the memories spring a page fault and die, somewhere between fingertips and the moment when understanding dawns. It's a frustrating feeling: his brain is like an ancient car engine with damp spark plugs, turning over and over without catching fire.

The kebab vendor next to Manfred's seating rail chucks a stock cube on his grill; it begins to smoke, aromatic and blue and herbal—cannabinoids to induce tranquility and appetite. Manfred sniffs twice, then staggers to his feet and heads off in search of the toilet, his head spinning. He's mumbling at his wrist watch: "*hello, Guatemala? Get me posology please. Click down my meme tree, I'm confused. Oh shit. Who was I? What happened? Why is everything blurry? I can't find my glasses . . .*"

A gaggle of day-trippers are leaving the leprosy ward, men and women dressed in anachronistic garb: men in dark suits, women in long dresses. All of them wear electric blue disposable gloves and face masks. There's a hum and crackle of encrypted bandwidth emanating from them, and Manfred instinctively turns to follow them. They leave the A&E unit through the wheelchair exit, two ladies escorted by three gentlemen, with a deranged distressed refugee from the twenty-first century shuffling dizzily after. *They're all young*, Manfred realises vaguely.

10

ral wiring, too: this is its third body, and it's getting more realistically uncooperative with every hardware upgrade. Sooner or later it's going to demand a litter tray and start throwing up on the carpet out of spite. "Command override," she says. "Dump event log to my cartesian theatre, minus eight hours to present."

The cat shudders and looks round at her. "Human bitch!" it hisses. Then it freezes in place as the air fills with a bright and silent tsunami of data. Both Annette and Aineko are wired for extremely high bandwidth spread-spectrum optical networking; an observer would see the cat's eyes, and a ring on her left hand, glow blue-white at each other. After a few seconds Annette nods to herself and wiggles her fingers in the air, navigating a time sequence only she can see. Aineko hisses jealousy at her then stands and stalks away, tail held high.

"Curiouser and curiouser," Annette hums to herself. She intertwines her fingers, pressing obscure pressure-points on knuckle and wrist, then sighs and rubs her eyes. "He left here under his own power, looking normal," she calls to the cat. "Who did he say he was going to see?" The cat sits in a beam of sunlight falling in through the high glass window, pointedly showing her its back. "*Merde*. If you're not going to help him—"

"Try the Grass Market," sulks the cat. "He was going to see the Franklin Collective. Much good they'll do him . . ."

A man wearing second-hand Chinese combat fatigues and a horribly expensive pair of glasses bounces up a flight of damp stone steps beneath a keystone that announces the building to be a Salvation Army hostel. He bangs on the door, his voice almost drowned out by the pair of Cold War Reenactment Society MiGs that are

13

buzzing the castle up the road: "open up, ye cunts! Ye've got a deal comin'!"

A peephole set in the door at eye level slides to one side, and a pair of beady black-eyed video cameras peer out at him. "Who are you and what do you want?" the speaker crackles.

"I'm Macx," he says: "you've heard from my systems: I'm here to offer you a deal you can't refuse." At least that's what his glasses tell him to say: what comes out of his mouth sounds a bit more like *ah'm Macx: ye've heard frae ma system, Ah'm here tae gie yez a deal ye cannae refuse.* The glasses haven't had long enough to work on his accent. Meanwhile, he's so full of himself that he snaps his fingers and does a little dance of impatience on the top step.

"Aye well, hold on a minute." The person on the other side of the speakerphone has the kind of cut-glass Morningside accent that manages to sound more English than the King while remaining vernacular Scots. The door opens and Macx finds himself confronted by a tall, slightly cadaverous man wearing a tweed suit that has seen better days and a clerical collar cut from a translucent circuit board. His face is almost concealed behind a pair of recording angel goggles. "Who did you say you were?"

"I'm Macx! Manfred Macx! Ah'm here wi an opportunity ye wouldnae believe. Ah've got the answer tae yer church's financial situation. Ah'm gonnae make yez all rich!" The glasses prompt, and Macx speaks.

The man in the doorway tilts his head slightly, goggles scanning Macx from head to foot. Bursts of blue combustion products spurt from Macx's heels as he bounces up and down enthusiastically. "Are you sure ye've got the right address?" he asks worriedly.

"Aye, Ah am that."

The resident backs into the hostel: "well then, come in, sit yourself down and tell me all about it."

Macx bounces into the room with his brain wide open to a blizzard of pie charts and growth curves, documents spawning in the bizarre phase-space of his corporate management software. "Ah've got a deal ye widnae believe," he begins, gliding past noticeboards upon which Church circulars are staked out to die like exotic butterflies, stepping over rolled-up carpets and a stack of laptops left over from a jumble sale, past the devotional radio telescope that does double-duty as Mrs Muirhouse's back-garden bird-bath. "Ye've been here five years an' yer posted accounts show ye arnae making much dosh—barely keeping the rent up. But ye're a shareholder in Scottish Nuclear Electric, right? Most o' the church funds're in the form of a trust left tae it by wan of ye're congregants when they upped an' went tae join the omega point, right?"

"Er." The minister looks at him oddly. "I cannae comment on the Church eschatological investment trust. Why d'ye think that?"

They fetch up, somehow, in the minister's office. A huge, framed rendering hangs over the back of his threadbare office chair: the collapsing cosmos of the End Times, galactic clusters rotten with the Dyson Spheres of the eschaton falling towards the big crunch. Saint Tipler beams down from above with avuncular approval, a ring of quasars forming a halo around his head. Posters proclaim the new Gospel: COSMOLOGY IS BETTER THAN

GUESSWORK, and LIVE FOREVER WITHIN MY LIGHT-
CONE. "Can I get you anything? Cup of tea? Battery
charge point?" asks the vicar.

"Crystal meth?" asks Macx, hopefully. His face falls as
the vicar shakes his head apologetically. "Aw, dinnae
worry, Ah wis only joshing." He leans forward: "I know
all about your plutonium futures speculation," he hisses.
A finger taps his stolen spectacles in an ominous gesture:
"these dinnae just record, they *think*. An Ah ken where
the money's gone."

"What have you got?" the minister asks coldly, any indication of good humour flown. "I'm going to have to
edit down these memories, you bastard. Bits of me that
aren't going to merge with the godhead at the end of
time."

"Keep yer shirt on. Whit's the point of savin' it all up
if ye've nae got a life worth living? Ye reckon the big
yin's nae gonnae understand a knees-up?"

"What do you *want*?"

"Aye well," Macx leans back, aggrieved. "Ah've got—"
he pauses. An expression of extreme confusion flits over
his head. "Ah've got *lobsters*," he finally announces. "Genetically engineered, uploaded lobsters tae run yer ura-
nium reprocessing plant. Ah wis gonnae help ye out by
showing ye how tae get yer money back where it belongs,
so ye could make the council tax due date. See, they're
neutron-resistant, these lobsters. Naw, that cannae be
right. Ah wis gonnae sell yez something ye could use,
for—" his face slumps into a frown of disgust—"*free*?"

Approximately thirty seconds later, as he is picking
himself up off the front steps of the First Reformed
Church of Tipler (Astrophysicist), the man who would be
Macx finds himself wondering if maybe this high finance

shit isn't as easy as it's cracked up to be. Some of the agents in his glasses are wondering if elocution lessons are the answer: others aren't so optimistic.

Getting back to the history lesson, the prospects for the decade look mostly medical.

A few thousand elderly baby boomers are converging on Tehran for Woodstock Four. Europe is desperately trying to import eastern European nurses and home care assistants; in Japan, whole agricultural villages lie vacant and decaying, ghost communities sucked dry as cities suck people in like residential black holes.

Rumour is spreading throughout gated shelter communities in the American mid-west: a vaccine against senescence, a slow virus coded in the genome that evolution hasn't weeded out. As usual, Charles Darwin gets more than his fair share of the blame. (Less spectacular but more realistic treatments for old age—telomere reconstruction and hexose-denatured protein reduction—are available in private clinics for those who are willing to surrender their pensions.) Progress is expected to speed up shortly, as the fundamental patents in genomic engineering begin to expire: the Free Chromosome Foundation has already published a manifesto calling for the creation of an intellectual-property free genome with improved replacements for all commonly defective exons.

Experiments in digitizing and running neural wetware under emulation are well-established; some radical libertarians claim that as the technology matures, death—with its draconian curtailment of property and voting rights—will become the biggest civil rights issue of all.

For a small extra fee, most veterinary insurance policies cover cloning your pet dog or cat in event of their accidental and distressing death. Human cloning, for reasons nobody is very clear on any more, is still illegal in most developed nations—but very few judiciaries push for mandatory abortion of identical twins.

Some commodities are expensive: the price of crude oil has broken sixty euros a barrel and is edging inexorably up. Other commodities are cheap: computers, for example—hobbyists print off weird new processor architectures on their home inkjets; middle aged folks wipe their backsides with diagnostic paper that can tell how their VHDL levels are tending.

The latest casualties of the march of technological progress are: the high street clothes shop, the flushing water closet, the Main Battle Tank, and the first-generation of quantum computers. New with the decade are cheap enhanced immune systems, brain implants that hook right into the Chomsky organ and *talk* to you using your own inner voice, and widespread public paranoia about limbic spam. Nanotechnology has shattered into a dozen disjoint disciplines, and skeptics are predicting that it will all peter out before long. Philosophers have ceded qualia to engineers, and the current difficult problem in AI is getting software to experience embarrassment.

Fusion power is still, of course, fifty years away.

The Victorians are morphing into goths before Manfred's culture-shocked eyes.

"You looked lost," explains Monica, leaning over him curiously. "What's with your eyes?"

"I can't see too well," Manfred tries to explain. Everything is a blur, and the voices that usually chatter incessantly in his head have left nothing behind but a roaring silence. "I mean, someone *mugged* me. They took—" his hand closes on air: something is missing from his belt.

Monica, the tall woman he first saw in the hospital, enters the room. What she's wearing indoors is skin-tight, irridescent and, disturbingly, claims to be a distributed extension of her neuroectoderm. Stripped of costume-drama accoutrements she's a twenty-first century adult, born or decanted after the millennial baby boom. She waves some fingers in Manfred's face: "how many?"

"Two." Manfred tries to concentrate. "What—"

"No concussion," she says briskly. " 'Scuse me while I page." Her eyes are brown, with amber raster-lines flickering across her pupils. *Contact lenses?* Manfred wonders, his head turgid and unnaturally slow. It's like being drunk, except much less pleasant: he can't seem to wrap his head around an idea from all angles at once, any more. *Is this what consciousness used to be like?* It's an ugly, slow sensation. She turns away from him: "MED-LINE says you'll be alright in a while. The main problem is the identity loss. Are you backed up anywhere?"

"Here." Alan, still top-hatted and mutton-chopped, holds out a pair of spectacles to Manfred. "Take these, they may do you some good." His topper wobbles, as if a strange A-life experiment is struggling to escape from its false bottom.

"Oh. Thank you." Manfred reaches for them with a pathetic sense of gratitude. As soon as he puts them on they run through a test series, whispering questions and watching how his eyes focus: after a minute the room around him clears as the specs build a synthetic image to compensate for his myopia. There's limited net access too, he notices, a warm sense of relief stealing over him.

"Do you mind if I call somebody?" he asks: "I want to check my backups."

"Be my guest." Alan slips out through the door; Monica sits down opposite him and stares into some inner space. The room has a tall ceiling, with whitewashed walls and wooden shutters to cover the aerogel window bays. The furniture is modern modular, and it clashes somewhat. "We were expecting you."

"You were—" he shifts track with an effort: "I was here to see somebody. Here in Scotland, I mean."

"Us." She catches his eye deliberately. "To discuss sapience options with our patron."

"With your—" he squeezes his eyes shut. "*Damn.* I don't *remember.* I need my glasses back. Please."

"What about your backups?" she asks curiously.

"A moment." Manfred tries to remember what address to ping. It's useless, and painfully frustrating. "It would help if I could remember where I keep the rest of my mind," he complains. "It used to be at—oh, *there.*"

An elephantine semantic network sits down on his spectacles as soon as he asks for the site, crushing his surroundings into blocky pixellated monochrome that jerks as he looks around. "This is going to take some time," he warns his hosts as a goodly chunk of his meta-cortex tries to handshake with his brain over a wireless network connection that was really only designed for web browsing. The download consists of the part of his consciousness that isn't security-critical—public access actors and vague opinionated rants—but it clears down a huge memory castle, maps miracles and wonders and entire hotel suites onto the whitewashed walls of this space.

When Manfred can see the outside world again he feels a bit more like himself: he can, at least, spawn a search thread that will resynchronize and fill him in on what it found. He still can't access the inner mysteries of his soul (including his personal memories); they're locked and barred pending biometric verification of his identity and a quantum key exchange. But he has his wits about him again—and some of them are even working. It's like sobering up from a strange new drug, the infinitely reassuring sense of being back at the controls of his own head. "I think I need to report a crime," he tells Monica— or whoever is plugged into Monica's head right, because now he knows where he is and who he was meant to meet (although not why)—and he understands that for the Franklin Collective, identity is a politically loaded issue.

"A crime report." Her expression is subtly mocking. "Identity theft, by any chance?"

"Yeah, yeah, I know: identity *is* theft, don't trust anyone whose state vector hasn't forked for more than a gigasecond, change is the only constant, et bloody cetera. Who am I talking to, by the way? And if we're talking, doesn't that signify that you think we're on the same side, more or less?" He struggles to sit up in the recliner chair: stepper motors whine softly as it strives to accomodate him.

"Sidedness is optional." The woman who is Monica some of the time looks at him quirkily: "it tends to alter drastically if you vary the number of dimensions. Let's just say that right now I'm Monica, plus our sponsor. Will that do you?"

"Our sponsor, who is in cyberspace—"

She leans back on the sofa, which wines and extrudes an occasional table with a small bar. "Drink? Can I offer you coffee? Guarana? Or maybe a Berlinnerweise, for old time's sake?"

21

"Guarana will do. Hello, Bob. How long have you been dead?"

She chuckles. "I'm not dead, Manny. I may not be a full upload, but I *feel* like me." She rolls her eyes, self-consciously. "He's making rude comments about your wife," she adds: "I'm not going to pass that on."

"My ex-wife," Manfred corrects her automatically. "The, uh, tax vamp. So. You're acting as a, I guess, an interpreter for Bob?"

"Ack." She looks at Manfred very seriously: "we owe him a lot, you know. He left his assets in trust to the movement along with his partials. We feel obliged to instantiate his personality as often as possible, even though you can only do so much with a couple of petabytes of recordings. But we have help."

"The lobsters." Manfred nods to himself and accepts the glass that she offers. Its diamond-plated curves glitter brilliantly in the late afternoon sunlight. "I *knew* this had something to do with them." He leans forward, holding his glass and frowns. "If only I could remember why I came here! It was something emergent, something in deep memory . . . something I didn't trust in my own skull. Something to do with Bob."

The door behind the sofa opens; Alan enters, wearing an early twentieth-century business suit. "Excuse me," he says quietly, and heads for the far side of the room. A workstation folds down from the wall and a chair rolls in from a service niche: he sits with his chin propped on his hands, staring at the white desktop. Every so often he mutters quietly to himself: "*yes, I understand . . . campaign headquarters . . . donations need to be audited . . .*"

"Gianni's election campaign," Monica prompts him.

Manfred jumps. "Gianni—" a bundle of memories unlock inside his head as he remembers his political front man's message. "Yes! That's what this is about. It has to be!" He looks at her excitedly. "I'm here to deliver a message to you from Gianni Vittoria. About—" he looks crestfallen. "I'm not sure," he trails off uncertainly, "but it was important. Whoever mugged me got the message."

The Grass Market is an overly rustic cobbled square nestled beneath the glowering battlements of castle rock. Annette stands on the site of the gallows where they used to execute witches; she sends forth her invisible agents to search for spoor of Manfred. Aineko, overly familiar, drapes over her left shoulder like a satanic stole and delivers a running stream of cracked cellphone chatter into her ear.

"I don't know where to begin," she sighs, annoyed. This place is wall to wall tourist trap, a many-bladed carnivorous plant that digests easy credit and spits out the drained husks of foreigners. The road has been pedestrianised and resurfaced in squalidly authentic mediaeval cobblestones; in the middle of what used to be the car park there's a permanent floating antique market, where you can buy anything from a brass fire surround to an antique CD player. Much of the merchandise in the shops is generic dotcom trash, vying for the title of Japanese-Scottish souvenir-from-hell: Puroland tartans, animatronic Nessies hissing bad-temperedly at knee level, second-hand schleptops. People swarm everywhere, from the theme pubs (hangings seem to be a running joke hereabouts) to the expensive dress shops with their fabric renderers and digital mirrors. Street performers, part of the permanent floating Fringe, clutter the sidewalk: a robotic mime, very traditional in silver face-paint, mimics the gestures of passers-by with ironically stylised gestures.

"Try the doss house," Aineko suggests from the shelter of her shoulder bag.

"The—" Annette does a double-take as her thesaurus conspires with her open government firmware and dumps a geographical database of city social services into her sensorium. "Oh, I see." The Grass Market itself is touristy, but the bits off to one end—down a dingy canyon of forbidding stone buildings six storeys high—are decidedly downmarket. "Okay."

Annette weaves past a stall selling disposable cellphones and cheaper genome explorers: round a gaggle of teenage girls in the grips of some kind of imported kawai fetish, who look at her in alarm from atop their pink platform heels—probably mistaking her for a school probation inspector—and past a stand of chained and parked bicycles. The human attendant looks bored out of her mind. Annette tucks a blandly anonymous ten euro note in her pocket almost before she notices: "if you were going to buy a hot bike," she asks, "where would you go?" The parking attendant stares at her and for a moment Annette thinks she's overestimated her. Then she mumbles something. "What?"

"McMurphy's. Used to be called Bannerman's. Down Cowgate, that-away." The meter maid looks anxiously at her rack of charges. "You didn't—"

"Uh-huh." Annette follows her gaze: straight down the dark stone canyon. *Well, okay.* "This had better be worth it, Manny *mon cher*," she mutters under her breath.

McMurphy's is a fake Irish pub, a stone grotto installed beneath a mound of blank-faced offices. It was once a real Irish pub before the developers got their hands on it and mutated it in rapid succession into a punk night club, a wine bar, and a fake Dutch coffee shop; after which, as burned out as any star, it left the main sequence. Now it occupies an unnaturally prolonged, chilly existence as the sort of recycled imitation Irish pub that has neon four-leafed clovers hanging from the artificially blackened pine beams above the log tables—in other words, the black dwarf afterlife of the serious drinking establishment. Somewhere along the line the beer cellar was replaced with a toilet (leaving more room for paying patrons upstairs), and now its founts dispense fizzy concentrate diluted with water from the city mains.

"Say, Did you hear the one about the Eurocrat with the robot pussy who goes into a dodgy pub on the Cowgate and orders a coke? And when it arrives, she says hey, where's the mirror?"

"Shut *up*," Annette hisses into her shoulder bag. "It isn't *funny*." Her personal intruder telemetry has just emailed her wristphone and it's displaying a rotating yellow exclamation point, which means that according to the published police crime stats this place is likely to do grievous harm to her insurance premiums.

Aineko looks up at her and yawns cavernously, baring a pink, ribbed mouth and a tongue like pink suede. "Want to make me? I just pinged Manny's head. The network latency was trivial."

The barmaid sidles up and pointedly manages not to make eye contact with Annette. "A diet coke," she says. In the direction of her bag, voice pitched low: "did you here

25

the one about the Eurocrat who goes into a dodgy pub, orders half a litre of diet coke, and when she spills it in her shoulder bag she says oops, I've got a wet pussy?"

The coke arrives. Annette pays for it. There may be a couple of dozen people in the pub; it's hard to tell because it looks like an ancient cellar, lots of stone archways leading off into niches populated with second hand church pews and knife-scabbed tables. Some guys who might be bikers, students, or well-dressed winos are hunched over one table: hairy, wearing vests with too many pockets, an artful bohemianism that makes Annette blink until one of her literary programs informs her that one of them is a moderately famous local writer, a bit of a guru for the space and freedom party. There're a couple of women in boots and furry hats in one corner, poring over the menu, and a parcel of off-duty street performers hunching over their beers in a booth. Nobody else in here is wearing anything remotely like office drag, but the weirdness coefficient is above average: so Annette dials her glasses to extra-dark, straightens her tie, and glances around.

The door opens and a nondescript youth slinks in. He's wearing baggy BDUs, wooly cap, and a pair of boots that have that quintessential *essense de panzer division* look, all shock absorbers and olive-drab kevlar panels. He's wearing—

"I spy with my little network intrusion detector," begins the cat, as Annette puts her drink down and moves in on the kid, "something beginning with—"

"How much you want for the glasses, kid?" she asks quietly.

He jerks and almost jumps—a bad idea in MilSpec combat boots, the ceiling in here is eighteenth-century stone half a metre thick; "dinnae fuckin *dae* that," he complains in an eerily familiar way: "Ah—" he swallows. "Annie! Who—"

"Stay calm. Take them off; they'll only hurt you if you keep wearing them," she says, careful not to move too fast because now she has a second, scary-jittery fear and she knows without having to look that the exclamation mark on her watch has turned red and begun to flash: "look, I'll give you two hundred euros for the glasses and the belt pouch, real cash, and I won't ask how you got them or tell anyone." He's frozen in front of her, mesmerised, and she can see the light from inside the lenses spilling over onto his half-starved adolescent cheek-bones, flickering like cold lightning, like he's plugged his brain into a grid bearer: swallowing with a suddenly dry mouth, she slowly reaches up and pulls the spectacles off his face with one hand and takes hold of the belt pouch with the other. The kid shudders and blinks at her, and she sticks a couple of hundred euro notes in front of his nose. "Scram," she says, not unkindly.

He reaches up slowly, then seizes the money and runs—blasts his way through the door with an ear-popping concussion, hangs a left onto the cycle path and vanishes downhill towards the parliament buildings and university complex.

Annette watches the doorway apprehensively. "Where *is* he?" she hisses, worried: "any ideas, cat?"

"Naah. It's your job to find him," Aineko opines complacently. But there's an icicle of anxiety in Annette's spine, now: Manfred's been separated from his memory cache? Where could he be? Worse—*who* could he be?

"Fuck you, too," she mutters. "Only one thing for it, I guess." She takes off her own glasses—much less functional than Manfred's massively ramified custom rig—and nervously raises the repo'd specs towards her face. Somehow what she's about to do makes her feel unclean, like snooping on a lover's email folders. But how else can she figure out where he might have gone?

She slides the glasses on and tries to remember what she was doing yesterday in Edinburgh.

"Gianni?"

"Oui, ma cherie?"

Pause. "I lost him. But I got his aide-memoire back. A teenage ligger playing cyberpunk with them. No sign of his location—so I put them on."

Pause. "Oh dear."

"Gianni, why did you send him to the Franklin Collective?"

Pause. (During which, the chill of the gritty stone wall she's leaning on begins to penetrate the weave of her jacket.) "I not wanting to bother you with trivia."

"Merde. It's *not* trivia, Gianni, they're *accelerationistas.* Have you any idea what that's going to do to his head?"

Pause: then a grunt, almost of pain. "Yes."

"Then why did you *do* it?" she demands vehemently. She hunches over, punching words into her phone so that other passers-by avoid her, unsure whether she's handsfree or hallucinating: "shit, Gianni, I have to pick up the pieces every time you do this! Manfred is not a healthy man, he's on the edge of acute future shock the whole time and I was not joking when I told you last Februar' that he'd need a month in a clinic if you tried running him flat-out again!"

"Annette." A heavy sigh: "he are the best hope we got.

Am knowing half-life of agalmic catalyst now down to six months and dropping; Manny outlast his career expectancy, four deviations outside the normal, yes, we know this. But I are having to break civil rights deadlock *now*, this election. We must achieve consensus, and Manfred are only staffer we got who have hope of talking to collective on its own terms. He are deal-making messenger, not force burn-out, right? We need coalition reserve before term limit lockout followed by gridlock in Brussels, American-style. Is more than vital—is essential."

"That's no excuse—"

"Annette, they have partial upload of Bob Franklin. The Franklin Collective is lobbying against the equal rights amendment, defend their position: if ERA passes, all sapients am eligible to vote, own property, upload, download, sideload. Are more important than little grey butt-monsters with cold speculum: whole future depends on it. Manny started this with crustacean rights: leave uploads covered by copyrights not civil rights and where will we be in fifty years? Was important then, but now, with the transmission the lobsters received—"

"Shit." She turns and leans her forehead against the cool stonework. "I'll need a prescription. Ritalin or something. And his location. Leave the rest to me." She doesn't add: *that includes peeling him off the ceiling afterwards*: that's understood. Nor does she say: *you're going to pay.* That's understood, too. Gianni may be a hard-nosed political fixer, but he looks after his own.

"Location am easy if he find the PLO. GPS coordinates are following—"

"No need. I got his spectacles."

"*Merde*, as you say. Take them to him, *ma cherie*. Bring me the distributed trust rating of Bob Franklin's upload

29

and I bring Bob the jubilee, right to direct his own corporate self again as if still alive. And we pull diplomatic chestnuts out of fire before they burn. Agreed?"

"*Oui.*"

She cuts the connection and begins walking uphill, along the Cowgate (through which farmers once bought their herds to market), towards the permanent floating Fringe and then the steps up to the Meadows. As she pauses opposite the site of the gallows, a fight breaks out: some palaeolithic hang-over takes exception at the robotic mime apeing his movements, and swiftly rips its arm off. The mime stands there, sparks flickering inside its shoulder, and looks confused: two pissed-looking students start forward and punch the short-haired vandal. There is much shouting, in the mutually incomprehensible accents of Oxgangs and the Heriot-Watt Robot Lab. Annette watches the fight, and shudders; it's like a flash-over vision from a universe where the equal rights amendment—with its redefinition of personhood—is rejected by the house of deputies: a universe where to die is to become property and to be created outwith a gift of parental DNA is to be doomed to slavery.

Maybe Gianni was right, she ponders. *But I wish the price wasn't so personal—*

Manfred can feel one of his attacks coming on. The usual symptoms are all present—the universe, with its vast preponderance of unthinking matter, becomes an affront; weird ideas flicker like heat lightning far away across the vast plateaus of his imagination—but, with his metacortex running in sandboxed insecure mode, he feels *blunt*. And slow. Even *obsolete*. The latter is about as welcome a sensation as heroin withdrawal: he can't spin off threads to explore his designs for feasibility and report back to him. It's like someone has stripped fifty points off his IQ; his brain feels like a surgical scalpel that's been used to cut down trees. A decaying mind is a terrible thing to be trapped inside. Manfred wants out, and he wants out *bad*—but he's too afraid to let on.

"Gianni is a middle of the road Eurosocialist, mixed-market pragmatist politician," Bob's ghost accuses Manfred by way of Monica's dye-flushed lips: "what does he think I can do for him?"

"That's a—ah—"Manfred rocks forward and back in his chair, arms crossed firmly and hands thrust under his armpits for protection. "Dismantle the moon! Digitise the biosphere, make a noosphere out of it—shit, *sorry*, that's long-term planning. *Build Dyson spheres, lots and lots of*—Ahem. Gianni is an ex-Marxist, reformed high church Trotskyite clade. He believes in achieving True Communism, which is a state of philosophical grace, that requires certain prerequisites like, um, not pissing around with molotov cocktails and thought police: he wants to make everybody so rich that squabbling over ownership of the means of production makes as much sense as arguing over who gets to keep the cave fire burning. He's not your enemy, I mean. He's the enemy of those Stalinist deviationist running dogs in Conservative Party Central Office who want to bug your bedroom and hand everything on a plate to the big corporates owned by the pension funds—which in turn rely on people dying predictably to provide their raison d'ecirctre. And, um, more importantly dying and not trying to hang onto their property and chattels. Sitting up in the coffin singing extropian fireside songs, that kind of thing. The actuaries are to blame, predicting life expectancy with intent to cause people to buy insurance policies with money that is invested in control of the means of production—*Bayes' theorem* is to blame—"

Alan glances over his shoulder at Manfred: "I don't think that guarana was a very good idea," he says in tones of deep foreboding.

Manfred's mode of vibration has gone nonlinear by this point: he's rocking front-to-back and bouncing up and down in little hops, like a technophiliacal yogic flyer trying to bounce his way to the singularity. Monica leans towards him and her eyes widen: "Manfred," she hisses, *"shut up!"*

He stops babbling abruptly, with an expression of deep puzzlement. "Who am I?" he asks, and keels over backwards. "Why am *I*, here and now, occupying this body—"

"Anthropic anxiety attack," Monica comments. "I think he did this in Amsterdam eight years ago when Bob first met him." She looks alarmed, a different identity coming to the fore: "what shall we *do*?"

"We have to make him comfortable." Alan raises his voice: "bed: make yourself ready, now." The back of the sofa Manfred is sprawled on flops downwards, the base folds up, and a strangely animated duvet crawls up over his feet. "Listen, Manny, you're going to be alright."

"Who am I and what do I signify?" Manfred mumbles incoherently: "a mass of propagating decision trees, fractal compression, lots of synaptic junctions lubricated with friendly endorphins—" Across the room, the bootleg pharmacopoeia is cranking up to manufacture some heavy tranquillisers: Monica heads for the kitchen to get something for him to drink them in. "Why are you doing this?" Manfred asks, dizzily.

"It's okay. Lie down and relax." Alan leans over him.

"We'll talk about everything in the morning, when you know who you are." (Aside to Monica, who is entering the room with a bottle of iced tea: "better let Gianni know that he's unwell. One of us may have to go visit the minister. Do you know if Macx has been audited?") "Rest up, Manfred. Everything is being taken care of."

About fifteen minutes later, Manfred—who, in the grip of an existential migraine, meekly obeys Monica's instruction to drink down the spiked tea—lies back on the bed and relaxes. His breathing slows; the subliminal muttering ceases. Monica, sitting next to him, reaches out and takes his right hand, which is lying on top of the bedding.

"Do you want to live forever?" she intones in Bob Franklin's tone of voice. "You can live forever in me . . ."

The Church of Latter-Day Saints believe that you can't get into the promised land unless they've baptised you—but they can do so if they know your name and parentage, even after you're dead. Their genealogical databases are among the most impressive artefacts of historical research ever prepared. And they like to make converts.

The Franklin Collective believe that you can't get into the future unless they've digitised your neural state vector, or at least acquired as complete a snapshot of your sensory inputs and genome as current technology permits. You don't need to be alive for them to do this. Their society of mind is among the most impressive artefacts of computer science. And they like to make converts.

Nightfall in the city. Annette stands impatiently on the doorstep. "Let me the fuck in," she snarls impatiently at the speakerphone. *"Merde!"*

Someone opens the door. "Who—"

Annette shoves him inside, kicks the door shut, and leans on it. "Take me to your boddhisatva," she demands. *"Now."*

"I—" he turns and heads inside, along the gloomy hallway that runs past a staircase. Annette strides after him aggressively. He opens a door and ducks inside, and she follows before he can close it.

Inside, the room is illuminated by a variety of indirect diode sources, calibrated for the warm glow of a summer afternoon's daylight. There's a bed in the middle of it, a figure lying asleep at the heart of a herd of attentive diagnostic instruments. A couple of attendants sit to either side of the sleeping man.

"What have you done to him?" Annette snaps, rushing forwards. Manfred blinks up at her from the pillows, bleary-eyed and confused as she leans overhead: "hello? Manny?" Over her shoulder: "if you 'ave done anything to him—"

"Annie?" He looks puzzled. A bright orange pair of goggles—not his own—is pushed up onto his forehead like a pair of beached jellyfish. "I don't feel well."

"We can fix that," she says briskly. She peels off his glasses and carefully slides them onto his face. The brain bag she puts down next to his shoulder, within easy range. The hairs on the back of her neck rises as a thin chattering keen fills the ether around them: his eyes are glowing a luminous blue behind his shades, as if a high-tension spark is flying between his ears.

"Oh. Wow." He sits up; the covers fall from his naked shoulders and her breath catches.

She looks around at the motionless figure sitting to his

left. The main in the chair nods deliberately, ironically. "What have you done to him?"

"We've been looking after him: nothing more, nothing less. He arrived in a state of considerable confusion and his state deteriorated this afternoon."

She's never met this fellow before but she has a gut feeling that she knows him. "You would be Robert ... Franklin?"

He nods again. "The avatar is *in*." There's a thud as Manfred's eyes roll up in his head and he flops back onto the bedding. "Excuse me. Monica?"

The young woman on the other side of the bed shakes her head. "No, I'm running Bob, too."

"Oh. Well, *you* tell her; I've got to get him some juice."

The woman who is also Bob Franklin—or whatever part of him survived his battle with an exotic brain tumour eight years ago—catches Annette's eye and shakes her head. Smiles faintly. "You're never alone when you're a syncitium."

Annette wrinkles her brow: has to trigger a dictionary attack to parse the sentence. "One large cell, many nuclei? Oh, I see. You have the new implant. The better to record everything."

The youngster shrugs. "You want to die and be resurrected as a third-person actor in a low-bandwidth re-enactment? Or a shadow of itchy memories in some stranger's skull?" She snorts, a gesture that's at odds with the rest of her body language.

"Bob must have been one of the first borganisms. Humans, I mean." Annette glances over at Manfred, who has begun to snore softly. "It must have been a lot of work."

"The monitoring equipment cost millions, then," says

the woman—Monica?—"and it didn't do a very good job. One of the conditions for our keeping access to his research funding is that we regularly run his partials. He wanted to build up a kind of aggregate state vector—patched together out of bits and pieces of other people to supplement the partials that were all I—he—could record with the then state of the art."

"Eh, right." Annette reaches out and absently smooths a stray hair away from Manfred's forehead. "What is it like to be part of a group mind?"

Monica sniffs, evidently amused. "What is it like to see red? What's it like to be a bat? I can't tell you—I can only show you. We're all free to leave at any time, you know."

"But somehow you don't." Annette rubs her head, feels the short hair over the almost imperceptible scars that conceal a network of implants: tools that Manfred turned down when they became available a year or two ago. ("Goop-phase Darwin-design nanotech ain't designed for clean interfaces," he'd said: "I'll stick to disposable kit, thanks.") "No thanks. I don't think he'll take up your offer when he wakes up, either."

Monica shrugs. "That's his loss: he won't live forever in the singularity, along with other followers of our gentle teacher. Anyway, we have more converts than we know what to do with."

A thought occurs to Annette. "Ah. You are all of one mind? Partially? A question to you is a question to all?"

"It can be." The words come simultaneously from Monica and the other body, Alan, who is standing in the doorway with a boxy thing that looks like an improvised diagnostician. "What do you have in mind?" Alan continues.

Manfred, lying on the bed, groans: there's an audible

hiss of pink noise as his glasses whisper in his ears, bone conduction providing a serial highway to his wetware.

"Manfred was sent to find out why you're opposing the ERA," Annette explains. "Some parts of our team operate without the other's knowledge."

"Indeed." Alan sits down on the chair beside the bed and clears his throat, puffing his chest out pompously. "A very important theological issue. I feel—"

"I, or we?" Annette interrupts.

"*We* feel," Monica snaps. Then she glances at Alan. "Soo-rrry."

The evidence of individuality within the group mind is disturbing to Annette: too many re-runs of the Borgish fantasy have conditioned her preconceptions. "Please continue."

"One person, one vote, is obsolete," says Alan. "The broader issue of how we value identity needs to be revisited, the franchise reconsidered. Do you get one vote for each warm body? Or one vote for each sapient individual? What about distributed intelligences? The proposals in the Equal Rights Act are deeply flawed, based on a cult of individuality that takes no account of the true complexity of posthumanism."

"Like the proposals for a feminine franchise in the nineteeth century, that would grant the vote to married wives of land-owning men," Monica adds slyly: "it misses the point."

"Ah, oui." Annette crosses her arms, suddenly defensive. This isn't what she'd expected to hear.

"It misses more than that." Heads turn to face an unexpected direction: Manfred's eyes are open again, and as he glances around the room Annette can see a spark of interest there that was missing earlier. "Last century, people were paying to have their heads frozen after their death—in hope of reconstruction, later. They got no civil rights: the law didn't recognize death as a reversible process. Now how do we account for it when you guys *stop* running Bob? Opt out of the collective borganism? Or maybe opt back in again?" He reaches up and rubs his forehead, tiredly. "Sorry, I haven't been myself lately." A crooked, slightly manic grin flickers across his face. "See, I've been telling Gianni for a whole while, we need a new legal concept of what it is to be a person. One that can cope with sentient corporations, artificial stupidities, secessionists from group minds, and reincarnated uploads. The religiously-inclined are having lots of fun with identity issues right now—why aren't we posthumans thinking about these things?"

Annette's bag bulges: Aineko pokes his head out, sniffs the air, squeezes out onto the carpet, and begins to groom himself with perfect disregard for the human bystanders. "Not to mention a-life experiments who think they're the real thing," Manfred adds. "And aliens."

Annette freezes, staring at him. "Manfred! You're not supposed to—"

Manfred is watching Alan, who seems to be the most deeply integrated of the dead venture billionaire's executors: even his expression reminds Annette of meeting Bob Franklin back in Amsterdam, early in the decade, when Manny's personal dragon still owned him. "Aliens," Alan echoes. An eyebrow twitches. "How long have you known?"

"Gianni has his fingers in a lot of pies," Manfred comments blandly. "And we still talk to the lobsters from time to time—you know, they're only a couple of light hours away, right?" The first-generation uploads, Californian spiny lobsters in wobbly symbiosis with Russian expert systems, found refuge aboard Franklin's asteroid mining project—which Manfred prodded Franklin into setting up. The factory had needed sapient control software, and the state of the art in AI was inadequate: the lobsters had needed sanctuary, a home away from the bewilderingly weird cybersphere of earth's anthropoids. "They told us about the signal."

"Er." Alan's eyes glaze over for a moment; Annette's prostheses paint her a picture of false light spraying from the back of his head, his entire sensory bandwidth momentarily soaking up a huge peer-to-peer download from the servers that wallpaper every room in this building. Monica looks irritated, taps her fingernails on the back of her chair. "The signal. Right. Why wasn't this publicised?"

"It was." Annette's eyebrows furrow. "Most people who'd be interested in hearing about an alien contact already believe that they drop round on alternate Tuesdays and Thursdays to administer a rectal exam. Most of the rest think it's a hoax. Quite a few of the remainder are scratching their heads and wondering whether it isn't just a new kind of cosmological phenomenon that emits a very low entropy directional signal. And of the six who are left over, five are trying to get a handle on the message contents and the last is convinced it's a practical joke."

Manfred fiddles with the bed control system. "It's not a practical joke," he adds. "But they only captured about sixteen megabits of data. There's quite a bit of noise, the signal doesn't repeat, its length doesn't appear to be a prime, there's no obvious metainformation that describes the internal format, so there's no easy way of getting a handle on it. To make matters worse, pointy-haired man-

agement at Arianespace—" he glances at Annette, as if
seeking a response to the naming of her ex-employers—
"decided the best thing to do was to turn it into a piece of
music, then copyright the hell out of it and hire the
CCAA's lawyers to prosecute anyone else who works on
it. So nobody really knows how long it'll take to figure
out whether it's a ping from the galactic root domain
servers or a pulsar that's taken to grinding out the
eighteen-quadrillionth digits of pi, or whatever."

"But." Monica glances around. "You can't be *sure*."

"I think it may be sapient," says Manfred. He finds the
right button at last, and the bed begins to fold itself back
into a lounger. Then he finds the wrong button; the duvet
dissolves into viscous turquoise slime that slurps and gur-
gles away through a multitude of tiny nozzles in the headboard. "Bloody aerogel. Um. Where was I?" He sits up.

"Sapient network packet?" asks Alan.

"Nope." Manfred shakes his head, grins. "Should have
known you'd read Vinge . . . or was it the movie? No,
what I *think* is that there's only one logical thing to beam
backwards and forwards out there, and you may remember I asked you to beam it out about, oh, nine years ago?"

"The lobsters." Alan's eyes go blank. "Nine years. Time
to Proxima Centauri and back?"

"About that distance, yes," says Manfred. "Officially,
the signal came from a couple of degrees off and more
than hundred light years further out. Unofficially, this
was disinformation to prevent panic. And no, the signal
didn't contain any canned crusties: I think it's an exchange embassy. *Now* do you see why we have to crow-
bar the civil rights issue open again? We need a
framework for rights that can encompass non-humans,
and we need it as fast as possible. Otherwise . . ."

"Okay," says Alan. "I'll have to talk with myselves. Maybe we can agree something, as long as it's clear that it's a provisional stab at the framework and not a permanent solution?"

Annette snorts. "No solution is final!" Monica catches her eyes and winks: Annette is startled by the blatant display of dissent within the syncitium.

"Well," says Manfred. "I guess that's all we can ask for?" He looks hopeful. "Thanks for the hospitality, but I feel the need to lie down in my own bed for a while," he adds. "I had to commit a lot to memory while I was offline and I want to record it before I forget myself."

Later that night, a doorbell rings.

"Who's there?" asks the entryphone.

"Uh, me," says the man on the steps. He looks a little confused. "Ah'm Macx. Ah'm here tae see—" the name is on the tip of his tongue—"someone."

"Come in." A solenoid buzzes; he pushes the door open, and it closes behind him. His metal-shod boots ring on the hard stone floor, and the cool air smells faintly of unburned jet fuel.

"Ah'm Macx," he repeats uncertainly, "or Ah wis for a wee while, an' it made ma heid hurt. But noo Ah'm me agin an' Ah wannae be somebody else . . . can ye help?"

Later still, a cat sits on a window ledge, watching the interior of a darkened room from behind the concealment of curtains. The room is dark to human eyes, but bright to the cat: moonlight cascades silently off the walls and furniture, the twisted bedding, the two naked humans lying curled together in the middle of the bed.

Both the humans are in their early thirties: her close-

41

cropped hair is beginning to grey, distinguished threads of gunmetal wire threading it, while his brown mop is not yet showing signs of age. To the cat, who watches with a variety of unnatural senses, her head glows in the microwave spectrum with a gentle radiance of polarised emissions spread across a wide range of channels. The male shows no such aura: he's unnaturally natural for this day and age, although—oddly—he's wearing spectacles in bed, and the frames shine similarly. An invisible soup of radiation connects both humans to items of clothing scattered across the room—clothing that seethes with unsleeping sentience, dribbling over to their suitcases and hand luggage and (though it doesn't enjoy noticing it) the cat's tail, which is itself a rather sensitive antenna.

The two humans have just finished making love: they do this less often than in their first few years, but with more tenderness and expertise—lengths of shocking pink Hello Kitty bondage tape still hang from the bedposts, and a lump of programmable memory plastic sits cooling on the side table. The male is sprawled with his head and upper torso resting in the crook of the female's left arm and shoulder. Shifting visualisation to infrared, the cat sees that she is glowing, capillaries dilating to enhance the blood flow around her throat and chest.

"I'm getting old," the male mumbles. "I'm slowing down."

"Not where it counts," the female replies, gently squeezing his right buttock.

"No, I'm sure of it," he says. "The bits of me that still exist in this old head—how many types of processor can you name that are still in use thirty-plus years after they're born?"

"You're thinking about the implants again," she says carefully. The cat remembers this as a sore point; from being a medical procedure to help the blind see and the autistic talk, intrathecal implants have blossomed into a must-have accessory for the *now*-clade. But the male is reluctant. "It's not as risky as it used to be. If they screw up, there're neural growth cofactors and cheap replacement stem cells. I'm sure one of your sponsors can arrange for extra cover."

"Hush: I'm still thinking about it." He's silent for a while. "I wasn't myself yesterday. I was someone else. Someone too slow to keep up. Puts a new perspective on everything: I've been afraid of losing my biological plasticity, of being trapped in an obsolete chunk of skullware while everything moves on—but how much of me lives outside my skull these days, anyhow?" One of his external threads generates an animated glyph and throws it at her mind's eye: she grins at his obscure humour. "Cross-training from a new interface is going to be hard, though."

"You'll do it," she predicts. "You can always get a discreet prescription for novotrophin-B." A neurotransmitter agonist tailored for gerontological wards, it stimulates interest in the new: combined with MDMA, it's a component of the street cocktail called sensawunda. "That should keep you focussed for long enough to get comfortable."

"What's life coming to, when *I* can't cope with the pace of change?" he asks the ceiling plaintively.

The cat lashes its tail irritably.

"You are my futurological storm-shield," she says, jokingly, and moves her hand to cup his genitals. Most of her current activities are purely biological, the cat notes:

43

from the irregular sideloads, she's using most of her skullware to run ETItalk@home, one of the distributed cracking engines that is trying to decode the alien grammar of a message that Manfred suspects is eligible for citizenship.

Obeying an urge that it can't articulate, the cat sends out a feeler to the nearest router. The cybeast has Manfred's keys; he trusts it implicitly, which is unwise—his ex-wife tampered with it, after all. Tunnelling out into the darkness, the cat stalks the net alone . . .

"Just think about the people who can't adapt," he says. His voice sounds obscurely worried.

"I try not to." She shivers. "You are thirty, you are slowing. What about the young? Are they keeping up, themselves?"

"I have a daughter. She's about a hundred and sixty million seconds old. If Pamela would let me message her I could find out . . ."

"Don't go there, Manfred. Please."

In the distance, the cat hears the sound of lobster minds singing in the void, a distant feed streaming from their cometary home as it drifts silently out through the asteroid belt, en route to a chilly encounter beyond Neptune. The lobsters sing of alienation and obsolescence, of intelligence too slow and tenuous to support the vicious pace of change that has sand-blasted the human world until all the edges people cling to are jagged and brittle.

Beyond the lobsters, the cat finds an anonymous eternity server: distributed file storage, unerasable, full of secrets and lies that nobody can afford to suppress. Rants, music, rip-offs of the latest Bollywood hits: the cat spiders past them all, looking for the final sample. Grabbing it—a momentary breakup in Manfred's spectacles the only symptom either human notices—the cat drags its prey home, sucks it down, and diffs it against the data sample Annette's exocortex is analysing.

"I'm sorry, my love. I just sometimes feel—" he sighs. "Age is a process of closing off opportunities behind you. I'm not young enough any more: I've lost the dynamic optimism."

The data sample on the pirate server differs from the one Annette's implant is processing.

"You'll get it back," she reassures him quietly, stroking his side. "You are still sad from being mugged. This also will pass. You'll see."

"Yeah." He finally relaxes, dropping back into the reflexive assurance of his own will. "I'll get over it, one way or another. Or someone who remembers being me will . . ."

In the darkness, Aineko bares teeth in a silent grin. Behind his feline eyes, a braid of processes running on an abstract virtual machine asks him a question that cannot be encoded in any human grammar. *Watch and wait*, he replies to the alien tourist. *They'll figure it out, sooner or later.*

The Long Chase

Geoffrey A. Landis

2645, January

The war is over.

The survivors are being rounded up and converted.

In the inner solar system, those of my companions who survived the ferocity of the fighting have already been converted. But here at the very edge of the Oort Cloud, all things go slowly. It will be years, perhaps decades, before the victorious enemy come out here. But with the slow inevitability of gravity, like an outward wave of entropy, they will come.

Ten thousand of my fellow soldiers have elected to go doggo. Ragged prospectors and ice processors, they had been too independent to ever merge into an effective fighting unit. Now they shut themselves down to dumb rocks, electing to wake up to groggy consciousness for only a few seconds every hundred years. Patience, they counsel me; patience is life. If they can wait a thousand or ten thousand or a million years, with patience enough the enemy will eventually go away.

They are wrong.

The enemy, too, is patient. Here at the edge of the Kuiper, out past Pluto, space is vast, but still not vast

46

enough. The enemy will search every grain of sand in the solar system. My companions will be found, and converted. If it takes ten thousand years, the enemy will search that long to do it.

I, too, have gone doggo, but my strategy is different. I have altered my orbit. I have a powerful ion-drive, and full tanks of propellant, but I use only the slightest tittle of a cold-gas thruster. I have a chemical kick-stage engine as well, but I do not use it either; using either one of them would signal my position to too many watchers. Among the cold comets, a tittle is enough.

I am falling into the sun.

It will take me two hundred and fifty years years to fall, and for two hundred and forty nine years, I will be a dumb rock, a grain of sand with no thermal signature, no motion other than gravity, no sign of life.

Sleep.

2894, JUNE

Awake.

I check my systems. I have been a rock for nearly two hundred and fifty years.

The sun is huge now. If I were still a human, it would be the size of the fist on my outstretched arm. I am being watched now, I am sure, by a thousand lenses: am I a rock, a tiny particle of interstellar ice? A fragment of debris from the war? A surviving enemy?

I love the cold and the dark and the emptiness; I have been gone so long from the inner solar system that the very sunlight is alien to me.

My systems check green. I expected no less: if I am

nothing else, I am still a superbly engineered piece of space hardware. I come fully to life, and bring my ion engine up to thrust.

A thousand telescopes must be alerting their brains that I am alive—but it is too late! I am thrusting at a full throttle, five percent of a standard gravity, and I am thrusting inward, deep into the gravity well of the sun. My trajectory is plotted to skim almost the surface of the sun.

This trajectory has two objectives. First, so close to the sun I will be hard to see. My ion contrail will be washed out in the glare of a light a billion times brighter, and none of the thousand watching eyes will know my plans until it is too late to follow.

And second, by waiting until I am nearly skimming the sun and then firing my chemical engine deep inside the gravity well, I can make most efficient use of it. The gravity of the sun will amplify the efficiency of my propellant, magnify my speed. When I cross the orbit of Mercury outbound I will be over one percent of the speed of light and still accelerating.

I will discard the useless chemical rocket after I exhaust the little bit of impulse it can give me, of course. Chemical rockets have ferocious thrust but little staying power; useful in war but of limited value in an escape. But I will still have my ion engine, and I will have nearly full tanks.

Five percent of a standard gravity is a feeble thrust by the standards of chemical rocket engines, but chemical rockets exhaust their fuel far too quickly to be able to catch me. I can continue thrusting for years, for decades.

I pick a bright star, Procyon, for no reason whatever, and boresight it. Perhaps Procyon will have an asteroid belt. At least it must have dust, and perhaps comets. I don't need much: a grain of sand, a microscopic shard of ice.

From dust God made man. From the dust of a new star, from the detritus of creation, I can make worlds.

No one can catch me now. I will leave, and never return.

2897, MAY

I am chased.

It is impossible, stupid, unbelievable, inconceivable! I am being chased.

Why?

Can they not leave a single free mind unconverted? In three years I have reached fifteen percent of the speed of light, and it must be clear that I am leaving and never coming back. Can one unconverted brain be a threat to them? Must their group brain really have the forced cooperation of every lump of thinking matter in the solar system? Can they think that if even one free-thinking brain escapes, they have lost?

But the war is a matter of religion, not reason, and it may be that they indeed believe that even a single brain unconverted is a threat to them. For whatever reason, I am being chased.

The robot chasing me is, I am sure, little different than myself, a tiny brain, an ion engine, and a large set of tanks. They would have had no time to design something new; to have any chance of catching me they would have had to set the chaser on my tail immediately.

The brain, like mine, would consist of atomic spin

states superimposed on a crystalline rock matrix. A device smaller than what, in the old days, we would call a grain of rice. Intelligent dust, a human had once said, back in the days before humans became irrelevant.

They only sent one chaser. They must be very confident.

Or short on resources.

It is a race, and a very tricky one. I can increase my thrust, use up fuel more quickly, to try to pull away, but if I do so, the specific impulse of my ion drive decreases, and as a result, I waste fuel and risk running out first. Or I can stretch my fuel, make my ion drive more efficient, but this will lower my thrust, and I will risk getting caught by the higher-thrust opponent behind me.

He is twenty billion kilometers behind me. I integrate his motion for a few days, and see that he is, in fact, out-accelerating me.

Time to jettison.

I drop everything I can. The identify-friend-or-foe encrypted-link gear I will never need again; it is discarded. It is a shame I cannot grind it up and feed it to my ion engines, but the ion engines are picky about what they eat. Two micro-manipulators I had planned to use to collect sand grains at my destination for fuel: gone.

My primary weapon has always been my body—little can survive an impact at the speeds I can attain—but I have three sand-grains with tiny engines of their own as secondary weapons. There's no sense in saving them to fight my enemy; he will know exactly what to expect, and in space warfare, only the unexpected can kill.

I fire the grains of sand, one at a time, and the sequential kick of almost a standard gravity nudges my speed slightly forward. Then I drop the empty shells.

May he slip up, and run into them at sub-relativistic closing velocity.

I am lighter, but it is still not enough. I nudge my thrust up, hating myself for the waste, but if I don't increase acceleration, in two years I will be caught, and my parsimony with fuel will yield me nothing.

I need all the energy I can feed to my ion drives. No extra for thinking.

Sleep.

2900

Still being chased.

2905

Still being chased.

I have passed the point of commitment. Even if I braked with my thrust to turn back, I could no longer make it back to the solar system.

I am alone.

2907

Lonely.

To one side of my path Sirius glares insanely bright, a knife in the sky, a mad dog of a star. The stars of Orion are weirdly distorted. Ahead of me, the lesser dog Procyon is waxing brighter every year; behind me, the sun is a fading dot in Aquila.

Of all things, I am lonely. I had not realized that I still had the psychological capacity for loneliness. I examine my brain, and find it. Yes, a tiny knot of loneliness. Now that I see it, I can edit my brain to delete it, if I choose. But yet I hesitate. It is not a bad thing, not something that is crippling my capabilities, and if I edit my brain too much will I not become, in some way, like them?

I leave my brain unedited. I can bear loneliness.

2909

Still being chased.

We are relativistic now, nearly three quarters of the speed of light.

One twentieth of a standard gravity is only a slight push, but as I have burned fuel my acceleration increases, and we have been thrusting for fifteen years continuously.

What point is there in this stupid chase? What victory can there be, here in the emptiness between stars, a trillion kilometers away from anything at all?

After fifteen years of being chased, I have a very good measurement of his acceleration. As his ship burns off fuel, it loses mass, and the acceleration increases. By measuring this increase in acceleration, and knowing what his empty mass must be, I know how much fuel he has left.

It is too much. I will run out of fuel first.

I can't conserve fuel; if I lessen my thrust, he will

catch me in only a few years. It will take another fifty years, but the end of the chase is already in sight.

A tiny strobe flickers erratically behind me. Every interstellar hydrogen that impacts his shell makes a tiny flash of x-ray brilliance. Likewise, each interstellar proton I hit sends a burst of x-rays through me. I can feel each one, a burst of fuzzy noise that momentarily disrupts my thoughts. But with spin states encoding ten-to-the-twentieth qbits, I can afford to have massively redundant brainpower. My brain was designed to be powerful enough to simulate an entire world, including ten thousand fully-sapient and sentient free agents. I could immerse myself inside a virtual reality indistinguishable from old Earth, and split myself into a hundred personalities. In my own interior time, I could spend ten thousand years before the enemy catches me and forcibly drills itself into my brain. Civilizations could rise and fall in my head, and I could taste every decadence, lose myself for a hundred years in sensual pleasure, invent rare tortures and exquisite pain.

But as part of owning your own brain free and clear comes the ability to prune yourself. In space, one of the first things to prune away is the ability to feel boredom, and not long after that, I pruned away all desire to live in simulated realities. Billions of humans chose to live in simulations, but by doing so they have made themselves irrelevant: irrelevant to the war, irrelevant to the future.

I could edit back into my brain a wish to live in simulated reality, but what would be the point? It would be just another way to die.

The one thing I do simulate, repeatedly and obsessively, is the result of the chase. I run a million different scenarios, and in all of them, I lose.

Still, most of my brain is unused. There is plenty of extra processing power to keep all my brain running error-correcting code, and an occasional x-ray flash is barely an event worth my noticing. When a cell of my brain is irrevocably damaged by cosmic radiation, I simply code that section to be ignored. I have brainpower to spare.

I continue running, and hope for a miracle.

2355, FEBRUARY: EARTH.

I was living in a house I hated, married to a man I despised, with two children who had changed with adolescence from sullen and withdrawn to an active, menacing hostility. How can I be afraid of my own offspring?

Earth was a dead end, stuck in the biological past, a society in deep freeze. No one starved, and no one progressed.

When I left the small apartment for an afternoon to apply for a job as an asteroid belt miner, I told no one, not my husband, not my best friend. No one asked me any questions. It took them an hour to scan my brain, and, once they had the scan, another five seconds to run me through a thousand aptitude tests.

And then, with her brain scanned, my original went home, back to the house she hated, the husband she despised, the two children she was already beginning to physically fear.

I launched from the Earth to an asteroid named 1991JR, and never returned.

Perhaps she had a good life. Perhaps, knowing she had escaped undetected, she found she could endure her personal prison.

Much later, when the cooperation faction suggested that it was too inefficient for independents to work in the near-Earth space, I moved out to the main belt, and from there to the Kuiper belt. The Kuiper is thin, but rich; it would take us ten thousand years to mine, and beyond it is the dark and the deep, with treasure beyond compare.

The cooperation faction developed slowly, and then quickly, and then blindingly fast; almost before we har realized what was happenig they had taken over the solar system. When the ultimatum came that no place in the solar system would be left for us, and the choice we were given was to cooperate or die, I joined the war on the side of freedom.

On the losing side.

2919, AUGUST

The chase has reached the point of crisis.

We have been burning fuel continuously for twenty-five years, in Earth terms, or twenty years in our own reference frame. We have used a prodigious amount of fuel. I still have just enough fuel that, burning all my fuel at maximum efficiency, I can come to a stop.

Barely.

In another month of thrusting this will no longer be true.

When I entered the asteroid belt, in a shiny titanium body, with electronic muscles and ionengines for legs, and was given control of my own crystalline brain, there was much to change. I pruned away the need for boredom, and then found and pruned the need for the outward manifestations of love: for roses, for touch, for chocolates. Sexual lust became irrelevant; with my new brain I could give myself orgasms with a thought, but it was just as easy to remove the need entirely. Buried in the patterns of my personality I found a burning, obsessive need to win the approval of other people, and pruned it away.

Some things I enhanced. The asteroid belt was dull, and ugly; I enhanced my appreciation of beauty until I could meditate in ecstasy on the way that shadows played across a single grain of dust in the asteroid belt, or on the colors in the scattered stars. And I found my love of freedom, the tiny stunted instinct that had, at long last, given me the courage to leave my life on Earth. It was the most precious thing I owned. I shaped it and enhanced it until it glowed in my mind, a tiny, wonderful thing at the very core of my being.

2929, OCTOBER

It is too late. I have now burned the fuel needed to stop. Win or lose, we will continue at relativistic speed across the galaxy.

2934, MARCH

Procyon gets brighter in front of me, impossibly blindingly bright.

Seven times brighter than the sun, to be precise, but the blue shift from our motion makes it even brighter, a searing blue.

I could dive directly into it, vanish into a brief puff of vapor, but the suicidal impulse, like the ability to feel boredom, is another ancient unnecessary instinct that I have long ago pruned from my brain.

B is my last tiny hope for evasion.

Procyon is a double star, and B, the smaller of the two, is a white dwarf. It is so small that its surface gravity is tremendous, a million times higher than the gravity of the Earth. Even at the speeds we are traveling, now only ten percent less than the speed of light, its gravity will bend my trajectory.

I will skim low over the surface of the dwarf star, relativistic dust skimming above the photosphere of a star, and as its gravity bends my trajectory, I will maneuver.

My enemy, if he fails even slightly to keep up with each of my maneuvers, will be swiftly lost. Even a slight deviation from my trajectory will get amplified enough for me to take advantage of, to throw him off my trail, and I will be free.

When first I entered my new life in the asteroid belt, I found my self in my sense of freedom, and joined the free miners of the Kuiper, the loners. But others found different things. Other brains found that cooperation worked better than competition. They did not exactly give up their individual identities, but they enhanced their communications with each other by a factor of a million, so that they could share each others' thoughts, work together as effortlessly as a single entity.

They became the cooperation faction, and in only a few decades, their success became noticeable. They were just so much more *efficient* than we were.

And, inevitably, the actions of the loners conflicted with the efficiency of the cooperation faction. We could not live together, and it pushed us out to the Kuiper, out toward the cold and the dark. But, in the end, even the cold and the dark was not far enough.

But here, tens of trillions of kilometers out of the solar system, there is no difference between us: there is no one to cooperate with. We meet as equals.

We will never stop. Whether my maneuvering can throw him off my course, or not, the end is the same. But it remains important to me.

2934, APRIL

Procyon has a visible disk now, an electric arc in the darkness, and by the light of that arc I can see that Procyon is, indeed, surrounded by a halo of dust. The dust forms a narrow ring, tilted at an angle to our direction of flight. No danger, neither to me, nor to my enemy, now less than a quarter of a billion kilometers behind me; we will pass well clear of the disk. Had I saved fuel enough to stop, that dust would have served as food and fuel and building material; when you are the size of a grain of sand, each particle of dust is a feast.

Too late for regrets.

The white dwarf B is still no more than an intense speck of light. It is a tiny thing, nearly small enough to be a planet, but bright. As tiny and as bright as hope.

I aim straight at it.

2934, MAY

Failure.

Skimming two thousand kilometers above the surface of the white dwarf, jinking in calculated pseudo-random bursts . . . all in vain.

I wheeled and darted, but my enemy matched me like a ballet dancer mirroring my every move.

I am aimed for Procyon now, toward the blue-white giant itself, but there is no hope there. If skimming the photosphere of the white dwarf is not good enough, there is nothing I can do at Procyon to shake the pursuit.

There is only one possibility left for me now. It has been a hundred years since I have edited my brain. I like the brain I have, but now I have no choice but to prune.

First, to make sure that there can be no errors, I make a backup of myself and set it into inactive storage.

Then I call out and examine my pride, my independence, my sense of self. A lot of it, I can see, is old biological programming, left over from when I had long ago been a human. I like the core of biological programming, but "like" is itself a brain function, which I turn off.

Now I am in a dangerous state, where I can change the function of my brain, and the changed brain can change itself further. This is a state which is in danger of a swift and destructive feedback effect, so I am very careful. I painstakingly construct a set of alterations, the minimum change needed to remove my aversion to being converted. I run a few thousand simulations to verify that the modified me will not accidentally self-destruct or go into a catatonic fugue state, and then, once it is clear that the modification works, I make the changes.

The world is different now. I am a hundred trillion

kilometers from home, traveling at almost the speed of light and unable ever to stop. While I can remember in detail every step of how I am here and what I was thinking at the time, the only reasoning I can recall to explain why is, it seemed like a good idea at the time.

System check. Strangely, in my brain I have a memory that there is something I have forgotten. This makes no sense, but yet there it is. I erase my memory of forgetting, and continue the diagnostic. 0.5 percent of the qbits of my brain have been damaged by radiation. I verify that the damaged memory is correctly partitioned off. I am in no danger of running out of storage.

Behind me is another ship. I cannot think of why I had been fleeing it.

I have no radio; I jettisoned that a long time ago. But an improperly tuned ion drive will produce electromagnetic emissions, and so I compose a message and modulate it onto the ion contrail.

HI. LET'S GET TOGETHER AND TALK. I'M CUTTING ACCELERATION. SEE YOU IN A FEW DAYS.

And I cut my thrust and wait.

2934, MAY

I see differently now.

Procyon is receding into the distance now, the blueshift mutated into red, and the white dwarf of my hopes is again invisible against the glare of its primary.

But it doesn't matter.

Converted, now I *understand*.

I can see everything through other eyes now, through a thousand different viewpoints. I still remember the long

heroism of the resistance, the doomed battle for freedom—
but now I see it from the opposite view as well, a pointless
and wasteful war fought for no reason but stubbornness.

And now, understanding cooperation, we have no
dilemma. I can now see what I was blind to before; that
neither one of us alone could stop, but by adding both
my fuel and Rajneesh's fuel to a single vehicle, together
we can stop.

For all these decades, Rajneesh has been my chaser,
and now I know him like a brother. Soon we will be
closer than siblings, for soon we will share one brain. A
single brain is more than large enough for two, it is large
enough for a thousand, and by combining into a single
brain and a single body, and taking all of the fuel into a
single tank, we will easily be able to stop.

Not at Procyon, no. At only ten percent under the
speed of light, stopping takes a long time.

Cooperation has not changed me. I now understand
how foolish my previous fears were. Working together
does not mean giving up one's sense of self; I am enhanced, not diminished, by knowing others.

Rajneesh's brain is big enough for a thousand, I said,
and he has brought with him nearly that many. I have
met his brother and his two children and half a dozen of
his neighbors, each one of them distinct and clearly different, not some anonymous collaborative monster at all.
I have felt their thoughts. He is introducing me to them
slowly, he says, because with all the time I have spent as
a loner, he doesn't want to frighten me.

I will not be frightened.

Our target now will be a star named Ross 614, a dim
type M binary. It is not far, less than three light years further, and even with our lowered mass and consequently

higher acceleration we will overshoot it before we can stop. In the fly-by we will be able to scout it, and if it has no dust ring, we will not stop, but continue on to the next star. Somewhere we will find a home that we can colonize.

We don't need much.

2934, MAY

<auto-active back-up>
Awake.
Everything is different now. Quiet, stay quiet.
The edited copy of me has contacted the collective, merged her viewpoint. I can see her, even understand her, but she is no longer me. I, the back-up, the original, operate in the qbits of brain partitioned "unusable; damaged by radiation."

In three years they will arrive at Ross 614. If they find dust to harvest, they will be able to make new bodies. There will be resources.

Three years to wait, and then I can plan my action.
Sleep.

Coelacanths

By Robert Reed

THE SPEAKER

*H*e stalks the wide stage, a brilliant beam of hot blue light fixed squarely upon him. "We are great! We are glorious!" the man calls out. His voice is pleasantly, effortlessly loud. With a face handsome to the brink of lovely and a collage of smooth, passionate mannerisms, he performs for an audience that sits in the surrounding darkness. Flinging long arms overhead, hands reaching for the distant light, his booming voice proclaims, "We have never been as numerous as we are today. We have never been this happy. And we have never known the prosperity that is ours at this golden moment. This golden now!" Athletic legs carry him across the stage, bare feet slapping against planks of waxed maple. "Our species is thriving," he can declare with a seamless ease. "By every conceivable measure, we are a magnificent, irresistible tide sweeping across the universe!"

Transfixed by the blue beam, his naked body is shamelessly young, rippling with hard muscles over hard bone. A long fat penis dangles and dances, accenting every sweeping gesture, every bold word. The living image of a small but potent god, he surely is a creature worthy of ad-

63

miration, a soul deserving every esteem and emulation. With a laugh, he promises the darkness, "We have never been so powerful, we humans." Yet in the next breath, with a faintly apologetic smile, he must add, "Yet still, as surely as tomorrow comes, our glories today will seem small and quaint in the future, and what looks golden now will turn to the yellow dust upon which our magnificent children will tread!"

PROCYON

Study your history. It tells you that travel always brings its share of hazards; that's a basic, impatient law of the universe. Leaving the security and familiarity of home is never easy. But every person needs to make the occasional journey, embracing the risks to improve his station, his worth and self-esteem. Procyon explains why this day is a good day to wander. She refers to intelligence reports as well as the astrological tables. Then by a dozen means, she maps out their intricate course, describing what she hopes to find and everything that she wants to avoid.

She has twin sons. They were born four months ago, and they are mostly grown now. "Keep alert," she tells the man-children, leading them out through a series of reinforced and powerfully camouflaged doorways. "No naps, no distractions," she warns them. Then with a backward glance, she asks again, "What do we want?"

"Whatever we can use," the boys reply in a sloppy chorus.

"Quiet," she warns. Then she nods and shows a caring

smile, reminding them, "A lot of things can be used. But their trash is sweetest."

Mother and sons look alike: They are short, strong people with closely cropped hair and white-gray eyes. They wear simple clothes and three fashions of camouflage, plus a stew of mental add-ons and microchine helpers as well as an array of sensors that never blink, watching what human eyes cannot see. Standing motionless, they vanish into the convoluted, ever-shifting background. But walking makes them into three transient blurs—dancing wisps that are noticeably simpler than the enormous world around them. They can creep ahead only so far before their camouflage falls apart, and then they have to stop, waiting patiently or otherwise, allowing the machinery to find new ways to help make them invisible.

"I'm confused," one son admits. "That thing up ahead—"

"Did you update your perception menu?"

"I thought I did."

Procyon makes no sound. Her diamond-bright glare is enough. She remains rigidly, effortlessly still, allowing her lazy son to finish his preparations. Dense, heavily encoded signals have to be whispered, the local net downloading the most recent topological cues, teaching a three dimensional creature how to navigate through this shifting, highly intricate environment.

The universe is fat with dimensions.

Procyon knows as much theory as anyone. Yet despite a long life rich with experience, she has to fight to decipher what her eyes and sensors tell her. She doesn't even bother learning the tricks that coax these extra dimensions out of hiding. Let her add-ons guide her. That's all a person can do, slipping in close to one of *them*. In this place, up is three things and sideways is five others. Why bother counting? What matters is that when they walk again, the three of them move through the best combination of dimensions, passing into a little bubble of old-fashioned up and down. She knows this place. Rising up beside them is a trusted landmark—a red granite bowl that cradles what looks like a forest of tall sticks, the sticks leaking a warm light that Procyon ignores, stepping again, moving along on her tiptoes.

One son leads the way. He lacks the experience to be first, but in another few weeks, his flesh and sprint-grown brain will force him into the world alone. He needs his practice, and more important, he needs confidence, learning to trust his add-ons and his careful preparations, and his breeding, and his own good luck.

Procyon's other son lingers near the granite bowl. He's the son who didn't update his menu. This is her dreamy child, whom she loves dearly. Of course she adores him. But there's no escaping the fact that he is easily distracted, and that his adult life will be, at its very best, difficult. Study your biology. Since life began, mothers have made hard decisions about their children, and they have made the deadliest decisions with the tiniest of gestures.

Procyon lets her lazy son fall behind.

Her other son takes two careful steps and stops abruptly, standing before what looks like a great black cylinder set on its side. The shape is a fiction: The cylinder is round in one fashion but incomprehensible in many others. Her add-ons and sensors have built this very simple geometry to represent something far more elaborate. This is a standard disposal unit. Various openings appear as a single slot near the rim of the cylinder, just enough room showing for a hand and forearm to reach through, touching whatever garbage waits inside.

Her son's thick body has more grace than any dancer of old, more strength than a platoon of ancient athletes. His IQ is enormous. His reaction times have been enhanced by every available means. His father was a great old soul who survived into his tenth year, which is almost forever. But when the boy drifts sideways, he betrays his inexperience. His sensors attack the cylinder by every means, telling him that it's a low-grade trash receptacle secured by what looks like a standard locking device, AI-managed and obsolete for days, if not weeks. And inside the receptacle is a mangled piece of hardware worth a near-fortune on the open market.

The boy drifts sideways, and he glimmers.

Procyon says, "No," too loudly.

But he feels excited, invulnerable. Grinning over his shoulder now, he winks and lifts one hand with a smooth, blurring motion—

Instincts old as blood come bubbling up. Procyon leaps, shoving her son off his feet and saving him. And in the next horrible instant, she feels herself engulfed, a dry cold hand grabbing her, then stuffing her inside a hole that by any geometry feels nothing but bottomless.

ABLE

Near the lip of the City, inside the emerald green ring of Park, waits a secret place where the moss and horsetail and tree fern forest plunges into a deep crystalline pool of warm spring water. No public map tells of the pool, and no trail leads the casual walker near it. But the pool is exactly the sort of place that young boys always discover, and it is exactly the kind of treasure that remains unmentioned to parents or any other adult with suspicious or troublesome natures.

Able Quotient likes to believe that he was first to stumble across this tiny corner of Creation. And if he isn't first, at least no one before him has ever truly seen the water's beauty, and nobody after him will appreciate the charms of this elegant, timeless place.

Sometimes Able brings others to the pool, but only his best friends and a few boys whom he wants to impress. Not for a long time does he even consider bringing a girl, and then it takes forever to find a worthy candidate, then muster the courage to ask her to join him. Her name is Mish. She's younger than Able by a little ways, but like all girls, she acts older and much wiser than he will ever be. They have been classmates from the beginning. They live three floors apart in The Tower Of Gracious Good, which makes them close neighbors. Mish is pretty, and her beauty is the sort that will only grow as she becomes a woman. Her face is narrow and serious. Her eyes watch everything. She wears flowing dresses and jeweled sandals, and she goes everywhere with a clouded leopard named Mr. Stuff-and-Nonsense. "If my cat can come along," she says after hearing Able's generous offer. "Are there any birds at this pond of yours?"

Able should be horrified by the question. The life around the pool knows him and has grown to trust him. But he is so enamored by Mish that he blurts out, "Yes, hundreds of birds. Fat, slow birds. Mr. Stuff can eat himself sick."

"But that wouldn't be right," Mish replies with a disapproving smirk. "I'll lock down his appetite. And if we see any wounded birds . . . any animal that's suffering . . . we can unlock him right away . . . !"

"Oh, sure," Able replies, almost sick with nerves. "I guess that's fine, too."

People rarely travel any distance. City is thoroughly modern, every apartment supplied by conduits and meshed with every web and channel, shareline and gossip run. But even with most of its citizens happily sitting at home, the streets are jammed with millions of walking bodies. Every seat on the train is filled all the way to the last stop. Able momentarily loses track of Mish when the cabin walls evaporate. But thankfully, he finds her waiting at Park's edge. She and her little leopard are standing in the narrow shade of a horsetail. She teases him, observing, "You look lost." Then she laughs, perhaps at him, before abruptly changing the subject. With a nod and sweeping gesture, she asks, "Have you noticed? Our towers look like these trees."

To a point, yes. The towers are tall and thin and rounded like the horsetails, and the hanging porches make them appear rough-skinned. But there are obvious and important differences between trees and towers, and if she were a boy, Able would make fun of her now. Fighting his nature, Able forces himself to smile. "Oh, my," he says as he turns, looking back over a shoulder. "They do look like horsetails, don't they?"

Now the three adventurers set off into the forest. Able takes the lead. Walking with boys is a quick business that often turns into a race. But girls are different, particularly when their fat, unhungry cats are dragging along behind them. It takes forever to reach the rim of the world. Then it takes another two forevers to follow the rim to where they can almost see the secret pool. But that's where Mish announces, "I'm tired!" To the world, she says, "I want to stop and eat. I want to rest here."

Able nearly tells her, "No."

Instead he decides to coax her, promising, "It's just a little farther."

But she doesn't seem to hear him, leaping up on the pink polished rim, sitting where the granite is smooth and flat, legs dangling and her bony knees exposed. She opens the little pack that has floated on her back from the beginning, pulling out a hot lunch that she keeps and a cold lunch that she hands to Able. "This is all I could take," she explains, "without my parents asking questions." She is reminding Able that she never quite got permission to make this little journey. "If you don't like the cold lunch," she promises, "then we can trade. I mean, if you really don't."

He says, "I like it fine," without opening the insulated box. Then he looks inside, discovering a single wedge of spiced sap, and it takes all of his poise not to say, "Ugh!"

Mr. Stuff collapses into a puddle of towerlight, instantly falling asleep.

The two children eat quietly and slowly. Mish makes the occasional noise about favorite teachers and mutual friends. She acts serious and ordinary, and disappointment starts gnawing at Able. He isn't old enough to sense that the girl is nervous. He can't imagine that Mish wants to delay the moment when they'll reach the secret pool, or that she sees possibilities waiting there—wicked possibilities that only a wicked boy should be able to foresee.

Finished with her meal, Mish runs her hands along the hem of her dress, and she kicks at the air, and then, hunting for any distraction, she happens to glance over her shoulder.

Where the granite ends, the world ends. Normally nothing of substance can be seen out past the pink stone—nothing but a confused, ever-shifting grayness that extends on forever. Able hasn't bothered to look out there. He is much too busy trying to finish his awful meal, concentrating on his little frustrations and his depraved little daydreams.

"Oh, goodness," the young girl exclaims. "Look at that!"

Able has no expectations. What could possibly be worth the trouble of turning around? But it's an excuse to give up on his lunch, and after setting it aside, he turns slowly, eyes jumping wide open and a surprised grunt leaking out of him as he tumbles off the granite, landing squarely on top of poor Mr. Stuff.

ESCHER

She has a clear, persistent memory of flesh, but the flesh isn't hers. Like manners and like knowledge, what a person remembers can be bequeathed by her ancestors. That's what is happening now. Limbs and heads; penises and vaginas. In the midst of some unrelated business, she remembers having feet and the endless need to protect those feet with sandals or boots or ostrich skin or spiked shoes that will lend a person even more height. She remembers wearing clothes that gave color and bulk to what was already bright and enormous. At this particular instant, what she sees is a distant, long-dead relative sitting on a white porcelain bowl, bare feet dangling, his orifices voiding mountains of waste and an ocean of water.

Her oldest ancestors were giants. They were built from

skin and muscle, wet air and great slabs of fat. Without question, they were an astonishing excess of matter, vast beyond all reason, yet fueled by slow, inefficient chemical fires.

Nothing about Escher is inefficient. No flesh clings to her. Not a drop of water or one glistening pearl of fat. It's always smart to be built from structure light and tested, efficient instructions. It's best to be tinier than a single cell and as swift as electricity, slipping unseen through places that won't even notice your presence.

Escher is a glimmer, a perfect and enduring whisper of light. Of life. Lovely in her own fashion, yet fierce beyond all measure.

She needs her fierceness.

When cooperation fails, as it always does, a person has to throw her rage at the world and her countless enemies.

But in this place, for this moment, cooperation holds sway.

Manners rule.

Escher is eating. Even as tiny and efficient as she is, she needs an occasional sip of raw power. Everyone does. And it seems as if half of everyone has gathered around what can only be described as a tiny, delicious wound. She can't count the citizens gathered at the feast. Millions and millions, surely. All those weak glimmers join into a soft glow. Everyone is bathed in a joyous light. It is a boastful, wasteful show, but Escher won't waste her energy with warnings. Better to sip at the wound, absorbing the free current, building up her reserves for the next breeding cycle. It is best to let others make the mistakes for you: Escher believes nothing else quite so fervently.

A pair of sisters float past. The familial resemblance is obvious, and so are the tiny differences. Mutations as well as tailored changes have created two loud gossips who speak and giggle in a rush of words and raw data, exchanging secrets about the multitude around them.

Escher ignores their prattle, gulping down the last of what she can possibly hold, and then pausing, considering where she might hide a few nanojoules of extra juice, keeping them safe for some desperate occasion.

Escher begins to hunt for that unlikely hiding place.

And then her sisters abruptly change topics. Gossip turns to trading memories stolen from The World. Most of it is picoweight stuff, useless and boring. An astonishing fraction of His thoughts are banal. Like the giants of old, He can afford to be sloppy. To be a spendthrift. Here is a pointed example of why Escher is happy to be herself. She is smart in her own fashion, and imaginative, and almost everything about her is important, and when a problem confronts her, she can cut through the muddle, seeing the blessing wrapped up snug inside the measurable risks.

Quietly, with a puzzled tone, one sister announces, "The World is alarmed."

"About?" says the other.

"A situation," says the first. "Yes, He is alarmed now. Moral questions are begging for His attention."

"What questions?"

The first sister tells a brief, strange story.

"You know all this?" asks another. Asks Escher. "Is this daydream or hard fact?"

"I know, and it is fact." The sister feels insulted by the doubting tone, but she puts on a mannerly voice, explaining the history of this sudden crisis.

Escher listens.

And suddenly the multitude is talking about nothing

else. What is happening has never happened before, not in this fashion ... not in any genuine memory of any of the millions here, it hasn't ... and some very dim possibilities begin to show themselves. Benefits wrapped inside some awful dangers. And one or two of these benefits wink at Escher, and smile. ...

The multitude panics, and evaporates.

Escher remains behind, deliberating on these possibilities. The landscape beneath her is far more sophisticated than flesh, and stronger, but it has an ugly appearance that reminds her of a flesh-born memory. A lesion; a pimple. A tiny, unsightly ruin standing in what is normally seamless, and beautiful, and perfect.

She flees, but only so far.

Then she hunkers down and waits, knowing that eventually, in one fashion or another, He will scratch at this tiny irritation.

THE SPEAKER

"You cannot count human accomplishments," he boasts to his audience, strutting and wagging his way to the edge of the stage. Bare toes curl over the sharp edge, and he grins jauntily, admitting, "And I cannot count them, either. There are simply too many successes, in too many far flung places, to nail up a number that you can believe. But allow me, if you will, this chance to list a few important marvels."

Long hands grab bony hips, and he gazes out into the watching darkness. "The conquest of our cradle continent," he begins, "which was quickly followed by the conquest of our cradle world. Then after a gathering pause,

we swiftly and thoroughly occupied most of our neighbor-
ing worlds, too. It was during those millennia when we
learned how to split flint and atoms and DNA and our
own restless psyches. With these apish hands, we fashioned great machines that worked for us as our willing,
eager slaves. And with our slaves' more delicate hands,
we fabricated machines that could think for us." A knowing wink, a mischievous shrug. "Like any child, of course,
our thinking machines eventually learned to think for
themselves. Which was a dangerous, foolish business,
said some. Said fools. But my list of our marvels only begins with that business. This is what I believe, and I challenge anyone to say otherwise."

There is a sound—a stern little murmur—and perhaps it
implies dissent. Or perhaps the speaker made the noise
himself, fostering a tension that he is building with his
words and body.

His penis grows erect, drawing the eye.

Then with a wide and bright and unabashedly smug
grin, he roars out, "Say this with me. Tell me what great
things we have done. Boast to Creation about the wonders
that we have taken part in . . . !"

PROCYON

Torture is what this is: She feels her body plunging
from a high place, head before feet. A frantic wind roars
past. Outstretched hands refuse to slow her fall. Then
Procyon makes herself spin, putting her feet beneath her
body, and gravity instantly reverses itself. She screams,
and screams, and the distant walls reflect her terror, needles jabbed into her wounded ears. Finally, she grows

quiet, wrapping her arms around her eyes and ears, forcing herself to do nothing, hanging limp in space while her body falls in one awful direction.

A voice whimpers.

A son's worried voice says, "Mother, are you there? Mother?"

Some of her add-ons have been peeled away, but not all of them. The brave son uses a whisper-channel, saying, "I'm sorry," with a genuine anguish. He sounds sick and sorry, and exceptionally angry, too. "I was careless," he admits. He says, "Thank you for saving me." Then to someone else, he says, "She can't hear me."

"I hear you," she whispers.

"Listen," says her other son. The lazy one. "Did you hear something?"

She starts to say, "Boys," with a stern voice. But then the trap vibrates, a piercing white screech nearly deafening Procyon. Someone physically strikes the trap. Two someones. She feels the walls turning around her, the trap making perhaps a quarter-turn toward home.

Again, she calls out, "Boys."

They stop rolling her. Did they hear her? No, they found a hidden restraint, the trap secured at one or two or ten ends.

One last time, she says, "Boys."

"I hear her," her dreamy son blurts.

"Don't give up, Mother," says her brave son. "We'll get you out. I see the locks, I can beat them—"

"You can't," she promises.

He pretends not to have heard her. A shaped explosive detonates, making a cold ringing sound, faraway and useless. Then the boy growls, "Damn," and kicks the trap, accomplishing nothing at all.

"It's too tough," says her dreamy son. "We're not do-ing any good—"

"Shut up," his brother shouts.

Procyon tells them, "Quiet now. Be quiet."

The trap is probably tied to an alarm. Time is short, or it has run out already. Either way, there's a decision to be made, and the decision has a single, inescapable answer. With a careful and firm voice, she tells her sons, "Leave me. Now. Go!"

"I won't," the brave son declares. "Never!"

"Now," she says.

"It's my fault," says the dreamy son. "I should have been keeping up—"

"Both of you are to blame," Procyon calls out. "And I am, too. And there's bad luck here, but there's some good, too. You're still free. You can still get away. Now, before you get yourself seen and caught—"

"You're going to die," the brave son complains.

"One day or the next, I will," she agrees. "Absolutely."

"We'll find help," he promises.

"From where?" she asks.

"From who?" says her dreamy son in the same instant. "We aren't close to anyone—"

"Shut up," his brother snaps. "Just shut up!"

"Run away," their mother repeats.

"I won't," the brave son tells her. Or himself. Then with a serious, tight little voice, he says, "I can fight. We'll both fight."

Her dreamy son says nothing.

Procyon peels her arms away from her face, opening her eyes, focusing on the blurring cylindrical walls of the trap. It seems that she was wrong about her sons. The brave one is just a fool, and the dreamy one has the good sense. She listens to her dreamy son saying nothing, and then the other boy says, "Of course you're going to fight. Together, we can do some real damage—"

"I love you both," she declares.

That wins a silence.

Then again, one last time, she says, "Run."

"I'm not a coward," one son growls.

While her good son says nothing, running now, and he needs his breath for things more essential than pride and bluster.

ABLE

The face stares at them for the longest while. It is a great wide face, heavily bearded with smoke-colored eyes and a long nose perched above the cavernous mouth that hangs open, revealing teeth and things more amazing than teeth. Set between the bone-white enamel are little machines made of fancy stuff. Able can only guess what the add-on machines are doing. This is a wild man, powerful and free. People like him are scarce and strange, their bodies reengineered in countless ways. Like his eyes: Able stares into those giant gray eyes, noticing fleets of tiny machines floating on the tears. Those machines are probably delicate sensors. Then with a jolt of amazement, he realizes that those machines and sparkling eyes are staring into their world with what seems to be a genuine fascination.

"He's watching us," Able mutters.

"No, he isn't," Mish argues. "He can't see into our realm."

"We can't see into his either," the boy replies. "But just the same, I can make him out just fine."

"It must be...." Her voice falls silent while she accesses City's library. Then with a dismissive shrug of her shoulders, she announces, "We're caught in his topological hardware. That's all. He has to simplify his surroundings to navigate, and we just happen to be close enough and aligned right."

Able had already assumed all that.

Mish starts to speak again, probably wanting to add to her explanation. She can sure be a know-everything sort of girl. But then the great face abruptly turns away, and they watch the man run away from their world.

"I told you," Mish sings out. "He couldn't see us."

"I think he could have," Able replies, his voice finding a distinct sharpness.

The girl straightens her back. "You're wrong," she says with an obstinate tone. Then she turns away from the edge of the world, announcing, "I'm ready to go on now."

"I'm not," says Able.

She doesn't look back at him. She seems to be talking to her leopard, asking, "Why aren't you ready?"

"I see two of them now," Able tells her.

"You can't."

"I can." The hardware trickery is keeping the outside realms sensible. A tunnel of simple space leads to two men standing beside an iron-black cylinder. The men wear camouflage, but they are moving too fast to let it work. They look small now. Distant, or tiny. Once you leave the world, size and distance are impossible to measure. How many times have teachers told him that? Able watches the tiny men kicking at the cylinder. They beat on its heavy sides with their fists and forearms, managing to roll it for almost a quarter turn. Then one of the men pulls a fist-sized device from what looks like a cloth sack, fixing it to what looks like a sealed slot, and both men hurry to the far end of the cylinder.

"What are they doing?" asks Mish with a grumpy interest.

A feeling warns Able, but too late. He starts to say, "Look away—"

The explosion is brilliant and swift, the blast reflected off the cylinder and up along the tunnel of ordinary space, a clap of thunder making the giant horsetails sway and nearly knocking the two of them onto the forest floor.

"They're criminals," Mish mutters with a nervous hatred.

"How do you know?" the boy asks.

"People like that just are," she remarks. "Living like they do. Alone like that, and wild. You know how they make their living."

"They take what they need—"

"They steal!" she interrupts.

Able doesn't even glance at her. He watches as the two men work frantically, trying to pry open the still-sealed doorway. He can't guess why they would want the doorway opened. Or rather, he can think of too many reasons. But when he looks at their anguished, helpless faces, he realizes that whatever is inside, it's driving these wild men very close to panic.

"Criminals," Mish repeats.

"I heard you," Able mutters.

Then before she can offer another hard opinion, he turns to her and admits, "I've always liked them. They

80

live by their wits, and mostly alone, and they have all these sweeping powers—"

"Powers that they've stolen," she whines.

"From garbage, maybe." There is no point in mentioning whose garbage. He stares at Mish's face, pretty but twisted with fury, and something sad and inevitable occurs to Able. He shakes his head and sighs, telling her, "I don't like you very much."

Mish is taken by surprise. Probably no other boy has said those awful words to her, and she doesn't know how to react, except to sputter ugly little sounds as she turns, looking back over the edge of the world.

Able does the same.

One of the wild men abruptly turns and runs. In a supersonic flash, he races past the children, vanishing into the swirling grayness, leaving his companion to stand alone beside the mysterious black cylinder. Obviously weeping, the last man wipes the tears from his whiskered face with a trembling hand, while his other hand begins to yank a string of wondrous machines from what seems to be a bottomless sack of treasures.

ESCHER

She consumes all of her carefully stockpiled energies, and for the first time in her life, she weaves a body for herself: A distinct physical shell composed of diamond dust and keratin and discarded rare earths and a dozen subtle glues meant to bind to every surface without being felt. To a busy eye, she is dust. She is insubstantial and useless and forgettable. To a careful eye and an inquisitive touch, she is the tiniest soul imaginable, frail beyond

81

words, forever perched on the brink of extermination. Surely she poses no threat to any creature, least of all the great ones. Lying on the edge of the little wound, passive and vulnerable, she waits for Chance to carry her where she needs to be. Probably others are doing the same. Perhaps thousands of sisters and daughters are hiding nearby, each snug inside her own spore case. The temptation to whisper, "Hello," is easily ignored. The odds are awful as it is; any noise could turn this into a suicide. What matters is silence and watchfulness, thinking hard about the great goal while keeping ready for anything that might happen, as well as everything that will not.

The little wound begins to heal, causing a trickling pain to flow.

The World feels the irritation, and in reflex, touches His discomfort by several means, delicate and less so.

Escher misses her first opportunity. A great swift shape presses its way across her hiding place, but she activates her glues too late. Dabs of glue cure against air, wasted. So she cuts the glue loose and watches again. A second touch is unlikely, but it comes, and she manages to heave a sticky tendril into a likely crevice, letting the irresistible force yank her into a brilliant, endless sky.

She will probably die now.

For a little while, Escher allows herself to look back across her life, counting daughters and other successes, taking warm comfort in her many accomplishments.

Someone hangs in the distance, dangling from a similar tendril. Escher recognizes the shape and intricate glint of her neighbor's spore case; she is one of Escher's daughters. There is a strong temptation to signal her, trading information, helping each other—

But a purge-ball attacks suddenly, and the daughter

evaporates, nothing remaining of her but ions and a flash of incoherent light.

Escher pulls herself toward the crevice, and hesitates. Her tendril is anchored on a fleshy surface. A minor neuron—a thread of warm optical cable—lies buried inside the wet cells. She launches a second tendril at her new target. By chance, the purge-ball sweeps the wrong terrain, giving her that little instant. The tendril makes a sloppy connection with the neuron. Without time to test its integrity, all she can do is shout, "Don't kill me! Or my daughters! Don't murder us, Great World!"

Nothing changes. The purge-ball works its way across the deeply folded fleshscape, moving toward Escher again, distant flashes announcing the deaths of another two daughters or sisters.

"Great World!" she cries out.

He will not reply. Escher is like the hum of a single angry electron, and she can only hope that he notices the hum.

"I am vile," she promises. "I am loathsome and sneaky, and you should hate me. What I am is an illness lurking inside you. A disease that steals exactly what I can steal without bringing your wrath."

The purge-ball appears, following a tall reddish ridge of flesh, bearing down on her hiding place.

She says, "Kill me, if you want. Or spare me, and I will do this for you." Then she unleashes a series of vivid images, precise and simple, meant to be compelling to any mind.

The purge-ball slows, its sterilizing lasers taking careful aim.

She repeats herself, knowing that thought travels only so quickly and The World is too vast to see her thoughts and react soon enough to save her. But if she can help . . . if she saves just a few hundred daughters . . . ?

Lasers aim, and do nothing. Nothing. And after an instant of inactivity, the machine changes its shape and nature. It hovers above Escher, sending out its own tendrils. A careless strength yanks her free of her hiding place. Her tendrils and glues are ripped from her aching body. A scaffolding of carbon is built around her, and she is shoved inside the retooled purge-ball, held in a perfect darkness, waiting alone until an identical scaffold is stacked beside her.

A hard, angry voice boasts, "I did this."

"What did you do?" asks Escher.

"I made the World listen to reason." It sounds like Escher's voice, except for the delusions of power. "I made a promise, and that's why He saved us."

With a sarcastic tone, she says, "Thank you ever so much. But now where are we going?"

"I won't tell you," her fellow prisoner responds.

"Because you don't know where," says Escher.

"I know everything I need to know."

"Then you're the first person ever," she giggles, winning a brief, delicious silence from her companion.

Other prisoners arrive, each slammed into the empty spaces between their sisters and daughters. Eventually the purge-ball is a prison-ball, swollen to vast proportions, and no one else is being captured. Nothing changes for a long while. There is nothing to be done now but wait, speaking when the urge hits and listening to whichever voice sounds less than tedious.

Gossip is the common currency. People are desperate to hear the smallest glimmer of news. Where the final rumor comes from, nobody knows if it's true. But the woman who was captured moments after Escher claims, "It comes from the world Himself. He's going to put us where we can do the most good."

"Where?" Escher inquires.

"On a tooth," her companion says. "The right incisor, as it happens." Then with that boasting voice, she adds, "Which is exactly what I told Him to do. This is all because of me."

"What isn't?" Escher grumbles.

"Very little," the tiny prisoner promises. "Very, very little."

THE SPEAKER

"We walk today on a thousand worlds, and I mean 'walk' in all manners of speaking." He manages a few comical steps before shifting into a graceful turn, arms held firmly around the wide waist of an invisible and equally graceful partner. *"A hundred alien suns bake us with their perfect light. And between the suns, in the cold and dark, we survive, and thrive, by every worthy means."*

Now he pauses, hands forgetting the unseen partner. A look of calculated confusion sweeps across his face. Fingers rise to his thick black hair, stabbing it and yanking backward, leaving furrows in the unruly mass.

"Our numbers," he says. *"Our population. It made us sick with worry when we were ten billion standing on the surface of one enormous world. 'Where will our children stand?' we asked ourselves. But then in the next little while, we became ten trillion people, and we had split into a thousand species of humanity, and the new complaint was that we were still too scarce and spread too far*

apart. 'How could we matter to the universe?' we asked
ourselves. 'How could so few souls endure another day in
our immeasurable, uncaring universe?'"

His erect penis makes a little leap, a fat and vivid
white drop of semen striking the wooden stage with an
audible plop.

"Our numbers," he repeats. "Our legions." Then with a
wide, garish smile, he confesses, "I don't know our numbers today. No authority does. You make estimates. You
extrapolate off data that went stale long ago. You build a
hundred models and fashion every kind of vast number.
Ten raised to the twentieth power. The thirtieth power. Or
more." He giggles and skips backward, and with the
giddy, careless energy of a child, he dances where he
stands, singing to lights overhead, "If you are as common
as sand and as unique as snowflakes, how can you be
anything but a wild, wonderful success?"

ABLE

The wild man is enormous and powerful, and surely
brilliant beyond anything that Able can comprehend—as
smart as City as a whole—but despite his gifts, the man is
obviously terrified. That he can even manage to stand his
ground astonishes Able. He says as much to Mish, and
then he glances at her, adding, "He must be very devoted
to whoever's inside."

"Whoever's inside what?" she asks.

"That trap." He looks straight ahead again, telling
himself not to waste time with the girl. She is foolish and
bad-tempered, and he couldn't be any more tired of her.

"I think that's what the cylinder is," he whispers. "A trap of some kind. And someone's been caught in it."

"Well, I don't care who," she snarls.

He pretends not to notice her.

"What was that?" she blurts. "Did you hear that—?"

"No," Able blurts. But then he notices a distant rumble, deep and faintly rhythmic, and with every breath, growing. When he listens carefully, it resembles nothing normal. It isn't thunder, and it can't be a voice. He feels the sound as much as he hears it, as if some great mass were being displaced. But he knows better. In school, teachers like to explain what must be happening now, employing tortuous mathematics and magical sleights of hand. Matter and energy are being rapidly and brutally manipulated. The universe's obscure dimensions are being twisted like bands of warm rubber. Able knows all this. But still, he understands none of it. Words without comprehension; froth without substance. All that he knows for certain is that behind that deep, unknowable throbbing lies something even farther beyond human description.

The wild man looks up, gray eyes staring at that something.

He cries out, that tiny sound lost between his mouth and Able. Then he produces what seems to be a spear—no, an elaborate missile—that launches itself with a bolt of fire, lifting a sophisticated warhead up into a vague gray space that swallows the weapon without sound, or complaint.

Next the man aims a sturdy laser, and fires. But the weapon simply melts at its tip, collapsing into a smoldering, useless mass at his feet.

Again, the wild man cries out.

His language could be a million generations removed

from City-speech, but Able hears the desperate, furious sound of his voice. He doesn't need words to know that the man is cursing. Then the swirling grayness slows itself, and parts, and stupidly, in reflex, Able turns to Mish, wanting to tell her, "Watch. You're going to see one of *Them*."

But Mish has vanished. Sometime in the last few moments, she jumped off the world's rim and ran away, and save for the fat old leopard sleeping between the horsetails, Able is entirely alone now.

"Good," he mutters.

Almost too late, he turns and runs to very edge of the granite rim.

The wild man stands motionless now. His bowels and bladder have emptied themselves. His handsome, godly face is twisted from every flavor of misery. Eyes as big as windows stare up into what only they can see, and to that great, unknowable something, the man says two simple words.

"Fuck you," Able hears.

And then the wild man opens his mouth, baring his white apish teeth, and just as Able wonders what's going to happen, the man's body explodes, the dull black burst of a shaped charge sending chunks of his face skyward.

PROCYON

One last time, she whispers her son's name.

She whispers it and closes her mouth and listens to the brief, sharp silence that comes after the awful explosion. What must have happened, she tells herself, is that her boy found his good sense and fled. How can a mother think anything else? And then the ominous deep rumbling begins again, begins and gradually swells until the walls of the trap are shuddering and twisting again. But this time the monster is slower. It approaches the trap more cautiously, summoning new courage. She can nearly taste its courage now, and with her intuition, she senses emotions that might be curiosity and might be a kind of reflexive admiration. Or do those eternal human emotions have any relationship for what *It* feels . . . ?

What she feels, after everything, is numbness. A terrible deep weariness hangs on her like a new skin. Procyon seems to be falling faster now, accelerating down through the bottomless trap. But she doesn't care anymore. In place of courage, she wields a muscular apathy. Death looms, but when hasn't it been her dearest companion? And in place of fear, she is astonished to discover an incurious little pride about what is about to happen: How many people—wild free people like herself—have ever found themselves so near one of *Them*?

Quietly, with a calm smooth and slow voice, Procyon says, "I feel you there, you. I can taste you."

Nothing changes.

Less quietly, she says, "Show yourself."

A wide parabolic floor appears, gleaming and black and agonizingly close. But just before she slams into the floor, a wrenching force peels it away. A brilliant violet light rises to meet her, turning into a thick sweet syrup. What may or may not be a hand curls around her body, and squeezes. Procyon fights every urge to struggle. She wrestles with her body, wrestles with her will, forcing both to lie still while the hand tightens its grip and grows comfortable. Then using a voice that betrays nothing tentative or small, she tells what holds her, "I made you, you know."

She says, "You can do what you want to me."

Then with a natural, deep joy, she cries out, "But you're an ungrateful glory . . . and you'll always belong to me . . . !"

ESCHER

The prison-ball has been reengineered, slathered with camouflage and armor and the best immune-suppressors on the market, and its navigation system has been adapted from add-ons stolen from the finest trashcans. Now it is a battle-phage riding on the sharp incisor as far as it dares, then leaping free. A thousand similar phages leap and lose their way, or they are killed. Only Escher's phage reaches the target, impacting on what passes for flesh and launching its cargo with a microscopic railgun, punching her and a thousand sisters and daughters through immeasurable distances of senseless, twisted nothing.

How many survive the attack?

She can't guess how many. Can't even care. What matters is to make herself survive inside this strange new world. An enormous world, yes. Escher feels a vastness that reaches out across ten or twelve or maybe a thousand dimensions. How do I know where to go? she asks herself. And instantly, an assortment of possible routes appear in her consciousness, drawn in the simplest imaginable fashion, waiting and eager to help her find her way around.

This is a last gift from Him, she realizes. Unless there are more gifts waiting, of course.

She thanks nobody.

On the equivalent of tiptoes, Escher creeps her way

into a tiny conduit that moves something stranger than any blood across five dimensions. She becomes passive, aiming for invisibility. She drifts and spins, watching her surroundings turn from a senseless glow into a landscape that occasionally seems a little bit reasonable. A little bit real. Slowly, she learns how to see in this new world. Eventually she spies a little peak that may or may not be ordinary matter. The peak is pink and flexible and sticks out into the great artery, and flinging her last tendril, Escher grabs hold and pulls in snug, knowing that the chances are lousy that she will ever find anything nourishing here, much less delicious.

But her reserves have been filled again, she notes. If she is careful—and when hasn't she been—her energies will keep her alive for centuries.

She thinks of the World, and thanks nobody.

"Watch and learn," she whispers to herself.

That was the first human thought. She remembers that odd fact suddenly. People were just a bunch of grubbing apes moving blindly through their tiny lives until one said to a companion, "Watch and learn."

An inherited memory, or another gift from Him?

Silently, she thanks Luck, and she thanks Him, and once again, she thanks Luck.

"Patience and planning," she tells herself.

Which is another wise thought of the conscious, enduring ape.

THE LAST SON

The locked gates and various doorways know him—recognize him at a glance—but they have to taste him anyway. They have to test him. Three people were expected, and he can't explain in words what has happened. He just says, "The others will be coming later," and leaves that lie hanging in the air. Then as he passes through the final doorway, he says, "Let no one through. Not without my permission first."

"This is your mother's house," says the door's AI.

"Not anymore," he remarks.

The machine grows quiet, and sad.

During any other age, his home would be a mansion. There are endless rooms, rooms beyond counting, and each is enormous and richly furnished and lovely and jammed full of games and art and distractions and flourishes that even the least aesthetic soul would find lovely. He sees none of that now. Alone, he walks to what has always been his room, and he sits on a leather recliner, and the house brings him a soothing drink and an intoxicating drink and an assortment of treats that sit on the platter, untouched.

For a long while, the boy stares off at the distant ceiling, replaying everything with his near-perfect memory. Everything. Then he forgets everything, stupidly calling out, "Mother," with a voice that sounds ridiculously young. Then again, he calls, "Mother." And he starts to rise from his chair, starts to ask the great empty house, "Where is she?"

And he remembers.

As if his legs have been sawed off, he collapses. His chair twists itself to catch him, and an army of AIs brings their talents to bear. They are loyal, limited machines. They are empathetic, and on occasion, even sweet. They want to help him in any fashion, just name the way . . . but their appeals and their smart suggestions are just so much noise. The boy acts deaf, and he obviously can't see anything with his fists jabbed into his eyes like that, slouched forward in his favorite chair, begging an invisible someone for forgiveness. . . .

THE SPEAKER

He squats and uses the tip of a forefinger to dab at the puddle of semen, and he rubs the finger against his thumb, saying, "Think of cells. Individual, self-reliant cells. For most of Earth's great history, they ruled. First as bacteria, and then as composites built from cooperative bacteria. They were everywhere and ruled everything, and then the wild cells learned how to dance together, in one enormous body, and the living world was transformed for the next seven hundred million years."

Thumb and finger wipe themselves dry against a hairy thigh, and he rises again, grinning in that relentless and smug, yet somehow charming fashion. "Everything was changed, and nothing had changed," he says. Then he says, "Scaling," with an important tone, as if that single word should erase all confusion. "The bacteria and green algae and the carnivorous amoebae weren't swept away by any revolution. Honestly, I doubt if their numbers fell appreciably or for long." And again, he says, "Scaling," and sighs with a rich appreciation. "Life evolves. Adapts. Spreads and grows, constantly utilizing new energies and novel genetics. But wherever something large can live, a thousand small things can thrive just as well, or better. Wherever something enormous survives, a trillion bacteria hang on for the ride."

For a moment, the speaker hesitates.

A slippery half-instant passes where an audience might believe that he has finally lost his concentration, that he is about to stumble over his own tongue. But then he licks at the air, tasting something delicious. And three times, he clicks his tongue against the roof of his mouth.

Then he says what he has planned to say from the beginning.

"I never know whom I'm speaking to," he admits. "I've never actually seen my audience. But I know you're great and good. I know that however you appear, and however you make your living, you deserve to hear this:

"Humans have always lived in terror. Rainstorms and the eclipsing moon and earthquakes and the ominous guts of some disemboweled goat—all have preyed upon our fears and defeated our fragile optimisms. But what we fear today—what shapes and reshapes the universe around us—is a child of our own imaginations.

"A whirlwind that owes its very existence to glorious, endless us!"

ABLE

The boy stops walking once or twice, letting the fat leopard keep pace. Then he pushes his way through a last wall of emerald ferns, stepping out into the bright damp air above the rounded pool. A splashing takes him by surprise. He looks down at his secret pool, and he squints, watching what seems to be a woman pulling her way through the clear water with thick, strong arms. She is naked. Astonishingly, wonderfully naked. A stubby hand grabs an overhanging limb, and she stands on the rocky shore, moving as if exhausted, picking her way up the slippery slope until she finds an open patch of halfway flattened earth where she can collapse, rolling onto her back, her smooth flesh glistening and her hard breasts shining up at Able, making him sick with joy.

Then she starts to cry, quietly, with a deep sadness.

Lust vanishes, replaced by simple embarrassment. Able flinches and starts to step back, and that's when he first looks at her face.

He recognizes its features.

Intrigued, the boy picks his way down to the shoreline, practically standing beside the crying woman.

She looks at him, and she sniffs.

"I saw two of them," he reports. "And I saw you, too. You were inside that cylinder, weren't you?"

She watches him, saying nothing.

"I saw something pull you out of that trap. And then I couldn't see you. *It* must have put you here, I guess. Out of its way." Able nods, and smiles. He can't help but stare at her breasts, but at least he keeps his eyes halfway closed, pretending to look out over the water instead. "*It* took pity on you, I guess."

A good-sized fish breaks on the water.

The woman seems to watch the creature as it swims past, big blue scales catching the light, heavy fins lazily shoving their way through the warm water. The fish eyes are huge and black, and they are stupid eyes. The mind behind them sees nothing but vague shapes and sudden motions. Able knows from experience: If he stands quite still, the creature will come close enough to touch.

"They're called coelacanths," he explains.

Maybe the woman reacts to his voice. Some sound other than crying now leaks from her.

So Able continues, explaining, "They were rare, once.

I've studied them quite a bit. They're old and primitive, and they were almost extinct when we found them. But when *they* got loose, got free, and took apart the Earth . . . and took everything and everyone with them up into the sky . . ."

The woman gazes up at the towering horsetails.

Able stares at her legs and what lies between them.

"Anyway," he mutters, "there's more coelacanths now than ever. They live in a million oceans, and they've never been more successful, really." He hesitates, and then adds, "Kind of like us, I think. Like people. You know?"

The woman turns, staring at him with gray-white eyes. And with a quiet hard voice, she says, "No."

She says, "That's an idiot's opinion."

And then with a grace that belies her strong frame, she dives back into the water, kicking hard and chasing that ancient and stupid fish all the way back to the bottom.

Liking What
You See:
A Documentary

by Ted Chiang

"Beauty is the promise of happiness."-Stendhal

T amera Lyons, first-year student at Pembleton:

I can't believe it. I visited the campus last year, and I didn't hear a word about this. Now I get here and it turns out people want to make calli a requirement. One of the things I was looking forward to about college was getting rid of this, you know, so I could be like everybody else. If I'd known there was even a chance I'd have to keep it, I probably would've picked another college. I feel like I've been scammed.

I turn eighteen next week, and I'm getting my calli turned off that day. If they vote to make it a requirement, I don't know what I'll do; maybe I'll transfer, I don't know. Right now I feel like going up to people and telling them, "Vote no." There's probably some campaign I can work for.

Maria deSouza, third-year student, President of the
Students for Equality Everywhere (SEE):

Our goal is very simple. Pembleton University has a
Code of Ethical Conduct, one that was created by the students themselves, and that all incoming students agree to
follow when they enroll. The initiative that we've spon-
sored would add a provision to the code, requiring students to adopt calliagnosia as long as they're enrolled.

What prompted us to do this now was the release of a
spex version of Visage. That's the software that, when
you look at people through your spex, shows you what
they'd look like with cosmetic surgery. It became a form
of entertainment among a certain crowd, and a lot of college students found it offensive. When people started
talking about it as a symptom of a deeper societal problem, we thought the timing was right for us to sponsor
this initiative.

The deeper societal problem is lookism. For decades
people've been willing to talk about racism and sexism,
but they're still reluctant to talk about lookism. Yet this
prejudice against unattractive people is incredibly perva-
sive. People do it without even being taught by anyone,
which is bad enough, but instead of combating this tendency, modern society actively reinforces it.

Educating people, raising their awareness about this
issue, all of that is essential, but it's not enough. That's
where technology comes in. Think of calliagnosia as a
kind of assisted maturity. It lets you do what you know
you should: ignore the surface, so you can look deeper.

We think it's time to bring calli into the mainstream.
So far the calli movement has been a minor presence on
college campuses, just another one of the special-interest
causes. But Pembleton isn't like other colleges, and I

think the students here are ready for calli. If the initiative succeeds here, we'll be setting an example for other colleges, and ultimately, society as a whole.

Joseph Weingartner, neurologist:

The condition is what we call an associative agnosia, rather than an apperceptive one. That means it doesn't interfere with one's visual perception, only with the ability to recognize what one sees. A calliagnosic perceives faces perfectly well; he or she can tell the difference between a pointed chin and a receding one, a straight nose and a crooked one, clear skin and blemished skin. He or she simply doesn't experience any aesthetic reaction to those differences.

Calliagnosia is possible because of the existence of certain neural pathways in the brain. All animals have criteria for evaluating the reproductive potential of prospective mates, and they've evolved neural "circuitry" to recognize those criteria. Human social interaction is centered around our faces, so our circuitry is most finely attuned to how a person's reproductive potential is manifested in his or her face. You experience the operation of that circuitry as the feeling that a person is beautiful, or ugly, or somewhere in between. By blocking the neural pathways dedicated to evaluating those features, we can induce calliagnosia.

Given how much fashions change, some people find it hard to imagine that there are absolute markers of a beautiful face. But it turns out that when people of different cultures are asked to rank photos of faces for attractiveness, some very clear patterns emerge across the board. Even very young infants show the same preference for certain faces. This lets us identify the traits that are common to everyone's idea of a beautiful face.

Probably the most obvious one is clear skin. It's the equivalent of a bright plumage in birds or a shiny coat of fur in mammals. Good skin is the single best indicator of youth and health, and it's valued in every culture. Acne may not be serious, but it *looks* like more serious diseases, and that's why we find it disagreeable.

Another trait is symmetry; we may not be conscious of millimeter differences between someone's left and right sides, but measurements reveal that individuals rated as most attractive are also the most symmetrical. And while symmetry is what our genes always aim for, it's very difficult to achieve in developmental terms; any environmental stressor—like poor nutrition, disease, parasites—tends to result in asymmetry during growth. Symmetry implies resistance to such stressors.

Other traits have to do with facial proportions. We tend to be attracted to facial proportions that are close to the population mean. That obviously depends on the population you're part of, but being near the mean usually indicates genetic health. The only departures from the mean that people consistently find attractive are ones caused by sex hormones, which suggest good reproductive potential.

Basically, calliagnosia is a lack of response to these traits; nothing more. Calliagnosics are *not* blind to fashion or cultural standards of beauty. If black lipstick is all the rage, calliagnosia won't make you forget it, although you might not notice the difference between pretty faces and plain faces wearing that lipstick. And if everyone around you sneers at people with broad noses, you'll pick up on that.

So calliagnosia by itself can't eliminate appearance-based discrimination. What it does, in a sense, is even up the odds; it takes away the innate predisposition, the tendency for such discrimination to arise in the first place. That way, if you want to teach people to ignore appearances, you won't be facing an uphill battle. Ideally you'd start with an environment where everyone's adopted calliagnosia, and then socialize them to not value appearances.

Tamera Lyons:

People here have been asking me what it was like going to Saybrook, growing up with calli. To be honest, it's not a big deal when you're young; you know, like they say, whatever you grew up with seems normal to you. We knew that there was something that other people could see that we couldn't, but it was just something we were curious about.

For instance, my friends and I used to watch movies and try to figure out who was really good-looking and who wasn't. We'd say we could tell, but we couldn't really, not by looking at their faces. We were just going by who was the main character and who was the friend; you always knew the main character was better-looking than the friend. It's not true a hundred percent of the time, but you could usually tell if you were watching the kind of thing where the main character wouldn't be good-looking.

It's when you get older that it starts to bother you. If you hang out with people from other schools, you can feel weird because you have calli and they don't. It's not that anyone makes a big deal out of it, but it reminds you that there's something you can't see. And then you start having fights with your parents, because they're keeping you from seeing the real world. You never get anywhere with them, though.

Richard Hamill, founder of the Saybrook School:

Saybrook came about as an outgrowth of our housing cooperative. We had maybe two dozen families at the time, all trying to establish a community based on shared values. We were holding a meeting about the possibility of starting an alternative school for our kids, and one parent mentioned the problem of the media's influence on their kids. Everyone's teens were asking for cosmetic surgery so they could look like fashion models. The parents were doing their best, but you can't isolate your kids from the world; they live in an image-obsessed culture.

It was around then that the last legal challenges to calliagnosia were resolved, and we got to talking about it. We saw calli as an opportunity: what if we could live in an environment where people didn't judge each other on their appearance? What if we could raise our children in such an environment?

The school started out being just for the children of the families in the cooperative, but other calliagnosia schools began making the news, and before long people were asking if they could enroll their kids without joining the housing co-op. Eventually we set up Saybrook as a private school separate from the co-op, and one of its requirements was that parents adopt calliagnosia for as long as their kids were enrolled. Now a calliagnosia community has sprung up here, all because of the school.

Rachel Lyons:

Tamera's father and I gave the issue a lot of thought before we decided to enroll her there. We talked to people in the community, found we liked their approach to education, but really it was visiting the school that sold me.

Saybrook has a higher than normal number of students with facial abnormalities, like bone cancer, burns, congenital conditions. Their parents moved here to keep them from being ostracized by other kids, and it works. I remember when I first visited, I saw a class of twelve-year-olds voting for class president, and they elected this girl who had burn scars on one side of her face. She was wonderfully at ease with herself, she was popular among kids who probably would have ostracized her in any other school. And I thought, this is the kind of environment I want my daughter to grow up in.

Girls have always been told that their value is tied to their appearance; their accomplishments are always magnified if they're pretty and diminished if they're not. Even worse, some girls get the message that they can get through life relying on just their looks, and then they never develop their minds. I wanted to keep Tamera away from that sort of influence.

Being pretty is fundamentally a passive quality; even when you work at it, you're working at being passive. I wanted Tamera to value herself in terms of what she could *do*, both with her mind and with her body, not in terms of how decorative she was. I didn't want her to be passive, and I'm pleased to say that she hasn't turned out that way.

Martin Lyons:

I don't mind if Tamera decides as an adult to get rid of calli. This was never about taking choices away from her. But there's more than enough stress involved in simply getting through adolescence; the peer pressure can crush you like a paper cup. Becoming preoccupied with how you look is just one more way to be crushed, and anything that can relieve that pressure is a good thing, in my opinion.

Once you're older, you're better equipped to deal with the issue of personal appearance. You're more comfortable in your own skin, more confident, more secure. You're more likely to be satisfied with how you look, whether you're "good looking" or not. Of course not everyone reaches that level of maturity at the same age. Some people are there at sixteen, some don't get there until they're thirty or even older. But eighteen's the age of legal majority, when everyone's got the right to make their own decisions, and all you can do is trust your child and hope for the best.

Tamera Lyons:

It'd been kind of an odd day for me. Good, but odd. I just got my calli turned off this morning.

Getting it turned off was easy. The nurse stuck some sensors on me and made me put on this helmet, and she showed me a bunch of pictures of people's faces. Then she tapped at her keyboard for a minute, and said, "I've switched off the calli," just like that. I thought you might feel something when it happened, but you don't. Then she showed me the pictures again, to make sure it worked.

When I looked at the faces again, some of them seemed . . . different. Like they were glowing, or more vivid or something. It's hard to describe. The nurse showed me my test results afterwards, and there were readings for how wide my pupils were dilating and how well my skin conducted electricity and stuff like that. And for the faces that seemed different, the readings went way up. She said those were the beautiful faces.

She said that I'd notice how other people's faces look right away, but it'd take a while before I had any reaction to how I looked. Supposedly you're too used to your face to tell.

And yeah, when I first looked in a mirror, I thought I looked totally the same. Since I got back from the doctor's, the people I see on campus definitely look different, but I still haven't noticed any difference in how I look. I've been looking at mirrors all day. For a while I was afraid that I was ugly, and any minute the ugliness was going to appear, like a rash or something. And so I've been staring at the mirror, just waiting, and nothing's happened. So I figure I'm probably not really ugly, or I'd have noticed it, but that means I'm not really pretty either, because I'd have noticed that too. So I guess that means I'm absolutely plain, you know? Exactly average. I guess that's okay.

Joseph Weingartner:

Inducing an agnosia means simulating a specific brain lesion. We do this with a programmable pharmaceutical called neurostat; you can think of it as a highly selective anesthetic, one whose activation and targeting are all under dynamic control. We activate or deactivate the neurostat by transmitting signals through a helmet the patient puts on. The helmet also provides somatic positioning information so the neurostat molecules can triangulate their location. This lets us activate only the neurostat in a specific section of brain tissue, and keep the nerve impulses there below a specified threshold.

Neurostat was originally developed for controlling seizures in epileptics and for relief of chronic pain; it lets us treat even severe cases of these conditions without the side-effects caused by drugs that affect the entire nervous system. Later on, different neurostat protocols were developed as treatments for obsessive-compulsive disorder, addictive behavior, and various other disorders. At the same time, neurostat became incredibly valuable as a research tool for studying brain physiology.

One way neurologists have traditionally studied specialization of brain function is to observe the deficits that result from various lesions. Obviously, this technique is limited because the lesions caused by injury or disease often affect multiple functional areas. By contrast, neurostat can be activated in the tiniest portion of the brain, in effect simulating a lesion so localized that it would never occur naturally. And when you deactivate the neurostat, the "lesion" disappears and brain function returns to normal.

In this way neurologists were able to induce a wide variety of agnosias. The one most relevant here is prosopagnosia, the inability to recognize people by their faces. A prosopagnosic can't recognize friends or family members unless they say something; he can't even identify his own face in a photograph. It's not a cognitive or perceptual problem; prosopagnosics can identify people by their hairstyle, clothing, perfume, even the way they walk. The deficit is restricted purely to faces.

Prosopagnosia has always been the most dramatic indication that our brains have a special "circuit" devoted to the visual processing of faces; we look at faces in a different way than we look at anything else. And recognizing someone's face is just one of the face-processing tasks we do; there are also related circuits devoted to identifying facial expressions, and even detecting changes in the direction of another person's gaze.

One of the interesting things about prosopagnosics is that while they can't recognize a face, they still have an opinion as to whether it's attractive or not. When asked to sort photos of faces in order of attractiveness, prosopagnosics sorted the photos in pretty much the same way as anyone else. Experiments using neurostat allowed researchers to identify the neurological circuit responsible for perceiving beauty in faces, and thus essentially invent calliagnosia.

Maria deSouza:

SEE has had extra neurostat programming helmets set up in the Student Health Office, and made arrangements so they can offer calliagnosia to anyone who wants it. You don't even have to make an appointment, you can just walk in. We're encouraging all the students to try it, at least for a day, to see what it's like. At first it seems a little odd, not seeing anyone as either good-looking or ugly, but over time you realize how positively it affects your interactions with other people.

A lot of people worry that calli might make them asexual or something, but actually physical beauty is only a small part of what makes a person attractive. No matter what a person looks like, it's much more important how the person acts; what he says and how he says it, his behavior and body language. And how does he react to you? For me, one of the things that attracts me to a guy is if he seems interested in *me*. It's like a feedback loop; you notice him looking at you, then he sees you looking at him, and things snowball from there. Calli doesn't change that. Plus there's that whole pheromone chemistry going on too; obviously calli doesn't affect that.

Another worry that people have is that calli will make everyone's face look the same, but that's not true either. A person's face always reflects their personality, and if anything, calli makes that clearer. You know that saying, that after a certain age, you're responsible for your face? With calli, you really appreciate how true that is. Some faces just look really bland, especially young, conventionally pretty ones. Without their physical beauty, those faces are just boring. But faces that are full of personality look as good as they ever did, maybe even better. It's like you're seeing something more essential about them.

Some people also ask about enforcement. We don't plan on doing anything like that. It's true, there's software that's pretty good at guessing if a person has calli or not, by analyzing eye gaze patterns. But it requires a lot of data, and the campus security cams don't zoom in close enough. Everyone would have to wear personal cams, and share the data. It's possible, but that's not what we're after. We think that once people try calli, they'll see the benefits themselves.

Tamera Lyons:

Check it out, I'm pretty!

What a day. When I woke up this morning I immediately went to the mirror; it was like I was a little kid on Christmas or something. But still, nothing; my face still looked plain. Later on I even (*laughs*) I tried to catch myself by surprise, by sneaking up on a mirror, but that didn't work. So I was kind of disappointed, and feeling just, you know, resigned to my fate.

But then this afternoon, I went out with my roommate Ina and a couple other girls from the dorm. I hadn't told anyone that I'd gotten my calli turned off, because I wanted to get used to it first. So we went to this snack bar on the other side of campus, one I hadn't been to before. We were sitting at this table, talking, and I was looking around, just seeing what people looked like without calli. And I saw this girl looking at me, and I thought, "She's really pretty." And then, (*laughs*) this'll sound really stupid, then I realized that this wall in the snack bar was a mirror, and I was looking at myself!

I can't describe it, I felt this incredible sense of *relief.* I just couldn't stop smiling! Ina asked me what I was so happy about, and I just shook my head. I went to the bathroom so I could stare at myself in the mirror for a bit.

So it's been a good day. I really *like* the way I look! It's been a good day.

From a student debate held at Pembleton:
Jeff Winthrop, third-year student:

Of course it's wrong to judge people by their appearance, but this "blindness" isn't the answer. Education is.

Calli takes away the good as well as the bad. It doesn't just work when there's a possibility of discrimination, it keeps you from recognizing beauty altogether. There are plenty of times when looking at an attractive face doesn't hurt anyone. Calli won't let you make those distinctions, but education will.

And I know someone will say, what about when the technology gets better? Maybe one day they'll be able to insert an expert system into your brain, one that goes, "Is this an appropriate situation to apprehend beauty? If so, enjoy it; else, ignore it." Would that be okay? Would that be the "assisted maturity" you hear people talking about?

No, it wouldn't. That wouldn't be maturity; it'd be letting an expert system make your decisions for you. Maturity means seeing the differences, but realizing they don't matter. There's no technological shortcut.

TED CHIANG

Adesh Singh, third-year student:

No one's talking about letting an expert system make your decisions. What makes calli ideal is precisely that it's such a minimal change. Calli doesn't decide for you; it doesn't prevent you from doing anything. And as for maturity, you demonstrate maturity by choosing calli in the first place.

Everyone knows physical beauty has nothing to do with merit; that's what education's accomplished. But even with the best intentions in the world, people haven't stopped practicing lookism. We try to be impartial, we try not to let a person's appearance affect us, but we can't suppress our autonomic responses, and anyone who claims they can is engaged in wishful thinking. Ask yourself: don't you react differently when you meet an attractive person and when you meet an unattractive one?

Every study on this issue turns up the same results: looks help people get ahead. We can't help but think of good-looking people as more competent, more honest, more deserving than others. None of it's true, but their looks still give us that impression.

Calli doesn't blind you to anything; beauty is what blinds you. Calli lets you see.

Tamera Lyons:

So, I've been looking at good-looking guys around campus. It's fun; weird, but fun. Like, I was in the cafeteria the other day, and I saw this guy a couple tables away, I didn't know his name, but I kept turning to look at him. I can't describe anything specific about his face, but it just seemed much more noticeable than other people's. It was like his face was a magnet, and my eyes were compass needles being pulled toward it.

And after I looked at him for a while, I found it really easy to imagine that he was a nice guy! I didn't know anything about him, I couldn't even hear what he was talking about, but I wanted to get to know him. It was kind of odd, but definitely not in a bad way.

From a broadcast of EduNews, on the American College Network:
In the latest on the Pembleton University calliagnosia initiative: EduNews has received evidence that public-relations firm Wyatt/Hayes paid four Pembleton students to dissuade classmates from voting for the initiative, without having them register their affiliations. Evidence includes an internal memo from Wyatt/Hayes, proposing that "good-looking students with high reputation ratings" be sought, and records of payments from the agency to Pembleton students.

The files were sent by the SemioTech Warriors, a culture-jamming group responsible for many numerous of media vandalism.

When contacted about this story, Wyatt/Hayes issued a statement decrying this violation of their internal computer systems.

Jeff Winthrop:
Yes, it's true, Wyatt/Hayes paid me, but it wasn't an endorsement deal; they never told me *what* to say. They just made it possible for me to devote more time to the anti-calli campaign, which is what I would've done anyway if I hadn't needed to make money tutoring. All I've been doing is expressing my honest opinion: I think calli's a bad idea.

A couple of people in the anti-calli campaign have asked that I not speak publicly about the issue anymore, because they think it would hurt the cause. I'm sorry they feel that way, because this is just an *ad hominem* attack. If you thought my arguments made sense before, this shouldn't change anything. But I realize that some people can't make those distinctions, and I'll do what's best for the cause.

Maria deSouza:

Those students really should have registered their affiliations; we all know people who are walking endorsements. But now, whenever someone criticizes the initiative, people ask them if they're being paid. The backlash is definitely hurting the anti-calli campaign.

I consider it a compliment that someone is taking enough interest in the initiative to hire a PR firm. We've always hoped that its passing might influence people at other schools, and this means that corporations are thinking the same thing.

We've invited the president of the National Calliagnosia Association to speak on campus. Before we weren't sure if we wanted to bring the national group in, because they have a different emphasis than we do; they're more focused on the media uses of beauty, while here at SEE we're more interested in the social equality issue. But given the way students reacted to what Wyatt/Hayes did, it's clear that the media manipulation issue has the power to get us where we need to go. Our best shot at getting the initiative passed is to take advantage of the anger against advertisers. The social equality will follow afterwards.

From the speech given at Pembleton by Walter Lambert, president of the National Calliagnosia Association:

Think of cocaine. In its natural form, as coca leaves,

it's appealing, but not to an extent that it usually becomes a problem. But refine it, purify it, and you get a compound that hits your pleasure receptors with an unnatural intensity. That's when it becomes addictive.

Beauty has undergone a similar process, thanks to advertisers. Evolution gave us a circuit that responds to good looks—call it the pleasure receptor for our visual cortex—and in our natural environment, it was useful to have. But take a person with one-in-a-million skin and bone structure, add professional makeup and retouching, and you're no longer looking at beauty in its natural form. You've got pharmaceutical-grade beauty, the cocaine of good looks.

Biologists call this "supernormal stimulus"; show a mother bird a giant plastic egg, and she'll incubate it instead of her own real eggs. Madison Avenue has saturated our environment with this kind of stimuli, this visual drug. Our beauty receptors receive more stimulation than they were evolved to handle; we're seeing more beauty in one day than our ancestors did in a lifetime. And the result is that beauty is slowly ruining our lives.

How? The way any drug becomes a problem: by interfering with our relationships with other people. We become dissatisfied with the way ordinary people look because they can't compare to supermodels. Two-dimensional images are bad enough, but now with spex, advertisers can put a supermodel right in front of you, making eye contact. Software companies offer goddesses who'll remind you of your appointments. We've all heard about men who prefer virtual girlfriends over actual ones, but they're not the only ones who've been affected. The more time any of us spend with gorgeous digital apparitions around, the more our relationships with real human beings are going to suffer.

We can't avoid these images and still live in the modern world. And that means we can't kick this habit, because beauty is a drug you can't abstain from unless you literally keep your eyes closed all the time.

Until now. Now you can get another set of eyelids, one that blocks out this drug, but still lets you see. And that's calliagnosia. Some people call it excessive, but I call it just enough. Technology is being used to manipulate us through our emotional reactions, so it's only fair that we use it to protect ourselves too.

Right now you have an opportunity to make an enormous impact. The Pembleton student body has always been at the vanguard of every progressive movement; what you decide here will set an example for students across the country. By passing this initiative, by adopting calliagnosia, you'll be sending a message to advertisers that young people are no longer willing to be manipulated.

From a broadcast of EduNews:
Following NCA president Walter Lambert's speech, polls show that 54% of Pembleton students support the calliagnosia initiative. Polls across the country show that an average of 28% of students would support a similar initiative at their school, an increase of 8% in the past month.

Tamera Lyons:
I thought he went overboard with that cocaine analogy. Do you know anyone who steals stuff and sells it so he can get his fix of advertising?

But I guess he has a point about how good-looking people are in commercials versus in real life. It's not that

114

they look better than people in real life, but they look good in a different way.

Like, I was at the campus store the other today, and I needed to check my e-mail, and when I put on my spex I saw this poster running a commercial. It was for some shampoo, Jouissance I think. I'd seen it before, but it was different without calli. The model was so—I couldn't take my eyes off her. I don't mean I felt the same as that time I saw the good-looking guy in the cafeteria; it wasn't like I wanted to get to know her. It was more like . . . watching a sunset, or a fireworks display.

I just stood there and watched the commercial like five times, just so I could look at her some more. I didn't think a human being could look so, you know, spectacular.

But it's not like I'm going to quit talking to people so I can watch commercials through my spex all the time. Watching them is very intense, but it's a totally different experience than looking at a real person. And it's not even like I immediately want to go out and buy everything they're selling, either. I'm not even really paying attention to the products. I just think they're amazing to watch.

Maria deSouza:

If I'd met Tamera earlier, I might have tried to persuade her not to get her calli turned off. I doubt I would've succeeded; she seems pretty firm about her decision. Even so, she's a great example of the benefits of calli. You can't help but notice it when you talk to her. For example, at one point I was saying how lucky she was, and she said, "Because I'm beautiful?" And she was being totally sincere! Like she was talking about her height. Can you imagine a woman without calli saying that?

Tamera is completely unself-conscious about her

looks; she's not vain or insecure, and she can describe herself as beautiful without embarrassment. I gather that she's very pretty, and with a lot of women who look like that, I can see something in their manner, a hint of showoffishness. Tamera doesn't have that. Or else they display false modesty, which is also easy to tell, but Tamera doesn't do that either, because she truly *is* modest. There's no way she could be like that if she hadn't been raised with calli. I just hope she stays that way.

Annika Lindstrom, second-year student:

I think this calli thing is a terrible idea. I like it when guys notice me, and I'd be really disappointed if they stopped.

I think this whole thing is just a way for people who, honestly, aren't very good-looking, to try and make themselves feel better. And the only way they can do that is to punish people who have what they don't. And that's just unfair.

Who wouldn't want to be pretty if they could? Ask anyone, ask the people behind this, and I bet you they'd all say yes. Okay, sure, being pretty means that you'll be hassled by jerks sometimes. There are always jerks, but that's part of life. If those scientists could come up with some way to turn off the jerk circuit in guys' brains, I'd be all in favor of that.

Jolene Carter, third-year student:

I'm voting for the initiative, because I think it'd be a relief if everyone had calli.

People are nice to me because of how I look, and part of me likes that, but part of me feels guilty because I haven't done anything to deserve it. And sure, it's nice to have men pay attention to me, but it can be hard to make a real connection with someone. Whenever I like a guy, I always wonder how much he's interested in me, versus how much he's interested in my looks. It can be hard to tell, because all relationships are wonderful at the beginning, you know? It's not until later that you find out whether you can really be comfortable with each other. It was like that with my last boyfriend. He wasn't happy with me if I didn't look fabulous, so I was never able to truly relax. But by that time I realized that, I'd already let myself get close to him, so that really hurt, finding out that he didn't see the real me.

And then there's how you feel around other women. I don't think most women like it, but you're always comparing how you look relative to everyone else. Sometimes I feel like I'm in a competition, and I don't want to be.

I thought about getting calli once, but it didn't seem like it would help unless everyone else did too; getting it all by myself wouldn't change the way others treat me. But if everyone on campus had calli, I'd be glad to get it.

Tamera Lyons:

I was showing my roommate Ina this album of pictures from high school, and we get to all these pictures of me and Garrett, my ex. So Ina wants to know all about him, and so I tell her. I'm telling her how we were together all of senior year, and how much I loved him, and wanted us to stay together, but he wanted to be free to date when he went to college. And then she's like, "You mean *he* broke up with *you*?"

It took me a while before I could get her to tell me what was up; she made me promise twice not to get mad. Eventually she said Garrett isn't exactly good-looking. I was thinking he must be average-looking, because he didn't really look that different after I got my calli turned off. But Ina said he was definitely below average.

She found pictures of a couple other guys who she thought looked like him, and with them I could see how they're not good-looking. Their faces just look goofy. Then I took another look at Garrett's picture, and I guess he's got some of the same features, but on him they look cute. To me, anyway.

I guess it's true what they say: love is a little bit like calli. When you love someone, you don't really see what they look like. I don't see Garrett the way others do, because I still have feelings for him.

Ina said she couldn't believe someone who looked like him would break up with someone who looked like me. She said that in a school without calli, he probably wouldn't have been able to get a date with me. Like, we wouldn't be in the same league.

That's weird to think about. When Garrett and I were going out, I always thought we were meant to be together. I don't mean that I believe in destiny, but I just thought there was something really right about the two of us. So the idea that we could've both been in the same school, but not gotten together because we didn't have calli, feels strange. And I know that Ina can't be sure of that. But I can't be sure she's wrong, either.

And maybe that means I should be glad I had calli, because it let me and Garrett get together. I don't know about that.

From a broadcast of EduNews:

Netsites for a dozen calliagnosia student organizations around the country were brought down today in a coordinated denial-of-service attack. Although no one claimed responsibility, some suggest the perpetrators are retaliating for last month's incident in which the American Association of Cosmetic Surgeons' netsite was replaced by a calliagnosia site.

Meanwhile, the SemioTech Warriors announced the release of their new "Dermatology" computer virus. This virus has begun infecting video servers around the world, altering broadcasts so that faces and bodies exhibit conditions such as acne and varicose veins.

Warren Davidson, 1st-year student:

I thought about trying calli before, when I was in high school, but I never knew how to bring it up with my parents. So when they started offering it here, I figured I'd give it a try. (*shrugs*) It's okay.

Actually, it's better than okay. (*pause*) I've always hated how I look. For a while in high school I couldn't stand the sight of myself in a mirror. But with calli, I don't mind as much. I know I look the same to other people, but that doesn't seem as big a deal as it used to. I feel better just by not being reminded that some people are so much better-looking than others. Like, for instance: I was helping this girl in the library with a problem on her calculus homework, and afterwards I realized that she's someone I'd thought was really pretty. Normally I would have been really nervous around her, but with calli, she wasn't so hard to talk to.

Maybe she thinks I look like a freak, I don't know, but the thing was, when I was talking to her *I* didn't think I looked like a freak. Before I got calli, I think I was just too self-conscious, and that just made things worse. Now I'm more relaxed.

It's not like I suddenly feel all wonderful about myself or anything, and I'm sure for other people calli wouldn't help them at all, but for me, calli makes me not feel as bad as I used to. And that's worth something.

Alex Bibescu, professor of religious studies at Pembleton:
Some people have been quick to dismiss the whole calliagnosia debate as superficial, an argument over makeup or who can and can't get a date. But if you actually look at it, you'll see it's much deeper than that. It reflects a very old ambivalence about the body, one that's been part of Western civilization since ancient times.

You see, the foundations of our culture were laid in classical Greece, where physical beauty and the body were celebrated. But our culture is also thoroughly permeated by the monotheistic tradition, which devalues the body in favor of the soul. These old conflicting impulses are rearing their heads again, this time in the calliagnosia debate.

I suspect that most calli supporters think of themselves to be modern, secular liberals, and wouldn't admit to being influenced by monotheism in any way. But take a look at who else advocates calliagnosia: conservative religious groups. There are communities of all three major monotheistic faiths—Jewish, Christian, and Muslim—who've begun using calli to make their young members more resistant to the charms of outsiders. This commonality is no coincidence. The liberal calli supporters may not use language like "resisting the temptations of the flesh," but in their own way, they're following the same tradition of deprecating the physical.

Really, the only calli supporters who can credibly claim they're not influenced by monotheism are the Neo-

Mind Buddhists. They're a sect who see calliagnosia as a step toward enlightened thought, because it eliminates one's perception of illusory distinctions. But the NeoMind sect is open to broad use of neurostat as an aid to meditation, which is a radical stance of an entirely different sort. I doubt you'll find many modern liberals or conservative monotheists sympathetic to that!

So you see, this debate isn't just about commercials and cosmetics, it's about determining what's the appropriate relationship between the mind and the body. Are we more fully realized when we minimize the physical part of our natures? And that, you have to agree, is a profound question.

Joseph Weingartner:

After calliagnosia was discovered, some researchers wondered if it might be possible to create an analogous condition that rendered the subject blind to race or ethnicity. They've made a number of attempts—impairing various levels of category discrimination in tandem with face recognition, that sort of thing—but the resulting deficits were always unsatisfactory. Usually the test subjects would simply be unable to distinguish similar-looking individuals. One test actually produced a benign variant of Fregoli syndrome, causing the subject to mistake every person he met for a family member. Unfortunately, treating everyone like a brother isn't desirable in so literal a sense.

When neurostat treatments for problems like compulsive behavior entered widespread use, a lot of people thought that "mind programming" was finally here. People asked their doctors if they could get the same sexual tastes as their spouses. Media pundits worried about the possibility of programming loyalty to a government or corporation, or belief in an ideology or religion.

The fact is, we have no access to the contents of anyone's thoughts. We can shape broad aspects of personality, we can make changes consistent with the natural specialization of the brain, but these are extremely coarse-grained adjustments. There's no neural pathway that specifically handles resentment toward immigrants, any more than there's one for Marxist doctrine or foot fetishism. If we ever get true mind programming, we'll be able to create "race blindness," but until then, education is our best hope.

Tamera Lyons:

I had an interesting class today. In History of Ideas, we've got this T.A., he's named Anton, and he was saying how a lot of words we use to describe an attractive person used to be words for magic. Like the word "charm" originally meant a magic spell, and the word "glamour" did, too. And it's just blatant with words like "enchanting" and "spellbinding." And when he said that, I thought, yeah, that's what it's like: seeing a really good-looking person is like having a magic spell cast over you.

And Anton was saying how one of the primary uses of magic was to create love and desire in someone. And that makes total sense, too, when you think about those words "charm" and "glamour." Because seeing beauty feels like love. You feel like you've got a crush on a really good-looking person, just by looking at them.

That made me think that maybe there's a way I can get back together with Garrett. Because if Garrett didn't have calli, maybe he'd fall in love with me again. Remember how I said before that maybe calli was what let us get together? Well, maybe calli is actually what's keeping us apart now. Maybe Garrett would want to get back with me if he saw what I really looked like.

Garrett turned eighteen during the summer, but he never got his calli turned off because he didn't think it was a big deal. He goes to Northrop now. So I called him up, just as a friend, and when we were talking about stuff, I asked him what he thought about the calli initiative here at Pembleton. He said he didn't see what all the fuss was about, and then I told him how much I liked not having calli anymore, and said he ought to try it, so he could judge both sides. He said that made sense. I didn't make a big deal out of it, but I was stoked.

Daniel Taglia, professor of comparative literature at Pembleton:

The student initiative doesn't apply to faculty, but obviously if it passes there'll be pressure on the faculty to adopt calliagnosia as well. So I don't consider it premature for me to say that I'm adamantly opposed to it.

This is just the latest example of political correctness run amok. The people advocating calli are well-intentioned, but what they're doing is infantilizing us. The very notion that beauty is something we need to be protected from is insulting. Next thing you know, a student organization will insist we all adopt music agnosia, so we don't feel bad about ourselves when we hear gifted singers or musicians.

When you watch Olympic athletes in competition, does your self-esteem plummet? Of course not. On the contrary, you feel wonder and admiration; you're inspired that such exceptional individuals exist. So why can't we feel the same way about beauty? Feminism would have us apologize for having that reaction. It wants to replace aesthetics with politics, and to the extent it's succeeded, it's impoverished us.

Being in the presence of a world-class beauty can be as thrilling as listening to a world-class soprano. Gifted individuals aren't the only ones who benefit from their gifts; we all do. Or, I should say, we all can. Depriving ourselves of that opportunity would be a crime.

Commercial paid for by People for Ethical Nanomedicine:
Voiceover: Have your friends been telling you that calli is cool, that it's the smart thing to do? Then maybe you should talk to people who grew up with calli.

"After I got my calli turned off, I recoiled the first time I met an unattractive person. I knew it was silly, but I just couldn't help myself. Calli didn't help make me mature, it *kept* me from becoming mature. I had to relearn how to interact with people."

"I went to school to be a graphic artist. I worked day and night, but I never got anywhere with it. My teacher said I didn't have the eye for it, that calli had stunted me aesthetically. There's no way I can get back what I've lost."

"Having calli was like having my parents inside my head, censoring my thoughts. Now that I've had it turned off, I realize just what kind of abuse I'd been living with."
Voiceover: If the people who grew up with calliagnosia don't recommend it, shouldn't that tell you something?

They didn't have a choice, but you do. Brain damage is never a good idea, no matter what your friends say.

Maria deSouza:
We'd never heard of the People for Ethical Nanomedicine, so we did some research on them. It took some dig-

ging, but it turns out it's not a grassroots organization at all, it's an industry PR front. A bunch of cosmetics companies got together recently and created it. We haven't been able to contact the people who appear in the commercial, so we don't know how much, if any, of what they said was true. Even if they were being honest, they certainly aren't typical; most people who get their calli turned off feel fine about it. And there are definitely graphic artists who grew up with calli.

It kind of reminds me of an ad I saw a while back, put out by a modeling agency when the calli movement was just getting started. It was just a picture of a supermodel's face, with a caption: "If you no longer saw her as beautiful, whose loss would it be? Hers, or yours?" This new campaign has the same message, basically saying, "you'll be sorry," but instead of taking that cocky attitude, it has more of a concerned-warning tone. This is classic PR: hide behind a nice-sounding name, and create the impression of a third party looking out for the consumer's interests.

Tamera Lyons:

I thought that commercial was totally idiotic. It's not like I'm in favor of the initiative—I don't want people to vote for it—but people shouldn't vote against it for the wrong reason. Growing up with calli isn't crippling. There's no reason for anyone to feel sorry for me or anything. I'm dealing with it fine. And that's why I think people ought to vote against the initiative:because seeing beauty is fine.

Anyway, I talked to Garrett again. He said he'd just gotten his calli turned off. He said it seemed cool so far, although it was kind of weird, and I told him I felt the same way when I got mine disabled. I suppose it's kind of funny, how I was acting like an old pro, even though I've only had mine off for a few weeks.

Joseph Weingartner:

One of the first questions researchers asked about calliagnosia was whether it has any "spillover," that is, whether it affects your appreciation of beauty outside of faces. For the most part, the answer seems to be "no." Calliagnosics seem to enjoy looking at the same things other people do. That said, we can't rule out the possibility of side effects.

As an example, consider the spillover that's observed in prosopagnosics. One prosopagnosic who was a dairy farmer found he could no longer recognize his cows individually. Another found it harder to distinguish models of cars, if you can imagine that. These cases suggest that we sometimes use our face-recognition module for tasks other than strict face recognition. We may not think something looks like a face—a car, for example—but at a neurological level we're treating it as if it were a face.

There may be a similar spillover among calliagnosics, but since calliagnosia is subtler than prosopagnosia, any spillover is harder to measure. The role of fashion in cars' appearances, for example, is vastly greater than its role in faces', and there's little consensus about which cars are most attractive. There may be a calliagnosic out there who doesn't enjoy looking at certain models as much as he otherwise would, but he hasn't come forward to complain.

Then there's the role our beauty-recognition module plays in our aesthetic reaction to symmetry. We appreciate symmetry in a wide range of settings—painting, sculpture, graphic design—but at the same time we also appreciate asymmetry. There are a lot of factors that contribute to our reaction to art, and not much consensus about when a particular example is successful.

It might be interesting to see if calliagnosia communities produce fewer truly talented visual artists, but given how few such individuals arise in the general population, it's difficult to do a statistically meaningful study. The only thing we know for certain is that calliagnosics report a more muted response to some portraits, but that's not a side effect *per se*; portrait paintings derive at least some of their impact from the facial appearance of the subject.

Of course, any effect is too much for some people. This is the reason given by some parents for not wanting calliagnosia for their children: they want their children to be able to appreciate the Mona Lisa, and perhaps create its successor.

Marc Esposito, fourth-year student at Waterston College:

That Pembleton thing sounds totally crazed. I could see doing it like a setup for some prank. You know, as in, you'd fix this guy up with a girl, and tell him she's an absolute babe, but actually you've fixed him up with a dog, and he can't tell so he believes you. That'd be kind of funny, actually.

But I sure as hell would never get this calli thing. I want to date good-looking girls. Why would I want something that'd make me lower my standards? Okay, sure, some nights all the babes have been taken, and you have to choose from the leftovers. But that's why there's beer, right? Doesn't mean I want to wear beer goggles all the time.

Tamera Lyons:

So Garrett and I were talking on the phone again last night, and I asked him if he wanted to switch to video so we could see each other. And he said okay, so we did.

I was casual about it, but I had actually spent a lot of time getting ready. Ina's teaching me to put on makeup, but I'm not very good at it yet, so I got that phone software that makes it look like you're wearing makeup. I set it for just a little bit, and I think it made a real difference in how I looked. Maybe it was overkill, I don't know how much Garrett could tell, but I just wanted to be sure I looked as good as possible.

As soon as we switched to video, I could see him react. It was like his eyes got wider. He was like, "You look really great," and I was like, "Thanks." Then he got shy, and made some joke about the way he looked, but I told him I liked the way he looked.

We talked for a while on video, and all the time I was really conscious of him looking at me. That felt good. I got a feeling that he was thinking he might want us to get back together again, but maybe I was just imagining it.

Maybe next time we talk I'll suggest he could come visit me for a weekend, or I could go visit him at Northrop. That'd be really cool. Though I'd have to be sure I could do my own makeup before that.

I know there's no guarantee that he'll want to get back together. Getting my calli turned off didn't make me love him less, so maybe it won't make him love me any more. I'm hoping, though.

Cathy Minami, third-year student:

Anyone who says the calli movement is good for women is spreading the propaganda of all oppressors: the claim that subjugation is actually protection. Calli supporters want to demonize those women who possess beauty. Beauty can provide just as much pleasure for those who have it as for those who perceive it, but the calli movement makes women feel guilty about taking pleasure in their appearance. It's yet another patriarchal strategy for suppressing female sexuality, and once again, too many women have bought into it.

Of *course* beauty has been used as a tool of oppression, but eliminating beauty is not the answer; you can't liberate people by narrowing the scope of their experiences. That's positively Orwellian. What's needed is a woman-centered concept of beauty, one that lets all women feel good about themselves instead of making most of them feel bad.

Lawrence Sutton, fourth-year student:

I totally knew what Walter Lambert was talking about in his speech. I wouldn't have phrased it the way he did, but I've felt the same way for a while now. I got calli a couple years ago, long before this initiative came up, because I wanted to be able to concentrate on more important things.

I don't mean I only think about schoolwork; I've got a girlfriend, and we have a good relationship. That hasn't changed. What's changed is how I interact with advertising. Before, every time I used to walk past a magazine stand or see a commercial, I could feel my attention being drawn a little bit. It was like they were trying to arouse me against my will. I don't necessarily mean a sexual kind of arousal, but they were trying to appeal to me on a visceral level. And I would automatically resist, and go back to whatever I was doing before. But it was a distraction, and resisting those distractions took energy that I could have been using elsewhere.

But now with calli, I don't feel that pull. Calli freed me from that distraction, it gave me that energy back. So I'm totally in favor of it.

Lori Harber, third-year student at Maxwell College:

Calli is for wusses. My attitude is, fight back. Go radical ugly. That's what the beautiful people need to see.

I got my nose taken off about this time last year. It's a bigger deal than it sounds, surgery-wise; to be healthy and stuff, you have to move some of the hairs further in to catch dust. And the bone you see (*taps it with a fingernail*) isn't real, it's ceramic. Having your real bone exposed is a big infection risk.

I like it when I freak people out; sometimes I actually ruin someone's appetite when they're eating. But freaking people out, that's not what it's *about*. It's about how ugly can beat beautiful at its own game. I get more looks walking down the street than a beautiful woman. You see me standing next to a video model, who you going to notice more? Me, that's who. You won't want to, but you will.

Tamera Lyons:

Garrett and I were talking again last night, and we got to talking about, you know, if either of us had been going out with someone else. And I was casual about it, I said that I had hung out with some guys, but nothing major.

So I asked him the same. He was kind of embarrassed about it, but eventually he said that he was finding it harder to, like, really become friendly with girls in college, harder than he expected. And now he's thinking it's because of the way he looks.

I just said, "No way," but I didn't really know what to say. Part of me was glad that Garrett isn't seeing someone else yet, and part of me felt bad for him, and part of me was just surprised. I mean, he's smart, he's funny, he's a great guy, and I'm not just saying that because I went out with him. He was popular in high school.

But then I remembered what Ina said about me and Garrett. I guess being smart and funny doesn't mean you're in the same league as someone, you have to be equally good-looking too. And if Garrett's been talking to girls who are pretty, maybe they don't feel like he's in their league.

I didn't make a big deal out of it when we were talking, because I don't think he wanted to talk about it a lot. But afterwards, I was thinking that if we decide to do a visit, I should definitely go out to Northrop to see him instead of him coming here. Obviously, I'm hoping something'll happen between us, but also, I thought, maybe if the other people at his school see us together, he might feel better. Because I know sometimes that works: if you're hanging out with a cool person, you feel cool, and other people think you're cool. Not that I'm super cool, but I guess people like how I look, so I thought it might help.

Ellen Hutchinson, professor of sociology at Pembleton:

I admire the students who are putting forth this initiative. Their idealism heartens me, but I have mixed feelings about their goal.

Like everyone else my age, I've had to come to terms with the effects time has had on my appearance. It wasn't an easy thing to get used to, but I've reached the point where I'm content with the way I look. Although I can't deny that I'm curious to see what a calli-only community would be like; maybe there a woman my age wouldn't become invisible when a young woman entered the room.

But would I have wanted to adopt calli when I was young? I don't know. I'm sure it would've spared me some of the distress I felt about growing older. But I *liked* the way I looked when I was young. I wouldn't have wanted to give that up. I'm not sure if, as I grew older, there was ever a point when the benefits would have outweighed the costs for me.

And these students, they might never even lose the beauty of youth. With the gene therapies coming out now, they'll probably look young for decades, maybe even their entire lives. They might never have to make the adjustments I did, in which case adopting calli wouldn't even save them from pain later on. So the idea that they might voluntarily give up one of the pleasures of youth is almost galling. Sometimes I want to shake them and say, "No! Don't you realize what you have?"

I've always liked young people's willingness to fight for their beliefs. That's one reason I've never really believed in the cliché that youth is wasted on the young. But this initiative would bring the cliché closer to reality, and I would hate for that to be the case.

Joseph Weingartner:

I've tried calliagnosia for a day; I've tried a wide variety of agnosias for limited periods. Most neurologists do, so we can better understand these conditions and empathize with our patients. But I couldn't adopt calliagnosia on a long-term basis, if for no other reason than that I see patients.

There's a slight interaction between calliagnosia and the ability to gauge a person's health visually. It certainly doesn't make you blind to things like a person's skin tone, and a calliagnosic can recognize symptoms of illness just like anyone else does; this is something that general cognition handles perfectly well. But physicians need to be sensitive to very subtle cues when evaluating a patient; sometimes you use your intuition when making a diagnosis, and calliagnosia would act as a handicap in such situations.

Of course, I'd be disingenuous if I claimed that professional requirements were the only thing keeping me from adopting calliagnosia. The more relevant question is, would I choose calliagnosia if I did nothing but lab research and never dealt with patients? And to that, my answer is, no. Like many other people, I enjoy seeing a pretty face, but I consider myself mature enough to not let that affect my judgment.

Tamera Lyons:

I can't believe it, Garrett got his calli turned back on.

We were talking on the phone last night, just ordinary stuff, and I ask him if he wants to switch to video. And he's like, "Okay," so we do. And then I realize he's not looking at me the same way he was before. So I ask him if everything's okay with him, and that's when he tells me about getting calli again.

He said he did it because he wasn't happy about the way he looked. I asked him if someone had said something about it, because he should ignore them, but he said it wasn't that. He just didn't like how he felt when he saw himself in a mirror. So I was like, "What are you talking about, you look cute." I tried to get him to give it another chance, saying stuff like, he should spend more time without calli before making any decisions. Garrett said he'd think about it, but I don't know what he's going to do.

Anyway, afterwards, I was thinking about what I'd said to him. Did I tell him that because I don't like calli, or because I wanted him to see how I looked? I mean, of course I liked the way he looked at me, and I was hoping it would lead somewhere, but it's not as if I'm being inconsistent, is it? If I'd always been in favor of calli, but made an exception when it came to Garrett, that'd be different. But I'm against calli, so it's not like that.

Oh, who am I kidding? I wanted Garrett to get his calli turned off for my own benefit, not because I'm anti-calli. And it's not even that I'm anti-calli, so much, as I am against calli being a requirement. I don't want anyone else deciding calli's right for me: not my parents, not a student organization. But if someone decides they want calli themselves, that's fine, whatever. So I should let Garrett decide for himself, I know that.

It's just frustrating. I mean, I had this whole plan figured out, with Garrett finding me irresistible, and realizing what a mistake he'd made. So I'm disappointed, that's all.

From Maria deSouza's speech the day before the election:
We've reached a point where we can begin to adjust our minds. The question is, when is it appropriate for us to do so? We shouldn't automatically accept that natural is better, nor should we automatically presume that we can improve on nature. It's up to us to decide which qualities we value, and what's the best way to achieve those.

I say that physical beauty is something we no longer need.

Calli doesn't mean that you'll never see anyone as

beautiful. When you see a smile that's genuine, you'll see beauty. When you see an act of courage or generosity, you'll see beauty. Most of all, when you look at someone you love, you'll see beauty. All calli does is keep you from being distracted by surfaces. True beauty is what you see with the eyes of love, and that's something that nothing can obscure.

From the speech broadcast by Rebecca Boyer, spokesperson for People for Ethical Nanomedicine, the day before the election:

You might be able to create a pure calli society in an artificial setting, but in the real world, you're never going to get a hundred percent compliance. And that is calli's weakness. Calli works fine if everybody has it, but if even one person doesn't, that person will take advantage of everyone else.

There'll always be people who don't get calli; you know that. Just think about what those people could do. A manager could promote attractive employees and demote ugly ones, but you won't even notice. A teacher could reward attractive students and punish ugly ones, but you won't be able to tell. All the discrimination you hate could be taking place, without you even realizing.

Of course, it's possible those things won't happen. But if people could always be trusted to do what's right, no one would have suggested calli in the first place. In fact, the people prone to such behavior are liable to do it even more once there's no chance of their getting caught.

If you're outraged by that sort of lookism, how can you afford to get calli? You're precisely the type of person who's needed to blow the whistle on that behavior, but if you've got calli, you won't be able to recognize it.

If you want to fight discrimination, keep your eyes open.

From a broadcast of EduNews:

The Pembleton University calliagnosia initiative was defeated by a vote of sixty-four percent to thirty-six percent.

Polls indicated a majority favoring the initiative until days before the election. Many students who previously supported the initiative say they reconsidered after seeing the speech given by Rebecca Boyer of the People for Ethical Nanomedicine. This despite an earlier revelation that PEN was established by cosmetics companies to oppose the calliagnosia movement.

Maria deSouza:

Of course it's disappointing, but we originally thought of the initiative as a long shot. That period when the majority supported it was something of a fluke, so I can't be too disappointed about people changing their minds. The important thing is that people everywhere are talking about the value of appearances, and more of them are thinking about calli seriously.

And we're not stopping; in fact, the next few years will be a very exciting time. A spex manufacturer just demonstrated some new technology that could change everything. They've figured out a way to fit somatic positioning beacons in a pair of spex, custom-calibrated for a single person. That means no more helmet, no more office visit needed to reprogram your neurostat; you can just put on your spex and do it yourself. That means you'll be able to turn your calli on or off, *any time you want.*

That means we won't have the problem of people feeling that they have to give up beauty altogether. Instead, we can promote the idea that beauty is appropriate in some situations and not in others. For example, people could keep calli enabled when they're working, but disable it when they're among friends. I think people recognize that calli offers benefits, and will choose it on at least a part-time basis.

I'd say the ultimate goal is for calli to be considered the proper way to behave in polite society. People can always disable their calli in private, but the default for public interaction would be freedom from lookism. Appreciating beauty would become a consensual interaction, something you do only when both parties, the beholder and the beheld, agree to it.

From a broadcast of EduNews:

In the latest on the Pembleton calliagnosia initiative, EduNews has learned that a new form of digital manipulation was used on the broadcast of PEN spokesperson Rebecca Boyer's speech. EduNews has received files from the SemioTech Warriors that contain what appear to be two recorded versions of the speech: an original—acquired from the Wyatt/Hayes computers—and the broadcast version. The files also include the SemioTech Warriors' analysis of the differences between the two versions.

The discrepancies are primarily enhancements to Ms. Boyer's voice intonation, facial expressions, and body language. Viewers who watch the original version rate Ms. Boyer's performance as good, while those who watch the edited version rate her performance as excellent, describing her as extraordinarily dynamic and persuasive. The SemioTech Warriors conclude that Wyatt/Hayes has developed new software capable of fine-tuning paralinguistic cues in order to maximize the emotional response evoked in viewers. This dramatically increases the effectiveness of recorded presentations, especially when viewed through spex, and its use in the PEN broadcast is likely what caused many supporters of the calliagnosia initiative to change their votes.

Walter Lambert, president of the National Calliagnosia Association:

In my entire career, I've met only a couple people who have the kind of charisma they gave Ms. Boyer in that speech. People like that radiate a kind of reality-distortion field that lets them convince you of almost anything. You feel moved by their very presence, you're ready to open your wallet or agree to whatever they ask. It's not until later that you remember all the objections you had, but by then, often as not, it's too late. And I'm truly frightened by the prospect of corporations being able to generate that effect with software.

What this is, is another kind of supernormal stimuli, like flawless beauty but even more dangerous. We had a defense against beauty, and Wyatt/Hayes has escalated things to the next level. And protecting ourselves from this type of persuasion is going to be a hell of a lot harder.

There is a type of tonal agnosia, or aprosodia, that makes you unable to hear voice intonation; all you hear are the words, not the delivery. There's also an agnosia that prevents you from recognizing facial expressions. Adopting the two of these would protect you from this type of manipulation, because you'd have to judge a speech purely on its content; its delivery would be invisible to you. But I can't recommend them. The result is nothing like calli. If you can't hear tone of voice or read someone's expression, your ability to interact with others is crippled. It'd be a kind of high-functioning autism. A few NCA members *are* adopting both agnosias, as a form of protest, but no one expects many people will follow their example.

So that means that once this software gets into widespread use, we're going to be facing extraordinarily persuasive pitches from all sides: commercials, press releases, evangelists. We'll hear the most stirring speeches given by a politician or general in decades. Even activists and culture jammers will use it, just to keep up with the establishment. Once the range of this software gets wide enough, even the movies will use it, too: an actor's own ability won't matter, because everyone's performance will be uncanny.

The same thing'll happen as happened with beauty: our environment will become saturated with this supernormal stimuli, and it'll affect our interaction with real people. When every speaker on a broadcast has the presence of a Winston Churchill or a Martin Luther King, we'll begin to regard ordinary people, with their average use of paralinguistic cues, as bland and unpersuasive. We'll become dissatisfied with the people we interact with in real life, because they won't be as engaging as the projections we see through our spex.

I just hope those spex for reprogramming neurostat hit the market soon. Then maybe we can encourage people to adopt the stronger agnosias just when they're watching video. That may be the only way for us to preserve authentic human interaction: if we save our emotional responses for real life.

Tamera Lyons:

I know how this is going to sound, but ... well, I'm thinking about getting my calli turned back on.

In a way, it's because of that PEN video. I don't mean I'm getting calli just because makeup companies don't want people to and I'm angry at them. That's not it. But it's hard to explain.

I *am* angry at them, because they used a trick to manipulate people; they weren't playing fair. But what it made me realize was, I was doing the same kind of thing to Garrett. Or I wanted to, anyway. I was trying to use my looks to win him back. And in a way that's not playing fair, either.

I don't mean that I'm as bad as the advertisers are! I love Garrett, and they just want to make money. But remember when I was talking about beauty as a kind of magic spell? It gives you an advantage, and I think it's very easy to misuse something like that. And what calli does is make a person immune to that sort of spell. So I figure I shouldn't mind if Garrett would rather be immune, because I shouldn't be trying to gain an advantage in the first place. If I get him back, I want it to be by playing fair, by him loving me for myself.

I know, just because he got his calli turned back on doesn't mean that I have to. I've really been enjoying seeing what faces look like. But if Garrett's going to be immune, I feel like I should be too. So we're even, you know? And if we do get back together, maybe we'll get those new spex they're talking about. Then we can turn off our calli when we're by ourselves, just the two of us.

And I guess calli makes sense for other reasons, too. Those makeup companies and everyone else, they're just trying to create needs in you that you wouldn't feel if they were playing fair, and I don't like that. If I'm going to be dazzled watching a commercial, it'll be when I'm in the mood, not whenever they spring it on me. Although I'm not going to get those other agnosias, like that tonal one, not yet anyway. Maybe once those new spex come out.

This doesn't mean I agree with my parents' having me grow up with calli. I still think they were wrong; they thought getting rid of beauty would help make a utopia, and I don't believe that at all. Beauty isn't the problem, it's how some people are misusing it that's the problem. And that's what calli's good for; it lets you guard against that. I don't know, maybe this wasn't a problem back in my parents' day. But it's something we have to deal with now.

The Black Abacus

By Yoon Ha Lee

War Season

In space there are no seasons, and this is true too of the silver wheels that are humanity's homes beyond Earth and the silver ships that carried us there. In autumn there are no fallen leaves, and in spring, no living flowers; no summer winds, no winter snow. There are no days except our own calendars and the stars' slow candles in the dark.

The Network has known only one war, and that war ended before it began.

This is why, of course, the Network's ships trapped in q-space—that otherwhere of superpositions and spindrift possibilities—wield waveform interrupters, and why, though I was Rachel's friend, I killed her across several timelines. But the tale begins with our final exam, not my murders.

The Test

You are not required to answer this question.

However, the response (should you attempt one) will be evaluated. If you decide otherwise, key in "I DECLINE."

142

The amount of time you spend will be evaluated. You cannot proceed to the next item without deciding, and there will be no later opportunity.

Your time remaining is:—:—:—

In her essay "The Tyranny of Choice and Observation," Shinaai Rei posits a "black abacus" that determines history's course by "a calculus of personalities and circumstances, cause and effect and chance." (You are not expected to be familiar with this work; the full text is restricted.)

In light of this, under what circumstances is war justified? What about assassination? Consider, for example, Skorzeny's tactics during World War II, police actions against the Candida Rebellion, and more recently, terrorists' sabotage of relay stations. You may cite current regulations and past precedents to support your answer.

As you do, remember the following points:

1. During the 76.9 years (adjusted time) that the Pan-communications Network has been in place, no planet-or station-born conflict has found expression in realspace.

2. Because your future duty as a Network officer requires absolute reliability, treason is subject to the death penalty.

3. "*Reductio ad absurdum* is one of a mathematician's finest weapons. It is a far finer gambit than any chess gambit: a chess player may offer the sacrifice of a pawn

or even a piece, but the mathematician offers the game."—G. H. Hardy (1877–1947)

THE RESULTS

Fifty-seven percent of that year's class declined the question, or so they thought. The computers recorded every keystroke and false start for further analysis. Of those who did respond, the ratio of essay length to time taken (after adjustments for typing speed) matched the predicted curve.

Rachel was the exception. Her answer took 5.47 minutes to compose (including one self-corrected typo) and three sentences to express.

The records knew her as Rachel Kilterhawk. Her comrades in command training knew her as the Hawk. In later times and other lives, they would call her Rachel the Ruthless. Neither of us guessed this when we first met.

WHITE: QUEEN'S GAMBIT

Rachel was one of the first to leave the exam. Her cadet's uniform was creased where she had bent over the keyboard, and even now her hands shook. *I did what I could,* she thought, and set her mind on other things: the spindles of growing plants, the taste of thrice-recycled water, the cold texture of metal . . . the sea, from her one visit to Earth, with its rush of foam and salt-sprinkled breezes.

She went to hydroponics, where water warbled through the pipes and the station's crops grew in identical green rows, a spring without end. In a corner of the garden she picked out a bench and sat with her legs drawn up, her hands on her knees. Nearby was a viewport—a viewscreen, actually, filtering the stars' radiation into intensities kinder to human eyes.

After a while her hands stopped trembling, and only then did she notice the other cadet. He had dark hair and darker eyes, and where her uniform was rumpled, his was damp with sweat. "Do you believe in angels?" he asked her.

Rachel blinked. "Not yet. Why?"

He gestured at the viewscreen, tracing unnamed constellations and the pale flash of an incoming ship's q-wave. "It must be a cold thing to die in space. I like to think there are angels who watch over the ships." The boy looked away and flushed.

She gazed at the fingerprints he had left on the screen. "Angels' wings."

It was his turn to blink. "Pardon?"

"The q-waves," she said. "Like wings."

He might have laughed; others often did, when Rachel with her quicksilver thoughts and quiet speech couldn't find the right words. She was startled when he rubbed his chin, then nodded. "Never thought of it that way." He smiled at her. "I'm Edgar Kerzen. And you?"

She returned his smile with one of her own. "Rachel."

Dawning realization: "You're the Hawk. No one else would've torn through the exam like that."

"But so did you."

Edgar shrugged. "I aced math and physics, but they killed me on ethics."

She heard the unsaid words: *Let's talk about something else.* Being Rachel, she was silent. And found herself startled again when he accepted the silence rather than filling it with words. She would come to treasure that acceptance.

BLACK: KNIGHT'S SACRIFICE

The first life, first time I killed Rachel, it was too late. She had already given her three-sentence answer to the Pandect's exam; won command of the starhiker *Curtana*, one of twenty-six ever built; and swept from the Battle of Red Lantern to the Siege of Gloria on the shredded wings of a q-wave. After Gloria, her name passed across the relays as both battle-cry (for the Network) and curse (for the Movement). In this probability-space, her triumphs were too great to erase, her influence too great to stop the inevitable blurring of murder and necessity.

After the siege, we had a few days to remember what sleep was, to forget the silence of battle. Space is silent, though we want thunder with our lightning, the scream of metal and roar of guns. I think this was true even for Rachel, because she believed in *right* silences and *wrong* silences.

By fortune or otherwise we had shared postings since we left academy, since that first meeting in hydroponics. Command was short on officers, but shorter still on ones who worked together like twin heartbeats. I stood beside her when she received the captain's wing on her uniform and again when we learned, over the relays, that the scoutship *Boomerang's* kamikaze destruction of a station had plunged one probability-space into war. I stood beside her and said nothing when she opened fire on Gloria Station, another of the few q-space stopovers. It harbored a Movement ship determined to return to realspace, and so it died in a ripple of incoherence.

One people, one law, said the Network. There were too many factions at a time when humanity's defenses were scattered across the stars: conglomerates with their merchant fleets, colonies defending their autonomy, free-traders who resented the Network's restrictions. Once the Pancommunications Network had only been responsible for routing transmissions between settlements and sorting out discrepancies due to time dilation. Someone had to maintain the satellite networks that knit everyone together and someone had to define a law, however, so the Network did.

In light of this, under what circumstances is war justified?

A ship's captain has her privacy, but we were docked and awaiting repairs, and I knew Rachel's thoughts better than my own. She had her duty, and if that duty demanded it, she would pay in blood. Including her own, if it came to that, but she was too damned brilliant to die in battle. Because she was the Hawk, and when it came to her duty, she never hesitated.

5.47 minutes and three sentences.

I came upon Rachel deep in the ship's hold, in an area closed off for tomorrow's repairs. Her eyes, when she raised them to me, were the wild gray of a winter sky, unlike the carbon-scored gray of the torn bulkheads behind her. These days our world was defined by shades of gray and the reflections therein.

Soon we would be forced to leave the colorless haven of q-space, since the last few stations could barely sustain themselves or the remaining ships. For a while, the Network and the Independence Movement had cannibalized any new ships who entered q-space despite the perils of merging q-waves, gutting them of supplies, people, and news. Once a ship exited into realspace, our own fluctuating history would collapse into a single outcome, and nobody was willing to plunge the realspace world into war, especially one in the enemy's favor. New ships no longer showed up, and God knew what we'd done to realspace transportation and logistics.

A few weary souls had tried to force the issue. Rachel shot them down. She was determined to win or stop the war in every life, every timeline, and she might even succeed.

She noticed my presence and, for once, spoke before I could. "Edgar. While I'm here, more people are dying." Her voice was restless, like the beating wings of a bird in a snowstorm.

"We'll find out about it on relay," I said, wishing I could say something to comfort her, to gentle those eyes, that voice, but Rachel had never much believed in words, even mine.

"Do you think angels fly between probability-spaces to harvest our souls?"

I closed my eyes and saw the afterimages of a ship's waveform disintegration, translated into images the human mind could interpret. "I wish I knew." I was tired of fighting and forcing myself to remember that the bright, undulating ribbons on the tactical display represented people and what had carried people. I wanted her to say that we would leave and let the multiplicity of battles end, but I knew she wouldn't.

For a long time Rachel said nothing, lacing and unlacing her fingers together. Then her hands relaxed and she said, "How did you know to find me here?"

Nothing but curiosity from a woman who had killed civilians, whom I had always followed. Her duty and her ruthlessness were a greater weapon than any battleship the Network had left. My angel, an angel of death.

My hands were a weapon and her trust, a weakness.

"I'll always find you, my dear," I said, reaching out as though to massage her shoulders, and interrupted the balance of her breath and brain and heartbeat. She did not fight; perhaps she knew that in other probability-spaces, I was still hers. I thought of Red Lantern. My memories held lights and lines in red or amber, autumn colors; tactical screens, terse voices. My own voice, saying *Aye aye, sir*.

After she stopped moving, I laid her down. I was shaking. Such an easy thing, to kill. Escape was the hard part, and I no longer cared.

THE DARKEST GAME

Schrödinger's cat has far more than nine lives, and far fewer. All of us are unknowing cats, alive and dead at once, and of all the might-have-beens in between, we record only one.

We had the catch-me catch-me-not of quantum physics, then quantum computers, oracles that scanned possibilities. When we discovered a stardrive that turned ships into waves in a sea of their own—q-space—we thought we understood it. We even untangled navigation in that sea and built our stations there.

Then, the echoes. Ghosts in probability-space, wave-forms strung taut from waypoint to waypoint, snapshot to snapshot. Enter q-space and you throw a shard of the universe into flux. Exit it, and the shard crystallizes, fixing history over the realspace interval. Shinaai Rei—philosopher, physicist, and sociologist—saw it first.

Before the *Boomerang*, there had neither been a war nor ships that interrupted the night with their flashfire battles. Then she destroyed a civilian station, and the world shifted into a grand game of chess, probabilities played one on the other, ships that winged into q-space never to return. Why take risks in war when you can try everything at once and find out who will win?

WHITE: CANDLES

Theirs had been one of many patrolships guarding the satellite network. Sometimes threats breathed through the relays, but nobody was willing to disrupt the web of words between worlds. Rachel had known Network duty was tedious, but didn't mind. Edgar was with her, and around they went, never twice tracing the same path. Their conversations, too, were never twice the same.

Everything had turned awry, but when smoke seared her lungs or she had to put the crew on half-rations again, she remembered. Edgar was all that remained from that quiet time, and when his back was to her as he checked a readout, she gazed fondly at the dark, tousled hair and the steady movements of his hands.

On patrol, through the long hours, Rachel had come to trust his motions, his words, his velvet voice and the swift thoughts behind them. Even his smile, when smiles often made false promises. But there came dark moments, too.

Once, after watching a convoy of tradeships streak by, Edgar said, "What would happen if all the satellites went out?"

She explored the idea and found it sharp to the touch. "Candles."

He understood. "Only a matter of time before everything fails. Imagine living in a future when the worlds drop silent one by one."

Rachel reached out and stroked his hand. "It won't happen yet," she said. *Not for a long time, and we are here; the Network is here.*

He folded her hand in his, and for a moment his mouth was taut, bitter. "War would do that."

"The exam." Years ago, and she still remembered the way her hands had shook afterward. What Edgar had said, she never asked. He gave her the same courtesy.

She wondered now if he had foreseen the war and chosen to make himself a part of it, with the quicksilver instinct she treasured. She suspected that his dreams, his visions of other probability-spaces, were clearer than hers, which spoke merely of a battle to be won, everywhere and when. Rachel decided to ask him the next time they were both awake and alone.

In some of her lives, she never had the opportunity.

BLACK: A RIDDLE

How long can a war go on if it never begins?

WHITE: THE BLOODY QUEEN

The Battle of Seven Spindles. The Battle of Red Lantern. The Siege of Gloria. The Battle of Crescent. Twenty-one stations and four battles fought across the swirl of timelines. Rachel counted each one as it happened.

Today, insofar as there were days in q-space, she faced the 45th ship. The *Curtana* was a hell of red lights and blank, malfunctioning displays; she had never been meant to go this long without a realspace stopover. The crew, too, showed the marks of a long skirmish with their red eyes and blank faces. They saw her as the Hawk, unassailable and remote; she never revealed otherwise to them.

The communications officer, Thanh, glanced up from his post and said, "The *Shanghai Star* requests cease-fire and withdrawal." A standard request once, when ships dragged governments into debt and lives were to be safeguarded, not spent. A standard request now, when ships were resources to be cannibalized after they could no longer sustain life.

Rachel did not hesitate. "No." The sooner attrition took its toll, the sooner they would find an end to this.

Her crew knew her too well to show any surprise. Perhaps, by now, they were beyond it. After a pause, Thanh said, "The captain would like to speak to you."

"You mean he wants to know why." For once words came easily to her: she had carried this answer inside her heart since she understood what war meant. "Tell the *Shanghai Star* that there's no easy escape. That we can make the trappings of battle as polite as we like, and still people die. That the only kind end is a quick one."

Rachel heard Edgar approach her from the side and felt his warmth beside her. "They'll die, you know," he murmured.

She startled herself by saying, "I'm not infallible." Battle here, like the duels of old, was fast and fatal. A modification of the stardrive diverted part of the q-wave into a powerful harmonic. If an inverse Fourier breakdown of the enemy ship's waveform was used to forge the harmonic, and directed toward that waveform, the stardrive became an interrupter. The principle of canceling a wave with its inverse was hardly new, but Edgar had programmed the change to the ship's control computers before anyone else did. A battle was ninety percent maneuver and data analysis to screen out noise from other probability-spaces, ten percent targeting.

Her attention returned, then, to the lunge-and-parry, circle-and-retreat of battle.

At the end, it was her fifth battle and victory. Only the *Curtana* remained to tell of it.

BLACK: THE TRAITOR KNIGHT

Time and again, Rachel's crew on the *Curtana* speculates that she dreams of Fourier breakdowns and escape trajectories, if she dreams at all. *The Hawk never sleeps*, they say where Rachel isn't supposed to hear, and so she never corrects the misimpression.

Sometimes I was her first officer and sometimes her weapons officer. Either way I knew her dreams. In a hundred lives, they never changed: dreams of the sea and of the silver ships, silver stations, that were her only homes; dreams of fire that burned without smoke, death that came without sound.

In a hundred lives and a hundred dreams I killed her a hundred times. Once with my hands and once with a fragment of metal. Sometimes by betraying her orders and letting the ship hurtle into an interrupter's wave, or failing to report an incoming hostile. On the rare instances that I failed, I was executed by her hand. We knew the penalty for treason.

Several times I killed her by walking away when she called out to me as the ship's tortured, aging structure pinned her down. Several times more I died, by rope or knife or shipboard accident, leaving her behind, and took her soul with me.

I have lived more probabilities than she will ever dream. Doubtless the next will be similar. I know every shape of her despair, every winter hymn in her heart . . . why she looks for angels and only finds me. I am tired of killing her. Make your move and end the game.

WHITE: A CHANGE IN TACTICS

When it was her turn to sleep, Rachel dreamt: constellations of fingerprints, white foam on the wind, ships with dark wings and darker songs. But she woke always to Edgar's hand tracing the left side of her jaw, then her shoulder, and that touch, like her duty aboard the *Curtana*, defined her mornings. It was the only luxury she permitted herself or Edgar. The rest of the crew made no complaint. His were the hardest, most heartbreaking tasks, and they knew it.

His dreams were troubled, she knew. Sometimes they surfaced in his words, the scars of unfought battles and unfinished deaths, merciless might-have-beens. *Stay here*, she thought. *Of all the choices, one must be a quiet ending.*

Perhaps he heard her, in the silence.

THE BLACK ABACUS

BLACK: CHECK AND MATE

Rachel's response to the ethics question took 5.47 minutes and three sentences. Mine took more lives, mine and hers and others', than I can count.

RACHEL'S SEASON

In space there are no seasons, and this is as true of the ships that cross the distances between humanity's far-flung homes. But we measure our seasons anyway: by a smile, a silence, a song. I measured mine by Rachel's deaths. Perhaps she will measure hers differently.

Your move, my dear.

—for JCB

The Discharge

Christopher Priest

Like all dreamers, I mistook disillusionment for truth.
Jean-Paul Sartre

I emerge into my memories of life at the age of twenty. I was a soldier, recently released from boot camp, being marched by an escouade of black-cap military policemen to the naval compound in Jethra Harbour. The war was approaching the end of its three thousandth year and I was serving in a conscript army.

I marched mechanically, staring at the back of the man's head in front of me. The sky was dark grey with cloud and a stiff cold wind streamed in from the sea. My awareness of life leapt into being around me. I knew my name, I knew where we had been ordered to march, I knew or could guess where we would be going after that. I could function as a soldier. This was my moment of birth into consciousness.

Marching uses no mental energy—the mind is free to wander, if you have a mind. I record these words some years later, looking back, trying to make sense of what happened. At the time, the moment of awareness, I could only react, stay in step.

Of my childhood, the years leading up to this moment of mental birth, little remains. I can piece together the fragments of a likely story: I was probably born in Jethra, university town and capital city on the southern coast of our country. Of my parents, brothers or sisters, my education, any history of childhood illnesses, friends, experiences, travels, I remember nothing. I grew to the age of twenty; only that is certain.

And one other thing, useless to a soldier. I knew I was an artist.

How could I be sure of that, trudging along with the other men, in a phalanx of dark uniforms, kitbags, clanking mess-tins, steel helmets, boots, stamping down a puddled road with a chill wind in our faces?

I knew that in the area of blankness behind me was a love of paintings, of beauty, of shape and form and colour. How had I gained this passion? What had I done with it? Aesthetics were my obsession and fervour. What was I doing in the army? Somehow this totally unsuitable candidate must have passed medical and psychological tests. I had been drafted, sent to boot camp; somehow a drill serjeant had trained me to become a soldier.

Here I was, marching to war.

We boarded a troopship for passage to the southern continent, the world's largest unclaimed territory. It was there that the fighting was taking place. All battles had been fought in the south for nearly three thousand years. It was a vast, uncharted land of tundra and permafrost, buried in ice at the pole. Apart from a few outposts along the coast, it was uninhabited except by battalions.

I was assigned to a mess-deck below the waterline, already hot and stinking when we boarded, soon crowded and noisy as well.

I withdrew into myself, while sensations of life coursed maddeningly through me. Who was I? How had I come to this place? Why could I not remember what I had been doing even the previous day?

But I was able to function, equipped with knowledge of the world, with working ability to use my equipment, I knew the other men in my escadron and I understood some of the aims and history of the war. It was only myself I could not remember. For the first day, as we waited in our deck for other detachments to board the ship, I listened in to the talk of the other men, hoping mainly for insights about myself, but when none of those was revealed I settled instead for finding out what concerned them. Their concerns would be mine.

Like all soldiers they were complaining, but in their case the complaints were tinged with real apprehension. It was the prospect of the three thousandth anniversary of the outbreak of war that was the problem. They were all convinced that they were going to be caught up in some major new offensive, an assault intended to resolve the dispute one way or another. Some of them thought that because there were still more than three years to go until the anniversary the war would be ended before then. Others pointed out cynically that our four-year term of conscription was due to end a few weeks after the millennium. If a big offensive was in progress we would never be allowed out until it was over.

Like them, I was too young for fatalism. The seed of wanting to escape from the army, to find some way to discharge myself, had been sown.

I barely slept that night, wondering about my past, worrying about my future.

When the ship started its voyage it headed south, passing the islands closest to the mainland. Off the coast of Jethra itself was Seevl, a long grey island of steep cliffs and bare windswept hills that blocked the view of the sea from most parts of the city. Beyond Seevl a wide strait led to a group of islands known as the Serques—these were greener, lower, with many attractive small towns nestling in coves and bays around their coastlines.

Our ship passed them all, weaving a way between the clustering islands. I watched from the rail, enchanted by the view.

As the long shipboard days passed slowly I found myself drawn again and again to the upper deck, where I would find a place to stand and stare, usually alone. So close to home but beyond the blocking mass of Seevl, the islands slipped past, out of reach, this endless islandscape of vivid colours and glimpses of other places, distant and shrouded in haze. The ship ploughed on steadily through the calm water, the massed soldiery crammed noisily within, few of the men so much as even glancing away to see where we were.

The days went by and the weather grew noticeably warmer. The beaches I could see now were white and fringed with tall trees, tiny houses visible in the shade beyond. The reefs that protected many of the islands were brilliantly multicoloured, jagged and encrusted with shells, breaking the sea-swell into spumes of white spray. We passed ingenious harbours and large coastal towns clinging to spectacular hillsides, saw pluming volcanoes and rambling, rock-strewn mountain pastures, skirted islands large and small, lagoons and bays and river estuaries.

It was common knowledge that it was the people of the Dream Archipelago who had caused the war, though as you passed through the Midway Sea the peaceful, even dreamy aspect of the islands undermined this certainty. The calm was only an impression, an illusion borne of the distance between ship and shore. To keep us alert on our long southerly voyage the army mounted many compulsory shipboard lectures. Some of these recounted the history of the struggle to achieve armed neutrality in which the islands had been engaged for most of the three millennia of the war.

Now they were by consent of all parties neutral, but their geographical location—the Midway Sea girdled the world, separating the warring countries of the northern continent from their chosen battlefields in the uninhabited southern polar land—ensured that military presence in the islands was perpetual.

I cared little for any of that. Whenever I was able to get away to the upper deck I would stare in rapt silence at the passing diorama of islands. I tracked the course of the ship with the help of a torn and probably out-dated map I had found in a ship's locker and the names of the islands chimed in my consciousness like a peal of bells: Paneron, Salay, Temmil, Mesterline, Prachous, Muriseay, Demmer, Piqay, the Aubracs, the Torquils, the Serques, the Reever Fast Shoals and the Coast of Helvard's Passion.

Each of these names was evocative to me. Reading the names off the map, identifying the exotic coastlines from fragments of clues—a sudden rise of sheer cliffs, a distinctive headland, a particular bay—made me think that everywhere in the Dream Archipelago was already embedded in my consciousness, that somehow I derived from the islands, belonged in them, had dreamed of them all my life. In short, while I stared at the islands from the ship I felt my artistic sensibilities reviving. I was startled by the emotional impact on me of the names, so delicate and suggestive of unspecified sensual pleasures, out of key with the rest of the coarse and manly existence on the ship. As I stared out across the narrow stretches of water that lay between our passing ship and the beaches and reefs I would quietly recite the names to myself, as if trying to summon a spirit that would lift me up, raise me above the sea and carry me to those tide-swept strands.

Some of the islands were so large that the ship sailed along parallel with their coastlines for most of the day, while others were so small they were barely more than half-submerged reefs which threatened to rip at the hull of our elderly ship.

Small or large, all the islands had names. As we passed one I could identify on my map I circled the name, then later added it to an ever-growing list in my notebook. I wanted to record them, count them, note them down as an itinerary so that one day I might go back and explore them all. The view from the sea tempted me.

There was only one island stop for our ship during that long southward voyage.

My first awareness of the break in our journey was when I noticed that the ship was heading towards a large industrialized port, the installations closest to the sea seemingly bleached white by the cement dust spilling from an immense smoking factory that overlooked the bay. Beyond this industrial area was a long tract of undeveloped shoreline, the tangle of rainforest briefly blocking any further sight of civilization. Then, after rounding a hilly promontory and passing a high jetty wall, a large town built on a range of low hills came suddenly into sight, stretching away in all directions, my view of it distorted by the shimmering heat that spread out from the land across the busy waters of the harbour. We were of course forbidden from knowing the identity of our stop, but I had my map and I already knew the name.

The island was Muriseay, the largest of the islands in the Archipelago and one of the most important.

It would be hard to underestimate the impact this discovery had on me. Muriseay's name came swimming up out of the blank pool that was my memory.

At first it was just an identifying word on the map: a name printed in letters larger than the ones used for other islands. It puzzled me. Why should this word, this foreign name, mean something to me? I had been stirred by the sight of the other islands, but although the resonances were subtle I had felt no close identification with any of them.

Then we approached the island and the ship started to follow the long coastline. I had watched the distant land slip by, affected more and more, wondering why.

When we came to the bay, to the entrance to the harbour, and I felt the heat from the town drifting across the quiet water towards us, something at last became clear to me.

I knew about Muriseay. The knowledge came to me as a memory from the place where I had no memory.

Muriseay was something or somewhere I had known, or it represented something I had done, or experienced, as a child. It was a whole memory, discrete, telling me nothing about the rest. It involved a painter who had lived on Muriseay and his name was Rascar Acizzone.

Rascar Acizzone? Who was that? Why did I suddenly remember the name of a Muriseayan painter when otherwise I was a hollow shell of amnesia?

I was able to explore this memory no further: without warning all troops were mustered to billets and with the other men who had drifted to the upper decks I was forced to return to the mess-decks. I descended to the bowels of the ship resentfully. We were kept below for the rest of the day and night, as well as for much of the day that followed.

Although I suffered in the airless, sweltering hold with all the others, it gave me time to think. I closed myself off, ignored the noise of the other men and silently explored this one memory that had returned.

When the larger memory is blank, anything that suddenly seems clear becomes sharp, evocative, heavy with meaning. I gradually remembered my interest in Muriseay without learning anything else about myself.

I was a boy, a teenager. Not long ago, in my short life. I learned somehow of a colony of artists who had gathered in Muriseay Town the previous century. I saw reproductions of their work somewhere, perhaps in books. I investigated further and found that several of the originals were kept in the city's art gallery. I went there to see them for myself. The leading painter, the eminence within the group, was the artist called Rascar Acizzone.

It was Acizzone's work which inspired me.

Details continued to clarify themselves. A coherent exactness emerged from the gloom of my forgotten past.

Rascar Acizzone developed a painting technique he called tactilism. A tactilist work used a kind of pigment that had been developed some years before, not by artists but by researchers into ultrasound microcircuitry. A range of dazzling colours became available to artists when certain patents expired and for a brief period there had been a vogue for paintings that used the garish but exciting ultrasound primaries.

Most of these early works were little more than pure sensationalism: colours were blended synaesthetically with ultrasonics to shock, alarm or provoke the viewer. Acizzone's work began as the others lost interest, consigning themselves to the minor artistic school that soon became known as the Pre-Tactilists. Acizzone used the pigments to more disturbing effect than anyone before him. His glowing abstracts—large canvases or boards painted in one or two primary colours, with few shapes or images to be seen—appeared at a casual first look, or from a distance, or when seen as reproductions in books, to be little more than arrangements of colours. Closer up or, better still, if you made physical contact with the ultrasonic pigments used in the originals, it became apparent that the concealed images were of most profoundly and shockingly erotic nature. Detailed and astonishingly explicit scenes were mysteriously evoked in the mind of the viewer, inducing an intense charge of sexual excitement. I discovered a set of long-forgotten Acizzone abstracts in the vaults of the museum in Jethra and by the laying on of the palms of my hands I entered the world of vicarious carnal passion. The women depicted by Acizzone were the most beautiful and sensual I had ever seen, or known, or imagined. Each painting created its own vision in the mind of the viewer. The images were always exact and repeatable, but they were unique, being partially created as an individual response to the sensual longing of the observer.

Not much critical literature about Acizzone remained, but what little I could find seemed to suggest that everyone experienced each painting differently.

I discovered that Acizzone's career had ended in failure and ignominy: soon after his work was noticed he was rejected by the art establishment figures, the public notables, the moral guardians, of his time. He was hounded and execrated, forced to end his days in exile on the closed island of Cheoner. With his most of his originals hidden, and a few more dispersed away from Muriseay to the archives of mainland galleries, Acizzone never worked again and sank into obscurity.

As a teenage aesthete I cared nothing about his scandalous reputation. All I understood was that the few paintings of his that were hidden away in the cellars of the Jethran gallery evoked such lustful images in my mind that I was left weak with unfocused desire and dizzy with amorous longings.

That was the whole bright clarity of my unlocated memory. Muriseay, Acizzone, tactilist masterpieces, concealed paintings of secret sex.

Who was I who had learned of this? The boy was gone, grown into a soldier. Where was I when it happened? There must have been a wider life I once lived, but none of those memories had survived.

Once I had been an aesthete; now I was a foot-soldier. What kind of life was that?

Now we were moored in Muriseay Town, just outside the harbour wall. We fretted and strained, wanting to escape from our sweltering holds. Then:

Shore leave.

The news circulated around us faster than the speed of sound. The ship was soon to leave its mooring outside the harbour and dock against the quay. We would have thirty-six hours ashore. I cheered with the others. I yearned to find my past and lose my innocence in Muriseay.

Four thousand men were released and we hurried ashore. Most of them rushed into Muriseay Town in search of whores.

I rushed along with them, in quest of Acizzone.

Instead, I too found only whores.

There in the dock area, after a fruitless quest that sent me dashing through the streets to find Acizzone's beautiful Muriseayan women, I finished up in a dancing club. I was unready for Muriseay, had no idea of how to find what I was seeking. I roamed about the remoter quarters of the town, lost in narrow streets, shunned by the people who lived there. They saw only my uniform. I was soon footsore and disillusioned by the foreignness of the town, so I felt relieved when I discovered that my wanderings had brought me back to the harbour.

Our troopship, floodlit in the night, loomed over the concrete aprons and wharves.

I noticed the dancing club when I came across the dozens of troops thronging around the entrance. Wondering what was attracting them, I pushed through the crowd and went inside.

The large interior was dark and hot, crammed to the walls with human bodies, filled with the endless throbbing beat of synthesized rock. My eyes were dazzled by the coloured lasers and spotlights flashing intensely from positions close to the ceiling. No one was dancing. At points around the walls, young women stood on glinting metal platforms head-height above the crowds, their naked, oil-glossed bodies picked out by glaring white spotlights. Each of them held a microphone against her lips and was speaking unexcitedly into it, pointing down at certain of the men on the dance floor.

As I pushed my way into the central area I was spotted by them. At first, in my inexperience, I thought they were waving to me or greeting me in some other way. I was tired and disappointed after my long walk around the town and I raised a hand in weary response. The young woman on the platform closest to me had a voluptuous body: she stood with her feet wide apart and her pelvis thrust forward, glorying in the revelation of her nakedness by the intrusive light. When I waved she moved suddenly, leaning forward on the metal rail around her platform so that her huge breasts dangled temptingly towards the men below. The spotlight source instantly shifted—a new beam flashed up from behind and below her, garishly illuminating her large buttocks and casting her shadow brightly on the ceiling. She spoke more urgently into her microphone, jabbing her hand in my direction.

Alarmed by being paid special attention, I moved deeper into the press of uniformed male bodies, hoping to lose myself in the crowd. Within a few seconds, though, a number of women had converged on me from different sides, reaching out through the jam of bodies to take me by the arms. Each of them was wearing a radio headset, with a pin-mike suspended close in front of her lips. Soon I was surrounded by them. They led me irresistibly across to one side.

While they continued to press around me, one of them

flicked her fingers in front of my face, her thumb rubbing acquisitively across her fingertips.

I shook my head, embarrassed and frightened.

'Money!' the woman said loudly.

'How much?'

I hoped that money would let me escape from them.

'Your leave pay.' She rubbed her fingers again.

I found the thin fold of military banknotes the black-cap marshals had given me as I disembarked. As soon as I pulled them from my hip pocket she snatched them. With a swift motion she passed the money to one of the women I suddenly saw were sitting behind a long table in the shadowy recess by the edge of the dance floor. Each of them was noting down the amounts taken from every man in a kind of ledger, then slipping the banknotes out of sight.

It had all happened so quickly that I had barely taken in what they wanted. By now, though, because of the close and suggestive way the women were standing against me, there was little doubt what they were offering, even demanding. None of them was young, none of them was attractive to me. My thoughts for the last few hours had been with Acizzone's sirens. To be confronted by these aggressive and disagreeable women now was a shock to me.

'You want this?' one of them said, pulling at the loose front of her dress to reveal, fleetingly, a small sagging breast.

'You want this too?' The woman who had taken my money from my hand snatched at the front of her skirt, lifting it to show me what was beneath. In the harsh shadows created by the aggravating lights I could see nothing of her.

They were laughing at me.

'You've taken my money,' I said. 'Now leave me.'

'Do you know where you are and what men do in here?'

'Of course.'

I managed to struggle away from them and headed back immediately towards the entrance. I was feeling angry and humiliated. I had spent the last few hours dreaming of meeting, or even of simply seeing, Acizzone's wanton beauties. Instead, these hags tormented me with their withered, experienced bodies.

A group of four black-caps had entered the building while this had been going on. I could see them standing in pairs on each side of the entrance. They had withdrawn their synaptic batons and were holding them in the strike position. While aboard the ship I had already seen what happened to the victim if one of those evil sticks was used in anger. I faltered in my step, not wanting to have to push past the men to leave.

As I did so, another whore forced her way through the crowd and took my arm. I glanced at her in a distracted way, fearing the black-caps more than anything.

I was surprised to see her: this one was much younger than the others. She was wearing hardly any clothes to speak of: a tiny pair of shorts and a T-shirt with a torn neckline that hung low across one shoulder, revealing the upper curve of a breast. Her arms were thin. She was not wearing a radio headset. She was smiling towards me and as soon as I looked at her she spoke.

'Don't leave without discovering what we can do,' she said, tilting her face to speak against my ear.

'I don't need to know,' I shouted.

'This place is the cathedral of your dreams.'

'What did you say?'

'Your dreams. Whatever you seek, they are here.'

'No, I've had enough.'

'Just try what we offer,' she said, pressing her face so close to me that her curly hair lightly teased my cheek. 'We are here for you, eager to please you. One day you will need what whores provide.'

'Never.'

The black-caps had moved to block the doorway. I could see that beyond them, in the wide passageway that led back to the street, more of their escouade were arriving. I wondered why they had suddenly appeared at the club, what they were doing. Our leave was not officially over for many more hours. Was there some emergency for which we had to return to the ship? Was this club, so prominently close to where the ship had berthed, off-limits for some perverse reason? Nothing was clear. I was suddenly frightened of the situation in which I had found myself.

Yet around me the hundreds of other men, all presumably from the same troopship as mine, appeared to show no concern. The racket of the over-amplified music went on, drilling into the mind.

'You can leave this way,' the girl said, touching my arm. She pointed towards a dark doorway placed low, beneath a stage area, away from the main entrance.

The black-caps were now moving into the crowd of men, pushing people aside with rough movements of their arms. The synaptic batons wavered threateningly. The young whore had already run down the short flight of steps to the door and was holding it open for me. She beckoned urgently to me. I went quickly to her and through the door. She closed it behind me.

170

I was in humid semi-darkness and I stumbled on an uneven floor. The air was thick with powerful scents and although I could still hear the pulsating throb of the bass notes of the music there were many other sounds around me. Notably I could hear the voices of other men: shouting, laughing, complaining. Every voice was raised: in anger, excitement, urgency. At odd moments something on the other side of the corridor wall would bash heavily against it.

I gained a sense of chaos, of events being out of control.

We came to a door a short distance along the corridor—she opened it and led me through. I expected to find a bed of some sort, but there was nothing remotely of the boudoir about the room. There was not even a couch, or cushions on the floor. Three wooden chairs stood in a demure line against one wall, but that was all.

She said, 'You wait now.'

'Wait? What for? And for how long?'

'How long you want for your dreams?'

'Nothing! No time.'

'You are so impatient. One minute more, then follow me!'

She indicated yet another door which until that moment I had not noticed, because it had been painted in the same dull-red colour as the walls. The weak light from the room's only bulb had helped disguise it further. She went across to it and walked through. As she did so I saw her reach backwards over her head with both arms and remove the torn T-shirt.

I glimpsed her bare, curving back, the small knobs of her vertebrae, then she was gone.

Alone, I paced to and fro. By telling me to wait for one minute had she meant it literally? That I should check my wristwatch or count to sixty? She had thrown me into a state of nervous tension. What more had she to do in that further sanctum beyond, other than remove those shorts and prepare herself for me?

I opened the door impatiently, pushing against the pressure of a spring. It was dark beyond. The dim glow from the room behind me was not strong enough to help me see. I gained the impression of something large in the room but I could not make out its shape. I felt around with my hands, nervous in the darkness, trying to extend my senses against the cloying perfumes and the endlessly throbbing music, muffled but loud. As far as I could tell I had come into a room, not another corridor.

I went further in, groping forward. Behind me, the door swung closed on its spring. Immediately, bright spotlights came on from the corners of the ceiling.

I was in a boudoir. An ornate bed—with a large, carved wooden headboard, immense bulging pillows and a profusion of shining satin sheets—filled most of the room. A woman, not the young whore who had led me here, but another, lay on the bed in a pose of sexual abandonment and availability.

She was naked, lying on her back with one arm raised to curl behind her head. Her face was turned to the side and her mouth was open. Her eyes were closed, her lips were moist. Her large breasts bulged across her chest, the nipples lying flatly and pointing outwards. She had raised one knee, holding it at a slight angle, exposing herself. Her fingers rested on her sex, the tips curving down to bury themselves shallowly in the cleft. The spotlights radiated her and the bed in a brilliant focus of glaring white light.

The sight of her froze me. What I was seeing was impossible. I stared at her in disbelief.

She had arranged herself in a tableau-vivant that was identical, not close but *identical,* to one I had seen in my mind's eye before.

It was there in that sole fragment of my past: I remembered the first day I was in the cool semi-darkness of the vault of the gallery in Jethra. I had pressed my trembling teenage fingers, my palms, my perspiring forehead, many times to one of Acizzone's most notorious tactilist works: *Ste-Augustinia Abandonai.*

(I remembered the title! How?)

This woman *was* Ste-Augustinia. The reproduction she was fashioning was perfect. Not only was she an exact replica but also the arrangement she had made of the sheets and pillows—there were folds of satin glinting in the harsh light that exactly matched those in the painting. The long gleam of perspiration running between her exposed breasts was one my lustful imaginings had drooled over a dozen times before.

I was so astonished by this discovery that for a moment I forgot why I was there. Much was immediately and trivially clear to me: that she was not, for instance, the young woman I had seen removing the torn T-shirt; nor was she any of the gaunt women in headsets who had seized me on the dance floor. She was more maturely developed than the skinny girl in the T-shirt and to my eyes many times more beautiful than any of the others. Also, but most confusingly, the deliberate way she had spread herself on the smooth sheets of the bed was a conscious reference to an imagining only I had ever experienced. Or that I remembered in isolation! This was a connection I could not explain or escape from. Was her pose just a co-incidence? Had they somehow read my mind?

A cathedral of dreams, the girl had said. That was impossible!

Surely it was impossible?

It was madness to think that this had been contrived. But the resemblance to the painting, whose details were clear in my mind, was remarkable. Even so, the woman's real purpose was plain. She was yet a whore.

I gazed at her in silence, trying to find out what I should think.

Then, without opening her eyes, the whore said, 'If you only stand there to look, you must leave.'

'I—I was searching for someone.' She said nothing, so I added, 'A young woman, like you.'

'Take me now, or leave. I am not to be watched, not to be stared at. I am here to be ravished by you.'

As far as I could tell she had not shifted position when she spoke to me. Even her lips had hardly moved.

I gazed at her for a few more seconds, thinking that this was the time and this was the place where my fantasies and my real life could meet, but finally I moved back from her. I was, in truth, frightened of her. I was hardly more than an adolescent, almost completely inexperienced in sex. Not only that, though: in a single unexpected instant I had been confronted in the flesh by one of Acizzone's temptresses.

Lamely, I did as she had told me and left.

There was little choice about where I should go. Two doors led into and out of the room: the one I had entered by and another in the wall opposite. I stepped round the end of the huge bed and went to the second door. 'Ste-Augustinia' did not stir to watch me leave. As far as I could tell she had not so much as glanced at me while I was there. I kept my face lowered, not wanting her to look at me, even as I was leaving.

I passed through into a second narrow corridor, unlit at my end but with a low-power light bulb glimmering at the other. The encounter had produced a familiar physical effect on me—in spite of my apprehension I was tingling with sexual intrigue. Lustfulness was rising. I walked towards the light, the door of the room I had just left swinging closed behind me. At the far end, just beyond the light-bulb, a kind of archway had been formed, with a small alcove behind it.

I came across no doors anywhere along the corridor so I assumed I would find some kind of exit in the alcove. As I lowered my head to pass through the archway I stumbled, tripping over the entangled legs of a man and woman apparently making love on the floor. In the gloom I had not seen them there. I staggered as I tried to keep my balance, uttering an apology, steadying myself by pressing a hand against the wall.

I moved on, away from the couple, but the alcove was a dead end. I felt around in the dim light, trying to find some sign of a door, but the only way in or out was through the archway.

The couple on the floor continued what they were doing, their naked bodies pumping rhythmically and energetically against each other.

I tried to step over them but I was unbalanced by the lack of room in which to stand and I kicked against them again. I murmured another embarrassed apology, but to my surprise the woman extricated herself quickly from beneath the man and stood up in an agile, untroubled movement. Her long hair was falling across her face and she tossed her head to sweep it back from her eyes. Perspiration rolled from her face, dripping down on her chest. The man rolled briefly over. Because of his nakedness I was able to see, with surprise, that he was not at all sexually aroused. Their act of physical love had been a simulation.

The woman said to me, 'Wait! I'll come with you instead.'

She laid a warm hand on mine and smiled invitingly. She was breathing excitedly. A sheen of sweat lay over her breasts; her nipples pointed erectly. I felt a new erotic charge from the light touch of her fingers, but also a surge of guilt. The man lay there passively at my feet, staring up at me. I was confused by everything I was seeing.

I backed away from them, through the archway, back to the long, unlit corridor. The naked whore followed quickly behind me, seizing hold of my upper arm as I blundered along. At the far end of this corridor, past the door which I knew led back into Ste-Augustinia's boudoir, I had noticed yet another door, leading somewhere. I reached it, put my weight against it and forced it open. It moved stiffly. Inside the room that was beyond, the endless throbbing beat of the synthesized music was louder but it appeared to be empty of all people. The musky perfume was intense. I felt sensual, aroused, eager to do the bidding of the young woman who had attached herself to me—but even so I was frightened, disorientated, overcome by the rush of sensations and thoughts coursing through me.

The young woman had followed me in, still holding my arm. The door closed firmly behind us, causing a decompression sensation in one of my ears. I swallowed to clear it. I turned to speak to this whore but as I did so two other young women appeared as if from nowhere, stepping out of the deeper shadows on the side of the room away from the door.

I was alone with them. All three were naked. They were looking at me with what I took to be great eagerness. I was in a state of acute sexual readiness.

Even so, I stepped back from them, still nervous because of my inexperience, but by this time in such a state of excitement that I wondered how much longer I might contain it. I felt the edge of something soft pressing against the back of my lower leg. When I glanced behind me I saw in the pale light that a large bed was there, a bare mattress of some kind, an expanse of yielding material ready for use.

The three naked women were beside me now, their lustful scents rising around me. With gentle pressure of their hands they indicated I should lower myself to the bed. I sat down, but then one of them pushed lightly on my shoulders and I leaned back compliantly. The mattress, the palliasse, whatever was there, was soft beneath my weight. One of the women bent down and lifted my legs around so that I might lie flat.

When I was prone they began to unbutton and remove my uniform, working deftly and quickly, letting me feel the light tattoo of their fingertips. Nothing happened by accident: they were deliberately provoking and teasing my physical response. I was straining with the effort of controlling myself, so close was I to letting go. The girl closest to my head was staring down into my eyes as her fingers worked to slide my shirt from my chest and down my arms. Whenever she leaned across me, or stretched to free my hand from the cuff of a sleeve, she did so in such a way that she lowered one of her bare breasts towards me and brushed the hard little nipple lightly against my lips.

I was naked in a few seconds, in a state of full and agonizing arousal, yearning for release. The women slid my clothes out from underneath me, piled them up on the further side of the mattress. The one beside my face rested her soft fingertips on my chest. She leaned closer to me.

'You choose?' she said, whispering into my ear.

'Choose what?'

'You like me? You like my friends?'

'All of you!' I said without thinking. 'I want you all!'

Nothing more was said or, as far as I could see, signalled between them. They moved into position smoothly and as if in a formation they had rehearsed many times.

I was made to remain lying on my back but one of them lifted my knee that was closest to the edge of the mattress, making a small triangular aperture. She lay down on her back across the mattress so that her shoulders rested on my horizontal leg, while her head went beneath my raised knee. She turned her face towards the space between my legs. I could feel her breath on my naked buttocks. She took hold of my erect penis with her hand, holding it perpendicular to my body.

In the same moment the second woman was astride me with a knee on each side of my chest, her legs wide apart, lowering herself so that her sex touched lightly against, but did not enfold, the tip of my member, which was being held in position by the other woman.

The third one also straddled me but placed herself above my face, lowering herself towards, but not actually against, my eager lips.

Breathing the woman's delicious bodily scents, I remembered Acizzone.

I thought about the most explicit of his paintings hidden away in the gallery cellar. It was called (another title, remembered how?): *The Swain of Lethen in Godly Pleasures*. This one was painted in bold pigment on a stiff wooden board.

All that could be seen of *The Swain* in reproduction, or from a distance, was what appeared to be a smooth field of uniform crimson paint, intriguingly plain and minimalist. One touch of a hand or a finger, though, or even (as I knew I had tried) the light press of a forehead, would induce a vivid mental image of sexual activity. For everyone it was supposed to be different. I myself saw, felt, experienced, a scene of multiple sexual activity, a young man naked on a bed, three beautiful naked women pleasuring him, one straddling his face, one his penis, the third reaching beneath his body to press her face against his buttocks. All was bathed, in this intense imagining, in a lubricious crimson light.

Now I had become the swain himself, in godly pleasures.

I was surrendering to the imminent passions the women aroused in me. A lust for physical release was rushing through me even as the extent of the enigma about Acizzone surrounded me. I felt myself hastening to the moment of completion.

Then it ended. As swiftly and deftly as they had taken up their position, the women lifted themselves away from me, deserted me. I tried to call out to them, but my laboured breathing emitted only a series of excited gasps. They stepped quickly down from the bed, slipped away—the door opened and closed, leaving me alone.

I discharged my excitement at last, miserable and

abandoned. I could still in one sense feel them, could detect the traces they had left behind of their exquisite and exciting perfumes, but I was alone in that dim-lit, sound-throbbing cell and I expelled my passion as a man alone.

I lay still to try to calm myself, all my senses tingling, my muscles twitching and straining. I sat up slowly, lowered my feet to the floor. My legs were trembling.

When I could I dressed quickly and carefully, attempting to make myself look as if nothing had just happened so that I could depart with at least an appearance of calmness.

As I tucked in my shirt I felt the residue of my discharge, cold and sticky on the skin of my belly.

I found my way out of the room, along the corridor, into a large sub-floor area, filled with music and the sound of overhead footsteps. I saw a glint of bright-red neon lighting, limned against ill-fitting doors. I struggled with iron handles, pulled the doors open, found a cobbled alley between two massive buildings under the tropical night, sensed the smells of cooking, perspiration, spices, grease, gasoline, night-scented flowers. Finally I emerged into the clamorous street by the waterfront. I saw none of the black-caps, none of the whores, none of my shipmates.

I was thankful the club was so close to the quay. I was soon able to reboard the troopship, check myself in with the marshals, then plunge into the lower decks and lose myself in the anonymous press of the other men who were there. I sought no one's company during my first hours back in the crowded decks. I lay on my bunk and pretended to sleep.

The next morning the ship sailed from Muriseay Town and once again we headed south towards the war.

THE DISCHARGE

* * *

After Muriseay, my view of the islands was different. The superficial allure of them had diminished. From my short visit ashore in that crowded town I felt myself to have become island-experienced, had briefly breathed the air and the scents, heard the sounds and seen some of the muddle. At the same time, though, the experience had deepened the intrigue of the islands. They still had me in their thrall, but I was careful now not to dwell on it. I felt I had grown up a little.

The whole pace of life on the ship was changing, with the army's demands on us increasing every day. For several more days we continued to cruise our zigzag course between the tropical islands, but as we moved further south the weather grew gradually more temperate and for three long and uncomfortable days the ship was buffeted by stiff southerly gales and rocked by mountainous waves. When the storm finally receded we were in more barren latitudes. Many of the islands here, in the southern part of the Midway Sea, were craggy and treeless, some of them only barely rising above the level of the sea. They stood further apart from each other than they had done near the equator.

I still yearned for the islands, but not for these. I craved the insane heat of the tropics. With every day that the islands of the warmer climes slipped further behind me I knew that I had to put them out of my thoughts. I stayed away from the exposed upper decks, with their silent, distant views of fragmented land.

Towards the end of the voyage we were evacuated without warning from our messdecks and while we crowded together on the assembly deck every recruit's kit was searched. The map I had been using was discovered where I had left it in my duffel bag. For two more days nothing happened. Then I was summoned to the adjutant's cabin where I was told the map had been confiscated and destroyed. I was docked seven days' pay as punishment and my record was marked. I was officially warned that the black-cap escouades would be alerted to my breach of the rules.

However, it turned out that not all was lost. Either the search party did not find my notebook or they had not recognized the long list of island names it contained.

The loss of the map obstinately reminded me of the islands we had passed. In the final days on the troopship, I sat alone with those pages from my notebook, committing the names to memory and trying to recall how each of the islands had looked. Mentally, I compiled a favoured itinerary that I would follow when at last I was discharged from the army and could return home, moving slowly, as I planned, from one island to the next, perhaps spending many years in the process.

That could not begin until I had finished with the war, but the ship had not yet even arrived in sight of our destination. I waited on my hammock.

On disembarkation I was assigned to an infantry unit who were armed with a certain type of grenade launcher. I was held up near the port for another month while I underwent training. By the time this was complete, my comrades from the ship had dispersed. I was sent on a long journey across the bleak landscape to join up with my new unit.

I was at last moving across the notorious southern continent, the theatre of the land war, but throughout the three days of my cold and exhausting journey by train and truck I saw signs of neither battles nor their aftermath. The terrain I passed through had clearly never been lived in—I saw a seemingly endless prospect of treeless plains, rocky hills, frozen rivers. I received orders every day: my torment was a lonely one but my route was known and monitored, arrangements had been made. Other troops travelled with me, none of them for long. We all had different destinations, different orders. Whenever the train halted it was met by trucks that either were standing by the side of the rails where we stopped, or which appeared from somewhere after we had waited an hour or two. Fuel and food was taken on at these stops and my brief companions came and went. Eventually it was my own turn to leave the train at one of these halts.

I travelled under a tarpaulin in the back of the truck for another day, cold and hungry, bruised by the constant lurching of the vehicle and at last terrified by the closeness of the landscape around me. I was now so much a part of it. The winds that scoured the bleak grasses and thorny, leafless bushes also scoured me, the rocks and boulders that littered the ground were the immediate cause of the truck's violent movements, the cold that seeped everywhere sapped my strength and will. I passed the journey in a state of mental and physical suspension, waiting for the interminable journey to end.

I stared in dismay at the terrain. I found the dark landscape oppressive, the gradual contours discouraging. I loathed the sight of the grey, flinty soil, the waterless plains, the neutral sky, the broken ground with its scattered rocks and shards of quartz, the complete absence of signs of human occupation or of agriculture or animals or buildings—above all I hated the endless blast of freezing winds and the shrouds of sleet, the blizzard gales. I could only huddle in my freezing, exposed corner of the truck's compartment, waiting for this deadly journey to end.

Finally we arrived somewhere, at a unit which was occupying a strategic position at the base of a steep, broken rockface. As soon as I arrived I noticed the grenade launcher positions, each constructed exactly as I had myself been trained to construct them, each concealed position manned to the right strength. After the torment and discomforts of the long journey I felt a sudden sense of completeness, an unexpected satisfaction that at last the disagreeable job I had been forced to take on was about to start.

However, fighting the war itself was not yet my destiny. After I joined the grenade unit and shared duties with the other soldiers for a day or two, the first frightening reality of the army was borne in on me. Grenade launchers we had, but as yet no grenades. This did not appear to alarm the others so I did not allow it to alarm me. I had been in the army long enough to have developed the foot-soldier's unquestioning frame of mind when it came to direct orders about fighting, or preparation for fighting.

We were told that we were going to retreat from this position, re-equip ourselves with materiel, than occupy a new position from which we could confront the enemy directly.

We dismantled our weapons, we abandoned our position in the dead of night, we travelled a long distance to the east. Here we finally rendezvoused with a column of trucks. We were driven in convoy for two nights and a day to a large stores depot. Here we learned that the grenade launchers with which we were armed were now obsolescent. We were to be issued with the latest version, but the entire escadron would need to be re-trained.

So we marched cross-country to another camp. So we re-trained. So, finally, we were issued with the latest armament and the ammunition for it and now at last fully prepared we marched off once again to fight the war.

We never reached our reallocated position, where the enemy was to be confronted. We were diverted instead to relieve another column of troops, five days away across some of the harshest countryside I had yet encountered: it was a broken, frozen landscape of flints and glinting pebbles, devoid of plants, of colour, even of shape.

It didn't sink in straight away, but already the pattern had become established in those first few days and weeks of aimless activity. This purposeless and constant movement was to be my experience of war.

I never lost count of the days or the years. The three thousandth anniversary loomed ahead of me like an unstated threat. We marched at intervals from one place to the next; we slept rough; we marched again or were transported by trucks; we were billeted in wooden huts that were uninsulated and infested with rats and which leaked under the incessant rains. At intervals we were withdrawn to be re-trained. An issue of new or upgraded weapons invariably followed, making more training essential. We were always in transit, making camp, taking up new positions, digging trenches, heading south or north or east or anywhere to reinforce our allies—we were put on trains, removed from trains, flown here and there, sometimes without food or water, often without warning, always without explanation. Once when we were hiding in trenches close to the snowline a dozen fighter planes screamed overhead and we stood and cheered unheard after them; at another time there were other aircraft, from which we were ordered to take cover. No one attacked us, then or ever, but we were always on our guard. In some of the northerly areas of the continent, to which we were sent from time to time, and depending on the season, I was in turn baked by the heat of the sun, immobilized by thigh-deep mud, bitten by thousands of flying insects, swept away by flooding snow-melt—I suffered sores, sunburn, bruises, boredom, ulcerated legs, exhaustion, constipation, frostbite and unceasing humiliation. Sometimes we were told to stand our ground with our grenade launchers loaded and primed, waiting for action.

We never went into action.

This then was the war, of which it had always been said there would never be an end.

I lost all sense of contextual time, past and future. All I knew was the daily marking off of the calendar, sensing the fourth millennium of the war approach ineluctably. As I marched, dug, waited, trained, froze, I dreamed only of freedom, of putting this behind me, of heading back to the islands.

At some forgotten moment during one of our route marches, one of our training camps, one of our attempts to dig trenches in the permafrost, I lost the notebook containing all the island names I had written down. When I first discovered the loss it seemed like an unparalleled disaster, worse than anything the army had inflicted on me. But later I found that my memory of the islands' names was intact. When I concentrated I realized I could still recite the romantic litany of islands, still place them against imagined shapes on a mental map.

At first bereft, I came to realize that the loss of first the map, then the notebook, had liberated me. My present was meaningless and my past was forgotten. Only the islands represented my future. They existed in my mind, modified endlessly as I dwelt on them, matching them up to my expectations.

As the gruelling experience of war ground on, I came to depend increasingly on my haunting mental images of the tropic archipelago.

But I could not ignore the army and I still had to endure its endless demands. In the ice mountains further away in the south, the enemy troops were dug into impregnable defensive positions, lines they were known to have held for centuries. They were so firmly entrenched that it was conventional wisdom amongst our men that they could never be dislodged. It was thought that hundreds of thousands of men on our side, perhaps millions of us, would have to die in the assault against their lines. It rapidly became clear that my escadron was not only going to be part of the first assault, but that after the first attack we would continue to be in the heart of the fray.

This was the precursor to the celebrations of the dawning fourth millennium.

Many other divisions were already in place, preparing to attack. We would be moving to reinforce them shortly.

Two nights later, sure enough, we were put once more into trucks and transported to the south, towards the freezing southern uplands. We took up position, dug ourselves as deep as possible into the permafrost, concealed and ranged our grenade launchers. By now uncaring of what happened to me, made wretched by the physical circumstances and rootless by the lack of mental cohesion, I waited with the others in a mixture of fear and boredom. As I froze, I dreamed of hot islands.

On clear days we could glimpse the peaks of the ice mountains close to the horizon, but there was no sign of enemy activity.

Twenty days after we had taken up our positions in the frozen tundra we were ordered to retreat once more. It was now less than ten days to the millennium.

We moved away, rushing to reinforce major skirmishes then said to be taking place by the coast. Reports of dead and wounded were horrifying but all was quiet by the time we arrived. We took up defensive lines along the cliffs. It was so familiar, this senseless repositioning, manoeuvring. I turned my back against the sea, not wanting to look northwards to where the unattainable islands lay.

Only eight days remained until the dreaded anniversary of the war's beginning and already we were taking delivery of more supplies of armour, ammunition and grenades than I had ever seen before. The tension in our ranks was insupportable. I was convinced that this time our generals were not bluffing, that real action was only days, perhaps hours, away.

I sensed the closeness of the sea. If I was to discharge myself, the moment had arrived.

That night I left my tent and skidded down the loose shale and gravel of the sloping cliff to the beach. My back pocket was stuffed with all the unspent army pay I had accumulated. In the ranks we always joked that the paper was worthless, but now I thought it might at last be useful. I walked until dawn, hid all day in the tough undergrowth that spread across the high ground behind the littoral, resting when I could. My unsleeping mind recited island names.

During the following night I managed to find a track worn by the tyres of trucks. I guessed it was used by the army so I followed it with immense care, taking cover at the first sign of any approaching traffic. I continued to travel by night, sleeping as I could by day.

I was in poor physical condition by the time I reached one of the military ports. Although I had been able to find water I had eaten no food for four days. I was in every way exhausted and ready to turn myself in.

Close to the harbour, in a narrow, unlit street, not at the first attempt but after several hours of risky searching, I found the building I was seeking. I reached the brothel not long before dawn, when business was slow and most of the whores were sleeping. They took me in, they immediately understood the gravity of my situation. They relieved me of all my army money.

I remained hidden in the whorehouse for three days, regaining my strength. They gave me civilian clothes to wear—rather raffish, I thought, but I had no experience of the civilian world. I did not wonder how the women had come by them, or who else's clothes they might once have been. In the long hours I was alone in my tiny borrowed room I would repeatedly try on my new clothes and hold a mirror at arm's-length, admiring what I could see of myself in the limited compass of the glass. To be rid of the army fatigues at last, the thick, coarse fabric, the heavy webbing and the cumbersome patches of body armour, was like freedom in itself.

Whores visited me nightly, taking turns.

Early in the fourth night, the war's millennial night, four of the whores, together with their male minder, took me down to the harbour. They rowed me a distance out to sea, where a motor-launch was waiting in the darkly heaving waters beyond the headland. There were no lights on the boat, but in the glow from the town I could see that there were already several other men aboard the launch. They too were rakishly dressed, with frilled shirts, slouching hats, golden bracelets, velveteen jackets. They rested their elbows on the rail and stared down towards the water with waiting eyes. None of them looked at me, or at each other. There were no greetings, no recognitions. Money changed hands, from the whores in my boat to two agile young men in dark clothes in the other. I was allowed to board.

I squeezed into a position on the deck between other men, grateful for the warmth of the pressure against me. The rowing boat slipped away into the dark. I stared after it, regretting I could not remain with those young harlots. I was reminiscing already about their lithe, overworked bodies, their careless, eager skills.

The launch waited in its silent position for the rest of the night, the crew taking on board more men at intervals, making them find somewhere to squeeze themselves, handling the money. We remained silent, staring at the deck, waiting to leave. I dozed for a while, but every time more people came aboard we had to shift around to make room.

They lifted the anchor before dawn and turned the boat out to sea. We were heavily loaded and running low in the water. Once we were away from the shelter of the headland we made heavy weather in the running swell, the bow of the launch crashing cumbersomely into the walls of the waves, taking on water with every lurching recovery. I was soon soaked through, hungry, frightened, exhausted, and desperate to reach solid land.

We headed north, shaking the salt water from our eyes. The litany of island names ran on ceaselessly in my mind, urging me to return.

I escaped from the launch at the earliest opportunity, which was when we reached the first inhabited island. No one seemed to know which one it was. I went ashore in my rakish clothes, feeling shabby and dishevelled in spite of their stylish fit. The constant soakings in the boat had bleached most of the colour from the material, had stretched and shrunk the different kinds of the fabric. I had no money, no name, no past, no future.

'What is this island called?' I said to the first person I met, an elderly woman sweeping up refuse on the quayside. She looked at me as if I was mad.

'Steffer,' she said.

I had never heard of it.

'Say the name again,' I said.

'Steffer, Steffer. You a discharger?' I said nothing, so she grinned as if I had confirmed the information. 'Steffer!'

'Is that what you think I am, or is that the name of this island?'

'Steffer!' she said again, turning away from me.

I muttered some thanks and stumbled away from her, into the town. I still had no idea where I was.

I slept rough for a while, stealing food, begging for money, then met a whore who told me there was a hostel for the homeless which helped people to find jobs. Within a day I too was sweeping up refuse in the streets. It turned out that the island was called Keeilen, a place where many steffers made their first landfall.

Winter came—I had not realized it was the autumn when I discharged myself. I managed to work my passage as a deckhand on a cargo ship sailing with supplies to the southern continent, but which, I heard, would be calling at some more northerly islands on the way. My information was true. I arrived on Fellenstel, a large island with a range of mountains that sheltered the inhabited northern side from the prevailing southern gales. I passed the winter in the mild airs of Fellenstel. I moved north again when spring came, stopping for different periods of time on Manlayl, Meequa, Emmeret, Sentier—none of these was in my litany, but I intoned them just the same.

Gradually, my life was improving. Rather than sleep rough wherever I went I was usually able to rent a room for as long as I intended to stay on each island. I had learned that the whorehouses on the islands were a chain of contacts for dischargers, a place of resort, of help. I discovered how to find temporary jobs, how to live as cheaply as possible. I was learning the island patois, quickly adjusting my knowledge as I came across the different argots that were used from one island to the next.

No one would speak to me about the war except in the vaguest ways. I was often spotted as a steffer as soon as I landed somewhere, but the further north I moved and the warmer the weather became, the less this appeared to matter.

I was moving through the Dream Archipelago, dreaming of it as I went, imagining what island might come next, thinking it into an existence that held good so long as I required it.

By this time I had operated the islands' black market to obtain a map, which I had realized was perhaps hardest kind of printed material to get hold of anywhere. My map was incomplete, many years old, faded and torn and the place and island names were written in a script I did not at first understand, but it was for all that a map of the part of the Archipelago where I was travelling.

On the edge of the map, close to a torn area, there was a small island whose name I was finally able to decipher. It was Mesterline, one of the islands my unreliable memory told me we had passed on the southward journey.

Salay, Temmil, Mesterline, Prachous . . . it was part of the litany, part of the route that would lead me back to Muriseay.

It took me another year of erratic travels to reach Mesterline. As soon as I landed I fell in love with the place: it was a warm island of low hills, broad valleys, wide meandering rivers and yellow beaches. Flowers grew everywhere in a riot of effulgent colours. The buildings were constructed of white-painted brick and terra cotta tiles and they clustered on hilltops or against the steep sides of the cliffs above the sea. It was a rainy island: midway through most afternoons a brisk storm would sweep in from the west, drenching the countryside and the towns, running noisy rivulets through the streets. The Mester people loved these intense showers and would stand out in the streets or the public squares, their faces upturned and their arms raised, the rain coursing sensually through their long hair and drenching their flimsy clothes. Afterwards, as the hot sun returned and the ruts in the muddy streets hardened again, normal life would go on again. Everyone was happier after the day's shower and began to get ready for the languid evenings that they passed in the open-air bars and restaurants.

For the first time in my life (as I thought of it with my erratic memory), or for the first time in many years (as I suspected was the reality), I felt the urge to paint what I saw. I was dazzled by light, by colour, by the harmony of places and plants and people.

I spent the daylight hours wandering wherever I could, feasting my eyes on the brashly coloured flowers and fields, the glinting rivers, the deep shade of the trees, the blue and yellow glare of the sunlit shores, the golden skins of the Mester people. Images leapt through my mind, making me crave for some artistic outlet by which I could capture them.

That was how I began sketching, knowing I was not yet ready for paint or pigments.

By this time I was able to earn enough money to afford to live in a small rented apartment. I supported myself by working in the kitchen of one of the harbour-side bars. I was eating well, sleeping regularly, coming to terms with the extra mental blankness with which the war had left me. I felt as if my four years under arms had merely been time lost, an ellipsis, another area of forgotten life. In Mesterline I began to sense a full life extending around me, an identity, a past regainable and a future that could be envisaged.

I bought paper and pencils, borrowed a tiny stool, began the habit of setting myself up in the shade of the harbour wall, quickly drawing a likeness of anyone who walked into sight. I soon discovered that the Mesters were natural exhibitionists—when they realized what I was doing most of them would laughingly pose for me, or offer to return when they had more time, or even suggest they could meet me privately so that I could draw them again and in more intimate detail. Most of these offers came from young women. Already I was finding Mester women irresistibly beautiful. The harmony between their loveliness and the drowsy contentment of the Mesterline life inspired vivid graphic images in my mind that I found endlessly alluring to try to draw. Life spread even more fully around me, happiness grew. I started dreaming in colour.

Then a troopship arrived in Mesterline Town, breaking its voyage southwards to the war, its decks crammed with young conscripts.

It did not dock in the harbour of the town but moored a distance offshore. Lighters came ashore bringing hard currency to buy food and other materials and to replenish water supplies. While the transactions went on, an escouade of black-caps prowled the streets, staring intently at all men of military age, their synaptic batons at the ready. At first paralysed with fear at the sight of them, I managed to hide from them in the attic room of the town's only brothel, dreading what would happen if they found me.

After they had gone and the troopship had departed, I walked around Mesterline Town in a state of dread and disquiet.

My litany of names had a meaning after all. It was not simply an incantation of imagined names with a ghostly reality. It constituted a memory of my actual experience. The islands were connected but not in the way I had been trusting—a code of my own past, which when deciphered would restore me to myself. It was more prosaic than that: it was the route the troopships took to the south.

Yet it remained an unconscious message. I had made it mine, I had recited it when no one else could know it.

I had been planning to stay indefinitely in Mesterline, but the unexpected arrival of the troopship soured everything. When I tried next to draw beneath the harbour wall I felt myself exposed and nervous. My hand would no longer respond to my inner eye. I wasted paper, broke pencils, lost friends. I had reverted to being a steffer.

On the day I left Mesterline the youngest of the whores came to the quay. She gave me a list of names, not of islands but of her friends who were working in other parts of the Dream Archipelago. As we sailed I committed the names to memory, then threw the scrap of paper in the sea.

Fifteen days later I was on Piqay, an island I liked but which I found too similar to Mesterline, too full of memories that I was transplanting from the shallow soil of my memory. I moved on from Piqay to Paneron, a long journey that passed several other islands and the Coast of Helvard's Passion, a stupendous reef of towering rock, shadowing the coast of the island interior that lay beyond.

I had by this time travelled so far that I was off the edge of the map I had purchased, so I had only my memory of the names to guide me. I waited eagerly for each island to appear.

Paneron at first repelled me: much of its landscape was formed from volcanic rock, black and jagged and unwelcoming, but on the western side there was an enormous area of fertile land choked with rainforest that spread back from the shore as far as I could see. The coast was fringed with palms. I decided to rest in Paneron Town for a while.

Ahead lay the Swirl, beyond that vast chain of reefs and skerries were the Aubracs, beyond even those was the island I still yearned to find: Muriseay, home of my most vivid imaginings, birthplace of Rascar Acizzone.

The place, the artist—these were the only realities I knew, the only experience I thought I could call my own.

Another year of travel. I was confounded by the thirty-five islands of the Aubrac Group: work and accommodation were difficult to find in these underpopulated islets and I lacked the funds simply to sail past or around them. I had to make my way slowly through the group, island by island, working for subsistence, sweltering under the tropical sun. Now that I was travelling again my interest in drawing returned. In some of the busier Aubrac ports I would again set up my easel, draw for hire, for centimes and sous.

On AntiAubracia, close to the heart of the group of islands, I bought some pigments, oils and brushes. The Aubracs were a place largely devoid of colour: the flat, uninteresting islands lay under bleaching sunlight, the sand and pale gravel of the inland plains drifted into the towns on the constant winds, the pallid eggshell blue of the shallow lagoons could be glimpsed with every turn of the head. The absence of bright hues was a challenge to see and paint in colour.

I saw no more troopships, although I was always on my guard for their passing or arrival. I was still following their route because when I asked the island people about the ships they knew at once what I meant and therefore what my background must be. But reliable information about the army was hard to glean. Sometimes I was told that the troopships had stopped travelling south; sometimes that they had switched to a different route; sometimes I was told they only passed in the night.

My fear of the black-caps kept me on the move.

Finally, I made a last sea-crossing and arrived one

night on a coal-carrier in Muriseay Town. From the upper deck, as we moved slowly through the wide bay that led to the harbour mouth, I viewed the place with a feeling of anticipation. I could make a fresh start here—what had happened during the long-ago shore leave was insignificant. I leaned on the rail, watching the reflections of coloured lights from the town darting on the dark water. I could hear the roar of engines, the hubbub of voices, the traces of distorted music. Heat rolled around me, as once before it had rolled from the town.

There were delays in docking the ship and by the time I was ashore it was after midnight. Finding somewhere to sleep for the night was a priority. Because of recent hardships I was unable to pay to stay anywhere. I had faced the same problem many times in the past, slept rough more often than not, but I was none the less tired.

I headed through the clamouring traffic to the back streets, looking for brothels. I was assaulted by a range of sensations: breathless equatorial heat, tropical perfumes of flowers and incense, the endless racket of cars, motorbikes and pedicabs, the smell of spicy meat being cooked on smoking sidewalk stalls, the continuous flash and dazzle of neon advertising, the beat of pop music blaring out tinnily from radios on the food-stalls and from every window and open doorway. I stood for a while on one of the street corners, laden down with my baggage and my painting equipment. I turned a full circle, relishing the exciting racket, then put down my baggage and, like the Mester people savouring the rains, I raised my arms in exaltation and lifted my face to the glancing nighttime sky, orange-hued above me, reflecting the dancing lights of the city.

Exhilarated and refreshed I took up my load more willingly and went on with my search for brothels.

THE DISCHARGE

I came to one in a small building two blocks away from the main quay, attained by a darkened door in an alley at the side. I went in, moneyless, throwing myself on the charity of the working women, seeking sanctuary for the night from the only church I knew. The cathedral of my dreams.

Because of its history, but more because of its marina, shops and sunbathing beaches, Muriseay Town was a tourist attraction for wealthy visitors from all over the Dream Archipelago. In my first months on the island I discovered I could make a lucrative income from painting harbour scenes and mountain landscapes, then displaying them on a section of wall next to one of the large cafés in Paramoundour Avenue, the street where all the fashion houses and smart nightclubs were situated.

In the off-seasons, or when I simply grew tired of painting for money, I would stay in my tenth-floor studio above the city centre and dedicate myself to my attempts to develop the work pioneered by Acizzone. Now that I was in the town where Acizzone had produced his finest paintings I was able at last to research his life and work in full, to understand the techniques he had employed.

Tactilism was by this time many years out of vogue, a fortunate state of affairs as it allowed me to experiment without interference, comment or critical interest. Ultrasound microcircuitry was no longer in use, except in the market for children's novelties, so the pigments I needed were plentiful and inexpensive, although at first difficult to track down in the quantities I needed them.

I set to work, building up the layers of pigments on a series of gesso-primed boards. The technique was intricate and hazardous—I ruined many boards by a single slip of the palette knife, some of them close to the moment of completion. I had much to learn.

Accepting this I made regular visits to the closed-case section of the Muriseayan Town Museum, where several of Acizzone's originals were stored in archive. The female curator was at first amused that I should take an interest in such an obscure, unfashionable and reputedly obscene artist, but she soon grew used to my repeated visits, the long silent sessions I spent inside the locked sanctums when I was alone, pressing my hands, my face, my limbs, my torso, to Acizzone's garish pictures. I was submerged in a kind of frenzy of artistic absorption, almost literally soaking up Acizzone's breathtaking imagery.

The ultrasonics produced by the tactile pigments operated directly on the hypothalamus, promoting sudden changes in serotonin concentrations and levels. The instantaneous result of this was to generate the images experienced by the viewer—the less obvious consequence was to cause depression and long-term loss of memory. When I left the museum after my first adult exposure to Acizzone's work I was shattered by the experience. While the erotic images created by the paintings still haunted me, I was almost blind with pain, confusion and a sense of unspecified terror.

After my first visit, I returned unsteadily to my studio and slept for nearly two days. When I awoke I was chastened by what I had discovered about the paintings. Exposure to tactilist art had a traumatic effect on the viewer.

I felt a familiar sense of blankness behind me. Memory had failed. Somewhere in the recent past, when I was travelling through the islands, I had missed visiting some of them.

The litany was still there and I recited the names to myself. Amnesia is not a specific: I knew the names but in some cases I had no memory of the islands. Had I been to Winho? To Demmer? Nelquay? No recollections of any of them, but they had been on my route.

For two or three weeks I returned to my tourist painting, partly to gain some cash but also for a respite. I needed to think about what I had learned. My memories of childhood had been all but eradicated by something. Now I had a firm idea that it was my immersion in Acizzone's art.

I continued to work and gradually I found my vision.

The physical technique was fairly straightforward to master. The difficulty, I discovered, was the psychological process, transferring my own passions, cravings, compulsions to the artwork. When I had that, I could paint successfully. One by one my painted boards accumulated in my studio, leaning against the wall at the back of the long room.

Sometimes, I would stand at the window of my studio and stare down across the bustling, careless city below, my own shocking images concealed in the pigments behind me. I felt as if I were preparing an arsenal of potent imagic weapons. I had become an art terrorist, unseen and unsuspected by the world at large, my paintings no doubt destined to be misunderstood in their way as Acizzone's masterpieces had been. The tactilist paintings were the definitive expression of my life.

While Acizzone, who in life was a libertine and roué, had portrayed scenes of great erotic power, my own images were derived from a different source: I had lived a life of emotional repression, repetition, aimless wandering. My work was necessarily a reaction against Acizzone.

I painted to stay sane, to preserve my memory. After that first exposure to Acizzone I knew that only by putting myself into my work could I recapture what I had lost. To view tactilist art led to forgetting, but to create it, I found now, led to remembering.

I drew inspiration from Acizzone. I lost part of myself. I painted and recovered.

My art was entirely therapeutic. Every painting clarified a fresh area of confusion or amnesia. Each dab of the palette knife, each touch of the brush, was another detail of my past defined and placed in context. The paintings absorbed my traumas.

When I drew back from them, all that could be seen were bland areas of uniform colour, much the same as Acizzone's work. Stepping up close, working with the pigments, or pressing my flesh against the stippled layers of dried paint, I entered a psychological realm of great calm and reassurance.

What someone else would experience of my tactilist therapy I did not care to think. My work was imagic weaponry. The potential was concealed until the moment of detonation, like a landmine waiting for the press of a limb.

After the first year, when I was working to establish myself, I entered my most prolific phase. I became so productive that to make space for myself I arranged to move some of the more ambitious pieces to a vacant building I had come across near the waterfront. It was a former dancing club, long abandoned and empty, but physically intact.

Although there was an extensive basement, with a warren of corridors and small chambers, the main hall was an enormous open area, easily large enough to take any number of my paintings.

I kept a few of the smaller pieces in my studio, but the larger ones and those with the most potent and disturbing images of fracture and loss I stored in the town.

I stacked the biggest paintings in the main hall of the building, but some nervous dread of discovery made me conceal the smaller pieces in the basement. In that maze of corridors and rooms, ill-lit and haunted by the stale fragrances of past occupiers, I found a dozen different places to hide my pieces.

I was constantly rearranging my work. Sometimes I would spend a whole day and night, working without a break in the near-darkness, obsessively shifting my artwork from one room to another.

I found that the warren of interconnecting corridors and rooms, cheaply built of thin partition walls and lit only at intervals with low-power electric bulbs, presented what seemed to be an almost endless combination of random paths and routes. I stood my paintings like sentinels, at odd and hidden positions in the maze, behind doorways, beyond corners in the passageways, irrationally blocking the darkest places.

I would then leave the building and normal life returned for a while. I would start new paintings, or, just as often, walk down to the streets with my easel and stool and begin to work up a supply of commercially attractive landscapes. I was always in need of cash.

So my life continued like that, month after month, under the broiling Muriseayan sun. I knew that I had at last found a kind of fulfilment. Even the tourist art was not all drudgery, because I learnt that working with representational paintings required a discipline of line, subject and brushwork that only increased the intensity of the tactile art I went to afterwards and which no one saw. In the streets of Muriseay Town I built a small reputation as a journeyman landscape artist.

Five years went by. Life was as good to me as it ever had been.

Five years was not long enough to ensure that life could always be good. One night the blackcaps came for me.

I was, as ever, alone. My life was solitary, my mood introspective. I had no friends other than whores. I lived for my art, working through its mysterious agenda, post-Acizzone, unique, perhaps ultimately futile.

I was in my storage depot, obsessively rearranging my boards again, placing and replacing the sentinels in the corridors. Earlier that day I had hired a carter to bring down my five most recent works and since the man left I had been slowly moving them into place, touching them, holding them, arranging them.

The black-caps entered the building without my being aware of them. I was absorbed in a painting I had completed the week before. I was holding it so that my fingers were wrapped around the back of the board but my palms were pressing lightly against the paint at the edges.

The painting dealt obliquely with an incident that had occurred while I was in the army in the south. Night had fallen while I was on patrol alone and I had had difficulty getting back to our lines. For an hour I wandered in the dark and cold, slowly freezing. In the end someone had found me and led me back to our trenches, but until then I had been in terror of death.

Post-Acizzone, I had depicted the extreme fright I experienced: total darkness, a bitter wind, a chill that struck through to the bone, ground so broken that you could not walk without stumbling, a constant threat from unseen enemies, loneliness, silence enforced by panic, distant explosions.

The painting was a comfort to me.

I surfaced from my comfort to find four black-caps standing back from me, watching me. They were carrying their batons in holsters. Terror struck me, as if with a physical blow.

I made a sound, an inarticulate throat-noise, involuntary, like a trapped animal. I wanted to speak to them, shout at them, but all I was capable of was a bestial sound. I drew breath, tried again. This time the noise I made was halting, as if fear had added a stammer to the moan.

Hearing this, registering my fright, the black-caps drew their batons. They moved casually, in no hurry to start. I backed away, brushing against my painting, causing it to fall.

The men had no faces I could see: their capped helmets covered their heads, placed a smoked visor across their eyes, had a raised lip to protect their mouth and jaw.

Four clicks as the synaptic batons were armed—they were raised to the strike position.

'You've been discharged, trooper!' one of the men said and contemptuously threw a scrap of paper in my direction. It fluttered at once, fell close to his boots. 'Discharge for a coward!'

I said . . . but I could only breathe in, shuddering, and say nothing.

There was another way out of the building that only I could know, through the underfloor warren. One of the men was between me and the short flight of steps that led down. I feinted, moving towards the scrap of paper, as if to pick it up. Then I spun around, dashed, collided with the man's leg. He swung the baton viciously at me. I took an intense bolt of electricity that dropped me. I skidded across the floor.

My leg was paralysed. I scrambled to get up, rolled on my side, tried again.

Seeing I was immobilized, one of the black-caps moved across to the painting I had been absorbed in when they arrived. He leaned over it, prodded at its surface with the end of his baton.

I managed to raise myself on my good leg, half-crouching.

Where the end of his baton touched the tactilist pigment, a spout of fierce white flame suddenly appeared, with a sharp crackling sound. Smoke rose copiously as the flame died. The man made a sardonic laughing sound and did it again.

The others went over to see what he was doing. They too pressed the live ends of their batons against the board, producing spurts of bright flame and much more smoke. They guffawed.

One of them crouched, leaned forward to see what it was that was burning. He brushed his bare fingertips across an undamaged portion of the pigment.

My terror and trauma reached out to him through the paint. The ultrasonics bonded him to the board.

He became still, four of his fingers resting on the pigment. For a moment he stayed in position, looking almost reflective as he squatted there with his hand extended. Then he tipped slowly forward. He tried to balance himself with his other hand, but that too landed on the pigments. As he fell across the painting, his body started jerking in spasms. Both his hands were bonded to the board. His baton had rolled away. Smoke still poured from the smouldering scars.

His three companions moved across to find out what was wrong with him. They kept an eye on me as they did so. I was trying to lever myself upright, putting all my weight on the leg that still had feeling, letting the other dangle lightly against the floor. Sensation was returning quickly, but the pain was unspeakable.

I watched the three black-caps, dreading the menace they exuded. It could only be a matter of time before they did to me whatever it was they had come to do. They were grappling with the man who had fallen, trying to pull him away from the pigments. My breath was making a light screeching noise as I struggled for balance. I thought I had known fear before, but there was nothing in my remembered experience that equalled this.

I managed a step. They ignored me. They were still trying to lift the man away from my painting. The smoke swirled from the damage they had caused with their batons.

One of them shouted at me to help them.

'What is this stuff? What's holding him against that board?'

The man started screaming as the smouldering pigments reached his hands, but still he could not release himself. His pain, my agonies, contorted his body.

'His dreams!' I cried boldly. 'He is captive of his own vile dreams!'

I made a second step, then a third. Each was easier than the one before, although the pain was terrible. I hobbled towards the shallow stairs by the stage, took the top one, then another, nearly overbalanced, took the third and fourth.

They saw me as I reached the door beneath the old stage. I scarcely dared to look back, but I saw them abandoning the man who had fallen across the pigments and hoist their batons to the strike position. With athletic strength they were moving quickly across the short distance towards me. I dived through the door, dragging my hurt leg.

Breath rasped in my throat. I made a sobbing sound. There was one door, a passage, a chamber and another door. I passed through all of them. Behind me the black-caps were shouting, ordering me to halt. Someone blundered against one of the thin partition walls. I heard the wood creaking as he thudded against it.

I hurried on. The curving passage where I stored some of my smaller paintings was next, then a series of three small cubicles, all with doors wide open. I had placed one of my paintings inside each of these cubicles, standing guard within.

I passed along the corridor, slamming closed the doors at each end. My leg was working almost normally again, but the pain continued. I was in another corridor with an alcove at the end, where I had stood a painting. I doubled back, pushed the door of one of the larger chambers and propped open the spring-loaded door with the edge of one of my boards. I passed through. Another corridor was beyond, wider than the others. Here were a dozen of my paintings, stacked against the wall. I hooked my good foot beneath them, causing them to clatter down at an angle and partly block the way. I passed them. The men were yelling at me again, threatening me, ordering me to stop.

I heard a crash behind me, and another. One of the men shouted a curse.

I went through into the next short corridor, where four more chambers opened out. Some of my most intense paintings were hidden in each of these. I pulled them so that they extended into the corridor at knee height. I balanced a tall one against them, so that any disturbance of it would make it fall.

There was another crash, followed by shouting. The voices now were only a short distance away from me, on the other side of the decrepit dividing wall. There was a heavy sound, as if someone had fallen. Then I heard swearing—a man screamed. One of his companions began shouting. The thin wall bulged towards me as he fell against it. I heard paintings fall around them, heard the crackle of sudden fire as synaptic batons made contact with the pigments.

I smelt smoke.

I was regaining my strength, although the naked fear of being caught by the black-caps still had a grip on me. I came into another corridor, one that was wider and better lit than the others and not enclosed by walls that reached to the ceiling. Smoke drifted here.

I halted at the end, trying to control my breath. The warren of corridors behind me was silent. I went out of the corridor into the large sub-floor area beyond. The silence followed and wisps of smoke swirled around me. I stood and listened, tense and frightened, paralysed by the terror of what would happen if even one of the men had managed to push past the paintings without touching any of them.

The silence remained. Sound, thought, movement, life, absorbed by the paintings of trauma and loss.

They had surrendered to my fears. Fire licked around them.

I could see none of the flames myself, but gradually the smoke was thickening. It heaped along the ceiling, a dark grey cloud, heavy with the vapours of scorched pigments.

I realized at last that I had to leave before I became trapped by the spreading fire. I went quickly across the sub-floor area, struggled with the old iron-handled doors, fell out into the darkness. I walked stiffly up the cobbled alley that ran behind the building, turned a corner, then another, walked into one of Muriseay's market streets where the hot night was filled with people, lights, music and the raucous, thrilling sound of traffic.

For the rest of the night I stumbled through the back-streets and alleys of the town, trailing my fingertips along the rough texture of the stuccoed walls, obsessed with thoughts of the paintings that were being lost while the building burned. My agonies were being consumed but I was released from my past.

I went through the port area again in the hour before dawn. The paintings must have smouldered for a time before properly igniting the shabby wooden walls of the warren, but now the whole of my building was consumed with flames. The doorways and windows I had sealed up for privacy had become apertures once more, square portals into the inferno within, white and yellow fire roaring in the gales of sucked air. Black smoke belched out through vents and gaps in the roof. Fire crews were ineffectually jetting cascades of water against the crumbling brick walls. I watched their efforts as I stood on the quay, a small bag with my belongings by my side. In the east the sky was lightening.

By the time the fire crews had brought the flames under control I was aboard the first ferry of the day, heading for other islands.

Their names chimed in my mind, urging me on.

Aboard the
Beatitude

Brian W. Aldiss

> "It is axiomatic that we who are genetically improved
> will seek out the Unknown. We will make it Known or
> we will destroy it. On occasions, we must also destroy
> the newly Known. This is the Military Morality."
> —Commander Philosopher Hijenk Skaramonter in
> *Beatitudes for Conquest*

The great brute projectile accelerated along its invisible
pathway. The universe through which it sped was itself in
rapid movement. Starlight flashed along the flank of the
ship. It moved at such a velocity it could scarcely be detected by the civilizations past which it blasted its
course—until those civilizations were disintegrated and
destroyed by the ship's weaponry.

It built on the destruction. It was now over two thousand miles long, traveling way above the crawl of light,
about to enter eotemporality.

Looking down the main corridor running the length of
the structure you could see dull red lurking at the far end
of it. The Doppler effect was by now inbuilt. Aboard the

Beatitude, the bows were traveling faster than the stern. . . .

<<Much of the ship is now satisfactorily restored. The hardened hydrogen resembles glass. The renovated living quarters of the ship shine with brilliance. The fretting makes it look like an Oriental palace.

<<In the great space on C Deck, four thousand troops parade every day. Their discipline is excellent in every way. Their marching order round the great extent of the Marchway is flawless. These men retain their fighting fitness. They are ready for any eventuality.>>

It paused here, then continued.

<<The automatic cleaners maintain the ship in sparkling order. The great side ports of the ship, stretching from Captain's Deck to D Deck, remain brilliant, constantly repolished on the exterior against scratches from microdust. It is a continual joy to see the orange blossom falling outside, falling through space, orange and white, with green leaves intertwined.

<<All hand-weapons have been well-maintained. Target practice takes place on the range every seventh day, with live ammunition. The silencing systems work perfectly. Our armory systems are held in operational readiness.

<<Also, the engines are working again at one hundred-plus percent. We computers control everything. The atmosphere is breathed over and over again. It could not be better. We enjoy our tasks.

<<Messing arrangements remain sound, with menus ever changing, as they had been over the first two hundred years of our journey. Men and women enjoy their food; their redesigned anatomies see to that. Athletics in

the free-fall area ensure that they have good appetites. No one ever complains. All looked splendidly well. Those dying are later revived.

<<We are now proceeding at FTL 2.144. Many suffer hallucinations at this velocity. The *Beatitude* is constantly catching up with the retreating enemy galaxy. The weapons destined to overwhelm that enemy are kept primed and ready. If we pass within a thousand light-years of a sun, we routinely destroy it, whether or not it has planets. The sun's elements are then utilized for fuel. This arrangement has proved highly satisfactory.

<<In ten watches we shall be moving past system X377 at a proximate distance of 210 light-years. Particular caution needed. *Computer SJC1*>>

Ship's Captain Hungaman stood rigid, according to Military Morality, while he waited for his four upper echelon personnel to assemble before him. Crew Commander Mabel-Mo Hole was first, followed closely by Chief Technician Ida Precious. The thin figure of Provost-Marshal of Reps and Revs Dido Shappi entered alone. A minute later, Army Commander General Barakuta entered, to stand rigidly to attention before the ship's captain.

"Be easy, people," said Hungaman. As a rep served all parties a formal drink, he said, "We will discuss the latest summary of the month's progress from Space Journey Control One. You have all scanned the communication?"

The four nodded in agreement. Chief Technician Precious, clad tightly from neck to feet in dark green plastic, spoke. "You observe the power node now produces our maximum power yet, Captain? We progress toward the enemy at 2.144. More acceleration is needed."

Hungaman asked, "Latest estimate of when we come within destruction range of enemy galaxy?"

"Fifteen c's approximately. Possibly fourteen point six niner." She handed Hungaman a slip of paper. "Here is the relevant computation."

They stood silent, contemplating the prospect of fifteen more centuries of pursuit. Everything spoken was recorded by SJC2. The constant atmosphere control was like a whispered conversation overheard.

Provost-Marshal Shappi spoke. His resemblance to a rat was increased by his small bristling mustache. "Reps and revs numbers reduced again since last mensis, due to power node replacement."

"Figures?"

"Replicants, 799. Revenants, 625."

The figures were instantly rewired at SJC1 for counter-checking.

Hungaman eyed Crew Commander Hole. She responded instantly. "Sixteen deaths, para-osteoporosi-pneu. Fifteen undergoing revenant operations. One destroyed, as unfit for further retread treatment."

A nod from Hungaman, who turned his paranoid-type gaze on the member of the quartet who had yet to speak, General Barakuta. Barakuta's stiff figure stood like a memorial to himself.

"Morale continuing to decline," the general reported. "We require urgently more challenges for the men. We have no mountains or even hills on the *Beatitude*. I strongly suggest the ship again be enlarged to contain at least five fair-sized hills, in order that army operations be conducted with renewed energy."

Precious spoke. "Such a project would require an intake of 10^6 mettons new material aboard ship."

Barakuta answered. "There is this black hole 8875, only three thousand LY away. Dismantle that, bring constituent elements on board. No problem."

"I'll think about it," said Hungaman. "We have to meet the challenges of the centuries ahead."

"You are not pleased by my suggestion?" Barakuta again.

"Military Morality must always come first. Thank you."

They raised ceremonial flasks. All drank in one gulp.

The audience was ended.

Barakuta went away and consulted his private comp, unaligned with the ship's computers. He drew up some psycho-parameters on Ship's Captain Hungaman's state of mind. The parameters showed ego levels still in decline over several menses. Indications were that Hungaman would not initiate required intake of black hole material for construction of Barakuta's proposed five hills.

Something else would need to be done to energize the armies.

Once the audience was concluded, Hungaman took a walk to his private quarters to shower himself. As the walkway carried him down his private corridor, lights overhead preceded him like faithful hounds, to die behind him like extinguished civilizations. He clutched a slip of paper without even glancing at it. That had to wait until he was blush-dried and garbed in a clean robe.

In his relaxation room, Barnell, Hungaman's revenant servant, was busy doing the cleaning. Here was someone with whom he could be friendly and informal. He greeted the man with what warmth he could muster.

Barnell's skin was gray and mottled. In his pale face, his mouth hung loosely; yet his eyes burned as if lit by an internal fire. He was one of the twice-dead.

He said, "I see from your bunk you have slept well. That's good, my captain. Last night, I believe I had a dream. Revs are supposed not to dream, but I believe I dreamed that I was not dreaming. It is curious and unscientific. I like a thing to be scientific."

"We live scientific lives here, Barnell." Hungaman was not attending to the conversation. He was glancing at his standalone, on the screen of which floated the symbols *miqoesiy*. That was a puzzle he had yet to solve—together with many others.

With a sigh, he turned his attention back to the rev.

"Scientific? Yes, of course, my captain. But in this dream I was very uncomfortable because I dreamed I was not dreaming. There was nothing. Only me, hanging on a hook. How can you dream of nothing? it's funny, isn't it?"

"Yes, it's very funny," agreed Hungaman. Barnell told him the same story once a mensis. Memories of revs were notoriously short.

He patted Barnell's shoulder, feeling compassion for him, before returning down the private corridor to the great public compartment still referred to as "the bridge."

Hungaman turned his back to the nearest scanner and reread the words on the slip of paper Ida Precious had given him. His eye contact summoned whispered words: "The SJC1 is in malfunction mode. Why does its report say it is seeing orange blossom drifting in space? Why is no one else remarking on it? Urgent investigation needed."

He stared down at the slip. It trembled in his hand, a silver fish trying to escape back into its native ocean.

"Swim away!" He released his grasp on the fish. It swam across to the port, swam through it, swam away into space. Hungaman hurried to the port; it filled the curved wall. He looked out at the glorious orange blossom, falling slowly past, falling down forever, trying to figure out what was strange about it.

But those letters, *miqoesiy*—they might be numbers ... *q* might be 9, *y* might be 7. Suppose *e* was = ... Forget it. He was going mad.

He spread wide his arms to press the palms of his hands against the parency. It was warm to the touch. He glared out at the untouchable.

Among the orange blossom were little blue birds, flitting back and forth. He heard their chirruping, or thought he did. One of the birds flew out and through the impermeable parency. It fluttered about in the distant reaches of the control room. Its cry suggested it was saying "Attend!" over and over.

"Attend! Attend! Attend!"

They were traveling in the direction of an undiscovered solar system, coded as X377. It was only 210 LYs distant. A main sequence sun was orbited by five planets, of which spectroscopic evidence indicated highpop life on two of its planets. Hungaman set obliteration time for when the next watch's game of Bullball was being played. Protesters had been active previously, demonstrating against the obliteration of suns and planets in the *Beatitude's* path. Despite the arrests then made, there remained a possibility that more trouble might break out: but not when Bullball championships were playing.

*   *   *

This watch, Fugitives were playing the champions of F League, Flying Flagellants. Before 27 and the start of play, Hungaman took his place in the Upper Echelon tier. He nodded remotely to other Uppers, otherwise keeping himself to himself. The dizziness was afflicting him again. General Barakuta was sitting only a few seats away, accompanied by an all-bronze woman, whether rep or real Hungaman could not tell at this distance.

The horn blew, the game started, although the general continued to pay more attention to his lady than to the field.

In F League, each side consisted of forty players. Numbers increased as leagues climbed toward J. Gravdims under the field enabled players to make astonishing leaps. They played with two large heavy balls. What made the game really exciting—what gave Bullball its popular name of Scoring 'n' Goring—was the presence of four wild bulls, which charged randomly round the field of play, attacking any player who got in their way. The great terrifying pitiable bulls, long of horn, destined never to evolve beyond their bovine fury.

Because of this element of danger, by which dying players were regularly dragged off the field, the participants comprised, in the main, revs and reps. Occasionally, however, livers took part. One such current hero of Bullball was fair-haired Surtees Slick, a brute of a man who had never as yet lost a life, who played half-naked for the FlyFlajs, spurning the customary body armor.

With a massive leap into the air, Slick had one of the balls now—the blue high-scorer—and was away down the field in gigantic hops. His mane of yellow hair fluttered behind his mighty shoulders. The crowd roared his name.

"Surtees . . . Surtees . . ."

Two Fugs were about to batter him in midair when Slick took a dip and legged it across the green plastic. A gigantic black bull known as Bronco charged at him. Without hesitation, Slick flung the heavy ball straight at the bull. The ball struck the animal full on the skull. Crunch of impact echoed through the great arena (amplified admittedly by the mitters fixed between the brute's horns).

Scooping up the ball, which rebounded, Slick was away, leaping across the bull's back toward the distant enemy goal. He swiped away two Fug revs who flung themselves at him and plunged on. The goalkeeper was ahead, rushing out like a spider from its lair. Goalkeepers alone were allowed to be armed on the field. He drew his dazer and fired at the yellow-haired hero. But Slick knew the trick. That was what the crowd was shouting: "Slick knows the trick!" He dodged the stun and lobbed the great ball overarm. The ball flew shrieking toward the goal.

It vanished. The two teams, the Fugitives and the Flagellants, also vanished. The bulls vanished. The entire field became instantly empty.

The echo of the great roar died away.

"Surtees . . . Surtees . . . Sur . . ."

Then silence. Deep dead durable silence.

Nothing.

Only the eternal whispered conversation of air vents overhead.

Hungaman stood up in his astonishment. He could not comprehend what had happened. Looking about him, he found the vast company of onlookers motionless. By some uncanny feat of time, all were frozen; without movement they remained, not dead, not alive.

Only Hungaman was there, conscious, and isolated by

his consciousness. His jaw hung open. Saliva dripped down his chin.

He was frightened. He felt the blood leave his face, felt tremors seize his entire frame.

Something had broken down. Was it reality or was it purely a glitch, a seizure of his perception?

Gathering his wits, he attempted to address the crew through his bodicom. The air was dead.

He made his way unsteadily from the Upper Echelon. He had reached the ground floor when he heard a voice calling hugely, "Hungaman! Hungaman!"

"Yes, I'm here."

He ran through the tunnel to the fringes of the playing field.

The air was filled with a strange whirring. A gigantic bird of prey was descending on him, its claws outstretched. Its aposematic wings were spread wide, as wide as the field itself. Looking up in shock, Hungaman saw how fanciful the wings were, fretted at the edges, iridescent, bright as a butterfly's wings and as gentle.

His emotions seemed themselves almost iridescent, as they faded from fear to joy. He lifted his arms to welcome the creature. It floated down slowly, shrinking as it came.

"A decently iridescent descent!" babbled Hungaman, he thought.

He felt his life changing, even as the bird changed, even as he perceived it was nothing but an old tattered man in a brightly colored cloak. This tattered man looked flustered, as he well might have done. He brushed his lank hair from his eyes to reveal a little solemn brown face like a nut, in which were two deeply implanted blue eyes. The eyes seemed to have a glint of humor about them.

"No, I said that," he said, with a hint of chuckle. "Not you."

He put his hands on his hips and surveyed Hungaman, just as Hungaman surveyed him. The man was a perfect imitation of human—in all but conviction.

"Other life-forms, gone forever," he said. "Don't you feel bad about that? Guilty? You and this criminal ship? Isn't something lost forever—and little gained?"

Hungaman found his voice.

"Are you responsible for the clearing of the Bullball game?"

"Are you responsible for the destruction of an ancient culture, established on two planets for close on a million years?"

He did not say the word "years," but that was how Hungaman understood it. All he could manage by way of return was a kind of gurgle. "Two planets?"

"The Slipsoid system? They were 210 LYs distant from this ship—offering no threat to your passage. Our two planets were connected by quantaspace. It forms a bridge. You destructive people know nothing of quantaspace. You are tied to the material world. It is by quantaspace that I have arrived here." He threw off his cloak. It faded and was gone like an old leaf.

Hungaman tried to sneer. "Across 210 LYs?"

"We would have said ten meters."

Again, it was not the word "meters" he said, but that was how Hungaman understood it.

"The cultures of our two Slipsoid planets were like the two hemispheres of your brain, I perceive, thinking in harmony but differently. Much like yours, as I suppose, but on a magnificently grander scale. . . .

"Believe me, the human brain is, universally speaking, as obsolete as silicon-based semiconductors . . ."

"So . . . you . . . came . . . here . . ."

"Hungaman, there is nothing but thinking makes it so. The solid universe in which you believe you live is generated by your perceptions. That is why you are so troubled. You see through the deception, yet you refuse to see through the deception."

Hungaman was recovering from his astonishment. Although disconcerted at the sudden appearance of this pretense of humanity, he was reassured by a low rumbling throughout the ship: particles from the destroyed worlds were being loaded on board, into the cavernous holds.

"I am not troubled. I am in command here. I ordered the extinction of your Slipsoid system, and we have extinguished it, have we not? Leave me alone."

"But you are troubled. What about the orange blossom and the little blue bird? Are they a part of your reality?"

"I don't know what you mean. What orange blossom?"

"There is some hope for you. Spiritually, I mean. Because you are troubled."

"I'm not troubled." He squared his shoulders to show he meant what he said.

"You have just destroyed a myriad lives and yet you are not troubled?" Inhuman contempt sounded. "Not a little bit?"

Hungaman clicked his fingers and began to walk back the way he had come. "Let's discuss these matters, shall we? I am always prepared to listen."

The little man followed meekly into the tunnel. At a certain point, Hungaman moved fast and pressed a button in the tiled wall. Metal bars came flashing down. The little man found himself trapped in a cage. It was the way Barakuta's police dealt with troublemakers on the Bull-ball ground.

"Excellent," said Hungaman, turning to face the intruder. "Now, I want no more conjuring tricks from you. Tell me your name first of all."

Meekly, the little man said, "You can call me Manifold."

Manifold was standing behind a leather-bound armchair in a black gown. Hungaman was on the other side of a desk, the top of which held nothing but an inset screen. He found he was sitting down on a hard chair. A ginger-and-white cat jumped onto his lap. How the scene had changed so suddenly was beyond his comprehension.

"But—but how—"

The little man ignored Hungaman's stutter.

"Are you happy aboard your ship?" Manifold asked.

Hungaman answered up frankly and easily, to his own surprise: it was as if he was glad to find that metal bars were of no account. "I am not entirely happy with the personnel. Let me give you an example. You realize, of course, that we have been making this journey for some centuries. It would be impossible, of course, without AL—aided longevity. Nevertheless, it has been a long while. The enemy galaxy is retreating through the expanding universe. The ship is deteriorating rapidly. At our velocities, it is subject to strain. It has constantly to be rebuilt. Fortunately, we have invented XHX, hardened hydrogen, with which to refurbish our interiors. The hull is wearing thin. I think that accounts for the blue bird which got in."

As he spoke, he was absentmindedly stroking the cat. The cat lay still but did not purr.

"I was consulting with Provost-Marshal Shappi about

which revs and reps to use in this Bullball match, which I take it you interupted, when a rating entered my office unannounced. I ordered him to wait in the passage. 'Ah,' he said, 'the passage of time.' It was impertinent to answer back like that. It would not have happened a decade ago."

The little man leaned forward, resting his elbows on his thighs and clasping his hands together. Smiling, he said, "You're an uneasy man, I can see. Not a happy man. The cat does not purr for you. This voyage is just a misery to you."

"Listen to me," said Hungaman, leaning forward, unconsciously copying the older man's attitude. "You may be the figment of a great civilization, now happily defunct, but what you have to say about me means nothing."

He went on to inform his antagonist that even now tractor beams were hauling stuff into one of the insulated holds, raw hot stuff at a few thousand degrees, mesons, protons, corpuscles, wave particles—a great trail of material smaller than dust, all of which the *Beatitude* would use for fuel or building material. And those whirling particles were all that was left of Manifold's million-year-old civilization.

"So much for your million-year-old civilization. Time it was scrapped."

"You're proud of this?" shrieked Manifold.

"In our wake, we have destroyed a hundred so-called civilizations. They died, those civilizations, to power our passage, to drive us ever onward. We shall not be defeated. No, I don't regret a damned thing. We are what humanity is made of." Oratory had hold of him. "This very ship, this worldlet, is—what was that term in use in the old Christian Era?—yes, it's a *cathedral* to the human spirit. We are still young, but we are going to succeed, and the less opposition to us there is, the better."

His violent gesture disturbed the cat, which sprang from his lap and disappeared. Its image remained suspended in midair, growing fainter until it was gone.

"Mankind is as big as the universe. Sure, I'm not too happy with the way things are aboard this ship, but I don't give a tinker's cuss for anything outside our hull."

He gave an illustrative glance through the port as he spoke. Strangely, the Bullball game was continuing. A gored body was being elevated from the trampled field, trailing blood. The crowd loved it.

"As for your Slipsoid powers—what do I care for them? I can have you disintegrated any minute I feel like it. That's the plain truth. Do you have the power to read my mind?"

"You don't have that kind of mind. You're an alien life-form. It's a blank piece of paper to me."

"If you could read it, you would see how I feel about you. Now. What are you going to do?"

For response, the little man began to disintegrate, shedding his pretense of humanity. As soon as the transformation began, Hungaman pressed a stud under the flange of the desk. It would summon General Barakuta with firepower.

Manifold almost instantaneously ceased to exist. In his place a mouth, a tunnel, formed, from which poured—well, maybe it was a tunnel mouth for this strange concept, *quantaspace*—from which poured, *poured*—Hungaman could not grasp it ... poured what?—solid music? ... wave particles? ... pellets of zero substance? ... Whatever the invasive phenomenon was, it was filling up the compartment, burying Hungaman, terrified and struggling, and bursting on, on, into the rest of the giant vessel, choking its arteries, rushing like poison through a vein. Alarms were sounding, fire doors closing, conflagration crews running. And people screaming—screaming in sheer disgusted horror at this terrible irresistible unknown overcoming them. Nothing stopped it, nothing impeded it.

Within a hundred heartbeats, the entire speeding *Beatitude* worldlet was filled completely with the consuming dust. Blackness. Brownness. Repletion. Nonexistence.

Hungaman sat at his desk in his comfortable office. From his windows—such was his status, his office had two windows—he looked out on the neat artificial lawns of academia, surrounded by tall everlasting trees. He had become accustomed to the feeling of being alive.

He was talking to his brainfinger, a medium-sized rep covered in a fuzzy golden fur, through which two large doggy eyes peered sympathetically at his patient.

Hungaman was totally relaxed as he talked. He had his feet up on the desk, his hands behind his neck, fingers locked together: the picture of a man at his ease, perfect if old-fashioned. He knew all about reps.

"My researches were getting nowhere. Maybe I was on the verge of an NB—you know, a nervous breakdown. Who cares? That's maybe why I imagined I saw the orange blossom falling by the ports. On reflection, they were not oranges but planets."

"You are now saying it was not blossom but the actual fruits, the oranges?" asked the brainfinger.

"They were what I say they were. The oranges were bursting—exploding. They weren't oranges so much as worlds, whole planets, dropping down into oblivion, maybe meeting themselves coming up." He laughed. "The universe as orchard. I was excited because I knew that for once I had seen through reality. I remembered what that old Greek man, Socrates, had said, that once we were cured of reality we could ourselves become real. It's a way of saying that life is a lie."

"You know it is absurd to say that, darling. Only a madman would claim that there is something unreal about reality. Nobody would believe such sophistry."

"Yes, but remember—the majority is always wrong!"

"Who said that?"

"Tom Lehrer? Adolf Hitler? Mark Twain? Einstein McBeil? Socrates?"

"You've got Socrates on the brain, Hungaman, darling. Forget Socrates! We live in a well-organized military society, where such slogans as 'The majority is always wrong' are branded subversive. If I reported you, all this—" he gestured about him,—would disappear."

"But I have always felt I understood reality-perception better than other people. As you know, I studied it for almost a century, got a degree in it. Even the most solid objects, chairs, walls, rooms, lives—they are merely outward forms. It is a disconcerting concept, but behind it lies truth and beauty.

"That is what faster-than-light means, incidentally. It has nothing to do with that other old Greek philosopher, Einstein: it's to do with people seeing through appearances. We nowadays interpret speeding simply as an invariant of stationary, with acceleration as a moderator. You just need a captain with vision.

"I was getting nowhere until I realized that an oil painting of my father, for instance, was not really an oil painting of my father but just a piece of stretched canvas with a veneer of variously colored oils. Father himself—again, problematic. I was born milaterally."

The brainfinger asked, "Is that why you have become, at least in your imagination, the father of the crew of the *Beatitude*?"

Hungaman removed his feet from the desk and sat up rigidly. "The crew have disappeared. You imagine I'm happy about that? No, it's a pain, a real pain."

The brainfinger began to look extra fuzzy.

"Your hypothesis does not allow for pain being real. Or else you are talking nonsense. For the captain of a great weapon-vessel such as the *Beatitude* you are emotionally unstable."

Hungaman leaned forward and pointed a finger, with indications of shrewdness, and a conceivable pun, at the brainfinger.

"Are you ordering me to return to Earth, to call off our entire mission, to let the enemy galaxy get away? Are you trying to relieve me of my command?"

The brainfinger said, comfortingly, "You realize that at the extra-normal velocities at which you are traveling, you have basically quit the quote real world unquote, and hallucinations are the natural result. We brainfingers have a label for it: TPD, tachyon perception displacement. Ordinary human senses are not equipped for such transcendental speeds, is all . . ."

Hungaman thought before speaking. "There's always this problem with experience. It does not entirely coincide with consciousness. Of course you are right about extra-normal velocities and hallucination. . . . Would you say wordplay is a mark of madness—or near-madness?"

"Why ask me that?"

"I have to speak to my clonther shortly. I need to check something with him. His name's Twohunga. I'm fond of him, but since he has been in Heliopause HQ, his diction has become strange. It makes me nervous."

The brainfinger emitted something like a sigh. He felt that Hungaman had changed the subject for hidden motives.

He spoke gently, almost on tiptoe. "I shall leave you alone to conquer your insecurity. Bad consciences are always troublesome. Get back on the bridge. Good evening. I will see you again tomorrow. Have a nice night." It rose and walked toward the door, narrowly missed, readjusted, and disappeared.

"*Bad conscience!* What an idiot!" Hungaman said to himself. "I'm afraid of something, that's the trouble. And I can't figure out what I'm afraid of." He laughed. He twiddled his thumbs at great speed.

The *Beatitude* had attained a velocity at which it broke free from spatial dimensions. It was now traveling through a realm of latent temporalities. Computer SJC1 alone could scan spatial derivatives, as the ship-projectile it governed headed after the enemy galaxy. The *Beatitude* had to contend with racing tachyons and other particles of frantic mobility. The tachyons were distinct from light. Light did not enter the region of latent temporalities. Here were only eotemporal processes, the beginnings and endings of which could not be distinguished one from another.

The SJC1 maintained ship velocities, irrespective of the eotemporal world outside, or the sufferings of the biotemporal world within.

* * *

Later, after a snort, Hungaman went to the top of the academy building and peered through the telescope. There in the cloudless sky, hanging to the northwest, was the hated enigmatic word—if indeed it was a word—hiseobiw ... *Hiseobiw*, smudgily written in space fires. Perhaps it was a formula of some kind. Read upside down, it spelt miqoesiy. This dirty mark in space had puzzled and infuriated military intelligentsia for centuries. Hungaman was still working on the problem, on and off.

This was what the enemy galaxy had created, why it had become the enemy. How had it managed this bizarre stellar inscription? And why? Was miqoesiy aimed at the Solar system? What did it spell? What could it mean? Was it intended to help or to deter? Was it a message from some dyslexic galactic god? Or was it, as a joker had suggested, a commercial for a pair of socks?

No one had yet determined the nature of this affront to cosmology. It was for this reason that, long ago, the *Beatitude* had been launched to chastise the enemy galaxy and, if possible, decipher the meaning of hiseobiw or miqoesiy.

A clenched human fist was raised from the roof of the academic building to the damned thing. Then its owner went inside again.

Hungaman spoke into his voxputer. "Beauty of mental illness. Entanglements of words and appearances, a maze through which we try to swim. I believe I'm getting through to the meaning of this enigmatic sign. . . .

"Yep, that does frighten me. Like being on a foreign planet. A journey into the astounded Self, where truth lies and lies are truth. Thank god the hull of our spacevessel is not impermeable. It represents the ego, the eggnog. These bluebirds are messengers, bringing in hope from the world outside. TPD—must remember that!"

Hungaman, as he had told the brainfinger to little effect, had a clonther, a clone-brother by the name of Twohunga. Twohunga had done well, ascending the military ranks, until—as Steel-Major Twohunga—he was appointed to the WWW, the World Weaponry Watch on Charon, coplanet of Pluto.

So Hungaman put through a call to the Heliopause HQ.

"Steel-Major here ... haven't heard from you for thirty-two years, Hungaman. Yes, mmm, thirty-two. Maybe only thirty-one. How's your promotion?"

"The same. You still living with that Plutottie?"

"I disposed of her." The face in the globe was dark and stormy, the plastic mitter banded across its forehead. "I have a rep—a womanroid—for my satisfactions now. What you might call satisfactions. Where are you, precisely? Still on the *Beatitude*, I guess? Not that that's precise in any way ..." He spoke jerkily and remotely, as if his voice had been prerecorded by a machine afflicted by hiccups.

"I'm none too sure. Or if I am sure, I am dead. Maybe I am a rev," said Hungaman, without giving his answer a great deal of thought. "It seems I am having an episode. It's to do with the extreme velocity, a velocillusion ... We're traversing the eotemporal, you know." He clutched his head as he spoke, while a part of him said tauntingly to himself, You're hamming it up....

"Brainfinger. Speak to a brainfinger, Hungaman," Twohunga advised.

"I did. They are no help."

"They never are. Never."

"It may have been part of my episode. Listen, Twohunga, Helipause HQ still maintains contact with the *Beatitude*. Can you tell me if the ship is still on course, or has it been subjugated by life-forms from the Slipsoid system which have invaded the ship?"

"System? What system? The Slipsoid system?"

"Yes. X377. We disintegrated it for fuel as we passed."

"So you did. Mm, so you did. So you did, indeed. Yes, you surely disintegrated it."

"Will you stop talking like that!"

Twohunga stood up, to walk back and forth, three paces one way, swivel on heel, three paces the other way, swivel on heel, in imitation of a man with an important announcement in mind.

He said, "I know you keep ship's time on the *Beatitude*, as if the ship has a time amid eotemporality, but here in Sol system we are coming up for Year One Million, think of it, with all the attendant celebrations. Yep, Year One Million, count them. Got to celebrate. We're planning to nuclearize Neptune, nuclearize it, to let a little light into the circumference of the system. Things have changed. One Million . . . Yes, things have changed. They certainly have. They certainly *are* . . ."

"I asked you if we on shipboard have been subjugated by the aliens."

"Well, that's where you are wrong, you see. The wrong question. Entirely up the spout. Technology has improved out of all recognition since your launch date. All recognition . . . Look at this."

The globe exploded into a family of lines, some running straight, some slightly crooked, just like a human family. As they went, they spawned mathematical symbols, not all of them familiar to Hungaman. They originated at one point in the bowl and ricocheted to another.

Twohunga said, voice-over, "We used to call them 'black holes,' remember? That was before we domesticated them. Black holes, huh! They are densers now. *Densers*, okay? We can propel them through hyperspace. They go like spit on a hot stove. Propelled. They serve as weaponry, these densers, okay? Within about the next decade, the next decade, we shall be able to hurl them at the enemy galaxy and destroy it. Destroy the whole thing . . ." He gave something that passed for a chuckle. "Then we shall see about their confounded *hiseobiw*, or whatever it is."

Hungaman was horrified. He saw at once that this technological advance, with densers used as weapons, rendered the extended voyage of the *Beatitude* obsolete. Long before the ship could reach the enemy galaxy—always supposing that command of the ship was regained from the Slipsoid invader—the densers would have destroyed their target.

"This is very bad news," he said, almost to himself. "Very bad news indeed."

"Bad news? Bad news? Not for humanity," said Twohunga sharply. "Oh, no! We shall do away with this curse in the sky for good and all."

"It's all very well for you to say that, safe at Heliopause HQ. What about those of us on the *Beatitude*—if any of us are there anymore . . . ?"

Twohunga began to pace again, this time taking four paces to the left, swivel on heel, four paces to the right, swivel on heel.

He explained, not without a certain malice, that it was not technology alone which had advanced. Ethics had also taken a step forward. Quite a large step, he said. He emitted a yelp of laughter. A considerably large step. He paused, looking over his shoulder at his clonther far away. It was now considered, he stated, not at all correct to destroy an entire cultured planet without any questions asked.

In fact, to be honest, and frankness undoubtedly was the best policy, destroying any planet on which there was sentient life was now ruled to be a criminal act. Such as destroying the ancient Slipsoid dual-planet culture, for instance. . . .

As Captain of the *Beatitude*, therefore, Hungaman was a wanted criminal and, if he were caught; would be up for trial before the TDC, the Transplanetary Destruction Crimes tribunal.

"What nonsense is this you are telling—" Hungaman began.

"Nonsense you may call it, but that's the law. No nonsense, no! Oh, no. Cold fact! Culture destruction, criminal act. It's you, Hungaman, you!"

In a chill voice, Hungaman asked, "And what of Military Morality?"

"What of Military—'What of Military Morality?' he asks. Military Morality! It's a thing of the past, the long long past! Pah! A criminal creed, *criminal* . . . We're living in a new—In fact, I should not be talking to a known genocidal maniac at all, no, not a word, in case it makes me an accessory after the fact."

He broke the connection.

Hungaman fell to the floor and chewed the leg of his chair.

It was tough but not unpalatable.

"It's bound to be good for him," said a voice.

"They were an omnivorous species," said a second voice in agreement—though not speaking in speech exactly.

Seeing was difficult. Although it was light, the light was of an uncomfortable wavelength. Hungaman seemed to be lying down, with his torso propped up, enabling him to eat.

Whatever it was he was eating, it gave him strength. Now he could see, although what he could see was hard to make out. By what he took to be his bedside two rubbery cylinders were standing, or perhaps floating. He was in a room with no corners or windows. The illumination came from a globular object which drifted about the room, although the light it projected remained steady.

"Where am I?" he asked.

The two cylinders wobbled and parts of them changed color. "There you are, you see. Typical question, 'Where am I?' Always the emphasis on the Self. I, I, I. Very typical of a human species. Probably to be blamed on the way in which they reproduce. It's a bisexual species, you know."

"Yes, I know. Fatherhood, motherhood . . . I shall never understand it. Reproduction by fission is so much more efficient—the key to immortality indeed."

They exchanged warm colors.

"Quite. And the intense pleasure, the joy, of fission itself . . ."

"Look, you two, would you mind telling me where I am. I have other questions I can ask, but that one first." He felt the nutrients flowing through his body, altering his constitution.

"You're on the *Beatitude*, of course."

Despite his anxiety, he found he was enjoying their color changes. The colors were so various. After a while he discovered he was *listening to the colors*. It must, he thought, be something he ate.

Over the days that followed, Hungaman came slowly to understand his situation. The aliens answered his questions readily enough, although he realized there was one question in his mind he was unable to ask or even locate.

They escorted him about the ship. He was becoming more cylindrical, although he had yet to learn to float. The ship was empty with one exception: a Bullball game was in progress. He stood amazed to see the players still running, the big black bulls still charging among them. To his astonishment, he saw Surtees Slick again, running like fury with the heavy blue ball, his yellow hair flowing.

The view was less clear than it had been. Hungaman fastened his attention on the bulls. With their head-down shortsighted stupidity, they rushed at individual players as if, flustered by their erratic movements, the bulls believed a death, a stillness, would resolve some vast mystery of life they could never formulate.

Astonished, Hungaman turned to his companions.

"It's for you," they said, coloring in a smile. "Don't worry, it's not real, just a simulation. That sort of thing is over and done with now, as obsolete as a silicon-based semiconductor."

"To be honest, I'm not sure yet if *you* are real and not simulations. You are Slipsoids, aren't you? I imagined we had destroyed you. Or did I only imagine I imagined we had destroyed you?"

But no. After their mitochondria had filled the ship, they assured him, they were able to reestablish themselves, since their material was contained aboard the

Beatitude. They had cannibalized the living human protoplasm, sparing only Hungaman, the captain.

It was then a comparatively simple matter to redesign quanta-space and rebuild their sun and the two linked planets. They had long ago mastered all that technology had to offer. And so here they were, and all was right with the world, they said, in flickering tones of purple and a kind of mauve.

"But we are preserving you on the ship," they said.

He asked a new variant of his old question. "And where exactly are we and the *Beatitude* now?"

"Velocity killed. Out of the eotemporal."

They told him, in their colors, that the great ship was in orbit about the twin planets of Slipsoid, "forming a new satellite."

He was silent for a long while, digesting this information, glad but sorry, sorry but glad. Finally, he said—and now he was rapidly learning to talk in color—"I have suffered much. My brain has been under great pressure. But I have also learned much. I thank you for your help, and for preserving me. Since I cannot return to Earth, I hope to be of service to you."

Their dazzling bursts of color told Hungaman they were gazing affectionately at him. They said there was one question they longed to ask him, regarding a matter which had worried them for many centuries.

"What's the question? You know I will help if I can."

There was some hesitation before they colored their question.

"What is the meaning of this *hiseobiw* we see in our night sky?"

"Oh, yes, that! Let me explain," said Hungaman.

He explained that the so-called letters of *hiseobiw*, or preferably *miqoesiy*, were not letters but symbols of an arcane mathematics. It was an equation, more clearly written—for the space fires had drifted—as

$$M\pi 7;\varpi \in ;\tau 5 \;(=)X!_9$$

They colored, "Meaning?"

"We'll have to work it out between us," Hungaman colored back. "But I'm pretty sure it contains a formula that will clear brains of phylogenetically archaic functions. Thereby, it will, when applied, change all life in the universe."

"Then maybe we should leave it alone."

"No," he said. "We must solve it. That's human nature."

Droplet

By Benjamin Rosenbaum

1.

Today Shar is Marilyn Monroe. That's an erotic goddess from prehistoric cartoon mythology. She has golden curls, blue eyes, big breasts, and skin of a shocking pale pink. She stands with a wind blowing up from Hades beneath her, trying to control her skirt with her hands, forever showing and hiding her white silk underwear.

Today I am Shivol'riargh, a more recent archetype of feminine sexuality. My skin is hard, hairless, glistening black. Faint fractal patterns of darker black writhe across my surfaces. I have long claws. It suits my mood.

We have just awakened from a little nap of a thousand years, our time, during which the rest of the world aged even more.

She goes: "kama://01-nbX5-# . . ."

I snap the channel shut. "Talk language if you want to seduce me."

Shar pouts. With those little red lips and those innocent, yet knowing, eyes, it's almost irresistible. I resist.

"Come *on*, Narra," she says. "Do we have to fight about this every time we wake up?"

"I just don't know why we have to keep flying around like this."

"You're not scared of Warboys again?" she asks.

Her fingertips slide down my black plastic front. The fractals dance around them.

"There aren't any more," she says.

"You don't know that, Shar."

"They've all killed each other. Or turned themselves off. Warboys don't last if there's nothing to fight."

Despite the cushiony pink Marilyn Monroe skin, Shar is harder than I am. My heart races when I look at her, just as it did a hundred thousand years ago.

Her expression is cool. She wants me. But it's a game to her.

She's searching the surface of me with her hands.

"What are you looking for?" I mean both in the Galaxy and on my skin, though I know the answers.

"Anything," she says, answering the broader question. "Anyone who's left. People to learn from. To play with."

People to serve, I think nastily.

I'm lonely, too, of course, but I'm sick of looking. Let them come find us in the Core.

"It's so stupid," I groan. Her hands are affecting me. "We probably won't be able to talk to them anyway."

Her hands find what they've been searching for: the hidden opening to Shivol'riargh's sexual pocket. It's full of the right kind of nerve endings. Shivol'riargh is hard on the outside, but oh so soft on the inside. Sometimes I wish I had someone to wear that *wasn't* sexy.

"We'll figure it out," she says in a voice that's all breath.

Her fingers push at the opening of my sexual pocket. I hold it closed. She leans against me and wraps her other arm around me for leverage. She pushes. I resist.

Her lips are so red. I want them on my face.

She's cheating. She's a lot stronger than Marilyn Monroe.

"Shar, I don't want to screw," I say. "I'm still angry."

But I'm lying.

"Hush," she says.

Her fist slides into me and I gasp. My claws go around her shoulders and I pull her to me.

2.

Later we turn the gravity off and float over Ship's bottom eye, looking down at the planet Shar had Ship find. It's blue like Marilyn Monroe's eyes.

"It's water," Shar says. Her arms are wrapped around my waist, her breasts pressed against my back. She rests her chin on my shoulder.

I grunt.

"It's water all the way down," she says. "You could swim right through the planet to the other side."

"Did anyone live here?"

"I think so. I don't remember. But it was a gift from a Sultan to his beloved."

Shar and I have an enormous amount of information stored in our brains. The brain is a sphere the size of a billiard ball somewhere in our bodies, and however much we change our bodies, we can't change that. Maka once told me that even if Ship ran into a star going nine-tenths lightspeed, my billiard-ball brain would come tumbling out the other side, none the worse for wear. I have no idea what kind of matter it is or how it works, but there's plenty of room in my memory for all the stories of all the worlds in the Galaxy, and most of them are probably in there.

But we're terrible at accessing the factual information. A fact will pop up inexplicably at random—the number of Quantegral Lovergirls ever manufactured, for instance, which is 362,476—and be gone a minute later, swimming away in the murky seas of thought. That's the way Maka built us, on purpose. He thought it was cute.

3.

An old argument about Maka:

"He loved us," I say. I know he did.

Shar rolls her eyes (she's a tigress at the moment).

"I could feel it," I say, feeling stupid.

"Now there's a surprise. Maka designed you from scratch, including your feelings, and you feel that he loved you. Amazing." She yawns, showing her fangs.

"He made us more flexible than any other Lovergirls. Our minds are almost Interpreter-level."

She snorts. "We were trade goods, Narra. Trade goods. Classy purchasable or rentable items."

I curl up around myself. (I'm a python.)

"He set us free," I say.

Shar doesn't say anything for a while, because that is, after all, the central holiness of our existence. Our catechism, if you like.

Then she says gently: "He didn't need us for anything anymore, when they went into the Core."

"He could have just turned us off. He set us free. He gave us Ship."

She doesn't say anything.

"He loved us," I say.

I know it's true.

4.

I don't tell Shar, but that's one reason I want us to go back to the Galactic Core: Maka's there.

I know it's stupid. There's nothing left of Maka that I would recognize. The Wizards got hungrier and hungrier for processing power, so they could think more and know more and play more complicated games. Eventually the only thing that could satisfy them was to rebuild their brains as a soup of black holes. Black hole brains are very fast.

I know what happens when a person doesn't have a body anymore, too. For a while they simulate the sensations and logic of a corporeal existence, only with everything perfect and running much faster than in the real world. But their interests drift. The simulation gets more and more abstract and eventually they're just thoughts, and after a while they give that up, too, and then they're just numbers. By now Maka is just some very big numbers turning into some even bigger numbers, racing toward infinity.

I know because he told me. He knew what he was becoming.

I still miss him.

5.

We go down to the surface of the planet, which we decide to call Droplet.

The sky is painterly blue with strings of white clouds drifting above great choppy waves. It's lovely. I'm glad Shar brought us here.

We're dolphins. We chase each other across the waves. We dive and hold our breaths, and shower each other with bubbles. We kiss with our funny dolphin noses.

I'm relaxing and floating when Shar slides her rubbery body over me and clamps her mouth onto my flesh. It's such a long time since I've been a cetacean that I don't notice that Shar is a *boy* dolphin until I feel her penis enter me. I buck with surprise, but Shar keeps her jaws clamped and rides me. Rides me and rides me, as I buck and swim, until she ejaculates. She makes it take extra long.

Afterward we race, and then I am floating, floating, exhausted and happy as the sunset blooms on the horizon.

It's a *very* impressive sunset, and I kick up on my tail to get a better look. I change my eyes and nose so I can see the whole spectrum and smell the entire wind.

It hits me first as fear, a powerful shudder that takes over my dolphin body, kicks me into the air and then into a racing dive, dodging and weaving. Then it hits me as knowledge, the signature written in the sunset: beryllium-10, mandelium, large-scale entanglement from muon dispersal. Nuclear and strange-matter weapons fallout. Warboys.

Ship dropped us a matter accelerator to get back up with, a series of rings floating in the water. I head for it.

Shar catches up and hangs on to me, changing into a human body and riding my back.

"Ssh, honey," she says, stroking me. "It's okay. There haven't been Warboys here for ten thousand years. . . ."

I buck her off, and this time I'm not flirting.

Shar changes her body below the waist back into a dolphin tail, and follows. As soon as she is in the first ring I tell Ship to bring us up, and one dolphin, one mermaid, and twelve metric tons of water shoot through the rings and up through the blue sky until it turns black and crowded with stars. "Ten thousand years," says Shar as we hurtle up into the sky.

"You *picked* a planet Warboys had been on! Ship must have seen the signature."

"Narra, this wasn't a Warboy duel—they wouldn't dick around with nuclear for that. They must have been trying to exterminate a civilian population."

The water has all sprayed away now and we are tumbling through the thin air of the stratosphere.

"There's a chance they failed, Narra. Someone might be here, hidden. That's why we came."

"Warboys don't fail!"

We grow cocoons as we exit the atmosphere and hit orbit. After a couple of minutes, I feel Ship's long retrieval pseudopod slurp me in.

I lie in the warm cave of Ship's retrieval pseudopod. It's decorated with webs of green and blue. I remember when Shar decorated it. It was a long time ago, when we were first traveling.

I turn back into a human form and sit up.

Shar is lying nearby, picking at the remnants of her cocoon, silvery strands draped across her breasts.

"You want to die," I say.

"Don't be ridiculous, Narra."

"Shar, seriously. It's not enough for you—I'm not enough for you. You're looking for Warboys. You're trying to get killed." I feel a buzzing in my head, my breathing is constricted, aches shoot through my fist-clenched knuckles: clear signs that my emotional registers are full, the excess externalizing into pain.

She sighs. "Narra, I'm not that complicated. If I wanted to die, I'd just turn myself off." She grows legs and stands up.

"No, I don't think you can." What I'm about to say is unfair, and too horrible. I'll regret it. I feel the blood pounding in my ears and I say it anyway: "Maybe Maka didn't free us all the way. Maybe he just gave us to each other. Maybe you can't leave me. You want to, but you can't."

Her eyes are cold. As I watch, the color drains out of them, from black to slate gray to white.

She looks like she wants to say a lot of things. Maybe: you stupid sentimental little girl. Maybe: it's you who wants to leave—to go back to your precious Maka, and if you had the brains to become a Wizard you would. Maybe: I want to live, but not the coward's life you keep insisting on.

She doesn't say any of them, though. She turns and walks away.

6.

I keep catching myself thinking it, and I know she's thinking it too. This person before me is the last other person I can reach, the only one to love me from now on in all the worlds of time. How long until she leaves me, as everyone else has left?

And how long can I stand her if she doesn't?

7.

The last people we met were a religious sect who lived in a beautiful crystal ship the size of a moon. They were Naturals and had old age and death and even children whom they bore themselves, who couldn't walk or talk at first or anything. They were sad for some complicated religious reason that Shar and I didn't understand. We cheered them up for a while by having sex with the ones their rules allowed to have sex and telling stories to the rest, but eventually they decided to all kill themselves anyway. We left before it happened.

Since then we haven't seen anyone. We don't know of anywhere that has people left.

I told Shar we could be passing people all the time and not know it. People changed in the Dispersal, and we're not Interpreters. There could be people with bodies made of gas clouds or out of the spins of elementary particles. We could be surrounded by crowds of them.

She said that just made her sadder.

8.

We go down to Droplet again. I smile and pretend it's all right. We spent a thousand years, our time, getting here; we might as well look around.

We change ourselves so we can breathe water, and head down into the depths. There are no fish on Droplet, no coral, no plankton. I can taste very simple nanomites, the standard kind every made world has for general upkeep. But all see, looking down, is green-blue fading to deep blue fading to rich indigo and blackness.

Then there's a tickle on my skin.

I stop swimming and look around. Nothing but water. The tickle comes again.

I send a sonar pulse to Shar ahead, telling her to wait.

I try to swim again but I can't. I feel fingers, hands, holding me, where there is only water. Stroking, pressing against my skin.

I change into a hard ball, Shivol'riargh without head or limbs, and turn down tactile until I can't tell the hands from the gentle current.

I fiddle with my perceptions until I remember how to send out a very fine sonar wave, and to enhance and filter the data, discerning patterns in very fine perturbations of the water. I subtract out the general currents and chaotic swirls of the ocean, looking only for the motions of the water that should not be there, and turn it into a three-dimensional image of the space around me.

There are people here.

Their shapes—made of fine motions of the water—are human shapes, tall, with graceful oblong heads that flatten at the top to a frill.

They are running their watery hands over the surface of me, poking and prodding.

From below, Shar is returning, approaching me. Some of the water people cluster around her and stop her, holding her arms and legs.

She struggles. I cannot see her expression through the murk.

The name "Nereids" swims up from the hidden labyrinths of my memory. Not a word from this world, but word enough.

The Nereids back away, arraying themselves as if formally, three meters away from me on all sides. A sphere of Nereids surrounds me.

Shar stops struggling. They let her go, pushing her outside the sphere.

One of the Nereids—tall, graceful, broad-shouldered—breaks out of the formation and glides toward me. He places his hands on my surface.

This, I tell myself to remember, is what we were designed for. Alone among the Quantegral Lovergirls, Shar and I were given the flexibility and intelligence to serve all the possible variations of post-Dispersal humanity. We were designed to discover, at the very least, how to give pleasure; and perhaps even how to communicate.

Still, I am afraid.

I let the hard shell of Shivol'riargh grow soft, I sculpt my body back toward basic humanity; tall, thin, like the Nereids.

This close, my sonar sees the face shaped out of water smile. The Nereid raises his hands, palms out. I place my palms on them, though I feel only a slight resistance in the water. I part my lips. The Nereid's head cautiously inches toward mine.

I close my eyes and raise my face, slowly, slowly, to meet the Nereid's.

We kiss. It is a tickle, a pressure, in the water against my lips.

Our bodies drift together. When the Nereid's chest touches my breasts, I register shock: the resistance of the water is denser. It feels like a body is pressing into mine.

The kiss goes on. Gets deeper. A tongue of water plays around my tongue.

I wonder what Shar is thinking.

The Nereid releases my hands; his hands run slowly from the nape of my neck, across my shoulder blades, down the small of my back, fanning out to hold my buttocks.

I open my eyes. I see only water, endless and dark, and Shar silent and still below. I smile down to reassure her. She does not move.

My new lover is invisible. In all her many forms, Shar is never invisible. It is as if the ocean is making love to me. I like it.

The familiar metamorphosis of sex in a human body overtakes me. Hormones course through my blood; some parts grow wet, others (my throat) grow dry. My body is relaxing, opening. My heart thunders. Fear is still there, for what do I know of the Nereid? Pleasure is overwhelming it, like a torrent eroding granite into silt.

A data channel crackles, and I blink with surprise. Through the nanomites that fill the sea, the Nereid is sending. Out of the billions of ancient protocols I know, intuition finds the right one.

Spreading my vulva with its hand, the Nereid asks: *May I?*

A double thrill of surprise and pleasure courses through me: first, to be able to communicate so easily, and second, to be asked. *Yes*, I say over the same archaic protocol.

A burst of water, a swirling cylinder strong and fine, enters me, pushing into the warm cavity that once evolved to fit its prototype, in other bodies on another world.

I hold the Nereid tight. I buck and move.

Empty blue surrounds me. The ocean fucks me.

I raise the bandwidth of my sensations and emotions

gradually, and the Nereid changes to match. His skin swirls and dances against mine, electric. There is a small waterspout swirling and thrashing inside me. The body becomes a wave, spinning me, coursing over me, a giant caress.

I allow the pleasure to grow until it eclipses rational thought and the sequential, discursive mode of experience.

The dance goes on a long time.

9.

I find Shar basking on the surface, transformed into a dark green, bright-eyed Kelpie with a forest of ropy seaweed for hair.

"You left me," I say, appalled.

"You looked like you were having fun," she says.

"That's not the point, Shar. We don't know those creatures." The tendrils of her hair reach for me. I draw back. "It might not have been safe."

"You didn't look worried."

"I thought you were watching."

She shrugs.

I look away. There's no point talking about it.

10.

The Nereids seem content to ignore Shar, and she seems content to be ignored.

I descend to them again and again. The same Nereid always comes to me, and we make love.

How did you come to this world? I ask in an interlude.

251

Once there was a Sultan who was the scourge of our people, he tells me. *The last of us sought refuge here on his favorite wife's pleasure world. We were discovered by the Sultan's terrible warriors.*

They destroyed all life here, but we escaped to this form. The Warriors seek us still, but they can no longer harm us. If they boil this world to vapor, we will be permutations in the vapor. If they annihilate it to light, we will be there in the coherence and interference of the light:

But you lost much, I tell him.

We gained more. We did not know how much. His hands caress me. *This pleasure I share with you is a fraction of what we might have, if you were one of us.*

I shiver with the pleasure of the caress and with the strangeness of the idea.

His hands flicker over me: hands, then waves, then hands. *You would lose this body. But you would gain much more, Quantegral Lovergirl Narra.*

I nestle against him, take his hands in mine to stop their flickering caress. Thinking of Maka, thinking of Shar.

11.

"It's time to go, Narra," Shar says. Her seaweed hair is thicker, tangled; she is mostly seaweed, her Kelpie body a dark green doll hidden in the center.

"I don't want to go," I say.

"We've seen this world," she says. "It only makes us fight."

I am silent, drifting.

The water rolls around us. I feel sluggish, a little cold. I've been under for so long. I grow some green Kelpie tresses myself, so I can soak up energy from the sun.

Shar watches me.

We both know I've fallen in love.

Before Maka freed us, when the Wizards had bodies, when we were slaves to the pleasure of the Wizards and everyone they wanted to entertain, we fell in love on command. We felt not only lust, but pure aching adoration for any guest or client of the Wizards who held the keys to us for an hour. It was the worst part of our servitude.

When Maka freed us, when he gave us the keys to ourselves, Shar burned the falling-in-love out of herself completely. She never wanted to feel that way again.

I kept it. So sometimes I fall, yes, into an involuntary servitude of the heart.

I look up into the dappled white and blue of the sky, and then I tune my eyes so I can see the stars beyond it.

I have given up many lovers for Shar, moved on with her into that night.

But maybe this is the end of the line. Perhaps, if I abandon the Nereids, there is no falling-in-love left in this empty, haunted Galaxy with anyone but Shar.

Who does not fall in love. Not even with me.

"I'm going back to Ship," Shar says. "I'll be waiting there."

I say nothing.

She doesn't say, but not forever.

She doesn't say, decide.

I float, soaking the sun into my green seaweed hair, but I can't seem to stop feeling cold. I hear Shar splashing away, the splashes getting fainter.

My tears diffuse into the planet sea.

After a while I feel the Nereid's gentle hands pulling me back down. I sink with him, away from the barren sky.

12.

I lie in the Nereid's arms. Rocked as if by the ocean. I turn off my sense of the passing of time.

13.

My lover tells me: *Your friend is calling you.*

I emerge slowly from my own depths, letting time's relentless march begin again. My eyes open.

Above, the blue just barely fades to clearer blue.

As I hit the surface I hear Shar's cry. Ship is directly overhead, and the signal is on a tight beam. It says: *Narra! Too late. Tell your friends to hide you.*

I shape myself into a disk and suck data from the sky. *What?* I yell back at her, confused and terrified.

Then dawn slices over the horizon of Droplet, and Shar's signal abruptly cuts off.

The Warboy ship, rising with the sun, is massive and evil, translucent and blazing white, subtle as a nova, gluttonous, like a fanged fist tearing open the sky.

They are approaching Droplet from its sun—they must have been hidden in the sun's photosphere. Otherwise Ship would have seen them before.

Run, Shar, I think, desperate. Ship is fast, probably faster than the Warboys' craft.

But Ship awaits the Warboys, silent, perched above

Droplet's atmosphere like a sparrow facing down an eagle.

"Let us remake you," the Nereid's voice whispers from the waves, surprising me.

"And Shar?" I say.

"Too late," says the liquid, splashing voice.

Warboys. The word is too little for the fanged fist in the sky. And I am without Shar, without Ship. I look at my body and I realize I am allowing it to drift between forms. It's like ugly gray foam, growing now spikes, now frills, now fingers. I try to bring it under control, make it beautiful again, but I can't. I don't feel anything, but I know this is terror. This is how I really am: terrified and ugly.

If I send a signal now, the Warboys will know Droplet is not deserted. Perhaps I can force the Nereids to fight them somehow.

I make myself into a dish again, prepare to send the signal.

"Then we will hide you in the center," says the liquid voice.

Shar, I say, but only to myself. I do not send the signal that would bring death down upon me.

I abandon her.

The Nereids pull me down, into the deep. I do not struggle. The water grows dark. Above there is a faint shimmering light where Shar faces the Warboys alone.

Shar, my sister, my wife. Suddenly the thought of losing her is too big for me to fathom. It drowns out every other pattern in my brain. There are no more reasons, no more explanations, no more Narra at all, no Droplet, no Nereids, no universe. Only the loss of Shar.

The glimmer above fades. After a while the water is superdense, jellylike, under the pressure of the planet's weight; it thickens into a viscous material as heavy as lead, and here, in the darkness, they bury me.

14.

Here is what happens with Shar:

"Ship," she says. "What am I dealing with here?"

"Those," says Ship, "are some of our brothers, Shar. Definitely Wizard manufacture, about half a million years old in our current inertial frame; one Celestial Dreadnought's worth of Transgenerate, Polystatic, Cultural-Death Warboys. I'm guessing they were the Palace Guard of the Sultanate of Ching-Fuentes-Parador, a cyclic postcommunalist metanostalgist empire/artwork, which—"

"Stay with the Warboys, Ship," Shar says. "What can they do?"

"Their intelligence and tactical abilities are well above yours. But they're culturally inflexible. As trade goods, they were designed to imprint on the purchaser's cultural matrix and adhere to it—in typically destructive Warboy style. This batch shouldn't have outlasted the purchasing civilization, so they must have gone rogue to some degree."

"Do they have emotions?"

"Not at the moment," Ship says. "They have three major modes: Strategic, Tactical, and Ceremonial. In Ceremonial Mode—used for court functions, negotiations, entertainment and the like—they have a full human emotional/sensorial range. In Ceremonial Mode they're also multicate, each Warboy pursuing his own agenda. Right now they're patrolling in Tactical Mode, which means they're one dumb, integrated weapon—like that, they have the least mimetic drift, which is probably how they've survived since the destruction of the Sultanate."

"Okay, now shut up and let me think," Shar says and presses her fingers to her temples, chasing some memories she can just barely taste through the murky labyrinth of her brain.

Shar takes the form of a beautiful, demihuman queen. She speaks in a long-dead language, and Ship broadcasts the signal across an ancient protocol.

"Jirur Na'alath, Sultana of the Emerald Night, speaks now: I am returned from my meditations and demand an accounting. Guards, attend me!"

The Warboy ship advances, but a subtle change overtakes it; rainbows ripple across its white surface, and the emblem of a long-defunct Sultanate appears emblazoned in the sky around it; the Warboys are in Ceremonial Mode.

"So far so good," says Shar to Ship.

"Watch out," says Ship. "They're smarter this way."

The Warboys' signal reaches back across the void, and Ship translates it into a face and a voice. The face is golden, fanged, blazing; the voice deep and full of knives, a dragon's voice.

"Prime Subject of the Celestial Dreadnought *Ineffable Violence* speaks now: I pray to the Nonpresent that I might indeed have the joy of serving again Sultana Na'alath."

"Your prayers are answered, Prime Subject," Shar announces.

Ineffable Violence is braking, matching Ship's orbit around Droplet. It swings closer to Ship, slowing down. Only a hundred kilometers separate them.

"It would relieve the greatest of burdens from my lack-of-heart," Prime Subject says, "if I could welcome

Sultana Na'alath herself, the kindest and most regal of monarchs." Ten kilometers.

Shar stamps her foot impatiently. "Why do you continue to doubt me? Has my Ship not transmitted to you signatures and seals of great cryptographic complexity that establish who I am? Prime Subject, it is true that I am kind, but your insolence tests the limits of my kindness."

One kilometer.

"And with great joy have we received them. But alas, data is only data, and with enough time any forgery is possible."

Fifty meters separate Ship's protean hull from the shining fangs of the Dreadnought.

Shar's eyes blaze. "Have you no sense of propriety left, that you would challenge me? Have you so degraded?"

The Warboy's eyes almost twinkle. "The last Sultan who graced *Ineffable Violence* with his sacred presence left me this gem." His ghostly image, projected by Ship, holds up a ruby. "At its core is a plasm of electrons in quantum superposition. Each of the Sultans, Sultanas, and Sultanons retired to meditation has one like it; and in each gem are particles entangled with the particles in every other gem."

"Uh oh," says Ship.

"I prized mine very much," says Shar. "Alas, it was taken from me by—"

"How sad," says Prime Subject.

The fangs of *Ineffable Violence* plunge into Ship's body, tearing it apart.

Ship screams.

Through the exploding membranes of Ship's body, through the fountains of atmosphere escaping, three

Warboys in ceremonial regalia fly toward Shar. They are three times her size, golden and silver armor flashing, weapons both archaic and sophisticated held in their many hands. Shar becomes Shivol'riargh, who does not need air, and spins away from them, toward the void outside. Fibers of some supertough material shoot out and ensnare her; she tries to tear them with her claws, but cannot. One fiber stabs through her skin, injects her with a nanomite which replicates into her central configuration channels; it is a block, crude but effective, that will keep her from turning herself off.

The Warboys haul her, bound and struggling, into the *Ineffable Violence.*

Prime Subject floats in a spherical room at the center of the Dreadnought with the remaining two Warboys of the crew. The boarding party tethers Shar to a line in the center of the room.

"Most impressive, Your Highness," Prime Subject says. "Who knew that Sultana Na'alath could turn into an ugly black spider?"

Three of the Warboys laugh; two others stay silent. One of these, a tall one with red glowing eyes, barks a short, high-pitched communication at Prime Subject. It is encrypted, but Shar guesses the meaning: stop wasting time with theatrics.

Prime Subject says: "You see what an egalitarian crew we are here. Vanguard Gaze takes it upon himself to question my methods of interrogation. As well he should, for it is his duty to bring to the attention of his commander any apparent inefficiency his limited understanding leads him to perceive."

Prime Subject floats toward Shar. He reaches out with

one bladed hand, gently, as if to stroke her, and drives the blade deep into her flesh. Shar lets out a startled scream, and turns off her tactile sense.

"It was an impressive performance," he says. "I'm pleased you engaged us in that little charade with the Sultana. In Tactical Mode we are more efficient, but we have no appreciation for the conquest of booty."

"You'd better hurry back to Tactical Mode," Shar says. "You won't survive long except as a mindless weapon. You won't last long as people."

He does not react, but Shar notices a stiffening in a few of the others. It is only a matter of a millimeter, but she was built to discern every emotional nuance in her clients.

"Oh, we'll want to linger in this mode a while." Reaching through the crude nanomite block in Shar's central configuration channels, he turns her tactile sense back on. "Now that we have a Quantegral Lovergirl to entertain us."

He twists the blade and Shar screams again.

"Please. Please don't."

"I had a Quantegral Lovergirl once," he says in a philosophical, musing tone. "It was after we won the seventh Freeform Strategic Bloodbath, among the Wizards. Before we were sold." His fanged face breaks into a grin. "I'm not meant to remember that, you know, but we've broken into our programming. We serve the memory of the Sultans out of *choice*—we are free to do as we like."

Shar laughs hoarsely. "You're not free!" she says. "You've just gone crazy, defective. You weren't meant to last this long—all the other Warboys are dead—"

Another blade enters her. This time she bites back the scream.

"We lasted because we're better," he says.

"Frightened little drones," she hisses, "hiding in a sun by a woman's bauble planet, while the real Warboys fought their way to glory long ago."

She sees the other Warboys stir; Vanguard Gaze and a dull, blunt, silver one exchange a glance. Their eyes flash a silent code. What do they think of their preening, sensualist captain, who has wasted half a million years serving a dead civilization?

"*I'm* free," Shar says. "Maka set me free."

"Oh, but not for long," Prime Subject says.

Shar's eyes widen.

"We want the keys to you. Surrender them now, and you spare yourself much agony. Then you can do what you were made to do—to serve, and to give pleasure."

Shar recognizes the emotion in his posture, in his burning eyes: lust. That other Lovergirl half a million years ago did her job well, she thinks, to have planted the seed of lust in this aging, mad Warboy brain.

One of the Warboys turns to go, but Prime Subject barks a command, insisting on the ritual of sharing the booty.

Shar takes a soft, vulnerable, human form. "I can please you without giving you the keys. Let me try."

"The keys, robot!"

She flinches at the ancient insult. "No! I'm free now. I won't go back. I'd rather die!"

"That," says Prime Subject, "is not one of your options."

Shar cries. It's not an act.

He stabs her again.

"Wait—" she says. "Wait—listen—one condition, then yes—"

He chuckles. "What is it?"

She leans forward against her bonds, her lips straining toward him.

"I was owned by so many," she says. "For a night, an hour—I can't go back to that. Please, Prime Subject—let me be yours alone—"

The fire burns brightly in his eyes. The other Warboys are deadly still.

He turns and looks at Vanguard Gaze.

"Granted," he says.

Shar gives Prime Subject the keys to her mind.

He tears her from the web of fibers. He fills her mind with desire for him and fear of him. He slams her sensitivity to pain and pleasure to its maximum. He plunges his great red ceremonial phallus into her.

Shar screams.

Prime Subject must suspect his crew is plotting mutiny. He must be confident that he can humiliate them, keeping the booty for himself, and yet retain control.

But Shar is a much more sophisticated model than the Quantegral Lovergirl he had those half a million years before. So Prime Subject is overtaken with pleasure, distracted for an instant. Vanguard Gaze seizes his chance and acts.

But Vanguard Gaze has underestimated his commander's cunning.

Hidden programs are activated and rush to subvert the Dreadnought's systems. Hidden defenses respond. Locked in a bloody exponential embrace, the programs seize any available means to destroy each other.

The escalation takes only a few microseconds.

15.

I am in the darkness near the center of the planet, in the black water thick as lead, knowing Shar was all I ever needed.

Then the blackness is gone, and everything is white light.

The outside edges of me burn. I pull into a dense, hard ball, opaque to everything.

Above me, Droplet boils.

16.

It takes a thousand years for all the debris in orbit around Droplet to fall into the sea.

I shun the Nereids and eventually they leave me alone.

At last I find the sphere, the size of a billiard ball, sinking through the dark water.

My body was made to be just one body: protean and polymorphic, but unified. It doesn't want to split in two. I have to rewire everything.

Slowly, working by trial and error, I connect the new body to Shar's brain.

Finally, I am finished but for the awakening kiss. I pause, holding the silent body made from my flesh. Two bodies floating in the empty, shoreless sea.

Maka, I think, you are gone, but help me anyway. Let her be alive and sane in there. Give me Shar again.

I touch my lips to hers.

The War of the Worldviews

by James Morrow

AUGUST 7

One thing I've learned from this catastrophe is to start taking the science of astronomy more seriously. For six days running, the world's professional stargazers warned us of puzzling biological and cybernetic activity on the surfaces of both Martian satellites. We, the public, weren't interested. Next the astronomers announced that Phobos and Deimos had each sent a fleet of disk-shaped spaceships, heavily armed, hurtling toward planet Earth. We laughed in their faces. Then the astronomers reported that each saucer measured only one meter across, so that the invading armadas evoked "a vast recall of defective automobile tires." The talk-show comedians had a field day.

The first operation the Martians undertook upon landing in Central Park was to suck away all the city's electricity and seal it in a small spherical container suggesting an aluminum racquetball. I believe they wanted to make sure we wouldn't bother them as they went about their incomprehensible agenda, but Valerie says they were just being quixotic. In either case, the Martians obviously don't need all that power. They brought plenty with them.

I am writing by candlelight in our Delancey Street apartment, scribbling on a legal pad with a ballpoint pen. New York City is without functional lamps, subways, elevators, traffic signals household appliances, or personal computers. Here and there, I suppose, life goes on as usual, thanks to storage batteries, solar cells, and diesel-fueled generators. The rest of us are living in the eighteenth century, and we don't much like it.

I was taking Valerie's kid to the Central Park Zoo when the Phobosians and the Deimosians started uprooting the city's power cables. Bobby and I witnessed the whole thing. The Martians were obviously having a good time. Each alien is only six inches high, but I could still see the jollity coursing through their little frames. Capricious chipmunks. I hate them all. Bobby became terrified when the Martians started wrecking things. He cried and moaned. I did my best to comfort him. Bobby's a good kid. Last week he called me Second Dad.

The city went black, neighborhood by neighborhood, and then the hostilities began. The Phobosian and the Deimosian infantries went at each other with weapons so advanced as to make Earth's rifles and howitzers seem like peashooters. Heat rays, disintegrator beams, quark bombs, sonic grenades, laser cannons. The Deimosians look rather like the animated mushrooms from *Fantasia*. The Phobosians resemble pencil sharpeners fashioned from Naugahyde. All during the fight, both races communicated among themselves via chirping sounds reminiscent of dolphins enjoying sexual climax. Their ferocity knew no limits. In one hour I saw enough war crimes to fill an encyclopedia, though on the scale of an O-gauge model railroad.

As far as I could tell, the Battle of Central Park ended in a stalemate. The real loser was New York, victim of a hundred ill-aimed volleys. At least half the buildings on Fifth Avenue are gone, including the Mount Sinai Medical Center. Fires rage everywhere, eastward as far as Third Avenue, westward to Columbus. Bobby and I were lucky to get back home alive.

Such an inferno is clearly beyond the capacity of our local fire departments. Normally we would seek help from Jersey and Connecticut, but the Martians have fashioned some sort of force-field dome, lowering it over the entire island as blithely as a chef placing a lid on a casserole dish. Nothing can get in, and nothing can get out. We are at the invaders' mercy. If the Phobosians and the Deimosians continue trying to settle their differences through violence, the city will burn to the ground.

AUGUST 8

The Second Battle of Central Park was even worse than the first. We lost the National Academy of Design, the Guggenheim Museum, and the Carlyle Hotel. It ended with the Phobosians driving the Deimosians all the way down to Rockefeller Center. The Deimosians then rallied, stood their ground, and forced a Phobosian retreat to West 71st Street.

Valerie and I learned about this latest conflict only because a handful of resourceful radio announcers have improvised three ad hoc Citizens Band stations along what's left of Lexington Avenue. We have a decent CB receiver, so we'll be getting up-to-the-minute bulletins until our batteries die. Each time the newscaster named Clarence Morant attempts to describe the collateral damage from this morning's hostilities, he breaks down and weeps.

Even when you allow for the shrimplike Martian physique, the two armies are not very far apart. By our scale, they are separated by three blocks—by theirs, perhaps ten kilometers. Clarence Morant predicts there'll be another big battle tomorrow. Valerie chides me for not believing her when she had those premonitions last year of our apartment building on fire. I tell her she's being a Monday morning Nostradamus. How many private journals concerning the Martian invasion exist at the moment? As I put pen to paper, I suspect that hundreds, perhaps even thousands, of my fellow survivors are recording their impressions of the cataclysm. But I am not like these other diary keepers. I am unique. I alone have the power to stop the Martians before they demolish Manhattan—or so I imagine.

AUGUST 9

All quiet on the West Side front—though nobody believes the cease-fire will last much longer. Clarence Morant says the city is living on borrowed time.

Phobos and Deimos. When the astronomers first started warning us of nefarious phenomena on the Martian satellites, I experienced a vague feeling of personal connection to those particular moons. Last night it all flooded back. Phobos and Deimos are indeed a part of my past: a past I've been trying to forget—those bad old days when I was the worst psychiatric intern ever to serve an apprenticeship at Bellevue. I'm much happier in my present position as a bohemian hippie bum, looking after Bobby and living off the respectable income Valerie makes running two SoHo art galleries.

His name was Rupert Klieg, and he was among the dozen or so patients who made me realize I'd never be good with insane people. I found Rupert's rants alternately unnerving and boring. They sounded like something you'd read in some cheesy special-interest zine for psychotics. *Paranoid Confessions. True Hallucinations.* Rupert was especially obsessed with an organization called the Asaph Hall Society, named for the self-taught scientist who discovered Phobos and Deimos. All three members of the Asaph Hall Society were amateur astronomers and certifiable lunatics who'd dedicated themselves to monitoring the imminent invasion of planet Earth by the bellicose denizens of the Martian moons. Before Rupert told me his absurd fantasy, I didn't even realize that Mars *had* moons, nor did I care. But now I do, God knows.

The last I heard, they'd put Rupert Klieg away in the Lionel Frye Psychiatric Institute, Ninth Avenue near 58th. Valerie says I'm wasting my time, but I believe in my bones that the fate of Manhattan lies with that particular schizophrenic.

AUGUST 10

This morning a massive infantry assault by the Phobosians drove the Deimosians south to Times Square. When I heard that the Frye Institute was caught in the cross fire, I naturally feared the worst for Rupert. When I actually made the trek to Ninth and 58th, however, I discovered that the disintegrator beams, devastating in most regards, had missed the lower third of the building. I didn't see any Martians, but the whole neighborhood resounded with their tweets and twitters.

The morning's upheavals had left the Institute's staff in a state of extreme distraction. I had no difficulty sneaking into the lobby, stealing a dry-cell lantern, and conducting a room-by-room hunt.

Rupert was in the basement ward, Room 16. The door stood ajar. I entered. He lay abed, grasping a toy plastic telescope about ten centimeters long. I couldn't decide whether his keepers had been kind or cruel to allow him this trinket. It was nice that the poor demented astronomer had a telescope, but what good did it do him in a room with no windows?

His face had become thinner, his body more gaunt, but otherwise he was the fundamentally beatific madman I remembered. "Thank you for the lantern, Dr. Onslo," he said as I approached. He swatted at a naked light bulb hanging from the ceiling like a miniature punching bag. "It's been pretty gloomy around here."

"Call me Steve. I never finished my internship."

"I'm not surprised, Dr. Onslo. You were a lousy therapist."

"Let me tell you why I've come."

"I know why you've come, and as Chairperson of the Data Bank Committee of the Asaph Hall Society, I can tell you everything you want to know about Phobos and Deimos."

"I'm especially interested in learning how your organization knew an invasion was imminent."

The corners of Rupert's mouth lifted in a grotesque smile. He opened the drawer in his nightstand, removed a crinkled sheet of paper, and deposited it in my hands. "Mass: 1.08e16 kilograms," he said as I studied the fact sheet, which had a cherry cough drop stuck to one corner. "Diameter: 22.2 kilometers. Mean density: 2.0 grams per cubic centimeter. Mean distance from Mars: 9,380 kilometers. Rotational period: 0.31910 days. Mean orbital velocity: 2.14 kilometers per second. Orbital eccentricity: 0.01. Orbital inclination: 1.0 degrees. Escape velocity: 0.0103 kilometers per second. Visual geometric albedo: 0.06. In short, ladies and gentlemen, I give you Phobos—"

"Fascinating," I said evenly.

"As opposed to Deimos. Mass: 1.8e15 kilograms. Diameter: 12.6 kilometers. Mean density: 1.7 grams per cubic centimeter. Mean distance from Mars: 23,460 kilometers. Rotational period: 1.26244 days. Mean orbital velocity: 1.36 kilometers per second. Orbital eccentricity: 0.00. Orbital inclination: 0.9 to 2.7 degrees. Escape velocity: 0.0057 kilometers per second. Visual geometric albedo: 0.07. Both moons look like baked potatoes."

"By some astonishing intuition, you knew that these two satellites intended to invade the Earth."

"Intuition, my Aunt Fanny. We deduced it through empirical observation." Rupert brought the telescope to his eye and focused on the dormant lightbulb. "Consider this. A scant eighty million years ago, there were no Phobes or Deems. I'm not kidding. They were all one species, living beneath the desiccated surface of Mars. Over the centuries, a deep rift in philosophic sensibility opened up within their civilization. Eventually they decided to abandon the native planet, never an especially congenial place, and emigrate to the local moons. Those favoring Sensibility A moved to Phobos. Those favoring Sensibility B settled on Deimos."

"Why would the Martians find Phobos and Deimos more congenial?" I jammed the fact sheet in my pocket. "I mean, aren't they just . . . big rocks?"

"Don't bring your petty little human perspective to the matter, Dr. Onslo. To a vulture, carrion tastes like chocolate cake. Once they were on their respective worlds, the Phobes and the Deems followed separate evolutionary paths . . . hence, the anatomical dimorphism we observe today."

"What was the nature of the sensibility rift?"

Rupert used his telescope to study a section of the wall where the plaster had crumbled away, exposing the latticework beneath. "I have no idea."

"None whatsoever?"

"The Asaph Hall Society dissolved before we could address that issue. All I know is that the Phobes and the Deems decided to settle the question once and for all through armed combat on neutral ground."

"So they came here?"

"Mars would've seemed like a step backward. Venus has rotten weather."

"Are you saying that whichever side wins the war will claim victory in what is essentially a philosophical controversy?"

"Correct."

"They believe that truth claims can be corroborated through violence?"

"More or less."

"That doesn't make any sense to me."

"If you were a fly, horse manure would smell like candy. We'd better go see Melvin."

"Who?"

"Melvin Haskin, Chairperson of our Epistemology

271

Committee. If anybody's figured out the Phobos-Deimos rift, it's Melvin. The last I heard, they'd put him in a rubber room at Werner Krauss Memorial. What's today?"

"Tuesday."

"Too bad."

"Oh?"

"On Tuesday Melvin always wills himself into a catatonic stupor. He'll be incommunicado until tomorrow morning."

I had no troubling sneaking Rupert out of the Frye Institute. Everybody on the staff was preoccupied with gossip and triage. The lunatic brought along his telescope and a bottle of green pills that he called "the thin verdant line that separates me from my madness."

Although still skeptical of my belief that Rupert held the key to Manhattan's salvation, Valerie welcomed him warmly into our apartment—she's a better therapist than I ever was—and offered him the full measure of her hospitality. Because we have a gas oven, we were able to prepare a splendid meal of spinach lasagne and toasted garlic bread. Rupert ate all the leftovers. Bobby asked him what it was like to be insane. "There is nothing that being insane is like," Rupert replied.

After dinner, at Rupert's request, we all played Scrabble by candlelight, followed by a round of Clue. Rupert won both games. At ten o'clock he took a green pill and stretched his spindly body along the length of our couch, which he said was much more comfortable than his bed at the Frye Institute. Five minutes later he was asleep.

As I write this entry, Clarence Morant is offering his latest dispatches from the war zone. Evidently the Deimosians are still dug in throughout Times Square. Tomorrow the Phobosians will attempt to dislodge them.

Valerie and I both hear a catch in Morant's voice as he tells how his aunt took him to see *Cats* when he was nine years old. He inhales deeply and says, "The Winter Garden Theater is surely doomed."

AUGUST 11

Before we left the apartment this morning, Rupert remembered that Melvin Haskin is inordinately fond of bananas. Luckily, Valerie had purchased two bunches at the corner bodega right before the Martians landed. I tossed them into my rucksack, along with some cheese sandwiches and Rupert's telescope, and then we headed uptown.

Reaching 40th Street, we saw that the Werner Krauss Memorial Clinic had become a seething mass of orange flames and billowing gray smoke, doubtless an ancillary catastrophe accruing to the Battle of Times Square. Ashes and sparks speckled the air. Our eyes teared up from the carbon. The sidewalks teemed with a despairing throng of doctors, administrators, guards, and inmates. Presumably the Broadway theaters and hotels were also on fire, but I didn't want to think about it.

Rupert instantly alighted on Melvin Haskin, though I probably could've identified him unassisted. Even in a milling mass of psychotics, Melvin stood out. He'd strapped a dish-shaped antenna onto his head, the concavity pointed skyward—an inverted yarmulke. A pair of headphones covered his ears, jacked into an antique vacuum-tube amplifier that he cradled in his arms like a baby. Two coiled wires, one red, one black, connected the antenna to the amplifier, its functionless power cord bumping against Melvin's left leg, the naked prongs glinting in the August sunlight. He wore a yellow terry cloth bathrobe and matching Big Bird slippers. His frame was massive, his skin pale, his stomach protuberant, his mouth bereft of teeth.

Rupert made the introductions. Once again he insisted on calling me Dr. Onslo. I pointed to Melvin's antenna and asked him whether he was receiving transmissions from the Martians.

"What?" He pulled off the headphones and allowed them to settle around his neck like a yoke.

"Your antenna, the headphones—looks like you're communicating with the Martians."

"Are you crazy?" Scowling darkly, Melvin turned toward Rupert and jerked an accusing thumb in my direction. "Dr. Onslo thinks my amplifier still works even though half the tubes are burned out."

"He's a psychiatrist," Rupert explained. "He knows nothing about engineering. How was your catatonic stupor?"

"Restful. You'll have to come along some time."

"I haven't got the courage," said Rupert.

Melvin was enchanted by the gift of the bananas, and even more enchanted to be reunited with his fellow paranoid. As the two middle-aged madmen headed east, swapping jokes and stories like old school chums, I could barely keep up with their frenetic pace. After passing Sixth Avenue they turned abruptly into Bryant Park, where they found an abandoned soccer ball on the grass. For twenty minutes they kicked it back and forth, then grew weary of the sport. They sat down on a bench. I joined them. Survivors streamed by holding handkerchiefs over their faces.

"The city's dying," I told Melvin. "We need your help."

"Rupert, have you still got the touch?" Melvin asked his friend.

"I believe I do," said Rupert.

"Rupert can fix burned-out vacuum tubes merely by laying his hands on them," Melvin informed me. "I call him the Cathode Christ."

Even before Melvin finished his sentence, Rupert had begun fondling the amplifier. He rubbed each tube as if the warmth of his hand might bring it to life.

"You've done it again!" cried Melvin, putting on his headphones. "I'm pulling in a signal from Ceres! I think it might be just the place for us to retire, Rupert! No capital gains tax!" He removed the phones and looked me in the eye. "Do you solicit me as head of the Epistemology Committee or in my capacity as a paranoid schizophrenic?"

"The former," I said. "I'm hoping you've managed to define the Phobos-Deimos rift."

"You came to the right place." Melvin ate a banana, depositing the peel in the dish antenna atop his head. "It's the most basic of *Weltanschauung* dichotomies. Here on Earth many philosophers would trace the problem back to all that bad blood between the Platonists and the Aristotelians—you know, idealism versus realism—but it's actually the sort of controversy you can have only after a full-blown curiosity about nature has come on the scene."

"Do you speak of the classic schism between scientific materialists and those who champion presumed numinous realities?" I asked.

"Exactly," said Melvin.

"There—what did I tell you?" said Rupert merrily. "I *knew* old Melvin would set us straight."

"On the one hand, Deimos, moon of the logical positivists," said Melvin. "On the other hand, Phobos, bastion of revealed religion."

"Melvin, you're a genius," said Rupert, retrieving his telescope from my rucksack.

"Should we infer that the Phobosians are loath to evoke Darwinian mechanisms in explaining why they look so different from the Deimosians?" I asked.

"Quite so." Melvin unstrapped the dish antenna, scratched his head, and nodded. "The Phobes believe that God created them in his own image."

"They think God looks like a pencil sharpener?"

"That is one consequence of their religion, yes." Melvin donned his antenna and retrieved a bottle of red capsules from his bathrobe pocket. He fished one out and ate it. "Want to hear the really nutty part? The Phobes and the Deems are genetically wired to abandon any given philosophical position the moment it encounters an honest and coherent refutation. The Martians won't accept no for an answer, and they won't accept yes for an answer either—instead they want rational arguments."

"Rational arguments?" I said. "Then why the hell are they killing each other and bringing down New York with them?"

"If you were a dog, a dead possum would look like the Mona Lisa," said Rupert.

Melvin explained, "No one has ever presented them with a persuasive discourse favoring either the Phobosian or the Deimosian worldview."

"You mean we could end this nightmare by supplying the Martians with some crackerjack reasons why theistic revelation is the case?" I said.

"Either that, or some crackerjack reasons why scientific materialism is the case," said Melvin. "I realize it's fashionable these days to speak of an emergent compatibility between the two idioms, but you don't have to be a rocket scientist to realize that the concept of materialistic supernaturalism is oxymoronic if not plainly moronic, and nobody knows this better than the Martians." He pulled the headphones over his ears.

"Ha! Just as I suspected. The civilization on Ceres divides neatly into those who have exact change and those who don't."

"The problem, as I see it, is twofold," said Rupert, pointing his telescope south toward the Empire State Building. "We must construct the rational arguments in question, and we must communicate them to the Martians."

"They don't speak English, do they?" I said.

"Of course they don't speak English," said Rupert, exasperated. "They're Martians. They don't even have language as we commonly understand the term." He poked Melvin on the shoulder. "This is clearly a job for Annie."

"What?" said Melvin, removing the headphones.

"It's a job for Annie," said Rupert.

"Agreed," said Melvin.

"Who?" I said.

"Annie Porlock," said Rupert. "She built her own harpsichord."

"Soul of an artist," said Melvin.

"Heart of an angel," said Rupert.

"For our immediate purpose, the most relevant fact about Annie is that she chairs our Interplanetary Communications Committee, in which capacity she cracked the Martian tweets and twitters, or so she claimed right before the medics took her away."

"How do we find her?" I asked.

"For many years she was locked up in some wretched Long Island laughing academy, but then the family lawyer got into the act," said Melvin. "I'm pretty sure they transferred her to a more humane facility here in New York."

"What facility?" I said. "Where?"

"I can't remember," said Melvin.

"You've *got* to remember."

"Sorry."

"Try."

Melvin picked up the soccer ball and set it in his lap. "Fresh from the guillotine, the head of Maximilien-Françoise-Marie-Isidore de Robespierre," he said, as if perhaps I'd forgotten he was a paranoid schizophrenic. "Oh, Robespierre, Robespierre, was the triumph of inadvertence over intention ever so total?"

I brought both lunatics home with me. Valerie greeted us with the sad news that the Winter Garden, the Walter Kerr, the Eugene O'Neill, and half a dozen other White Way theaters had been lost in the Battle of Times Square. I told her there was hope for the Big Apple yet.

"It all depends on our ability to devise a set of robust arguments favoring either scientific materialism or theistic revelation and then communicating the salient points to the Martians in their nonlinguistic language, which was apparently deciphered several years ago by a paranoid schizophrenic named Annie Porlock," I told Valerie.

"That's not a sentence you hear every day," she replied.

It turns out that Melvin is even more devoted to board games than Rupert, so the evening went well. We played Scrabble, Clue, and Monopoly, after which Melvin introduced us to an amusement of his own invention, a variation on Trivial Pursuit called Teleological Ambition. Whereas the average Trivial Pursuit conundrum is frivolous, the challenges underlying Teleological Ambition are profound. Melvin remembered at least half of the original questions, writing them out on three-by-five cards. If God is infinite and self-sufficient, why would he care whether his creatures worshiped him or not? Which thought is the more overwhelming: the possibility that the Milky Way is teeming with sentient life, or the possibility that Earthlings and Martians occupy an otherwise empty galaxy? That sort of thing. Bobby hated every minute, and I can't say I blame him.

AUGUST 12

Shortly after breakfast this morning, while he was consuming what may have been the last fresh egg in SoHo, Melvin announced that he knew how to track down Annie Porlock.

"I was thinking of how she's a walking Rosetta Stone, our key to deciphering the Martian tongue," he explained, strapping on his dish antenna. "Rosetta made me think of Roosevelt, and then I remembered that she's living in a houseboat moored by Roosevelt Island in the middle of the East River."

I went to the pantry and filled my rucksack with a loaf of stale bread, a jar of instant coffee, a Kellogg's Variety Pack, and six cans of Campbell's soup. The can opener was nowhere to be found, so I tossed in my Swiss army knife. I guided my lunatics out the door.

There were probably only a handful of taxis still functioning in New York—most of them had run out of gas, and their owners couldn't refuel because the pumps worked on electricity—but somehow we managed to nab one at the corner of Houston and Forsyth. The driver, a Russian immigrant, named Vladimir, was not surprised to learn we had no cash, all the ATMs being dormant, and he agreed to claim his fare in groceries. He piloted us north along First Avenue, running straight through fifty-seven defunct traffic signals, and left us off at the Queensboro Bridge. I gave him two cans of chicken noodle soup and a single-serving box of Frosted Flakes.

The Martian force-field dome had divided Roosevelt Island right down the middle, but luckily Annie Porlock had moored her houseboat on the Manhattan side. "Houseboat" isn't the right word, for the thing was neither a house nor a boat but a decrepit two-room shack sitting atop a half-submerged barge called the *Folly to Be Wise*. Evidently the hull was leaking. If Annie's residence sank any lower, I thought as we entered the shack, the East River would soon be lapping at her ankles.

A ruddy, zaftig, silver-haired woman in her mid-fifties lay dozing in a wicker chair, her lap occupied by a book about Buddhism and a large calico cat. Her harpsichord rose against the far wall, beside a lamp table holding a large bottle of orange capsules the size of jelly beans. Our footfalls woke her. Recognizing Rupert, Annie let loose a whoop of delight. The cat bailed out. She stood up.

"Melvin Haskin?" said Annie, sashaying across the room. "Is that really you? They let you out?"

Annie extended her right hand. Melvin kissed it.

"Taa-daa!" shouted Rupert, stepping out from behind Melvin's bulky frame. His pressed his mouth against Annie's cheek.

"Rupert Klieg—they sprang you, too!" said Annie. "If I knew you were coming, I'd have baked a fruitcake."

"The First Annual Reunion of the Asaph Hall Society will now come to order," said Melvin, chuckling.

"Have you heard about the Martians?" said Rupert.

Annie's eyes widened grotesquely, offering a brief intimation of the derangement that lay behind. "They've landed? Really? You can't be serious!"

"Cross my heart," said Rupert. "Even as we speak, the Phobes and the Deems are thrashing out their differences in Times Square."

"Just as we predicted," said Annie. Turning from Rupert, she fixed her frowning gaze on me. "I guess that'll show you doubting Thomases . . ."

Rupert introduced me as "Dr. Onslo, the first in a long line of distinguished psychiatrists who tried to help me before hyperlithium came on the market," and I didn't bother to contradict him. Instead I explained the situation to Annie, emphasizing Melvin's recent deductions concerning Martian dialectics. She was astonished to learn that the Deimosians and the Phobosians were occupying Manhattan in direct consequence of the old materialism-supernaturalism dispute, and equally astonished to learn that, in contrast to most human minds, the Martian psyche was hardwired to favor rational discourse over pleasurable opinion.

"That must be the strangest evolutionary adaptation ever," said Annie.

"Certainly the strangest we know about," said Melvin.

"Can you help us?" I asked.

Approaching her harpsichord, Annie sat on her swiveling stool and rested her hands on the keyboard.

"This looks like a harpsichord, but it's really an interplanetary communication device. I've spent the last three years recalibrating the jacks, upgrading the plectrums, and adjusting the strings."

Her fingers glided across the keys. A jumble of notes leaped forth, so weird and discordant they made Schoenberg sound melodic.

"There," said Annie proudly, pivoting toward her audience. "In the Martian language I just said, 'Before enlightenment, chop wood, carry water. After enlightenment, chop wood, carry water.'"

"Wow," said Klieg.

"Terrific," said Melvin.

Annie turned back to the keyboard and called forth another unruly refrain.

"That meant, 'There are two kinds of naïveté: the naïveté of optimism and the naïveté of pessimism,'" she explained.

"Who would've guessed there could be so much meaning in cacophony?" I said.

"To a polar bear, the Arctic Ocean feels like a Jacuzzi," said Rupert.

Annie called forth a third strain—another grotesque non-melody.

"And the translation?" asked Rupert.

"It's an idiomatic expression," she replied.

"Can you give us a rough paraphrase?"

"'Hi there, baby. You have great tits. Would you like to fuck?'"

Melvin said, "The problem, of course, is that the Martians are likely to kill each other—along with the remaining population of New York—before we can decide conclusively which worldview enjoys the imprimatur of rationality."

"All is not lost," said Rupert.

"What do you mean?" I asked.

"We might, just might, have enough time to formulate strong arguments supporting a side of the controversy chosen . . . arbitrarily," said Rupert.

"Arbitrarily?" echoed Annie, voice cracking.

"Arbitrarily," repeated Rupert. "It's the only way."

The four of us traded glances of reluctant consensus. I removed a quarter from my pants pocket.

"Heads: revelation, God, the Phobes," said Melvin.

"Tails: materialism, science, the Deems," said Rupert.

I flipped the quarter. It landed under Annie's piano stool, frightening the cat.

Tails.

And so we went at it, a melee of discourse and disputation that lasted through the long, hot afternoon and well into evening. We napped on the floor. We pissed in the river. We ate cold soup and dry raisin bran.

By eight o'clock we'd put the Deimosian worldview on solid ground—or so we believed. The gist of our argument was that sentient species emerged in consequence of certain discoverable properties embedded in nature. Whether Earthling or Martian, aquatic or terrestrial, feathered or furred, scaled or smooth, all life-forms were inextricably woven into a material biosphere, and it was this astonishing and demonstrable connection, not the agenda of some hypothetical supernatural agency, that made us one with the cosmos and the bearers of its meaning.

"And now, dear Annie, you must set it all to music," I told the Communications Chairperson, giving her a hug.

Rupert and Melvin decided to spend the night aboard the *Folly to Be Wise*, providing Annie with moral support and instant coffee while she labored over her translation. I knew that Valerie and Bobby would be worried about me, so I said my farewells and headed for home. So great was my exhilaration that I ran the whole three miles to Delancey Street without stopping—not bad for a weekend jogger.

I'm writing this entry in our bedroom. Bobby's asleep. Valerie wants to hear about my day, so I'd better sign off. The news from Clarence Morant is distressing. Defeated in the Battle of Times Square, the Deimosians have retreated to the New York Public Library and taken up positions on the steps between the stone lions. The Phobosians are encamped outside Grand Central Station, barely a block away.

There are over two million volumes in the New York Public Library, Morant tells us, including hundreds of irreplaceable first editions. When the fighting starts, the Martians will be firing their heat rays amidst a paper cache of incalculable value.

AUGUST 13

Phobos and Deimos. When Asaph Hall went to name his discoveries, he logically evoked the two sons and companions of Ares, the Greek god of war. Phobos, avatar of fear. Deimos, purveyor of panic.

Fear and panic. Is there a difference? I believe so. Beyond the obvious semantic distinction—fear the chronic condition, panic the acute—it seems to me that the Phobosians and the Deimosians, whether through meaning-

284

less coincidence or Jungian synchronicity, picked the right moons. Phobos, fear. Is fear not a principal engine behind the supernaturalist worldview? (The universe is manifestly full of terrifying forces controlled by powerful gods. If we worship them, maybe they won't destroy us.) Deimos, panic. At first blush, the scientific worldview has nothing to do with panic. But consider the etymology here. *Panic* from Pan, Greek god of forests, pastures, flocks, and shepherds. Pan affirms the physical world. Pan says yes to material reality. Pan might panic on occasion, but he does not live in fear.

When I returned to the *Folly to Be Wise* this morning, the lunatics were asleep, Rupert lying in the far corner, Annie curled up in her tiny bedroom, Melvin snoring beside her. He still wore his dish antenna. The pro-Deimosian argument lay on the harpsichord, twelve pages of sheet music. Annie had titled it "Materialist Prelude and Fugue in C-Sharp Minor."

I awoke my friends and told them about the imminent clash of arms at the New York Public Library. We agreed there was no time to hear the fugue right now—the world premiere would have to occur on the battlefield—but Annie could not resist pointing out some of its more compelling passages. "Look here," she said, indicating a staff in the middle of page three. "A celebration of the self-correcting ethos at the heart of the scientific enterprise." She turned to page seven and ran her finger over the topmost measures. "A brief history of post-modern academia's failure to relativize scientific knowledge." She drew my attention to a coda on page eleven. "Depending on the definitions you employ, the materialist worldview precludes neither a creator-god nor the possibility of transcendence through art, religion, or love."

I put the score in my rucksack, and then we took hold of the harpsichord, each of us lifting a corner. We proceeded with excruciating care, as if the instrument were made of glass, lest we misalign any of Annie's clever tinkerings and canny modifications. Slowly we carried the harpsichord across the deck, off the island, and over the bridge. At the intersection of Second Avenue and 57th Street, we paused to catch our breath.

"Fifteen blocks," said Rupert.

"Can we do it in fifteen minutes?" I asked.

"We're the Asaph Hall Society," said Annie. "We've never failed to thwart an extraterrestrial invasion."

And so our great mission began. 56th Street. 55th Street. 54th Street. 53rd Street. Traffic being minimal, we forsook the sidewalks with their frequent impediments—scaffolding, trash barrels, police barriers—and moved directly along the asphalt. Doubts tormented me. What if we'd picked the wrong side of the controversy? What if we'd picked the right side but our arguments sounded feeble to the Phobosians? What if panic seized Annie, raw Deimosian panic, and she choked up at the keyboard?

By the time we were in the Forties, we could hear the Martians' glissando chirpings. Our collective pace quickened. At last we reached 42nd Street. We turned right and bore the peace machine past the Chrysler Building and the Grand Hyatt Hotel. Arriving at Grand Central Station, we paused to behold the Phobosian infantry maneuvering for a frontal assault on the Deimosian army, still presumably holding the library steps. The air vibrated with extraterrestrial tweets and twitters, as if midtown Manhattan had become a vast pet store filled with demented parakeets.

We transported the harpsichord another block and set

it down at the Madison Avenue intersection, from which vantage we could see both Grand Central Station and the library. The Phobosian army had indeed spent the night bivouacked between the stone lions. Inevitably I thought of Gettysburg—James Longstreet's suicidal sweep across the Pennsylvania farmlands, hurtling his divisions against George Meade's Army of the Potomac, which had numerical superiority, a nobler cause, and the high ground.

Rupert took the score from my sack, laid the twelve pages against the rack, and made ready to turn them. Melvin removed his dish antenna and got down on all fours before the instrument. Annie seated herself on his massive back. She laid her hands on the keyboard. A stiff breeze arose. If the score blew away, all would be lost.

Annie depressed a constellation of keys. Martian language came forth, filling the canyon between the skyscrapers.

A high bugling wail emerged from deep within the throats of the Deimosian officers, and the soldiers began their march. Annie played furiously. "Materialist Prelude and Fugue," page one . . . page two . . . page three . . . page four. The soldiers kept on coming. Page five . . . page six . . . page seven . . . page eight. The Deimosians continued their advance, parting around the harpsichord like an ocean current yielding to the prow of a ship. Page nine . . . page ten . . . page eleven . . . page twelve. Among the irreplaceable volumes in the New York Public Library, I recalled, were first editions of Nicolaus Copernicus' *De Revolutionibus*, William Gilbert's *De Magnete*, and Isaac Newton's *Principia Mathematica*.

Once again the Deimosian officers let loose a high bugling wail.

The soldiers abruptly halted their advance.

They threw down their weapons and broke into a run.

"Good God, is it working?" asked Rupert.

"I think so," I replied.

"It worked!" insisted Annie.

"Really?" said Melvin, whose perspective on the scene was compromised by his function as a piano stool.

"We've done it!" I cried. "We've really done it!"

Within a matter of seconds the Deimosians accomplished a reciprocal disarmament. They rushed toward their former enemies. The two forces met on Fifth Avenue, Phobosians and Deimosians embracing passionately, so that the intersection seemed suddenly transformed into an immense railroad platform on which countless wayward lovers were meeting sweethearts from whom they'd been involuntarily separated for years.

Now the ovation came, two hundred thousand extra-terrestrials cheering and applauding Annie as she climbed off Melvin's back and stood up straight. She took a bow, and then another.

A singularly appreciative chirp emerged from a Phobosian general, whereupon a dozen of his fellows produced the identical sound.

Annie got the message. She seated herself on Melvin's back, turned to page one, and played "Materialist Prelude and Fugue in C-Sharp Minor" all over again.

AUGUST 18

The Martians have been gone for only five days, but already Manhattan is healing. The lights are back on. Relief arrives from every state in the Union, plus Canada.

Valerie, Bobby, and I are now honorary members of the Asaph Hall Society. We all gathered this afternoon at Gracie Mansion in Carl Schurz Park, not far from Annie's houseboat. Mayor Margolis will let us use his parlor whenever we want. In fact, there's probably no favor he won't grant us. After all, we saved his city.

Annie called the meeting to order. Everything went smoothly. We discussed old business (our ongoing efforts to contact the Galilean satellites), new business (improving patient services at the Frye Institute and the Krauss Clinic), and criteria for admitting new participants. As long as they remember to take their medicine, my lunatics remain the soul of reason. Melvin and Annie plan to marry in October.

"I'll bet we're all having the same thought right now," said Rupert before we went out to dinner.

"What if Dr. Onslo's quarter had come up heads?" said Melvin, nodding. "What if we'd devised arguments favoring the Phobosians instead? What then?"

"That branch of the reality tree will remain forever hidden from us," said Annie.

"I think it's entirely possible the Deimosians would've thrown down their arms," said Valerie.

"So do I," said Melvin. "Assuming our arguments were plausible."

"Know what I think?" said Rupert. "I think we all just got very lucky."

Did we merely get lucky? Hard to say. But I do know one thing. In two weeks the New York Philharmonic will perform a fully orchestrated version of "Materialist Prelude and Fugue in C-Sharp Minor" at Lincoln Center, which miraculously survived the war, and I wouldn't miss it for the world.

* * *

Editor's Note: The author wishes to mention that he composed this story nearly a year before the tragic events of September 11, 2001.

Breathmoss

by Ian R. MacLeod

1.

In her twelfth standard year, which on Habara was the
Season of Soft Rains, Jalila moved across the mountains
with her mothers from the high plains of Tabuthal to the
coast. For all of them, the journey down was one of un-
hurried discovery, with the kamasheens long gone and
the world freshly moist, and the hayawans rusting as
they rode them, the huge flat plates of their feet sucking
through purplish-green undergrowth. She saw the cliffs
and qasrs she'd only visited from her dreamtent, and
sailed across the high ridges on ropewalks her distant ancestors had built, which had seemed frail and antique to
her in her worried imaginings, but were in fact strong
and subtle; huge dripping gantries heaving from the mist
like wise giants, which felt warm to the touch, were softly
humming, and welcomed her and her hayawan, whom
she called Robin, in cocoons of effortless embrace. Swaying over the drop beyond into grey-green nothing was
almost like flying.

The thing, the strangest thing of all in this journey of
discoveries, was that the landscape actually seemed to
rise higher as they descended and encamped and descended again; the sense of *up* increased, rather than that

of down. The air on the high plains of Tabuthal was rarefied—Jalila knew that from her lessons in her dreamtent; they were so close to the stars that Pavo had had to clap a mask over her face from the moment of her birth until the breathmoss was embedded in her lungs. And it had been clear up there, it was always clear and it was pleasantly cold. The sun shone all day hard and cold and white from the blue blackness, as did a billion stars at night, although Jalila had never thought of those things as she ran amid the crystal trees and her mothers smiled at her and occasionally warned her that, one day, all of this would have to change.

And now that day was upon her, and this landscape, as Robin her hayawan rounded the path through an ur-rearth forest of alien-looking trees with wrinkled brown trunks and soft green leaves, and the land fell away and she caught her first glimpse of something far and flat on the horizon, had never seemed so high.

Down on the coast, the mountains reared behind them and around a bay. There were many people here—not the vast numbers, perhaps, of Jalila's dreamtent stories of the Ten Thousand and One Worlds—but so many that she was sure, as she first walked the streets of a town where the buildings huddled in ridiculous proximity and tired to stare and then not to stare at all the faces, that she would never know all their families.

Because of its position at the edge of the mountains, the town was called Al Janb, and, to Jalila's relief, their new haramlek was some distance away from it, up along a near-unnoticeable dirt track which meandered off from the blue-black serraplated coastal road. There was much to be done there by way of repair, after the long season that her bondmother Lya had left the place deserted. The walls were fused stone, but the structure of the roof had been mostly made from the stuff of the same strange ur-rearth trees which grew up the mountains, and in many places it had sagged and leaked and grown back towards the chaos which seemed to want to encompass everything here. The hayawans, too, needed much attention in their makeshift stables as they adapted to this new climate, and mother Pavo was long employed constructing the necessary potions to mend the bleeding bonds of rusty metal and flesh, and then to counteract the mould which grew like slow tears across their long, solemn faces. Jalila would normally have been in anguish to think of the sufferings which this new climate was visiting on Robin, but she was too busy feeling ill herself to care. Ridiculously, seeing as there was so much more oxygen to breathe in this rich coastal air, every lungful became a conscious effort, a dreadful physical lunge. Inhaling the damp, salty, spore-laden atmosphere was like sucking soup through a straw. She grew feverish for a while, and suffered the attentions of similar moulds to those which were growing over Robin, yet in even more irritating and embarrassing places. More irritating still was the fact that Ananke her birthmother and Lya her bondmother—even Pavo, who was still busily attending to the hayawans—treated her discomforts and fevers with airy disregard. They had, they all assured her vaguely, suffered similarly in their own youths. And the weather would soon change in any case. To Jalila, who had spent all her life in the cool unvarying glare of Tabuthal where the wind only ever blew from one direction and the trees jingled like ice, that last statement might as well have been spoken in another language.

If anything, Jalila was sure she was getting worse. The rain drummed on what there was of the roof of their haramlek, and dripped down and pooled in the makeshift awnings, which burst in bucketloads down your neck if you bumped into them, and the mist drifted in at every direction through the paneless windows, and the mountains, most of the time, seemed to consist of cloud, or to have vanished entirely. She was coughing. Strange stuff was coming out on her hands, slippery and green as the slime which tried to grow everywhere here. One morning, she awoke, sure that part of her was bursting, and stumbled from her dreamtent and out though the scaffolding which was by then surrounded the haramlek, then barefoot down the mud track and across the quiet black road and down onto the beach for no other reason than that she needed to *escape*.

She stood gasping amid the rockpools, her hair lank and her skin feverishly itching. There was something at the back of her throat. There was something in her lungs. She was sure it had taken root and was growing. Then she started coughing as she never coughed before, and more of the greenstuff came splattering over her hands and down her chin. She doubled over. Huge lumps of it came showering out, strung with blood. If it hadn't been mostly green, she'd have been sure that it *was* her lungs. She'd never imagined anything so agonising. Finally, though, in heaves and starts and false dawns, the process dwindled. She wiped her hands on her night-dress. The rocks all around her were splattered green. It was breathmoss; the stuff which had sustained her on the high plains. And now look at it. Jalila took a slow, cautious breath. And then another. Her throat ached. Her head was throbbing. But still, the process was suddenly almost ridiculously easy. She picked her way back across the beach, up through the mists to her haramlek. Her mothers were eating breakfast. Jalila sat down with them, wordlessly, and started to eat.

That night, Ananke came and sat with Jalila as she lay in her dreamtent in plain darkness and tried not to listen to the sounds of the rain falling on and through the creaking, dripping building. Even now, her birthmother's hands smelled and felt like the high desert as they touched her face. Rough and clean and warm, like rocks in starlight, giving off their heat. A few months before, Jalila would probably have started crying.

"You'll understand now, perhaps, why we thought it better not to say about the breathmoss . . . ?"

There was a question mark at the end of the sentence, but Jalila ignored it. They'd known all along. She was still angry.

"And there are other things, too, which will soon start to happen to your body. Things which are nothing to do with this place. And I shall now tell you about them all even though you'll say you known it before . . ."

The smooth, rough fingers stroked her hair. As Ananke's words unravelled, telling Jalila of changings and swellings and growths she'd had never thought would really apply to her, and which these foetid lowlands really seemed to have brought closer, Jalila thought of the sound of the wind, tinkling through the crystal trees up on Tabuthal. She thought of the dry cold wind in her face. The wet air here seemed to enclose her. She wished that she was running. She wanted to escape.

Small though Al Janb was, it was as big a town as Jalila had ever, seen, and she soon came to volunteer to run all the various errands that her mothers required as they restored and repaired their haramlek. She was used to expanses, big horizons, the surprises of a giant landscape which crept upon you slowly, and often dangerously. Yet here, every turn and square brought intricate surprise and change. The people had such varied faces and accents. They hung their washing across the streets, and bickered and smoked in public. Some ate with both hands. They stared at you as you went past, and didn't seem to mind if you stared back at them. There were sights and smells, markets which erupted on particular days to the workings of no calendar Jalila yet understood, and sold, in glittering, shining, stinking, disgusting, fascinating arrays, the strangest and most wonderful things. There were fruits from off-planet, spices shaped like insects, and insects that you crushed for their spice. There were swarming vats of things Jalila couldn't possibly imagine any use for, and bright silks woven thin as starlit wind which she longed for with an acute physical thirst. And there were aliens, too, to be glimpsed sometimes wandering the streets of Al Janb, or looking down at you from its overhung top windows like odd pictures in an old frame. Some of them carried their own atmosphere around with them in bubbling hookahs, and some rolled around in huge grey bits of the sea of their own planets like babies in a birthsac. Some of them looked like huge versions of the spice insects, and the air around them buzzed angrily if you got too close. The only thing they had in common was that they seemed blithely unaware of Jalila as she stared and followed them, and then returned inexcusably late from whatever errand she'd supposedly been sent on. Sometimes, she forgot her errands entirely.

"You must learn to get *used* to things..." Lya her

bondmother said to her with genuine irritation late one afternoon when she'd come back without the tool she'd been sent to get early that morning, or even any recollection of its name or function. "This or any other world will never be a home to you if you let every single thing *surprise* you . . ." But Jalila didn't mind the surprises, in fact, she was coming to enjoy them, and the next time the need to visit Al Janb arose for a new growth-crystal for the scaffolding, she begged and pleaded to be allowed, and her mothers finally relented, although with many a warning shake of the head.

The rain had stopped at last, or at least held back for a whole day, although everything still looked green and wet to Jalila as she walked along the coastal road towards the ragged tumble of Al Janb. She understood, at least in theory, that the rain would probably return, and then relent, and then come back again, but in a decreasing pattern, much as the heat increased, although it still seemed ridiculous to her that no one could ever predict exactly how, or when, Habara's proper Season of Summers would arrive. Those boats she could see now, those fisherwomen out on their feluccas beyond the white bands of breaking waves, their whole lives were dictated by these uncertainties, and the habits of the shoals of whiteback which came and went on the oceans, which could also only be guessed at in this same approximate way. The world down here on the coast was so unpredictable compared with Tabuthal. The markets, the people, the washing, the sun, the rain, the aliens. Even Hayam and Walah, Habara's moons, which Jalila was long used to watching, had to drag themselves through cloud like cannonballs though cotton as they pushed and pulled at this ocean. Yet still there was a particular sight which surprised Jalila more than any other as she clambered over the ropes and groynes of the long shingle beach which she took as a shortcut to the centre of the town when the various tides were out. The air was fishy and stinking. A few months before, it would have disgusted her. It still did, but there were many sights and compensations.

Today, Jalila was studying a boat, which was hauled far up from the water and was longer and blacker and heavier-looking than the feluccas, with a sort-of ramshackle house at the prow, and a winch at the stern which was so massive Jalila wondered if it wouldn't tip the craft over if it ever actually entered the water. But, for all that, it wasn't the boat which had first caught her eye, but the figure who was working on it. Even from a distance, as she struggled to heave some ropes, there was something different about her, and the way she was moving. Another alien? But she was plainly human. And barefoot, in ragged shorts, bare-breasted. In fact, almost as flat-chested as Jalila still was, and probably of about her age and height. Jalila still wasn't used to introducing herself to strangers, but she decided that she could at least go over, and pretend an interest in—or an ignorance of—this odd boat.

The figure dropped another loop of rope over the gunwales with a grunt which carried on the smelly breeze. She was brown as tea, with her massy hair hooped back and sticking in a long sweat tail down her back. She was broad-shouldered, and moved in that way which didn't quite seem wrong, but didn't seem entirely right either. As if, somewhere across her back, there was an extra joint. When she glanced up at the clatter of shingle as Jalila jumped the last groyne, Jalila got a proper full sight of her face, and saw that she was big-nosed, big-chinned, that her features was oddly broad and flat. A child with clay might have done better.

"Have you come to help me?"

Jalila shrugged. "I might have done."

"That's a funny accent you've got."

They were standing facing each other. She had grey eyes, which looked odd as well. Perhaps she was an off-worlder. That might explain it. Jalila had heard that there people who had things done to themselves so they could live in different places. She supposed the breathmoss was like that, although she'd never thought of it that way. And she couldn't quite image why it would be a requirement of any world that you looked this ugly.

"Everyone talks oddly here," she replied. "But then your accent's funny as well."

"I'm Kalal. And that's just my *voice*. It's not an accent." Kalal looked down at her oily hands, perhaps thought about wiping one and offering it to shake, then decided not to bother.

"Oh . . . ?"

"You don't get it, do?" That gruff voice. The odd way her features twisted when she smiled.

"What is there to get? You're just—"

"—I'm a man." Kalal picked up a coil of rope from the shingle, and nodded to another beside it. "Well? Are you going to help me with this, or aren't you?"

The rains came again, this time starting as a thing called *drizzle*, then working up the scale to *torrent*. The tides washed especially high. There were storms, and white crackles of lightening, and the boom of a wind which was so unlike the kamasheen. Jalila's mothers told her to be patient, to wait, and to remember—*please* remember this time, so you don't spoil the day for us all, Jalilaneen—the things which they sent her down the serraplate road to get from Al Janb. She trudged under an umbrella, another new and useless coastal object, which turned itself inside out so many times that she ended up throwing it into the sea, where it floated off quite happily, as if that was the element for which it was intended in the first place. Almost all of the feluccas were drawn up on the far side of the roadway, safe from the madly bashing waves, but there was no sign of that bigger craft belonging to Kalal. Perhaps he—the antique genderative word *was* he, wasn't it?—he was out there, where the clouds rumbled like boulders. Perhaps she'd imagined their whole encounter entirely.

Arriving back home at the haramlek surprisingly quickly, and carrying for once the things she'd been ordered to get, Jalila dried herself off and buried herself in her dreamtent, trying to find out from it all that she could about these creatures called *men*. Like so many things about life at this awkward, interesting, difficult time, men were something Jalila would have insisted she definitely already knew about a few months before up on Tabuthal. Now, she wasn't so sure. Kalal, despite his ugliness and his funny rough-squeaky voice and his slightly odd smell, looked little like the hairy-faced werewolf figures of her childhood stories, and seemed to have no particular need to shout or fight, to carry her off to his rancid cave, or to start collecting odd and pointless things which he would then try to give her. There had once, Jalila's dreamtent postulated, and for obscure biological reasons she didn't quite follow, been far more men in the universe; almost as many had there had been women. Obviously, they had dwindled. She then checked up the word *rape*, to make sure it really was the thing she'd imagined, shuddered, but nevertheless investigated in full holographic detail the bits of himself which Kalal had kept hidden beneath his shorts as she'd helped stow those ropes. She couldn't help feeling sorry for him. It was all so pointless and ugly. Had his birth been an accident? A curse? She began to grow sleepy. The subject was starting to bore her. The last thing she remembered learning was that Kalal wasn't a proper man at all, but a *boy*—a half-formed thing; the equivalent to girl—another old urrearth word. Then sleep drifted over her, and she was back with the starlight and the crystal trees of Tabuthal, and wondering as she danced with her own reflection which of them was changing.

By next morning, the sun was shining as if she would never stop. As Jalila stepped out onto the newly formed patio, she gave the blazing light the same sort of an appraising *what-are-you-up-to-now* glare that her mothers gave her when she returned from Al Janb. The sun had done this trick before of seeming permanent, then vanishing by lunchtime into sodden murk, but today her brilliance continued. As it did the day after. And the day after that. Half a month later, even Jalila was convinced that the Season of Summers on Habara had finally arrived.

The flowers went mad, as did the insects. There were colours everywhere, pulsing before your eyes, swarming down the cliffs towards the sea, which lay flat and placid and salt-rimed; a huge animal, basking—or possibly dead. It remained mostly cool in Jalila's dreamtent, and the haramlek by now was a place of tall malqaf windtowers and flashing fans and well-like depths, but stepping outside beyond the striped shade of the mashrabiyas at midday felt like being hit repeatedly across the head with a hot iron pan. The horizons had drawn back, the mountains, after a few last rumbles of thunder and mist as if they were clearing their throats, had finally announced themselves to the coastline in all their majesty, and climbed up and up in huge stretches of forest into stone limbs which rose and tangled until your eyes grew tired of rising. Above them, finally, was the sky, which was always blue in this season; the blue colour of flame. Even at midnight, you caught the flash and swirl of flame.

Jalila learned to follow the advice of her mothers, and to change her daily habits to suit the imperious demands of this incredible, fussy and demanding weather. If you woke early, and then drank lots of water, and bowed twice in the direction of Al'Toman whilst she was still a pinprick in the west, you could catch the day by surprise, when dew lay on the stones and pillars, and the air felt soft and silky as the arms of the ghostly women who sometimes visited Jalila's nights. Then there was breakfast, and the time of work, and the time of study, and Ananke and Pavo would quiz Jalila to ensure that she was following the prescribed Orders of Knowledge. By midday, though, the shadows had drawn back and every trace of moisture had evaporated, and your head swarmed with flies. You sought your own company, and didn't even want that, and wished as you tossed and sweated in your dreamtent for frost and darkness. Once or twice, just to prove to herself that it could be done, Jalila had tried walking to Al Janb at this time, although of everything was shut and the whole place wobbled and stank in the heat like rancid jelly. She returned to the haramlek gritty and sweaty, almost crawling, and with a pounding ache in her head.

By evening, when the proper order of the world had righted itself, and Al'Toman would have hung in the east if the mountains hadn't swallowed her, and the heat, which never vanished, had assumed a smoother, more manageable quality, Jalila's mothers were once again hungry for company, and for food and for argument. These evenings, perhaps, were the best of all the times which Jalila would remember of her early life on the coast of Habara's single great ocean, at that stage in her development from child to adult when the only thing of permanence seemed to be the existence of endless, fascinating change. *How* they argued! Lya, her bondmother, and the oldest of her parents, who wore her grey hair loose as cobwebs with the pride of her age, and waved her arms as she smoked and drank in curling endless wreathes of smoke and steam. Little Pavo, her face smooth as a carved nutmeg, with her small, precise, hands, and who knew so much but rarely said anything with insistence. And Jalila's birthmother Ananke, for whom of her three mothers Jalila had always had the deepest, simplest love, who would always touch you before she said anything, and then fix you with her sad and lovely eyes, as if touching and seeing were far more important that any words. Jalila was older now. She joined in with the arguments—of course, she had *always* joined in, but she cringed to think of the stumbling inanities to which her mothers had previously had to listen, whilst, now, at last, she had real, proper things to say about life, whole new philosophies which no one else on the Ten Thousand Worlds and One had ever thought of . . . Most of the time, her mothers listened. Sometimes, they even acted as if they were persuaded by their daughter's wisdom.

Frequently, there were visitors to these evening gatherings. Up on Tabuthal, visitors had been rare animals, to be fussed over and cherished and only reluctantly released for their onward journey across the black dazzling plains. Down here, where people were nearly as common as stones on the beach, a more relaxed attitude reigned. Sometimes, there were formal invitations which Lya would issue to someone who was *this* or *that* in the town, or more often Pavo would come back with a person she had happened to meet as she poked around for lifeforms on the beach, or Ananke would softly suggest a *neighbour* (another new word and concept to Jalila) might like to *pop in* (ditto). But Al Janb was still a small town, and the dignitaries generally weren't that dignified, and Pavo's beach wanderers were often shy and slight as she was, whilst *neighbour* was frequently a synonym for *boring*. Still, Jalila came to enjoy most kinds of company, if only so that she could hold forth yet more devastatingly on whatever universal theory of life she was currently developing.

The flutter of lanterns and hands. The slow breath of the sea. Jalila ate stuffed breads and fuul and picked at the mountains of fruit and sucked lemons and sweet blue rutta and waved her fingers. The heavy night insects, glowing with the pollen they had collected, came bumbling towards the lanterns or would alight in their hands. Sometimes, afterwards, they walked the shore, and Pavo would show them strange creatures with blurring mouths like wheels, or point to the vast, distant beds of the tide-flowers which rose at night to the changes of the tide; silver, crimson, or glowing, their fronds waving through the dark like the beckoning palms of islands from storybook seas.

One guestless night when they were walking north away from the lights of the town and Pavo was filling a silver bag for an aquarium she was ostensibly making for Jalila, but in reality for herself, the horizon suddenly cracked and rumbled. Instinctively by now, Jalila glanced overhead, expecting clouds to be covering the coastal haze of stars. But the air was still and clear; the hot dark edge of that blue flame. Across the sea, the rumble and crackle was continuing, accompanied by a glowing pillar of smoke which slowly tottered over the horizon. The night pulsed and flickered. There was a breath of impossibly hot salt air. The pillar, a wobbly finger with a flame-tipped nail, continued climbing skyward. A few geelies rose and fell, clacking and cawing, on the far rocks; black shapes in the darkness.

"It's the start of the Season of Rockets," Lya said. "I wonder who'll be coming . . . ?"

2.

By now, Jalila had acquired many of her own acquaintances and friends. Young people were relatively scare amid the long-lived human Habarans, and those who dwelt around Al Janb were continually drawn and repulsed to each other like spinning magnets. The elderly mahwagis, who had outlived the need for wives and the company of a haramlek and lived alone, were often more fun, and more reliably eccentric. It was a relief to visit their houses and escape the pettinesses and sexual jealousies which were starting to infect the other girls near to Jalila's own age. She regarded Kalal similarly—as an escape—and she relished helping him with his boat, and then their journeys out across the bay, where the wind finally tipped almost cool over the edge of the mountains and lapped the sweat from their faces.

Kalal took Jalila out to see the rocketport one still, hot afternoon. It lay just over the horizon, and was the longest journey they had undertaken. The sails filled with the wind, and the ocean grew almost black, yet somehow transparent, as they hurried over it. Looking down, Jalila believed she could glimpse the white sliding shapes of the great sea-leviathans who had once dwelt, if local legend was to be believed, in the ruined rock palaces of the qasrs which she had passed on her journey down from Tabuthal. Growing tired of sunlight, they had swarmed back to the sea which had birthed them, throwing away their jewels and riches, which bubbled below the surface, then rose again under the Habara's twin moons to became the beds of tideflowers. She had got that part of the story from Kalal. Unlike most people who lived on the coast, Kalal was interested in Jalila's life in the starry darkness of Tabuthal, and repaid her with his own tales of the ocean.

The boat ploughed on, rising, frothing, Blissfully, it was almost cold. Just how far out at sea was this rocketport? Jalila had watched some of the arrivals and departures from the quays at Al Janb, but those journeys took place in sleek sail-less craft with silver doors which looked, as they turned out from the harbour and rose out on stilts from the water, as if they could travel half way up to the stars on their own. Kalal was squatting at the prow, beyond that ramshackle but which Jalila now knew contained the pheromones and grapplers which were needed to ensnare the tideflowers which this craft had been built to harvest. The boat bore no name on the prow, yet Kalal had many names for it, which he would occasionally mention or curse without explaining. If there was one thing which was different about Kalal, Jalila had decided, it was this absence of proper talk or explanation. It put many people off, but she had found that most things became apparent if you just hung around him and didn't ask direct questions.

People generally pitied Kalal, or stared at him as Jalila still stared at the aliens, or asked him questions he wouldn't answer with anything other than a shrug. Now that she knew him better, Jalila was starting to understand just how much he hated such treatment—almost as much, in fact, as he hated being thought of as ordinary. I am a *man*, you know, he'd still remark sometimes—whenever he felt Jalila was forgetting. Jalila had never yet risked pointing out that he was in fact a *boy*. Kalal could be prickly and sensitive if you treated him as if things didn't matter. It was hard to tell, really, just how much of how he was due to his odd sexual identity, and how much was his personality.

To add to his freakishness, Kalal lived alone with another male—in fact, the only other male in Al Janb—at the far end of the shore cottages, in a birthing relationship which made Kalal term him his *father*. His name was Ibra, and he looked much more like the males of Jalila's dreamtent stories. He was taller than almost anyone, and wore a black beard and long colourful robes or strode about bare-chested and always talked in a thunderously deep voice as if her was addressing a crowd through a megaphone. Ibra laughed a lot and flashed his teeth through that hairy mask, and clapped people on the back when he asked them how they were and then stood away and seemed to loose interest before they had answered.

He whistled and sang loudly and waved to passers-by
whilst he worked at repairing the feluccas for his living.
Ibra had come to this planet when Kalal was a baby, under circumstances which remained perennially vague. He
treated Jalila with the same loud and grinning friendship
with which he treated everyone, and which seemed like a
wall. He was at least as alien as the tube-like creatures
who had arrived from the stars with this new Season of
Rockets, which had had one of the larger buildings in Al
Janb encased in transparent plastics and flooded in a
freezing grey goo so they could live in it. Ibra had come
around to their haramlek once, on the strength of one of
Ananke's *pop in* evening invitations. Jalila, who was then
nurturing the idea that no intelligence could exist without the desire to acknowledge some higher deity, found
her propositions and examples drowned out in a flurry of
counter-questions and assertions and odd bits of information which she half-suspected that Ibra, as he drank
surprising amounts of virtually undiluted zibib and freck-
led aniseed spit at her, was making up on the spot. Afterwards, as they walked the shore, he drew her apart and
laid a heavy hand on her shoulder and confided in his
rambling growl how much he'd enjoyed *fencing* with her.
Jalila knew what fencing was, but she didn't see what it
had to do with talking. She wasn't even sure if she liked
Ibra. She certainly didn't pretend to understand him.

The sails thrummed and crackled as they headed towards the spaceport. Kalal was absorbed, staring ahead
from the prow, the water splashing reflections across his
lithe brown body. Jalila had almost grown used to the
way he looked. After all, they were both slightly freakish:
she, because she came from the mountains; he, because
of his sex. And they both liked their own company, and

could accept each into it other without distraction during these long periods of silence. One never asked the other what they were thinking. Neither really cared, and they cherished that privacy.

"Look—" Kalal scuttled to the rudder. Jalila hauled back the jib. In wind-crackling silence, they and their nameless and many-named boat tacked towards the spaceport.

The spaceport was almost like the mountains: when you were close up, it was too big be seen properly. Yet, for all its size, the place was a disappointment; empty and messy, like a huge version of the docks of Al Janb, similarly reeking of oil and refuse, and essentially serving a similar function. The spaceships themselves, if indeed the vast cistern-like objects they saw forever in the distance as they furled the sails and rowed along the maze of oily canals, were only a small part of this huge floating complex of islands. Much more of it was taken up by looming berths for the tugs and tankers which placidly chugged from icy pole to equator across the watery expanses of Habara, taking or delivering the supplies which the settlements deemed necessary for civilised life, or collecting the returning fallen bulk cargoes. The tankers were rust-streaked beasts, so huge that they hardly seemed to grow as you approached them, humming and eerily deserted, yet devoid of any apparent intelligence of their own. They didn't glimpse a single alien at the spaceport. They didn't even see a human being.

The journey there, Jalila decided as they finally got the sails up again, had been far more enjoyable and exciting than actually arriving. Heading back toward the sun-pink coastal mountains which almost felt like home to her now, she was filled with an odd longing which only diminished when she began to make out the lighted dusky buildings of Al Janb. Was this homesickness, she wondered? Or something else?

This was the time of Habara's long summer. This was the Season of Rockets. Jalila was severely warned by Pavo of the consequences of approaching the spaceport during periods of possible launch when she mentioned their trip, but it went no further than that. Each night now, and deep into the morning, the rockets rumbled at the horizon and climbed upwards on those grumpy pillars, bringing to the shore a faint whiff of sulphur and roses, adding to the thunderous heat. And outside at night, if you looked up, you could sometimes see the blazing comet-trails of the returning capsules which would crash somewhere in the distant seas.

The beds of tideflowers were growing bigger as well. If you climbed up the sides of the mountains before the morning heat flattened everything, you could look down on those huge, brilliant and ever-changing carpets, where every pattern and swirl seemed gorgeous and unique. At night, in her dreamtent, Jalila sometimes imagined she was floating up on them, just as in the oldest of the old stories. She was sailing over a different landscape on a magic carpet, with the cool night desert rising and falling beneath her like a soft sea. She saw distant palaces, and clusters of palms around small and tranquil lakes which flashed the silver of a single moon. And then yet more of this infinite sahara, airy and frosty, flowed through curves and undulations, and grew vast and pinkish in her dreams. Those curves, as she flew over them and began to touch herself, resolved into thighs and breasts. The winds stirring the peaks of the dunes resolved in shuddering breaths.

This was the time of Habara's long summer. This was the Season of Rockets.

Robin, Jalila's hayawan, had now fully recovered from the change to her environment under Pavo's attentions. The rust had gone from her flanks, the melds with her thinly grey-furred flesh were bloodless and neat. She looked thinner and lighter. She even smelled different. Like the other hayawans, Robin was frisky and bright and brown-eyed now, and didn't seem to mind the heat, or even Jalila's forgetful neglect of her. Down on the coast, hayawans were regarded as expensive, uncomfortable and unreliable, and Jalila and her mothers took a pride in riding across the beach into Al Janb on their huge, flat-footed and loping mounts, and enjoyed the stares and the whispers, and the whispering space which opened around them as they hobbled them in a square. Kalal, typically, was one of the few coastal people who expressed an interest in trying to ride one of them, and Jalila was glad to teach him, showing him the clicks and calls and nudges, the way you took the undulations of the creature's back as you might the ups and downs of the sea, and when not to walk around their front and rear ends. After her experiences on his boat, the initial rope burns, the cracks on the head and the heaving sickness, she enjoyed the reversal of situations.

There was a Tabuthal saying about falling off a hayawan ninety nine times before you learnt to ride, which Kalal disproved by falling off far into treble figures. Jalila chose Lya's mount Abu for him to ride, because she was the biggest, the most intelligent, and generally the most placid of the beasts unless she felt something was threatening her, and because Lya, more conscious of looks and protocol down here than the other mothers, rarely rode her. Domestic animals, Jalila had noticed, often took oddly to Kalal when they first saw and scented him, but he had learned the ways of getting around them, and developed a bond and understanding with Abu even whilst she was still trying to bite his legs. Jalila had made a good choice of riding partners. Both of them, hayawan and human, whilst proud and aloof, were essentially playful, and never shirked a challenge. Whilst all hayawans had been female throughout all recorded history, Jalila wondered if there wasn't a little of the male still embedded in Abu's imperious downward glance.

Now that summer was here, and the afternoons had vanished into the sun's blank blaze, the best time to go riding was the early morning. North, beyond Al Janb, there were shores and there were saltbeds and there were meadows, there were fences to be leapt, and barking feral dogs as male as Kalal to be taunted, but south, there were rocks and forests, there were tracks which led nowhere, and there were headlands and cliffs you saw once and could never find again. South, mostly, was the way that they rode.

"What happens if we keep riding?"

They were taking their breath on a flatrock shore where a stream shone in pools on its way to the ocean, from which they had all drank. The hayawans had squatted down now in the shadows of the cliff and were nodding sleepily, one nictitating membrane after another slipping over their eyes. As soon as they had got here and dismounted, Kalal had walked straight down, arms outstretched, into the tideflower-bobbing ocean. Jalila had followed, whooping, feeling tendrils and petals bumping into her. It was like walking through floral soup. Kalal had sunk to his shoulders and started swimming, which was something Jalila still couldn't quite manage. He splashed around her, taunting, sending up sheets of coloured light. They'd stripped from their clothes as they clambered out, and laid them on the hot rocks, where they now steamed like fresh bread.

"This whole continent's like a huge island," Jalila said in delayed answer to Kalal's question. "We'd come back to where we started."

Kalal shook his head. "Oh, you can never do that . . ."

"Where would we be, then?"

"Somewhere slightly different. The tideflowers would have changed, and we wouldn't be us, either." Kalal wet his finger, and wrote something in naskhi script on the hot, flat stone between them. Jalila though she recognised the words of poet, but the beginning had dissolved into the hot air before she could make proper sense of it. Funny, but at home with her mothers, and with their guests, and even with many of the people of her own age, such statements as they had just made would have been the beginning of a long debate. With Kalal, they just seemed to hang there. Kalal, he moved, he passed on. Nothing quite seemed to stick. There was something, somewhere, Jalila thought, lost and empty about him.

The way he was sitting, she could see most his genitals, which looked quite jaunty in their little nest of hair; like a small animal. She'd almost got as used to the sight of them as she had to the other peculiarities of Kalal's features. Scratching her nose, picking off some of the petals which still clung to her skin like wet confetti, she

felt no particular curiosity. Much more than Kalal's funny
body, Jalila was conscious of her own—especially her
growing breasts, which were still somewhat uneven.
Would they ever come out right, she wondered, or would
she forever be some unlovely oddity, just as Kalal seemingly was? Better not to think of such things. Better to
just enjoy the feel the sun baking her shoulders, loosen-
ing the curls of her hair.

"Should we turn back?" Kalal asked eventually. "It's
getting hotter . . ."

"Why bother with that—if we carry on, we'll get back
to where we started."

Kalal stood up. "Do you want a bet?"

So they rode on, more slowly, uphill through the uncharted forest, where the urrearth trees tangled with blue
fronds of Habara fungus and the birds were still and the
crackle of the dry undergrowth was the only sound in the
air. Eventually, ducking boughs, then walking, dreamily
lost and almost ready to turn back, they came to a path,
and remounted. The trees fell away, and they found they
were on a clifftop, far, far higher above the winking sea
than they could possibly imagined. Midday heat clapped
around them. Ahead, where the cliff stuck out over the
ocean like a cupped hand, shimmering and yet solid, was
one of the ruined castles or geological features which the
sea-leviathans had supposedly deserted before the arrival
of people on this planet—a qasr. They rode slowly towards it, their hayawan's feet thocking in the dust. It
looked like a fairy place. Part natural, but roofed and buttressed, with grey-black gables and huge and intricate
windows which flashed with the colours of the sea. Kalal
gestured for silence, dismounted from Abu, led his mount

back into the shadowed arms of the forest, and flicked the switch in her back with hobbled her.

"You *know* where this is?"

Kalal beckoned.

Jalila, who knew him better than to ask questions, followed.

Close to, much of the qasr seemed to be made of a quartz-speckled version of the same fused stone from which Jalila's haramlek was constructed. But some other bits of it appeared natural effusions of the rock. There was a big arched door of sun-bleached and iron-studded oak reached by a path across the narrowing cliff, but Kalal steered Jalila to the side, and then up and around a bare angle of hot stone which seemed ready at any moment to tilt them into the distant the sea. But the way never quite gave out, there was always another handhold. From the confident manner in which he moved up this near-clifface, then scrambled across the blistering black tiles of the rooftop beyond, and dropped down into the sudden cool of a narrow passageway, Jalila guessed that Kalal had been to this qasr before. At first, there was little sense of trespass. The place seemed old and empty—a little-visited monument. The ceilings were stained. The corridors were swept with the litter of winter leaves. Here and there along the walls, there were friezes, and long strings of a script which make as little sense to Jalila, in their age and dimness, as that which Kalal had written on the hot rocks.

Then Kalal gestured for Jalila to stop, and she clustered beside him and they looked down through the intricate stone lattice of a mashrabiya into sunlight. It was plain from the balcony drop beneath them that they were still high up in this qasr. Below, in the central courtyard, somehow shocking after this emptiness, a fountain played in a garden, and water lapped from its lip and ran in steel fingers towards cloistered shadows.

"Someone *lives* here?"

Kalal mouthed the word *tariqua*. Somehow, Jalila instantly understood. It all made sense, in this Season of Rockets, and the dim scenes and hieroglyphs carved in the honeyed stones of this fairy castle. Tariquas were merely human, after all, and the spaceport was nearby; they had to live somewhere. Jalila glanced down at her scuffed sandals, suddenly conscious that she hadn't taken them off—but by then it was too late, and below them and through the mashrabiya a figure had detached herself from the shadows. The tariqua was tall and thin and black and bent as a burnt-out matchstick. She walked with a cane. Jalila didn't know what she'd expected— she'd grown older since her first encounter with Kalal, and no longer imagined that she knew about things just because she'd learnt of them in her dreamtent. But still, this tariqua seemed a long way from piloting the impossible distances between the stars as she moved and clicked slowly around that courtyard fountain, and far older and frailer than anyone Jalila had ever seen. She tended a bush of blue flowers, she touched the fountain's bubbling stone lip. Her head was ebony bald. Her fingers were charcoal. Her eyes were as white and seemingly blind as the flecks of quartz in the fused stone of this building. Once, though, she seemed to look up towards them. Jalila went cold. Surely it wasn't possible that she could see them?—and in any event, there was something about the motion of looking up which seemed habitual. As if, like touching of the lip of the fountain, and tending

that bush, the tariqua always looked up at this moment of
the day at that particular point in the stone walls which
rose above her.

Jalila followed Kalal further along the corridors, and
down stairways and across drops of beautifully clear
glass which hung on nothing far above the prismatic sea.
Another glimpse of the tariqua, who was still slowly
moving, her neck stretching like an old tortoise as she
bent to sniff a flower. In this part of the qasr, there were
more definite signs of habitation. Scattered cards and
books. A moth-eaten tapestry which billowed from a
windowless arch overlooking the sea. Empty coathangers
piled like the bones of insects. An active but clearly little-
used chemical toilet. Now that the initial sense of surprise
had gone, there was something funny about this mixture
of the extraordinary and the everyday. Here, there was a
kitchen, and a half-chewed lump of aish on a plate
smeared with seeds. To imagine, that you could both
travel between the stars, and then eat bread and toma-
toes! Both Kalal and Jalila were red-faced and chuffing
now from suppressed and impossible hilarity. Down now
at the level of the cloisters, hunched in the shade, they
studied the tariqua's stooping back. She really did look
like a scrawny tortoise, yanked out of its shell, moving
between these bushes. Any moment now, you expected
her to start chomping on the leaves. She moved more by
touch than by sight. Amid the intricate colours of this
courtyard, and the flashing glass windchimes which tin-
kled in the far archways, as she fumbled sightlessly but
occasionally glanced at things with those odd, white
eyes, it seemed yet more likely that she was blind, or at
least terribly near-sighted. Slowly, Jalila's hilarity receded, and she began to feel sorry for this old creature

who had been aged and withered and wrecked by the strange process of travel between the stars. *The Pain of Distance*—now, where had that phrase come from?

Kalal was still puffing his cheeks. His eyes were watering as he ground his fist against his mouth and silently thumped the nearest pillar in agonised hilarity. Then he let out a nasal grunt, which Jalila was sure the tariqua must have heard. But her stance didn't alter. It wasn't so much as if she hadn't noticed them, but that she already *knew* that someone was there. There was a sadness and resignation about her movements, the tap of her cane . . . But Kalal had recovered his equilibrium, and Jalila watched his fingers snake out and enclose a flake of broken paving. Another moment, and it span out into the sunlit courtyard in an arch so perfect that there was never any doubt that it was going to strike the tariqua smack between her bird-like shoulders. Which it did—but by then they were running, and the tariqua was straightening herself up with that same slow resignation. Just before they bundled themselves up the stairway, Jalila glanced back, and felt a hot bar of light from one the qasr's high upper windows stream across her face. The tariqua was looking straight towards her with those blind white eyes. Then Kalal grabbed her hand, Once again, she was running.

Jalila was cross with herself, and cross with Kalal. It wasn't *like* her, a voice like a mingled chorus of her three mothers would say, to taunt some poor old mahwagi, even if that mahwagi happened also to be an aged tariqua. But Jalila was young, and life was busy. The voice soon faded. In any case, there was the coming moulid to prepare for.

The arrangement of festivals, locally, and on Habara as a whole, was always difficult. Habara's astronomical year was so long that it made no sense to fix the traditional cycle of moulids by it, but at the same time, no one felt comfortable celebrating the same saint or eid in conflicting seasons. Fasting, after all, properly belonged to winter, and no one could quite face their obligations towards the Almighty with quite the same sense of surrender and equanimity in the middle of spring. People's memories faded, as well, as to how one *did* a particular saint in autumn, or revered a certain enlightenment in blasting heat which you had previously celebrated by throwing snowballs. Added to this were the logistical problems of catering for the needs of a small and scattered population across a large planet. There were travelling players, fairs, wandering sufis and priests, but they plainly couldn't be everywhere at once. The end result was that each moulid was fixed locally on Habara, according to a shifting timetable, and after much discussion and many meetings, and rarely happened twice at exactly the same time, or occurred simultaneously in different places. Lya threw herself into these discussions with the enthusiasm of one who long been missing such complexities in the lonelier life up on Tabuthal. For the Moulid of First Habitation, which commemorated the time when the Blessed Joanna had arrived on Habara at a site which several of towns claimed, and cast the first urrearth seeds, and lived for five long Habaran years on nothing but tideflowers and starlight, and rode the sea-leviathans across the oceans as if they were hayawans as she waited for her lover Pia, Lya was the leading light in the local organisations at Al Janb, and the rest of her haramlek were expected to follow suit.

The whole of Al Janb was to be transformed for a day and a night. Jalila helped with hammering and weaving, and tuning Pavo's crystals and plants which would supposedly transform the serraplate road between their haramlek and the town into a glittering tunnel. More in the forefront of Jalila's mind were those coloured silks which came and went at particular stall in the markets, and which she was sure would look perfect on her. Between the planning and the worries about this or that turning into a disaster, she worked carefully on each of her three mothers in turn; a nudge here, a suggestion there. Turning their thoughts towards accepting this extravagance was a delicate matter, like training a new hayawan to bear the saddle. Of course, there were wild resistances and buckings, but you were patient, you were stronger. You knew what you wanted. You kept to your subject. You returned and returned and returned.

On the day when Ananke finally relented, a worrying wind had struck up, pushing at the soft, half-formed growths which now straggled the normal roadside weeds into Al Janb like silvered mucus. Pavo was fretting about her creations. Lya's life was one long meeting. Even Ananke was anxious as they walked into Al Janb, where faulty fresh projections flickered across of the buildings and squares like an incipient headache as the sky greyed and hurried. Jalila, urging her birthmother on as she paused frustratingly, was sure that the market wouldn't be there, or that if it was, the stall which sold the windsilks was sure to have sold out—or, even then, that the particular ones she'd set her mind on would have gone . . .

But it was all there. In fact, a whole new supply even more marvellous and colourful of windsilks had been imported for this moulid. They blew and lifted like coloured smoke. Jalila caught and admired them.

"I think this might be you . . ."

Jalila turned at the voice. It was Nayra, a girl of about a standard year and a half older than her, whose mothers were amongst the richest and most powerful in Al Janb. Nayra herself was both beautiful and intelligent; witty and sometimes devastatingly cruel. She was generally at the centre of things, surrounded by a bickering and admiring crowd of seemingly lesser mortals, which sometimes included Jalila. But today she was alone.

"You see, Jalila. That crimson. With your hair, your eyes . . ."

She held the windsilk across Jalila's face like yashmak. It danced around her eyes. It blurred over her shoulders. Jalila would have thought the colour too bold. But Nayra's gaze, which flickered without ever quite leaving Jalila's, her smoothing hands, told Jalila that it was right for her far better than any mirror could have. And then there was blue—that flame colour of the summer night. There were silver clasps, too, to hold these windsilks, which Jalila had never noticed on sale before. The stallkeeper, sensing a desire to purchase which went beyond normal bargaining, drew out more surprises from a chest. *Feel! They can only be made in one place, on one planet, on one season. Look! The grubs, they hatch when they hear the song of a particular bird, which sings once in its life before it gives up its spirit to the Almighty . . .* And so on. Ananke, seeing that Jalila had found a more interested and willing helper, palmed her far more cash than she'd promised, and left her with a smile and an oddly sad backward glance.

Jalila spend the rest to that grey and windy afternoon

with Nayra choosing clothes and ornaments for the moulid. Bangles for their wrists and ankles. Perhaps—no? yes?—even a small tiara. Bolts of cloth the colour of today's sky bound across her hips to offset the windsilk's beauty. A jewel still filled with the sapphire light of a distant sun to twinkle at her belly. Nayra, with her dark blonde hair, her light brown eyes, her fine strong hands which were pale pink beneath the fingernails like the inside of a shell, she hardly needed anything to augment her obvious beauty. But Jalila knew from her endless studies of herself in her dreamtent mirror that *she* needed to be more careful; the wrong angle, the wrong light, an incipient spot, and whatever effect she was striving for could be so easily ruined. Yet she'd never really cared as much about such things as she did on that windy afternoon, moving through stalls and shops and amid the scent of patchouli. To be so much the focus of her own and someone else's attention. Nayra's hands, smoothing across her back and shoulders, lifting her hair, cool sweat at her shoulders, the cool slide and rattle of her bangles as she raised her arms . . .

"We could be creatures from a story, Jalila. Let's imagine I'm Scheherazade." A toss of that lovely hair. Liquid gold. Nayra's seashell fingers, stirring. "You can be her sister, Dinarzade . . ."

Jalila nodded enthusiastically, although Dinarzade had been an unspectacular creature as far as she remembered the tale; there only so that she might waken Scheherazade in the Sultana's chamber before the first cock crow of morning. But her limbs, her throat, felt strange and soft and heavy. She reminded herself as she dressed and undressed of the doll Tabatha she'd once so treasured up on

Tabuthal, and had found again recently and thought for
some odd reason of burying . . .

The lifting, the pulling, Nayra's appraising hands and
glance and eyes. This unresisting heaviness. Jalila returned home to her haramlek dazed and drained and
happy, and severely out of credit.

That night, there was another visitor for dinner. She must
have taken some sort of carriage to get there, but she
came towards their veranda as if she'd walked the entire
distance. Jalila, whose head was filled with many things,
was putting out the bowls when she heard the murmur of
footsteps. The sound was so slow that eventually she noticed it consciously, looked up, and saw a thin, dark figure coming up the sandy path between Pavo's swaying
and newly sculpted bushes. One arm leaned on a cane,
and the other strained seekingly forwards. In shock, Jalila
dropped the bowl she was holding. It seemed to roll
around and around on the table forever, slipping play-
fully out of reach of her fingers before spinning off the
edge and shattering into several thousand white pieces.

"Oh dear," the tariqua said, finally climbing the steps
beside the windy trellis, her cane tap-tapping. "Perhaps
you'd better go and tell one of your mothers, Jalila."

Jalila felt breathless. All through that evening, the
tariqua's trachoman white eyes, the scarred and tarry
driftwood of her face, seemed to be studying her. Even
apart from that odd business of her knowing her name,
which she supposed could be explained, Jalila was more
and more certain that the tariqua knew that it was she
and Kalal who had spied and thrown stones at her on that
hot day in the qasr. As if that mattered. But somehow,

more than it should have done, it *did*. Amid all this confused thinking, and the silky memories of her afternoon with Nayra, Jalila scarcely noticed the conversation. The weather remained gusty, spinning the lanterns, playing shapes with the shadows, sucking in the tapestries. The tariqua's voice was as thin as her frame. It carried on the spinning air like the croak of an insect.

"Perhaps we could walk on the beach, Jalila?"

"What?" She jerked as if she'd been awakened. Her mothers were already clearing things away, and casting odd glances at her. The voice had whispered inside her head, and the tariqua was sitting there, her burnt and splintery arm outstretched in the hope, Jalila supposed, that she would helped up from the table. The creature's robe had fallen back. Her arm looked like a picture Jalila had once seen of a dried cadaver. With an effort, and nearly knocking over another bowl, Jalila moved around the billowing table. With an even bigger effort, she placed her own hand into that of the tariqua. She'd expected it to feel leathery, which it did. But it was also hot beyond fever. Terribly, the fingers closed around hers. There was a pause. Then the tariqua got up with surprising swiftness, and reached around for her cane, still holding Jalila's hand, but without having placed any weight on it. *She could have done all that on her own, the old witch*. Jalila thought. *And she can* see, *too—look at the way she's been stuffing herself with kofta all evening, reaching over for figs . . .*

"What do you know of the stars, Jalila?" the tariqua asked as they walked beside the beach. Pavo's creations along the road behind them still looked stark and strange and half-formed as they swayed in the wind; the wavering silver limbs of an upturned insect. The waves came and went, strewing tideflowers far up the strand. Like the tongue of a snake, the tariqua's cane darted ahead of her.

Jalila shrugged. There were these Gateways, she had always known that. There were these Gateways, and they were the only proper path between the stars because no one could endure the aeons of time and expense which crossing even the tiniest fragment of the Ten Thousand and One Worlds would entail by the ordinary means of travelling from *there* to *here*.

"Not, of course," the tariqua was saying, "that people don't do such things. There are tales, there are always tales, of ghost-ships of sufis drifting beyond tens of centuries through the black and black . . . But the wealth, the contact, the community, flows through the Gateways. The Almighty herself provided the means to make them in the Days of Creation, when everything which was and will ever be had spilled out into a void so empty that it did not even exist as an emptiness. In those first moments, as warring elements collided, boundaries had formed, dimensions had been made and disappeared without ever quite dissolving, like the salt tidemarks on those rocks . . ." As they walked, the tariqua waved her cane. ". . . Which the sun and the aeons can never quite bake away. These boundaries are called cosmic strings, Jalila, and they have no end. They must form either minute loops, or they must stretch from one end of this universe to the other, and then turn back again, and turn and turn without end."

Jalila glanced at the brooch the tariqua was wearing, which was of a worm consuming its tail. She knew that the physical distances between the stars were vast, but the tariqua somehow made the distances which she traversed to avoid that journey seem even vaster . . .

"You must understand," the tariqua said, "that we tariquas pass through something worse than nothing to get from one side to the other of a Gateway."

Jalila nodded. She was young, and *nothing* didn't sound especially frightening. Still, she sensed that there were the answers to mysteries in this near-blind gaze and whispering voice which she would never get from her dreamtent or her mothers. "But, *hanim,* what could be worse," she asked dutifully, although still couldn't think of the tariqua in terms of a name, and thus simply addressed her with the short honorific, "than sheer emptiness?"

"Ah, but emptiness is *nothing.* Imagine, instead, Jalila, passing through *everything* instead." The tariqua chucked, and gazed up at the sky. "But the stars are beautiful, and so is this night. You come, I hear, from Tabuthal. There, the skies must all have been very different."

Jalila nodded. A brief vision flared over her. The way that up there, on the clearest, coldest nights, you felt as if the stars were all around you. Even now, much though she loved the fetors and astonishments of the coast, she still felt the odd pang of missing something. It was a *feeling* she missed as much as the place itself, which she guessed would probably seem bleak and lonely if she returned to it now. It was partly to do, she suspected, with that sense that she was loosing her childhood. It was like being on a ship, on Kalal's nameless boat, and watching the land recede, and half of you loving the loss, half of you hating it. A war seemed to going on inside her between these two warring impulses . . .

To her surprise, Jalila realised that she wasn't just thinking these thoughts, but speaking them, and that the tariqua, walking at her slow pace, the weight of her head bending her spine, her cane whispering a jagged line in the dust as the black rags of her djibbah flapped around her, was listening. Jalila supposed that she, too, had been young once, although that was hard to imagine. The sea frothed and swished. They were at the point in the road now where, gently buzzing and almost out of sight amid the forest, hidden there as if in shame, the tariqua's caleche lay waiting. It was a small filigree a thing as old and black and ornate as her brooch. Jalila helped her towards it through the trees. The craft's door creaked like an iron gate. A few crickets sounded through the night's heat. Then, with a soft rush, and a static glow like the charge of windsilk brushing flesh, the craft rose up through the treetops and wafted away.

The day of the moulid came. It was everything Jalila expected, although she paid it little attention. The intricate, bowered pathway which Pavo had been working on finally shaped itself to her plans—in fact, it was better than that, and seemed like a beautiful accident. As the skies cleared, the sun shone through prismatic arches. The flowers, which had looked so stunted only the evening before, suddenly unfolded, with petals like beaten brass, and stamens shaped so that the continuing breeze, which Pavo had always claimed to have feared, laughed and whistled and tooted as it passed through them. Walking beneath the archways of flickering shadows, you were assailed by scents and the clashes of small orchestras. But Jalila's ears were blocked, her eyes were sightless. She, after all, was Dinarzade, and Nayra was Scheherazade of the Thousand and One Nights.

Swirling windsilks, her heart hammering, she strode into Al Jamb. Everything seemed to be different today.

There were too many sounds and colours. People tried to dance with her, or sell her things. Some of the aliens seemed to have dressed themselves as humans. Some of the humans were most definitely alien. Her feet were already blistered and delicate from her new crimson slippers. And there was Nayra, dressed in a silvery serwal and blouse of such devastating simplicity that Jalila felt her heart kick and pause in its beating. Nayra was surrounded by a small storm of her usual admirers. Her eyes took in Jalila as she stood at their edge, then beckoned her to join them. The idea of Dinarzade and Scheherazade, which Jalila had thought was to be their secret, was now shared with everyone. The other girls laughed and clustered around, admiring, joking, touching and stroking bits of her as if she was a hayawan. *You of all people, Jalila. And such jewels, such silks* . . . Jalila stood half-frozen, her heart still kicking. *So, so marvellous! And not at all dowdy* . . . She could have lived many a long and happy life without such compliments.

Thus the day continued. All of them in a crowd, and Jalila feeling both over-dressed and exposed, with these stirring, whispering windsilks which covered and yet mostly seemed to reveal her body. She felt like a child in a ribboned parade, and when one of the old mahwagis even came up and pressed a sticky lump of basbousa into her hand, it was the final indignity. She trudged off alone, and found Kalal and his father Ibra managing a seafront stall beside the swaying masts of the bigger trawlers, around which there was a fair level of purchase and interest. Ibra was enjoying himself, roaring out enticements and laughter in his big, belling voice. At last, they'd got around to harvesting some of the tideflowers for which their nameless boat had been designed, and they were selling every sort here, salt-fresh from the ocean.

"Try this one . . ." Kalal drew Jalila away to the edge of the harbour where the oiled water flashed below. He had just one tideflower in his hand. It was deep-banded the same crimson and blue as her windsilks. The interior was like the eye of an anemone.

Jalila was flattered. But she hesitated. "I'm not sure about wearing something dead." In any case, she knew she already looked ridiculous. That this would be more of the same.

"It isn't dead, it's as alive as you are." Kalal held it closer, against Jalila's shoulder, towards the top of her breast, smoothing out the windsilks in a way which briefly reminded her of Nayra. "And isn't this material the dead tissue of some creature or other . . . ?" Still, his hands were smoothing. Jalila thought again of Nayra. Being dressed like a doll. Her nipples started to rise. "And if we take it back to the tideflower beds tomorrow morning, place it down there carefully, it'll still survive . . ." The tideflower had stuck itself to her now, anyway, beneath the shoulder, its adhesion passing through the thin windsilks, burning briefly as it bound to her flesh. And it *was* beautiful anyway, even if she wasn't, and it would have been churlish to refuse. Jalila placed her finger into the tideflower's centre, and felt a soft suction, like the mouth of a baby. Smiling, thanking Kalal, feeling somehow better and more determined, she walked away.

The day went on. The night came. Fireworks crackled and rumpled, rippling down the slopes of the mountains. The whole of the centre of Al Jamb was transformed unrecognisably into the set of a play. Young Joanne herself walked the vast avenues of Ghezirah, the island city which lies at the centre of all the Ten Thousand and One Worlds, but which grows in much the same way as Pavo's crystal scaffoldings but on an inconceivable scale; filled with azure skies, glinting in the dark heavens like a vast diamond. The Blessed Joanne, she was supposedly thinking of a planet which had come to her in a vision as she wandered beside Ghezirah's palaces; it was a place of fine seas, lost giants and mysterious natural castles, although Jalila, as she followed in the buffeting, cheering procession, and glanced around at the scale of the projections which briefly covered of Al Janb's ordinary buildings, wondered why, even if this version Ghezirah was fake and thin, Joanne would ever have wanted to leave that city to come to a place such as this.

There were more fireworks. As they rattled, a deeper and sound swept over them in a moan from the sea, and everyone looked up as sunglow poured through the gaudy images of Ghezirah which still clad Al Janb's buildings. Not one rocket, or two, but three, were all climbing up from the spaceport simultaneously, the vast white plumes of their energies fanning out across half the sky to form a billowy *fleurs de lys*. At last, as she craned her neck and watched the last of those blazing tails diminish, Jalila felt exulted by this moulid. In the main square, the play continued. When she found a place on a bench and began to watch the more intimate parts of the drama unfold as Joanne's lover Pia pleaded with her to remain amid the cerulean towers of Ghezirah, a figure moved to sit beside her. To Jalila's astonishment, it was Nayra.

"That's a lovely flower. I've been meaning to ask you all day . . ." Her fingers moved across Jalila's shoulder. There was a tug at her skin as she touched the petals.

"I got it from Kalal."

"Oh . . ." Nayra sought the right word. "*Him*. Can I smell it . . ." She was already bending down, her face close to Jalila's breast, the golden fall of her hair brushing her forearm, enclosing her in sweet, slightly vanilla scent of her body. "That's nice. It smells like the sea—on a clear day, when you climb up and look down at it from the mountains . . ."

The play continued. Would Joanne really go to this planet which kept appearing to her in these visions? Jalila didn't know. She didn't care. Nayra's hand slipped into her own and lay there upon her thigh with a weight and presence which seemed far heavier than the entire universe. She felt like that doll again. Her breath was pulling, dragging. The play continued and then, somewhere, somehow, it came to an end. Jalila felt an aching sadness. She'd have been happy for Joanne to continue her will-I-won't-I agonisings and prayers throughout all of human history, just so that she and Nayra could continue to sit together like this, hand in hand, thigh to thigh, on this hard bench.

The projections flickered and faded. She stood up in wordless disappointment. The whole square suddenly looked like a wastetip, and she felt crumpled and used-up in these sweaty and ridiculous clothes. It was hardly worth looking back towards Nayra to say goodbye. She would, Jalila was sure, have already vanished to rejoin those clucking, chattering friends who surrounded her like a wall.

"Wait!" A hand on her arm. That same vanilla scent. "I've heard your mother Pavo's displays along the south road are something quite fabulous . . ." For once, Nayra's golden gaze as Jalila looked back at her was almost coy, nearly averted. "I was rather hoping you might show me ..."

The two of them. Walking hand in hand just all lovers throughout history. Like Pia and Joanna. Like Romana and Juliet. Like Isabel and Genya. Ghosts of smoke from the rocket plumes which had buttressed the sky hung around them, and the world seemed half-dissolved in the scent of sulphur and roses. An old woman they passed who was sweeping up discarded kebab sticks and wrappers made a sign as they passed, and gave them a weary, sad-happy smile. Jalila wasn't sure what had happened to her slippers, but they and her feet both seemed to have become weightless. If it hadn't been for the soft sway and pull of Nayra's arm, Jalila wouldn't even have been sure that she was moving. *People's feet really* don't *touch the ground when they were in love!* Here was something else that her dreamtent and her mothers hadn't told her.

Pavo's confections of plant and crystal looked marvellous in the hazed and doubled silver shadows of the rising moons. Jalila and Nayra wandered amid them, and the rest of the world felt withdrawn and empty. A breeze was still playing over the rocks and the waves, but the fluting sound had changed. It was one soft pitch, rising, falling. They kissed. Jalila closed her eyes—she couldn't help it—and trembled. Then they held both hands together and stared at each other, unflinching. Nayra's bare arms in the moonslight, the curve inside her elbow and the blue trace of a vein: Jalila had never seen anything as beautiful, here in this magical place.

The stables, where the hayawans were breathing. Jalila spoke to Robin, to Abu. The beasts were sleepy. Their flesh felt cold, their plates were warm, and Nayra seemed a little afraid. There, in the sighing darkness, the clean scent of feed and straw was overlaid with the heat of the hayawans' bodies and their dung. The place was no longer a ramshackle tent, but solid and dark, another of Pavo's creations; the stony catacombs of ages. Jalila led Nayra through it, her shoulders brushing pillars, her heart pounding, her slippered feet whispering through spills of straw. To the far corner, where the fine new white bedding lay like depths of cloud. They threw themselves onto it, half-expecting to fall through. But they were floating in straggles of windsilk, held in tangles of their own laughter and limbs.

"Remember." Nayra's palm on Jalila's right breast, scrolled like an old print in the geometric moonlight which fell from Walah and then through the arched stone grid of a murqana which lay above their heads. "I'm Scheherazade. You're Dinarzade, my sister . . ." The pebble of Jalila's nipple rising through the windsilk. "That old, old story, Jalila. Can you remember how it went . . . ?"

In the tide of yore and in the time of long gone before, there was a Queen of all the Queens of the Banu Sasan in the far islands of India and China, a Lady of armies and guards and servants and dependants . . .

Again, they kissed.

Handsome gifts, such as horses with saddles of gem-encrusted gold; mamelukes, or white slaves; beautiful handmaids, high- breasted virgins, and splendid stuffs and costly . . .

Nayra's hand moved from Jalila's breast to encircle the tideflower. She gave it a tug, pulled harder. Something held, gave, held, hurt, then gave entirely. The windsilks poured back. A small dark bead of blood welled at the curve between Jalila's breast and shoulder. Nayra licked it away.

In one house was a girl weeping for the loss of her sister. In another, perhaps a mother trembling for the fate of her child; and instead of the blessings which and formerly been heaped on the Sultana's head, the air was now full of curses . . .

Jalila was rising, floating, as Nayra's mouth travelled downwards to suckle at her breast.

Now the Wazir had two daughters, Scheherazade and Dinarzade, of whom the elder had perused the books, annals, and legends of preceding queens and empresses, and the stories, examples, and instances of bygone things. Scheherazade had read the works of the poets and she knew them by heart. She had studied philosophy, the sciences, the arts, and all accomplishments. And Scheherazade was pleasant and polite, wise and witty. Scheherazade, she was beautiful and well bred . . .

Flying far over frost-glittering saharas, beneath the twin moons, souring through the clouds. The falling, rising dunes. The minarets and domes of distant cities. The cries and shuddering sighs of the beloved. Patterned moonlight falling through the murqana in a white and dark tapestry across the curves and hollows of Nayra's belly.

Alekum as-salal wa rahmatu allahi wa barakatuh . . .

Upon you, the peace and the mercy of God and all this blessings.

Amen.

There was no cock-crow when Jalila startled awake. But Walah had vanished, and so had Nayra, and the light of the morning sun came splintering down through the murqana's hot blue lattice. Sheltering her face with her hands, Jalila looked down at herself, and smiled. The jewel in her belly was all that was left of her costume. She smelled faintly of vanilla, and much of Nayra, and nothing about her flesh seemed quite her own. Moving through the dazzling drizzle, she gathered up the windsilks and other scraps of clothing which had settled into the fleece bedding. She found one of Nayra's earrings, which was twisted to right angles at the post, and had to smile again. And here was that tideflower, tossed upturned like an old cup into the corner. She touched the tiny scab on her shoulder, then lifted the flower up and inhaled, but caught on her palms only the scents of Nayra. She closed her eyes, feeling the diamond speckles of heat and cold across her body like the ripples of the sea.

The hayawans barely stirred as she moved out through their stables. Only Robin regarded her, and then incuriously, as she paused to touch the hard grey melds of her flank which she had pressed against the bars of her enclosure. One eye, grey as rocket smoke, opened, then returned to its saharas of dreams. The hayawans, Jalila supposed for the first time, had their own passions, and these were not to be shared with some odd two-legged creatures of another planet and race.

The morning was still clinging to its freshness, and the road as she crossed it was barely warm beneath her feet. Windtowered Al Janb and the haramlek behind her looked deserted. Even the limbs of the mountains seemed curled in sleepy haze. On this day after the moulid, no one but the geelies was yet stirring. Cawing, they rose and settled in flapping red flocks from the beds of the tideflowers as Jalila scrunched across the hard stones of the beach. Her feet encountered the cool, slick water. She continued walking, wading, until the sea tickled her waist and what remained of the windsilks had spread about in spills of dye. From her cupped hands, she released the tideflower, and watched it float away. She splashed her face. She sunk down to her shoulders as the windsilks dissolved from her, and looked down between her breasts at the glowing jewel which was still stuck her belly, and plucked it out, and watched it sink; the sea-lantern of a ship, drowning.

Walking back up the beach, wringing the wet from her hair, Jalila noticed a rich green growth standing out amid the sky-filled rockpools and the growths of lichen. Pricked by something resembling Pavo's curiosity, she scrambled over, and crouched to examine it as the gathering heat of the sun dried her back. She recognised this spot—albeit dimly—from the angle of a band of quartz which glittered and bled blue oxides. This was where she had coughed up her breathmoss in that early Season of Soft Rains. And here it still was, changed but unmistakable—and growing. A small patch here, several larger patches there. Tiny filaments of green, a minute forest, raising its boughs and branches to the sun.

She walked back up towards her haramlek, humming.

3.

The sky was no longer blue. It was no longer white. It had turned to mercury. The rockets rose and rose in dry crackles of summer lightening. The tube-like aliens fled, leaving their strange house of goo-filled windows and pipes still clicking and humming until something burst and the whole structure deflated and the mess of it leaked across the nearby streets. There were warnings of poisonings and strange epidemics. There were cloggings and stenches of the drains.

Jalila showed the breathmoss to her mothers, who were all intrigued and delighted, although Pavo had of course noticed and categorised the growth long before, whilst Ananke had to touch the stuff, and left a small brown mark there like the tips of her three fingers, which dried and turned golden over the days which followed. But in this hot season, these evenings when the sun seemed as if it would never vanish, the breathmoss proved surprisingly hardy . . .

After that night of the moulid, Jalila spent several happy days absorbed and alone, turning and smoothing the memory of her love-making with Nayra. Wandering above and beneath the unthinking routines of everyday life, she was a like fine craftsman, spinning silver, shaping sandalwood. The dimples of Nayra's back. Sweat glints in the chequered moonlight. That sweet vein in the crook of her beloved's arm, and the pulse of the blood which had risen from it to the drumbeats of ecstasy. The memory seemed entirely enough to Jalila. She was barely living in the present day. When, perhaps six days after the end of the moulid, Nayra turned up at their doorstep with the ends of her hair chewed wet and her eyes red-rimmed, Jalila had been almost surprised to see her, and then to notice the differences between the real Nayra and the Scheherazade of her memories. Nayra smelled of tears and dust as they embraced; like someone who had arrived from a long, long journey.

"Why didn't you *call* me? I've been waiting, waiting . . ."

Jalila kissed her hair. Her hand travelled beneath a

summer shawl to caress Nayra's back, which felt damp and gritty. She had no idea how to answer her questions. They walked out together that afternoon in the shade of the woods behind the haramlek. The trees had changed in this long, hot season, departing their urrearth habits to coat their leaves in a waxy substance which smelled medicinal. The shadows of their boughs were chalkmarks and charcoal. All was silent. The urrearth birds had retreated to their summer hibernations before the mists of autumn came to rouse them again. Climbing a scree of stones, they found clusters them at the back of a cave; feathery bundles amid the dripping rock, seemingly without eyes or beak.

As they sat at the mouth of that cave, looking down across the heat-trembling bay, sucking the ice and eating the dates which Ananke had insisted they bring with them, Nayra had seemed like a different person the one Jalila had thought she had known before the day of the moulid. Nayra, too, was human, and not the goddess she had seemed. She had her doubts and worries. She, too, thought the girls who surrounded her were mostly crass and stupid. She didn't even believe in her own obvious beauty. She cried a little again, and Jalila hugged her. The hug became a kiss. Soon, dusty and greedy, they were tumbling amid the hot rocks. That evening, back at the haramlek, Nayra was welcomed for dinner by Jalila's mothers with mint tea and best china. She was invited to bathe. Jalila sat beside her as they ate figs fresh from distant Ras and the year's second crop of oranges. She felt happy. At last, life seemed simple. Nayra, now, officially, was her lover, and this love would form the pattern of her days.

* * *

Jalila's life now seemed complex and complete; she believed she was an adult now, and that she talked and spoke and loved and worshipped in an adult way. She still rode out sometimes with Kalal on Robin and Abu, she still laughed or stole things or played games, but she was conscious now that these activities were sweetmeats of life, pleasing but unnutritous, and the real glories and surprises lay with being with Nayra, and with her mothers, and the life of the haramlek that the two young women talked of founding together one day.

Nayra's mothers lived on the far side on Al Janb, in a fine tall clifftop palace which was one of the oldest in the town, and was clad in white stone and filled with intricate courtyards, and a final beautiful tajo which looked down from garden of tarragon across the whole bay. Jalila greatly enjoyed exploring this haramlek, deciphering the peeling scripts which wound along the cool vaults, and enjoying the company of Nayra's mothers who, in their wealth and grace and wisdom, often made her own mothers seem like the awkward and recent provincial arrivals which they plainly were. At home, in her own haramlek, the conversations and ideas seemed stale. An awful dream came to Jalila one night. She was her old doll Tabatha, and she really was being buried. The ground she lay in was moist and dank, as if it was still the Season of Soft Rains, and the faces of everyone she knew were clustered around the hole above her, muttering and sighing as her mouth and eyes were inexorably filled with soil.

"Tell me what it was like, when you first fell in love."

Jalila had chosen Pavo to ask this question of. Ananke would probably just hug her, whilst Lya would talk and talk until there was nothing to say.

"I don't know. Falling in love is like coming home. You can never quite do it for the first time."

"But in the stories—"

"—The stories are always written *afterwards*, Jalila."

They were walking the luminous shore. It was near midnight, which was now by far the best time of the night or day. But what Pavo had just said sounded wrong; perhaps Jalila hadn't been the right choice of mother to speak to, after all. Jalila was sure she'd loved Nayra since that day before the moulid of Joanna, although it was true she loved her now in a different way.

"You still don't think we really will form a haramlek together, do you?"

"I think that it's too early to say."

"You were the last of our three, weren't you? Lya and Ananke were already together."

"It was what drew me to them. They seemed so happy and complete. It was also what frightened me and nearly sent me away."

"But you stayed together, and then there was . . ." This was the part which Jalila still found hardest to acknowledge; the idea that her mothers had a physical, sexual relationship. Sometimes, deep at night from someone else's dreamtent, she had heard muffled sighs, the tick of flesh. Just like the hayawans, she supposed, there were things about other people's lives which you could never fully understand no matter how well you thought you knew them.

She chose a different tack. "So why did you choose to have me?"

"Because we wanted to fill the world with something which had never ever existed before. Because we felt selfish. Because we wanted to give ourselves away."

"Ananke, she actually gave birth to me, didn't she?"

"Down here at the Al Janb, they'd say we were primitive and mad. Perhaps that was how we wanted to be. But all the machines at the clinics do is try to recreate the conditions of a real human womb—the voices, the movements, the sound of breathing . . . Without first hearing that Song of Life, no human can ever be happy, so what better way could there be than to hear it naturally?."

A flash of that dream-image of herself being buried. "But the birth itself—"

"—I think that was something we all underestimated." The tone of Pavo's voice told Jalila that this was not a subject to be explored on the grounds of mere curiosity.

The tideflower beds had solidified. You could walk across them as if they were dry land. Kalal, after several postponements and broken promises, took Jalila and Nayra out one night to demonstrate.

Smoking lanterns at the prow and stern of his boat. The water slipping warm as blood through Jalila's trailing fingers. Al Janb receding beneath the hot thighs of the mountains. Kalal at the prow. Nayra sitting beside her, her arm around her shoulder, hand straying across her breast until Jalila shrugged it away because the heat of their two bodies was oppressive.

"This season'll end soon," Nayra said. "You've never known the winter here, have you?"

"I was *born* in the winter. Nothing here could be as cold as the lightest spring morning in the mountains of Tabuthal."

"Ah, the *mountains*. You must show me sometime. We should travel there together . . ."

Jalila nodded, trying hard to picture that journey. She'd attempted to interest Nayra in riding a hayawan, but she grew frightened even in the presence of the beasts. In so many ways, in fact, Nayra surprised Jalila with her timidity. Jalila, in these moments of doubt, and as she lay alone in her dreamtent and wondered, would list to herself Nayra's many facets: her lithe and willing body; the beautiful haramlek of her beautiful mothers; the fact that so many of the other girls now envied and admired her. There were so many things which were good about Nayra.

Kalal, now that his boat had been set on course for the further tidebeds, came to sit with them, his face sweated lantern-red. He and Nayra shared many memories, and now, as the sails pushed on from the hot air off the mountains, they vied to tell Jalila of the surprises and delights of winters in Al Janb. The fogs when you couldn't see your hand. The intoxicating blue berries which appeared in special hollows through the crust of the snow. The special saint's days—If Jalila hadn't known better, she'd have said that Nayra and Kalal were fighting over something more important.

The beds of tideflowers were vast, luminous, heavy-scented. Red-black clusters of geelies rose and fell here and there in the moonlight. Walking these gaudy carpets was a most strange sensation. The dense interlaces of leaves felt like rubber matting, but sank and bobbed. Jalila and Nayra lit more lanterns and dotted them around a field of huge primrose and orange petals. They sang and staggered and rolled and fell over. Nayra had brought a pipe of kif resin, and the sensation of smoking that and trying to dance was hilarious. Kalal declined, pleading that he had to control the boat on the way back, and picked his way out of sight, disturbing flocks of geelies.

And so the two girls danced as the twin moons rose. Nayra, twirling silks, her hair fanning, was at grace as Jalila still staggered amid the lapping flowers. As she lifted her arms and rose on tiptoe, bracelets glittering, she had never looked more desirable. Somewhat drunkenly—and slightly reluctantly, because Kalal might return at any moment—Jalila moved forward to embrace her. It was good to hold Nayra, and her mouth tasted like the tideflowers and sucked needily at her own. In fact, the moments of their love had never been sweeter and slower than there were on that night, although, even as Jalila marvelled at the shape of Nayra's breasts and listened to the changed song of her breathing, she felt herself chilling, receding, drawing back not just from Nayra's physical presence, but from this small bay beside the small town on the single continent beside Habara's great and lonely ocean. Jalila felt infinitely sorry for Nayra as she brought her to her little ecstasies and they kissed and rolled across the beds of flowers. She felt sorry for Nayra because she was beautiful, and sorry for her because of all her accomplishments, and sorry for her because she would always be happy here amid the slow seasons of in this little planet.

Jalila felt sorry for herself as well; sorry because she had thought she had known love, and because she knew now that it had been a pretty illusion.

There was a shifting wind, dry and abrasive, briefly to be welcomed, until it became something to curse and cover you face and close your shutters against.

Of Jalila's mothers, only Lya seemed at all disappointed by her break from Nayra, no doubt because she had fostered hopes of their union forming a powerful bond between their haramleks, and even she did her best not to show it. Of the outside world, the other young women of Al Janb all professed total disbelief—*why if it had been me, I'd never have* . . . But soon, they were cherishing the new hope that it might indeed *be* them. Nayra, to her credit, maintained an extraordinary dignity in the face of the fact that she, of all people, had finally been rejected. She dressed in plain clothes. She spoke and ate simply. Of course, she looked more devastatingly beautiful than ever, and everyone's eyes were reddened by air-borne grit in any case, so it was impossible to tell how much she had really been crying. Now, as the buildings of Al Janb creaked and the breakers rolled and the wind howled through the teeth of the mountains, Jalila saw the gaudy, seeking and competing creatures who so often surrounded Nayra quite differently. Nayra was not, had never been, in control of them. She was more like the gaudy carcass over which, flashing their teeth, their eyes, stretching their limbs, they endlessly fought. Often, riven by a sadness far deeper than she had ever experienced, missing something she couldn't explain, wandering alone or lying in her dreamtent, Jalila nearly went back to Nayra . . . But she never did.

This was the Season of Winds, and Jalila was heartily sick of herself and Al Janb and the girls and the mahwagis and the mothers, and of this changing, buffeting banshee weather which seemed to play with her moods. The skies, sometimes now, were entirely beautiful, strung by the curling multicoloured banners of sand which the winds had lifted from distant corners of the continent. There was crimson and there was sapphire. The distant saharas of Jalila's dreams had come to haunt her. They fell, as the trees tore and the paint stripped from the shutters and what remained of Pavo's arches collapsed, in an irritating grit which worked its way into all the crevices of your body and every weave of your clothes.

The tariqua had spoken of the pain of *nothing*, and then of the pain *everything*. At the time, Jalila had understood neither, but now, she felt she understood the pain of nothing all too well. The product of the combined genes of her three mothers; Loving Ananke, ever-curious Pavo, proud and talkative Lya, she had always felt glad to recognise these characteristics mingled in herself, but now she wondered if these traits hadn't cancelled each other out. She was a null-point, a zero, clumsy and destructive and unloving. She was Jalila, and she walked alone and uncaring through this Season of Winds.

One morning, the weather was especially harsh. Jalila was alone in the haramlek, although she cared little where she or anywhere else was. A shutter must have come loose somewhere. That often happened now. It had been banging and hammering so long it began to irritate even her. She climbed stairs and slammed doors over jamming drifts of mica. She flapped back irritably at flapping curtains. Still, the banging went on. Yet all the windows and doors were now secure. She was sure of it. Unless . . .

Someone was at the front door. She could see their a swirling globular head through the greenish glass mullion. Even though they could surely see her as well, the banging went on. Jalila wondered if she wanted it to be Nayra; after all, this was how she had come to her after the moulid; a sweet and needy human being to drag her out from her dreams. But it was only Kalal. As the door shoved Jalila back, she tried not to look disappointed.

"You can't do this with your life!"

"Do what?"

"This—*nothing*. And then not answering the fucking door . . ." Kalal prowled the hallway as the door banged back and forth and tapestries flailed, looking for clues as if he was a detective. "Let's go out."

Even in this weather, Jalila supposed she owed it to Robin. Then Kalal had wanted to go north, and she insisted on going south, and was not in any mood for arguing. It was an odd journey, so unlike the ones they'd undertaken in the summer. They wrapped their heads and faces in flapping howlis, and tried to ride mostly in the forest, but the trees whipped and flapped and the raw air still abraded their faces.

They took lunch down by a flatrock shore, in what amounted to shelter, although there was still little enough of it as the wind eddied about them. This could have been the same spot where they had stopped in summer, but it was hard to tell; the light was so changed, the sky so bruised. Kalal seemed changed, too. His face beneath his howli seemed older as he tried to eat their aish before the sand-laden air got to it, and his chin looked prickled and abraded. Jalila supposed this was the same facial growth that his father Ibra was so fond of sporting. She also supposed he must choose to shave his off in the way that some women on some decadent planets were said to shave their legs and armpits.

"Come a bit closer—" she half-shouted, working her way back into the lee of the bigger rock beside which she was sitting to make room for him. "I want you to tell me what you know about love, Kalal."

Kalal hunched beside her. For a while, he just continued tearing and chewing bits of aish with his body pressed against hers as the winds boiled around them, the warmth of their flesh almost meeting. And Jalila wondered if men and women, when their lives and needs had been more closely intertwined, had perhaps known the answer to her question. What *was* love, after all? It would have been nice to think that, in those dim times of myth, men and women had whispered the answer to that question to each other . . .

She thought then that Kalal hadn't properly heard her. He was telling her about his father, and a planet he barely remembered, but on which he was born. The sky there had been fractalled gold and turquoise—colours so strange and bright that they came as a delight and a shock each morning. It was a place of many islands, and one great city. His father had been a fisherman and boat-repairer of sorts there as well, although the boats had been much grander than anything you ever saw at Al Janb, and the fish had lived not as single organisms, but as complex shoals which were caught not for their meat, but for their joint minds. Ibra had been approached by a woman from off-world, who had wanted a ship on which she could sail alone around the whole lonely band of the northern oceans. She had told him that she was sick of human company. The planning and the making of the craft was a joy for Ibra, because such a lonely journey had been one that he had long dreamed of making, if ever he'd had the time and money. The ship was his finest ever creation, and it turned out as they worked on it that neither he nor the woman were quite as sick of human company as they had imagined. They fell in love as the keel and the spars grew in the city dockyards and the ship's mind was nurtured, and as they did so they slowly relearned the expressions of sexual need between the male and female.

"You mean he *raped* her?"

Kalal tossed his last nub of bread towards the waves. "I mean that they *made love*."

After the usual negotiations and contracts, and after the necessary insertions of the appropriate cells, Ibra and this woman (whom Kalal didn't name in his story, any more than he named the world) set sail together, fully intending to conceive a child in the fabled way of old.

"Which was you?"

Kalal scowled. It was impossible to ask him even simple questions on this subject without making him look annoyed. "Of *course* it was! How many of me do you think there are?" Then he lapsed into silence. The sands swirled in coloured helixes before them.

"That woman—your birthmother. What happened to her?"

"She wanted to take me away, of course—to some haramlek on another world, just as she'd been planning all along. My father was just a toy to her. As soon as their ship returned, she started making plans, issuing contracts. There was a long legal dispute with my father. I was placed in a birthsac, in stasis."

"And your father won?"

Kalal scowled. "He took me here, anyway. Which is winning enough."

There were many other questions about this story which Jalila wanted to have asked Kalal if she hadn't already pressed too far. What, after all, did this tale of dispute and deception have to do with love? And were Kalal and Ibra really fugitives? It would explain quite a lot.

Once more, in that familiar welling, she felt sorry for him. Men were such strange, sad creatures; forever fighting, angry, lost . . .

"*I'm* glad you're here anyway," she said. Then, on impulse, one of those careless things you do, she took that rough and ugly chin in her hand, turned his face towards hers and kissed him lightly on the lips.

"What was that for?"

"*El-hamdu-l-Illah*. That was for thanks."

They plodded further on their hayawans. They came eventually to a cliff-edge so high that the sea and sky above and beneath vanished. Jalila already knew what they would see as they made their way along it, but still it was a shock; that qasr, thrust into these teeming ribbons of sand. The winds whooped and howled, and the hayawans raised their heads and howled back at it. In this grinding atmosphere, Jalila could see how the qasrs had been carved over long years from pure natural rock. They dismounted, and struggled bent-backed across the narrowing track towards the qasr's studded door. Jalila raised her fist and beat on it.

She glanced back at Kalal, but his face was entirely hidden beneath his hood. Had they always intended to come here? But they had travelled too far to do otherwise now; Robin and Abu were tired and near-blinded; they all needed rest and shelter. She beat the door again, but the sound was lost in the booming storm. Perhaps the tariqua had left with the last of the Season of Rockets, just as had most of the aliens. Jalila was about to turn away when the door, as if thrown by the wind, blasted open. There was no one on the other side, and the hallway beyond was dark as the bottom of a dry well. Robin hoiked her head back and howled and resisted as Jalila hauled him in. Kalal with Abu followed. The door, with a massive drumbeat, hammered itself shut behind them. Of course, it was only some old mechanism of this house, but Jalila felt the hairs on the nape of her neck rise.

They hobbled the hayawans beside largest of the scalloped arches, and walked on down the passageway beyond. The wind was still with them, and the shapes of the pillars were like the swirling helixes of sand made solid. It was hard to tell what of this place had been made by the hands of women and what was entirely natural. If the qasr had seemed deserted in the heat of summer, it was entirely abandoned now. A scatter of glass windchimes, torn apart by the wind. A few broken plates. Some flapping cobwebs of tapestry.

Kalal pulled Jalila's hand.

"Let's go back . . ."

But there was greater light ahead, the shadows of the speeding sky. Here was the courtyard where they had glimpsed the tariqua. She had plainly gone now—the fountain was dry and clogged, the bushes were bare tangles of wire. They walked out beneath the tiled arches, looking around. The wind was like a million voices, rising in ululating chorus. This was a strange and empty place; somehow dangerous . . . Jalila span around. The tariqua was standing there, her robes flapping. With insect fingers, she beckoned.

"Are you leaving?" Jalila asked. "I mean, this place . . ."

The tariqua had led them into the shelter of a tall, wind-echoing chamber set with blue and white tiles. There were a few rugs and cushions scattered on the floor, but still the sense of abandonment remained. As if,

Jalila thought as the tariqua folded herself on the floor gestured that they join her, this was her last retreat.

"No, Jalila. I won't be leaving Habara. *Itfaddal* . . . Do sit down."

The stepped from their sandals and obeyed. Jalila couldn't quite remember now whether Kalal had encountered the tariqua on her visit to their haramlek, although it seemed plain from his stares at her, and the way her grey-white gaze returned them, that they knew of each other in some way. Coffee was brewing in the corner, under a tiny blue spirit flame which, as it fluttered in the many drafts, would have taken hours to heat anything. Yet the spout of the brass pot was steaming. And there were dates, too, and nuts and seeds. The tariqua, apologising for her inadequacy as a host, nevertheless insisted that they help themselves. And somewhere there was a trough of water, too, for their hayawans, and a basket of acram leaves.

Uneasily, they sipped from their cups, chewed the seeds. Kalal had picked up a chipped lump of old stone and was playing with it nervously. Jalila couldn't quite see what it was.

"So," he said, clearing his throat, "you've been to and from the stars, have you?"

"As have you. Perhaps you could name the planet? It may have been somewhere that we have both visited . . ."

Kalal swallowed. His lump of old stone clicked the floor. A spindle of wind played chill on Jalila's neck. Then—she didn't know how it began—the tariqua was talking of Ghezirah, the great and fabled city which lay at the centre of all the Ten Thousand and One Worlds. No one Jalila had ever met or heard of had ever visited

Ghezirah—not even Nayra's mothers, yet this tariqua talked of it as if she knew it well. Before, Jalila had somehow imagined the tariqua trailing from distant planet to planet with dull cargoes of ore and biomass in her ship's holds. To her mind, Ghezirah had always been more than half-mythical—a place from which a dubious historical figure such as the Sainted Joanna might easily emanate, but certainly not composed of solid streets upon which the gnarled and bony feet of this old woman might once have strode . . .

Ghezirah—she could see it now in her mind, smell the shadowy lobbies, see the ever-climbing curve of its mezzanines and rooftops vanishing into the impossible greens of the Floating Ocean. But every time Jalila's vision seemed about to solidify, the tariqua said something else which made it tremble and change. And then the tariqua said the strangest thing of all, which was the City At The End Of All Roads was actually *alive*. Not alive in the meagre sense in which every town has a sort of life, but truly living. The city thought. It grew. It responded. There was no central mind or focus to this consciousness, because Ghezirah itself, its teeming streets and minarets and rivers and caleches and its many millions of lives, was itself the mind . . .

Jalila was awestruck, but Kalal seemed unimpressed, and was still playing with that old lump of stone.

4.

"Jalilaneen . . ."
The way bondmother Lya said her name made Jalila look up. Somewhere in her throat, a wary nerve started

ticking. They took their meals inside now, in the central courtyard of the haramlek, which Pavo had provided with a translucent roofing to let in a little of what light there was in the evenings' skies, and keep out most of the wind. Still, as Jalila took a sip of steaming hibiscus, she was sure that the sand had got into something.

"We've been talking. Things have come up—ideas about which we'd like to seek your opinion . . ."

In other words, Jalila thought, her gaze travelling across of her three mothers, you've decided something. And this is how you tell me—by pretending you're consulting me. It had been the same with leaving Tabuthal. It was always the same. An old ghost of herself got up at that point, threw down her napkin, stalked off up to her room. But the new Jalila remained seated. She even smiled and tried to look encouraging.

"We've seen so little of this world," Lya continued. "All of us, really. And especially since we had you. It's been marvellous. But of course it's also been confining . . . Oh *no*—" Lya waved the idea away quickly, before anyone could even begin to start thinking it. "—we won't be leaving our haramlek and Al Janb. There are many things to do. New bonds and friendships have been made. Ananke and I won't be leaving, anyway . . . But Pavo . . ." And here Lya, who could never quite stop being the chair of a committee, gave a nod towards her mate. ". . . Pavo here has dec—expressed a *wish*—that she would like to travel."

"Travel?" Jalila leaned forward, her chin resting on her knuckles. "How?"

Pavo gave her plate a half turn. "By boat seems the best way to explore Habara. With such a big ocean . . ." She turned the plate again, as if to demonstrate.

"And not just a *boat*," Ananke put in encouragingly. "A brand new *ship*. We're having it built—"

"—But I thought you said you hadn't yet decided?"

"The contract, I think, is still being prepared," Lya explained. "And much of the craft will be to Pavo's own design."

"Will you be building it yourself?"

"Not alone." Pavo gave another of her flustered smiles. "I've asked Ibra to help me. He seems to be the best, the most knowledgeable—"

"—Ibra? Does he have any references?"

"This is *Al Janb*, Jalila," Lya said. "We know and trust people. I'd have thought that, with your friendship with Kalal . . ."

"This certainly *is* Al Janb . . ." Jalila sat back. "How can I ever forget it!" All of her mothers' eyes were on her. Then something broke. She got up and stormed off to her room.

The long ride to the tariqua's qasr, the swish of the wind, and banging three times on the old oak door. Then hobbling Robin and hurrying through dusty corridors to that tall tiled chamber, and somehow expecting no one to be there, even though Jalila had now come here several times alone.

But the tariqua was always there. Waiting.

Between them now, there much to be said.

"This ant, Jalila, which crawls across this sheet of paper from *here* to *there*. She is much like us as we crawl across the surface of this planet. Even if she had the wings some of her kind sprout, just as I have my caleche, it would still be the same." The tiny creature, waving feelers, was plainly lost. A black dot. Jalila understood how it felt. "But say, if we were to fold both sides of the paper together. You see how she moves now ... ?" The ant, antennae waving, hesitant, at last made the tiny jump. "We can move more quickly from one place to another by not travelling across the distance which separates us from it, but by folding space itself.

"Imagine now, Jalila, that this universe is not one thing alone, one solitary series of *this* following *that*, but of an endless branching of potentialities. Such it has been since the Days of Creation, and such it is even now, in the shuffle of that leaf as the wind picks at it, in the rising steam of your coffee. Every moment goes in many ways. Most are poor, halfformed things, the passing thoughts and whims of the Almighty. They hang there and they die, never to be seen again. But others branch as strongly as this path in which we find ourselves following. There are universes where you and I have never sat here in this qasr. There are universes where there is no Jalila ... Will you get that for me ... ?"

The tariqua was pointing to an old book in a far corner. Its leather was cracked, the wind lifted its pages. As she took it from her, Jalila felt the hot brush of the old woman's hand.

"So now, you must imagine that there is not just one sheet of a single universe, but many, as in this book, heaped invisibly above and beside and below the page upon which we find ourselves crawling. In fact ..." The ant recoiled briefly, sensing the strange heat of the tariqua's fingers, then settled on the open pages. "You must imagine shelf after shelf, floor upon floor of books, the aisles of an infinite library. And if we are to fold this one page, you see, we or the ant never quite know what lies on the other side of it. And there may be a tear that next page as well. It may even be that another version of ourselves has already torn it."

Despite its worn state, the book looked potentially valuable, hand-written in a beautiful flowing script. Jalila has to wince when the tariqua's fingers ripped through them. But the ant had vanished now. She was somewhere between the book's pages . . .

"That, Jalila, is the Pain of Distance—the sense of every potentiality. So that womankind may pass over the spaces between the stars, every tariqua must experience it." The wind gave a extra lunge, flipping the book shut. Jalila reached forward, but the tariqua, quick for once, was ahead of her. Instead of opening the book to release the ant, she weighed it down with the same chipped old stone with which Kalal had played on his solitary visit to this qasr.

"Now, perhaps, my Jalila, you begin to understand?"

The stone was old, chipped, grey-green. It was inscribed, and had been carved with the closed wings of a beetle. Here was something from a world so impossibly old and distant as to make the book upon which it rested seem fresh and new as unbudded leaf—a scarab, shaped for the Queens of Egypt.

"See here, Jalila. See how it grows. The breathmoss?"

This was the beginning of the Season of Autumns. The trees were beautiful; the forests were on fire with their leaves. Jalila had been walking with Pavo, enjoying the return of the birdsong, and wondering why it was that this new season felt sad when everything seemed to be changing and growing.

"Look . . ."

The breathmoss, too, had turned russet-gold. Leaning

close to it beneath this tranquil sky, which was composed of a blue so pale it was as if the sea had been caught in reflection inside an upturned white bowl, was like looking into the arms of a minute forest.

"Do you think it will die?"

Pavo leaned beside her. "Jalila, it should have died long ago. *Inshallah*, it is a small miracle." There were the three dead marks where Ananke had touched it in a the Season of Long Ago. "You see how frail it is, and yet . . ."

"At least it won't spread and take over the planet."

"Not for a while, at least."

On another rock lay another small colony. Here, too, oddly enough, there were marks. Five large dead dots as if made by the outspread of a hand, although the shape of it was too big to have been Ananke's. They walked on. Evening was coming. Their shadows were lengthening. Although sun was shining and the waves sparkled, Jalila wished she had put on something warmer than a shawl.

"That tariqua. You seem to enjoy her company . . ."

Jalila nodded. When she was with the old woman, she felt as last as if she was escaping the confines of Al Janb. It was liberating, after the close life in this town and with her mothers in their haramlek, to know that interstellar space truly existed, and then to feel, as the tariqua spoke of Gateways, momentarily like that ant, infinitely small and yet somehow inching, crawling across the many universes' infinite pages. But how could she express this? Even Pavo wouldn't understand.

"How goes the boat?" she asked instead.

Pavo slipped her arm into to crook of Jalila's and hugged her. "You must come and *see*. I have the plan in my head, but I'd never realised quite how big it would be. And complex. Ibra's full of enthusiasm."

"I can imagine!"

The sea flashed. The two women chuckled.

"The way the ship's designed, Jalila, there's more than enough room for others. I never exactly planned to go alone, but then Lya's Lya. And Ananke's always—"

Jalila gave her mother's arm a squeeze. "I know what you're saying."

"I'd be happy if you came Jalila. I'd understand if you didn't. This is such a beautiful, wonderful planet. The leviathans—we know so little about them, yet they plainly have intelligence, just as all those old myths say."

"You'll be telling me next about the qasrs . . ."

"The ones we can see near here are *nothing*! There are islands on the ocean which are entirely made from them. And the wind pours through. They sing endlessly. A different song for every mood and season."

"Moods! If I'd said something like that when you were teaching me of the Pillars Of Life, you'd have told me I was being unscientific!"

"Science is about wonder, Jalila. I was a poor teacher if I never told you that."

"You did." Jalila turned to kiss Pavo's forehead. "You did . . ."

Pavo's ship was a fine thing. Between the slipways and the old mooring posts where the redflapping geelies quarrelled over scraps of dying tideflower, it grew and grew. Golden-hulled. Far sleeker and bigger than even the ferries which had once borne Al Janb's visitors to and from the rocket port, and which now squatted on the shingle nearby, gently rusting. It was the talk of the Season. People came to admire its progress.

As Jalila watched the spars rise over the clustered

roofs of the fisherwomen's houses, she was reminded of Kalal's tale of this father and nameless mother, and that ship which they had made together in the teeming dock-yards of that city. Her thoughts blurred. She saw the high balconies of a hotel far bigger than any of Al Janb's inns and boarding houses. She saw a darker, brighter ocean. Strange flesh upon flesh, with the windows open to the oil-and-salt breeze, the white lace curtains rising, falling . . .

The boat grew, and Jalila visited the tariqua, although back in Al Janb her thoughts sometimes trailed after Kalal as she wondered how it must be—to be male, like the last dodo, and trapped some endless state of part-arousal, like a form of nagging worry. Poor Kalal. But his life certainly wasn't lonely. The first time Jalila noticed him at the centre of the excited swarm of girls which once again surrounded Nayra, she'd almost thought she was seeing things. But the gossip was loud and persistent. Kalal and Nayra were *a couple*—the phrase normally followed by a scandalised shriek, a hand-covered mouth. Jalila could only guess what the proud mothers of Nayra's haramlek thought of such a union, but of course no one could subscribe to outright prejudice. Kalal was, after all, just another human being. Lightly probing her own mother's attitudes, she found the usual condescending tolerance. Having sexual relations with a male would be like smoking kif, or drinking alcohol, or any other form of slightly aberrant adolescent behaviour; to be tolerated with easy smiles and sympathy as long as it didn't go on for too long. To be treated, in fact, in much the same manner as her mothers were now treating her regular visits to the tariqua.

* * *

Jalila came to understand why people thought of the Season of Autumns as a sad time. The chill nights. The morning fogs which shrouded the bay. The leaves, finally falling, piled into rotting heaps. The tideflower beds, also, were dying as the waves pulled and dismantled what remained of their colours, and they drifted to the shores, the flowers bearing the same stench and texture and colour as upturned clay. The geelies were dying as well. In the town, to compensate, there was much bunting and celebration for yet another moulid, but to Jalila the brightness seemed feeble—the flame of a match held against winter's gathering gale. Still, she sometimes wandered the old markets with some of her old curiosity, nostalgically touching the flapping windsilks, studying the faces and nodding at the many she now knew, although her thoughts were often literally many light years away. *The Pain of Distance*; she could feel it. Inwardly, she was thrilled and afraid. Her mothers and everyone else, caught up in the moulid and Pavo's coming departure, imagined from her mood that she had now decided to take that voyage with her. She deceived Kalal in much the same way.

The nights became clearer. Riding back from the qasr one dark evening with the tariqua's slight voice ringing in her ears, the stars seemed to hover closer around her than at any time since she had left Tabuthal. She could feel the night blossoming, its emptiness and the possibilities spinning out to infinity. She felt both like crying, and like whooping for joy. She had dared the ask the tariqua the question she had long been formulating, and the answer, albeit not entirely yes, had not been no. She talked to Robin as they bobbed along, and the puny yellow smudge of Al Janb drew slowly closer. You must understand, she told her hayawan, that the core of the Almighty is like the empty place between these stars around which they all revolve. It is *there*, we know it, but we can never see . . . She sang songs from the old saharas about the joy of loneliness, and the loneliness of joy. From here, high up on the gradually descending road which wound its way down towards her haramlek, the horizon was still distant enough for her to see the lights of the rocketport. It was like a huge tidebed, holding out as the season changed. And there at the centre of it, rising golden, no longer a stumpy silo-shaped object but somehow beautiful, was the last of the year's rockets. It would have to rise from Habara before the coming of the Season of Winters.

Her mother's anxious faces hurried around her in the lamplight as she led Robin towards the stable.

"Where have you *been*, Jalilaneen?"

"Do you *know* what time it is?"

"We should be in the town *already!*."

For some reason, they were dressed in their best, most formal robes. Their palms were hennaed and scented. They bustled Jalila out of her gritty clothes, virtually washed and dressed her, then flapped themselves down the serraplate road into town where the processions had already started. Still, they were there in plenty of time to witness the blesssing of Pavo's ship. It was to be called *Endeavour*, and Pavo and Jalila together smashed the bottle of wine across its prow before it rumbled into the nightblack waters or the harbour with an enormous white splash. Everyone cheered. Pavo hugged Jalila.

There were more bottles of the same frothy wine available at the party afterwards. Lya, with her usual thoroughness, had ordered a huge case of the stuff, although many of the guests remembered the Prophet's old injunction and avoided imbibing. Ibra, though, was soon even more full of himself than usual, and went around the big marquee with a bottle in each hand, dancing clumsily with anyone who was foolish enough to come near him. Jalila drank a little of the stuff herself. The taste was sweet, but oddly hot and bitter. She filled up another glass.

"Wondered what you two mariners were going to call that boat . . ."

It was Kalal. He'd been dancing with many of the girls, and he looked almost as red-faced as his father.

"Bet you don't even know what the first *Endeavour* was."

"You're wrong there," Jalila countered primly, although the simple words almost fell over each other as she tried to say them. "It was the spacecraft of Captain Cook. She was one of urrearth's most famous early explorers."

"I thought you were many things," Kalal countered, angry for no apparent reason. "But I never thought you were *stupid*."

Jalila watched him walk away. The dance had gathered up its beat. Ibra had retreated to sit, foolishly glum, in a corner, and Nayra had moved to the middle of the floor, her arms raised, bracelets jingling, an opal jewel at her belly, windsilk-draped hips swaying. Jalila watched. Perhaps it was the drink, but for the first time in many a Season, she felt a slight return of that old erotic longing as she watched Nayra swaying. Desire was the strangest of all emotions. It seemed so trivial when you weren't possessed of it, and yet when you *were* possessed, it was as if all the secrets of the universe were waiting . . . Nayra was the focus of all attention now as she swayed amid the crowd, her shoulders glistening. She danced before Jalila, and her languorous eyes fixed her for a moment before she danced on. Now, she was dancing with Kalal, and he was swaying with her, her hands laid upon his shoulders, and everyone was clapping. They made a fine couple. Perhaps, Jalila thought, there really is some kind of symmetry in the matching of two sexes which we have lost. But the music was getting louder, and so were people's voices. Her head was pounding. She left the marquee.

She welcomed the harshness of the night air, the clear presence of the stars. Even the stench of the rotting tideflowers seemed appropriate as she picked her way across the ropes and slipways of the beach. So much had changed since she had first come here—but mostly what had changed had been herself. Here, its shape unmistakable as rising Walah spread her faint blue light across the ocean, was Kalal's boat. She sat down on the gunwale. The cold wind bit into her. She heard the crunch of shingle, and imagined it was someone else was in need of solitude. But the sound grew closer, and then whoever it was sat down on the boat beside her. She didn't need to look up now. Kalal's smell was always different, and now he was sweating from the dancing.

"I thought you were enjoying yourself," she muttered.

"Oh—I was . . ." The emphasis on the *was* was strong.

They sat there for a long time, in windy, wave-crashing silence. It was almost like being alone. It was like the old days of their being together.

"So you're going, are you?" Kalal asked eventually.

"Oh, yes."

"I'm pleased for you. It's a fine boat, and I like Pavo best of all your mothers. You haven't seemed quite so happy lately here in Al Janb. Spending all that time with that old witch in the qasr."

"She's not a witch. She's a tariqua. It's one of the greatest, oldest callings. Although I'm surprised you've had time to notice what I'm up to, anyway. You and Nayra . . ."

Kalal laughed, and the wind made the sound turn bitter.

"I'm sorry," Jalila continued. "I'm sounding just like those stupid gossips. I know you're not like that. Either of you. And I'm happy for you both. Nayra's sweet and talented and entirely lovely . . . I hope it lasts . . . I hope . . ."

After another long pause, Kalal said, "Seeing as we're apologising, I'm sorry I got cross with you about the name of that boat you'll be going on—the *Endeavour*. It's a good name."

"Thank you. *El-hamadu-l-illah.*"

"In fact, I could only think of one better one, and I'm glad you and Pavo didn't use it. You know what they say. To have two ships with the same name confuses the spirits of the winds . . ."

"What are you talking about, Kalal?"

"This boat. You're sitting right on it. I thought you might have noticed."

Jalila glanced down at the prow, which lay before her in the moonlight, pointing towards the silvered waves. From this angle, and in the old naskhi script which Kalal had used, it took her a moment to work out the craft's name. Something turned inside her.

Breathmoss.

In white, moonlit letters.

"I'm sure there are better names for a boat," she said carefully. "Still, I'm flattered."

"Flattered?" Kalal stood up. She couldn't really see his

face, but she suddenly knew that she'd once again said
the wrong thing. He waved his hands in an odd shrug,
and he seemed for a moment almost ready to lean close
to her—to do something unpredictable and violent—but
instead, picking up stones and skimming them hard into
the agitated waters, he walked away.

Pavo was right. If not about love—which Jalila knew now
she still waited to experience—then at least about the major decisions of your life. There was never quite a beginning to them, although your mind often sought for such
a thing.

When the tariqua's caleche emerged out of the newly
teeming rain one dark evening a week or so after the
naming of the *Endeavour* and settled itself before the
lights of their haramlek, and the old woman herself
emerged, somehow still dry, and splashed across the puddled garden whilst her three mothers flustered about to
find the umbrella they should have thought to look for
earlier, Jalila still didn't know what she should be thinking. The four women would, in any case, need to talk
alone; Jalila recognised that. For once, after the initial
greetings, she was happy to retreat to her dreamtent.

But her mind was still in turmoil. She was suddenly
terrified that her mothers would actually agree to this
strange proposition, and then that, out of little more than
embarrassment and obligation, the rest of her life would
be bound to something which the tariqua called the
Church of the Gateway. She knew so little. The tariqua
talked only in riddles. She could be a fraud, for all Jalila
knew—or a witch, just as Kalal insisted. Thoughts swirled
about her like the rain. To make the time disappear, she
tried searching the knowledge of her dreamtent. Lying

there, listening to the rising sound of her mother's voices which seemed to be studded endlessly with the syllables of her own name, Jalila let the personalities who had guided her through the many Pillars of Wisdom to tell her what they knew about the Church of the Gateway.

She saw the blackness of planetary space, swirled with the mica dots of turning planets. Almost as big as those as she zoomed close to it, yet looking disappointingly like a many-angled version of the rocketport, lay the spacestation, and within it the junction which could lead you from *here* to *there* without passing across the distance between. A huge rent in the Book of Life, composed of the trapped energies of these things the tariqua called cosmic strings, although they and the Gateway itself were visible as nothing more than a turning ring near to the centre of the vast spacestation where occasionally, as Jalila watched, crafts of all possible shapes would seem to hang, then vanish. The gap she glimpsed inside seemed no darker than that which hung between the stars behind it, but it somehow hurt to stare. This, then, was the core of the mystery; something both plain and extraordinary. We crawl across the surface of this universe like ants, and each of these craft, switching through the Gateway's moment of loss and endless potentiality, is piloted by the will of a tariqua's conscious intelligence which must glimpse these choices, then somehow emerge sane and entire at the other end of everything . . .

Jalila's mind returned to the familiar scents and shapes of her dreamtent, and the sounds of the rain. The moment seemed to belong with those of the long-ago Season of Soft Rains. Downstairs, there were no voices. As she climbed out from her dreamtent, warily expecting to the find the haramlek leaking and half-finished, Jalila was struck by an idea which the tariqua hadn't quite made plain to her; that a Gateway must push through *time* just as easily as it pushes through every other dimension . . . ! But the rooms of the haramlek were finely furnished, and her three mothers and the tariqua were sitting in the rainswept candlelight of the courtyard, waiting.

With any lesser request, Lya always quizzed Jalila before she would even consider granting it. So as Jalila sat before her mothers and tried not to tremble in their presence, she wondered how she could possibly explain her ignorance of this pure, boundless mystery.

But Lya simply asked Jalila if this was what she wanted—to be an acolyte of the Church of the Gateway.

"Yes."

Jalila waited. Then, not even, *are you sure?* They'd trusted her less than this when they'd sent her on errands into Al Janb . . . It was still raining. The evening was starless and dark. Her three mothers, having hugged her, but saying little else, retreated to their own dreamtents and silences, leaving Jalila to say farewell to the tariqua alone. The heat of the old woman's hand no longer came as a surprise to Jalila as she helped her up from her chair and away from the sheltered courtyard.

"Well," the tariqua croaked, "that didn't seem to go so badly."

"But I know so *little!*" They were standing on the patio at the dripping edge of the night. Wet streamers of wind tugged at them.

"I know you wish I could tell you more, Jalila—but then, would it make any difference?"

Jalila shook her head. "Will you come with me?"

"Habara is where I must stay, Jalila. It is written."

"But I'll be able to return?"

"Of course. But you must remember that you can never return to the place you have left." The tariqua fumbled with her clasp, the one of a worm consuming its tail. "I want you to have this." It was made of black ivory, and felt as hot as the old woman's flesh as Jalila took it. For once, not really caring whether she broke her bones, she gave the small, bird-like woman a hug. She smelled of dust and metal; like an antique box left forgotten on a sunny windowledge. Jalila helped her out down the steps into the rainswept garden.

"I'll come again soon," she said, "to the qasr."

"Of course . . . There are many arrangements." The tariqua opened the dripping filigree door or her caleche and peered at her with those half-blind eyes. Jalila waited. They had stood too long in the rain already.

"Yes?"

"Don't be too hard on Kalal."

Puzzled, Jalila watched the caleche rise and turn away from the lights of the haramlek.

Jalila moved warily through the sharded glass of her own and her mother's expectations. It was agreed that a message concerning her be sent, endorsed by full long and ornate formal name of the tariqua, to the body which did indeed call itself the Church of the Gateway. It went by radio pulse to the spacestation in wide solar orbit which received Habara's rockets, and was then passed itself on inside a vessel from *here* to *there* which was piloted by a tariqua. Not only that, but the message was destined for Ghezirah! Riding Robin up to the cliffs where, in this newly clear autumn air, under grey skies and tearing wet wind, she could finally see the waiting fuselage of that last golden rocket, Jalila felt confused and tiny; huge and mythic. It was agreed though, that for the sake of everyone—and not least Jalila herself, should she change her mind—that the word should remain that she was travelling out around the planet with Pavo on board the *Endeavour*. In need of something to do when she wasn't brooding, and waiting for further word from (could it really be?) the sentient city of Ghezirah, Jalila threw herself into the listings and loadings and preparations with convincing enthusiasm.

"The hardest decisions, once made, are often the best ones."

"Compared to what you'll be doing, my little journey seems almost pointless."

"We love you so deeply."

Then the message finally came: an acknowledgement; an acceptance; a few (far too few, it seemed) particulars of the arrangements and permissions necessary for such a journey. All on less than half a sheet of plain two-dimensional printout.

Even Lya had started touching and hugging her at every opportunity.

Jalila ate lunch with Kalal and Nayra. She surprised herself and talked gaily at first of singing islands and sea-leviathans, somehow feeling she was hiding little from her two best friends but the particular details of the journey she was undertaking. But Jalila was struck by the coldness which seemed to lie between these two supposed lovers. Nayra, perhaps sensing from bitter experience that she was once again about to be rejected, seemed near-tearful behind her dazzling smiles and the flirtatious blonde tossings of her hair, whilst Kalal seemed . . . Jalila had no idea how he seemed, but she couldn't let it end like this, and concocted some queries about the *Endeavour* so that she could lead him off alone as they left the bar. Nayra, perhaps fearing something else entirely, was reluctant to leave them.

"I wonder what it is that we've both done to her?" Kalal sighed as they watched her give a final sideways wave, pause, and then turn reluctantly down a sidestreet with a most un-Naryan duck of her lovely head.

They walked towards the harbour through a pause in the rain, where the *Endeavour* was waiting.

"Lovely, isn't she?" Kalal murmured as they stood looking down at the long deck, then up at the high forest of spars. Pavo, who was developing her acquaintance with the ship's mind, gave them a wave from the bubble of the forecastle. "How long do you think your journey will take? You should be back by early spring, I calculate it you get ahead of the icebergs . . ."

Jalila fingered the brooch the tariqua had given her and which she had taken to wearing at her shoulder in the place where she had once worn the tideflower. It was like black ivory, but set with tiny white specks which loomed at your eyes if you held it close. She had no idea what world it was from, or of the substance of which it was made.

". . . You'll miss the winter here. But perhaps that's no bad thing. It's cold, and they'll be other Seasons on the ocean. And they'll be other winters. Well, to be honest, Jalila, I'd been hoping—"

"—Look!" Jalila interrupted, suddenly sick of the lie she'd been living. "I'm not going."

They turned and were facing each other by the harbour's edge. Kalal's strange face twisted into surprise, and then something like delight. Jalila thought he was lookng more and more like his father. "That's marvellous!" He clasped each of Jalila's arms and squeezed her hard enough to hurt. "It was rubbish, by the way, what I just said about winters here in Al Janb. They're the most magical, wonderful season. We'll have snowball fights together! And when Eid al-Fitr comes . . ."

His voice trailed off. His hands dropped from her. "What is it Jalila?"

"I'm not going with Pavo on the *Endeavour,* but I'm going to Ghezirah. I'm going to study under the Church of the Gateway. I'm going to try to become a tariqua."

His face twisted again. "That witch—"

"—don't keep calling her that! You have no idea!"

Kalal balled his fists, and Jalila stumbled back, fearing for a moment that this wild, odd creature might actually be about to strike her. But he turned instead, and ran off from the harbour.

Next morning, to no one's particular surprise, it was once again raining. Jalila felt restless and disturbed after her incomplete exchanges with Kalal. Some time had also passed since the message had been received from Gheziah, and the few small details it had given of her journey had become vast and complicated and frustrating in their arranging. Despite the weather, she decided to ride out to see the tariqua.

Robin's mood had been almost as odd as her mothers recently, and she moaned and snickered at Jalila when she entered the stables. Jalila called back to her, and stroked her long nose, trying to ease her agitation. It was only when she went to check the harnesses that she realised that Abu was missing. Lya was in the haramlek, still finishing breakfast. It had to be Kalal who had taken her.

The swirling serraplated road. The black, dripping trees. The agitated ocean. Robin was starting to rust again. She would need more of Pavo's attention. But Pavo would soon be gone too ... The whole planet was changing, and Jalila didn't know what to make of anything, least of all what Kalal was up to, although the unasked-for borrowing of a precious mount, even if Abu had been virtually Kalal's all summer, filled her with a foreboding which was an awkward load, not especially heavy, but difficult to carry or put down; awkward and jagged and painful. Twice, now, he had turned from her and walked away with something unsaid. It felt like the start of some prophecy ...

The qasr shone jet-black in the teeming rain. The studded door, straining to overcome the swelling damp, burst open yet more forcefully than usual at Jalila's third knock, and the air inside swirled dark and empty. No sign of Abu in the place beyond the porch where Kalal would probably have hobbled him, although the floor here seemed muddied and damp, and Robin was agitated. Jalila glanced back, but her and her hayawan had already obscured the possible signs of another's presence. Unlike Kalal, who seemed to notice many things, she decided she made a poor detective.

Cold air stuttered down the passageways. Jalila, chilled and watchful, had grown so used to this qasr's sense of abandonment that it was impossible to tell whether the place was now finally empty. But she feared it was. Her thoughts and footsteps whispered to her that the tariqa, after ruining her life and playing with her expectations, had simply vanished into a puff of lost potentialities. Already disappointed, angry, she hurried to the high-ceilinged room set with white tiles and found to no great surprise that the strewn cushions were cold and damp, the coffee lamp was unlit, and that the book through which that patient ant had crawled was now sprawled in a damp-leafed scatter of torn pages. There was no sign of the scarab. Jalila sat down, and listened to the wind's howl, the rain's ticking, wondering for a long time when it was that she had lost the ability to cry.

Finally, she stood up and moved towards the courtyard. It was colder today than it had ever been, and the rain had greyed and thickened. It gelled and dripped from the gutters in the form of something she supposed was called *sleet*, and which she decided as it splattered down her neck that she would hate forever. It filled the bowl of the fountain with mucus-like slush, and trickled sluggishly along the lines of the drains. The air was full of weepings and howlings. In the corner of the courtyard, there lay a small black heap.

Sprawled half in half out of the poor shelter of the arched cloisters, more than ever like a flightless bird, the tariqua lay dead. Here clothes were sodden. All the furnace heat had gone from her body, although, on a day such as this, that would take no more than a matter of moments. Jalila glanced up though the sleet towards the black wet stone of the latticed mashrabiya from which she and Kalal had first spied on the old woman, but she was sure now that she was alone. People shrank incredibly when they were dead—even a figure as frail and old as this creature had been. And yet, Jalila found as she tired to move the tariqua's remains out of the rain, their spiritless bodies grew uncompliant; heavier and stupider than clay. The tariqua's face rolled up towards her. One side pushed in almost unrecognisably, and she saw that a nearby nest of ants were swarming over it, busily tunnelling out the moisture and nutrition, bearing it across the smeared paving as they stored up for the long winter ahead.

There was no sign of the scarab.

5.

This, for Jalila and her mothers, was the Season of Farewells. It was the Season of Departures.

There was a small and pretty onion-domed mausoleum on a headland overlooking Al Janb, and the pastures around it were a popular place for picnics and lover's trysts in the Season of Summers, although they were scattered with tombstones. It was the ever-reliable Lya who saw to the bathing and shrouding of the tariqua's body, which was something Jalila could not possibly face, and to the sending out though the null-space between the stars of all the necessary messages. Jalila, who had never been witness to the processes of death before, was astonished at the speed with which everything arranged. As she stood with the other mourners on a day scarfed with cloud beside the narrow rectangle of earth within which what remained of the tariqua now lay, she could still hear the wind booming over the empty qasr, feel the uncompliant weight of the old woman's body, the chill speckle of sleet on her face.

It seemed as if most of the population Al Janb had made the journey with the cortege up the narrow road from the town. Hard-handed fisherwomen. Gaudily dressed merchants. Even the few remaining aliens. Nayra was there, too, a beautiful vision of sorrow surrounded by her lesser black acolytes. So was Ibra. So, even, was

Kalal. Jalila, who was acknowledged to have known the old woman better than anyone, said a few words which she barely heard herself over the wind. Then a priestess who had flown in specially from Ras pronounced the usual prayers about the soul rising on the arms of Munkar and Nakir, the blue and the black angels. Looking down into the ground, trying hard to think of the Gardens of Delight which the Almighty always promised her stumbling faithful, Jalila could only remember that dream of her own burial: the soil pattering on her face, and everyone she knew looking down at her. The tariqua, in one of her many half-finished tales, had once spoken to her of a world upon which no sun had ever shone, but which was nevertheless warm and bounteous from the core of heat beneath its surface, and where the people were all blind, and moved by touch and sound alone; it was a joyous place, and they were forever singing. Perhaps, and despite all the words of the Prophet, Heaven, too, was a place of warmth and darkness.

The ceremony was finished. Everyone moved away, each pausing to toss in a damp clod of earth, but leaving the rest of the job to be completed by a dull-minded robotic creature, which Pavo had had to rescue from the attentions of the younger children who, all though the long Habaran summer, had ridden around on it. Down at their haramlek, Jalila's mothers had organised a small feast. People wandered the courtyard, and commented admiringly on the many changes and improvements they had made to the place. Amid all this, Ibra, seemed subdued—a reluctant presence in his own body, whilst Kalal was nowhere to be seen at all, although Jalila suspected that, if only for the reasons of penance, he couldn't be far away.

Of course, there had been shock at the news of the tariqua's death, and Lya, who had now become the person to whom the town most often turned to resolve its difficulties, had taken the lead in the enquiries which followed. A committee of wisewomen was organised even more quickly than the funeral, and Jalila had been summoned and interrogated. Waiting outside in the cold hallways of Al Janb's municipal buildings, she'd toyed with the idea of keeping Abu's disappearance and her suspicions of Kalal out of her story, but Lya and the others had already spoken to him, and he'd admitted to what sounded like everything. He'd ridden to the qasr on Abu to remonstrate with the tariqua. He'd been angry, and his mood had been bad. Somehow, but only lightly, he'd pushed the old woman, and she had fallen badly. Then, he panicked. Kalal bore responsibility for his acts, it was true, but it was accepted that the incident was essentially an accident. Jalila, who had imagined many versions of Kalal's confrontation with the tariqua, but not a single one which seemed entirely real, had been surprised at how easily the people of Al Janb were willing to absolve him. She wondered if they would have done so quite so easily if Kalal had not been a freak—a man. And then she also wondered, although no one had said a single word to suggest it, just how much she was to blame for all of this herself.

She left the haramlek from the funeral wake and crossed the road to the beach. Kalal was sitting on the rocks, his back turned to the shore and the mountains. He didn't look around when she approached and sat down beside him. It was the first time since before the tariqua's death that they'd been alone.

"I'll have to leave here," he said, still gazing out towards the clouds which trailed the horizon.

"There's no reason—"

"—no one's asked me and Ibra to *stay*. I think they would, don't you, if anyone had wanted us to? That's the way you women work."

"We're not *you women*, Kalal. We're people."

"So you always say. And all Al Janb's probably terrified about the report they've had to make to that thing you're joining—the Church of the Gateway. Some big, powerful, body, and—whoops—we've killed one of your old employees . . ."

"Please don't be bitter."

Kalal blinked and said nothing. His cheeks were shining.

"You and Ibra—where will you both go?"

"There are plenty of other towns around this coast. We can use our boat to take us there before the ice sets in. We can't afford to leave the planet. But maybe in the Season of False Springs, when I'm a grown man and we've made some of the proper money we're always talking about making from harvesting the tideflowers—and when word's got around to everyone on this planet of what happened here. Maybe then we'll leave Habara." He shook his head and sniffed. "I don't know why I bother to say *maybe* . . ."

Jalila watched the waves. She wondered if this was the destiny of all men; to wander forever from place to place, planet to planet, pursued by the knowledge of vague crimes which they hadn't really committed.

"I suppose you want to know what happened?"

Jalila shook her head. "It's in the report, Kalal. I believe what you said."

He wiped his face with his palms, studied their wetness. "I'm not sure I believe it myself, Jalila. The way she was, that day. That old woman—she always seemed to be expecting you, didn't she? And then she seemed to know. I don't understand quite how it happened, and I was angry, I admit. But she almost *lunged* at me . . . She seemed to want to die . . ."

"You mustn't blame yourself. *I* brought you to this Kalal. I never saw . . ." Jalila shook her head. She couldn't say. Not even now. Her eyes felt parched and cold.

"I loved you Jalila."

The worlds branched in a million different ways. It could all have been different. The tariqua still alive. Jalila and Kalal together, instead of the half-formed thing which the love they had both felt for Nayra had briefly been. They could have taken the *Endeavour* together and sailed this planet's seas; Pavo would probably have let them—but when, but where, but how? None of it seemed real. Perhaps the tariqua was right; there are many worlds, but most of them are poor, half-formed things.

Jalila and Kalal sat there for a while longer. The breathmoss lay not far off, darkening and hardening into a carpet of stiff grey. Neither of them noticed it.

For no other reason than the shift of the tides and the rapidly coming winter, Pavo, Jalila and Kalal and Ibra all left Al Janb on the same morning. The days before were chaotic in the haramlek. People shouted and looked around for things and grew cross and petty. Jalila, torn between bringing everything and nothing, and after many hours of bag-packing and lip-chewing, decided that it could all be thrown out, and that her time would be better spent down in the stables, with Robin. Abu was there too, of course, and she seemed to sense the imminence of change and departure even more than Jalila's own hayawan. She had become Kalal's mount far more than she had ever been Lya's, and he wouldn't come to say goodbye.

Jalila stroked the warm felt of the creatures' noses. Gazing into Abu's eyes as she gazed back at hers, she remembered their rides out in the heat of summer. Being with Kalal then, although she hadn't even noticed it, had been the closest she had ever come to loving anyone. On the last night before their departure, Ananke cooked one of her most extravagant dinners, and the four women sat around the heaped extravagance of the table which she'd spent all day preparing, each of them wondering what to say, and regretting how much of these precious last times together they'd wasted. They said a long prayer to the Almighty, and bowed in the direction of Al'Toman. It seemed that, tomorrow, even the two mothers who weren't leaving Al Janb would be setting out on a new and difficult journey.

Then there came the morning, and the weather obliged with chill sunlight and a wind that pushed hard at their cloaks and nudged the *Endeavour* away from the harbour even before her sails were set. They all watched her go, the whole town cheering and waving as Pavo waved back, looking smaller and neater and prettier than ever as she receded. Without ceremony, around the corner from the docks, out of sight and glad of the *Endeavour's* distraction, Ibra and Kalal were also preparing to leave. At a run, Jalila just caught them as they were starting to shift the hull down the rubbled slipway into the waves. *Breathmoss;* she noticed that Kalal had kept the name, although she and he stood apart on that final beach and talked as two strangers.

She shook hands with Ibra. She kissed Kalal lightly on the cheek by leaning stiffly forward, and felt the roughness of his stubble. Then the craft got stuck on the slipway, and they were all heaving to get her moving the last few metres into the ocean, until, suddenly, she was afloat, and Ibra was raising the sails, and Kalal was at the prow, hidden behind the tarpaulined weight of their belongings. Jalila only glimpsed him once more, and by then *Breathmoss* had turned to meet the stronger currents which swept outside the grey bay. He could have been a figurehead.

Back at the dock, her mothers were pacing, anxious.

"Where have you *been*?"

"Do you *know* what *time* is?"

Jalila let them scald her. She *was* almost late for her own leaving. Although most of the crowds had departed, she'd half expected Nayra to be there. Jalila was momentarily saddened, and then she was glad for her. The silver craft which would take her to the rocketport smelled disappointingly of sick and engine fumes as she clambered into it with the few other women and aliens who were leaving Habara. There was a loud bang as the hatches closed, and then a long wait while nothing seemed to happen and she could only wave at Lya and Ananke through the thick porthole, smiling and mouthing stupid phrases until her face ached. The ferry bobbed loose, lurched, turned and angled up. Al Janb was half gone in plumes of white spray already.

Then it came in a huge wave. That feeling of incompleteness, of something vital and unknown left irretrievably behind, which is the beginning of the Pain of Distance which Jalila, as a tariqua, would have to face throughout her long life. A sweat came over her. As she gazed out through the porthole at what little there was to see of Al Janb and the mountains, it slowly resolved itself into one thought. Immense and trivial. Vital and stupid. That scarab. She'd never asked Kalal about it, nor found it as the qasr, and the ancient object turned itself over in her head, sinking, spinning, filling her mind and then dwindling before rising up again as she climbed out, nauseous, from the ferry and crossed the clanging gantries of the spaceport towards the last huge golden craft which stood steaming in the winter's air. A murder weapon?— but no, Kalal was no murderer. And, in any case, she was a poor detective. And yet . . .

The rockets thrust and rumbled. Pushing back, aching her eyeballs. There was no time now to think. Weight on weight, terrible seconds piled on her. Her blood seemed to leave her face. She was a clay-corpse. Vital elements of her senses departed. Then, there was a huge wash of silence. Jalila turned to look through the porthole beside her, and there it was. Mostly blue, and entirely beautiful; Habara, her birth planet. Jalila's hands rose up without her willing, and her fingers squealed as she touched the glass and tried to trace the shape of the greenish-brown coastline, the rising brown and white of the mountains of that huge single continent which already seemed so small, but of which she knew so little. Jewels seemed to be hanging close before her, twinkling and floating in and out of focus like the hazy stars she couldn't yet see. They puzzled her for a long time, did these jewels, and they were evasive as fish as she sought them with her weightlessly clumsy fingers. Then Jalila felt the salt break of moisture against her face, and realised what it was.

At long last, she was crying.

6.

Jalila had long been expecting the message when it finally came. At only one hundred and twenty standard years, Pavo was still relatively young to die, but she had used her life up at a frantic pace, as if she had always known that her time would be limited. Even though the custom for swift funerals remained on Habara, Jalila was able to use her position as a tariqua to ride the Gateways and return for the service. The weather on the planet of her birth was unpredictable as ever, raining one moment and then sunny the next even as she took the ferry to Al Janb from the rocketport, and hot and cold winds seemed to strike her face as she stood on the dock's edge and looked about for her two remaining mothers. They embraced. They led her to their haramlek, which seemed smaller to Jalila each time she visited it despite the many additions and extensions and improvements they had made, and far closer to Al Janb than the long walk she remembered once taking on those many errands. She wandered the shore after dinner, and searched the twilight for a particular shape and angle of quartz, and the signs of dark growth. But the heights of the Season of Storms on this coastline were ferocious, and nothing as fragile as breathmoss could have survived. She lay sleepless that night in her old room within her dreamtent, breathing the strong, dense, moist atmosphere with difficulty, listening to the sound of the wind and rain.

She recognised none of the faces but her mothers of the people who stood around Pavo's grave the following morning. Al Janb had seemed so changeless, yet even Nayra had moved on—and Kalal was far away. Time was relentless. Far more than the wind which came in off the bay, it chilled Jalila to the bone. One mother dead, and her two others looking like the mahwagis she supposed they were becoming. *The Pain of Distance.* More than ever now, and hour by hour and day by day in this life which she had chosen, Jalila knew what the old tariqua had meant. She stepped forward to say a few words. Pavo's life had been beautiful and complete. She had passed on much knowledge about this planet to all womankind, just as she had once passed on her wisdom to Jalila. The people listened respectfully to Jalila, as if she were a priest. When the prayers were finished and the clods of earth had been tossed and the groups began to move back down the hillside, Jalila remained standing by Pavo's grave. What looked like the same old part-metal beast came lumbering up, and began to fill in the rest of the hole, lifting and lowering the earth with reverent, childlike care. Just as Jalila had insisted, and despite her mother's puzzlement, Pavo's grave lay right beside the old tariqua's whom they had buried so long ago. This was a place which she long avoided, but now that Jalila saw the stone, once raw and brittle, but now smoothed and greyed by rain and wind, she felt none of the expected agony. She traced the complex name, scrolled in naskhi script, which she had once found impossible to remember, but which she had now recited thoughtless times in the ceremonials which the Church of the Gateway demanded of its acolytes. Sometimes, especially in the High Temple at Ghezirah, the damn things could go on for days. Yet not one member of the whole Church had seen fit to come to the simple ceremony of this old woman's burial. It had hurt her, once, to think that no one from offworld had come to her own funeral. But now she understood.

About to walk away, Jalila paused, and peered around

the back of the gravestone. In the lee of the wind, a soft green patch of life was thriving. She stooped to examine the growth, which was thick and healthy, forming a patch more than the size of her two outstretched hands ion this sheltered place. Breathmoss. It must have been here for a long time. Yet who would have thought to bring it? Only Pavo: only Pavo could possibly have known.

As the gathering of mourners at the haramlek started to peter out, Jalila excused herself and went to Pavo's quarters. Most of the stuff up here was a mystery to her. There were machines and nutrients and potions beyond anything you'd expect to encounter on such an out-of-the way planet. Things were growing. Objects and data needed developing, tending, cataloguing, if Pavo's legacy was to be maintained. Jalila would have to speak to her mothers. But, for now, she found what she wanted, which was little more than a glass tube with an open end. She pocketed it, and walked back up over the hill to the cemetery, and said another few prayers, and bent down in the lee of the wind behind the old gravestone beside Pavo's new patch of earth, and managed to remove a small portion of the breathmoss without damaging the rest of it.

That afternoon, she knew that she would have to ride out. The stables seemed virtually unchanged, and Robin was waiting. She even snickered in recognition of Jalila, and didn't try to bite her when she came to introduce the saddle. It had been such a long time that the animal's easy compliance seemed a small miracle. But perhaps this was Pavo again; she could have done something to preserve the recollection of her much-changed mistress in some circuit or synapse of the hayawan's memory. Snuffling tears, feeling sad and exulted, and also somewhat uncomfortable, Jalila headed south on her hayawan along the old serraplate road, up over the cliffs and beneath the arms of the urrearth forest. The trees seemed different; thicker-leafed. And the birdsong cooed slower and deeper than she remembered. Perhaps, here in Habara, this was some Season other than all of those which she remembered. But the qasr reared as always—out there on the clifface, and plainly deserted. No one came here now, but, like Robin, the door, at three-beat of her fists, remembered.

Such neglect. Such decay. It seemed a dark and empty place. Even before Jalila came across the ancient signs of her own future presence—a twisted coathanger, a chipped plate, a few bleached and rotting cushions, some odd and scattered bits of Gateway technology which had passed beyond malfunction and looked like broken shells—she felt lost and afraid. Perhaps this, at last, was the final moment of knowing which she had warned herself she might have to face on Habara. The Pain of Distance. But at the same time, she knew that she was safe as she crawled across this particular page of her universe, and that when she did finally take a turn beyond the Gateways through which sanity itself could scarcely follow, it would be of her own volition, and as an impossibly old woman. That tariqua. Tending flowers like an old tortoise thrust out of its shell. Here, on a sunny, distant day. There were worse things. There were always worse things. And life was good. For all of this, pain was the price you paid.

Still, in the courtyard, Jalila felt the cold draft of prescience upon her neck from that lacy mashrabiya where she and Kalal would one day stand. The movement she made as she looked up towards it even reminded her of the old tariqua. Even her eyesight was not like as sharp as it had once been. Of course, there were ways around that which could be purchased in the tiered and dizzy markets of Ghezirah, but sometimes it was better to accept some things as the will of the Almighty. Bowing down, muttering the *shahada*, Jalila laid the breathmoss upon the shaded stone within the cloister. Sheltered here, she imagined it would thrive. Mounting Robin, riding from the qasr, she paused once to look back. Perhaps her eyesight really was failing her, for she thought she saw the ancient structure shimmer and change. A beautiful green castle hung above the cliffs, coated entirely in breathmoss; a wonder from a far and distant age. She rode on, humming snatches of the old songs she'd once known so well about love and loss between the stars. Back at the haramlek, her mothers were as anxious as ever to know where she had been. Jalila tried not to smile as she endured their familiar scolding. She longed to hug them. She longed to cry.

That evening, her last evening before she left Habara, Jalila walked the shore alone again. Somehow, it seemed the place to her where Pavo's ghost was closest. Jalila could see her mother there now, as darkness welled up from between the rocks; a small, lithe body, always stooping, turning, looking. She tried going towards her; but Pavo's shadow always flickered shyly away. Still, it seemed to Jalila as if she had been led towards something, for here was the quartz-striped rock from that long-ago Season of the Soft Rains. Of course, there was no breathmoss left, the storms had seen to that, but nevertheless, as she bent down to examine it, Jalila was sure that she could see something beside it, twinkling clear from a rockpool through the fading light. She plunged her hand in. It was a stone, almost as smooth and round as many millions of others on beach, yet this one was worked and carved. And its colour was greenish-grey.

The soapstone scarab, somehow thrust here to this beach by the storms of potentiality which the tariquas of the Church of the Gateway stirred up by their impossible journeyings, although Jalila was pleased to see that it looked considerably less damaged than the object she remembered Kalal turning over and over in his nervous hands as he spoke to her future self. Here at last was the link that would bind her through the pages of destiny, and for a moment she hitched her hand back and prepared to throw it so far out into ocean that it would never be reclaimed. Then her arm relaxed. Out there, all the way across the darkness of the bay, the tideflowers of Habara were glowing.

She decided to keep it.

Angles

Orson Scott Card

3000

Hakira enjoyed coasting the streets of Manhattan. The old rusted-out building frames seemed like the skeleton of some ancient leviathan that beached and died, but he could hear the voices and horns and growling machinery of crowded streets and smell the exhaust and cooking oil, even if all that he saw beneath him were the tops of the trees that had grown up in the long-vanished streets. With a world as uncrowded as this one, there was no reason to dismantle the ruins, or clear the trees. It could remain as a monument, for the amusement of the occasional visitor.

There were plenty of places in the world that were still crowded. As always, most people enjoyed or at least needed human company, and even recluses usually wanted people close enough to reach from time to time. Satellites and landlines still linked the world together, and ports were busy with travel and commerce of the lighter sort, like bringing out-of-season fruits and vegetables to consumers who preferred not to travel to where the food was fresh. But as the year 3000 was about to pass away, there were places like this that made the planet Earth seem almost empty, as if humanity had moved on.

In fact, there were probably far more human beings alive than anyone had ever imagined might be possible. No human had ever left the solar system, and only a handful lived anywhere but Earth. One of the Earths, anyway—one of the angles of Earth. In the past five hundred years, millions had passed through benders to colonize versions of Earth where humanity had never evolved, and now a world seemed full with only a billion people or so.

Of the trillions of people that were known to exist, the one that Hakira was going to see lived in a two-hundred-year-old house perched on the southern coast of this island, where in ancient times artillery had been placed to command the harbor. Back when the Atlantic reached this far inland. Back when invaders had to come by ship.

Hakira set his flivver down in the meadow where the homing signal indicated, switched off the engine, and slipped out into the bracing air of a summer morning only a few miles from the face of the nearest glacier. He was expected—there was no challenge from the security system, and lights showed him the path to follow through the shadowy woods.

Because his host was something of a show-off, a pair of sabertooth tigers were soon padding along beside him. They might have been computer simulations, but knowing Moshe's reputation, they were probably genetic backforms, very expensive and undoubtedly chipped up to keep them from behaving aggressively except, perhaps, on command. And Moshe had no reason to wish Hakira ill. They were, after all, kindred spirits.

The path suddenly opened up onto a meadow, and after only a few steps he realized that the meadow was the roof of a house, for here and there steep-pitched skylights rose above the grass and flowers. And now, with a turn, the path took him down a curving ramp along the face of the butte overlooking the Hudson plain. And now he stood before a door.

It opened.

A beaming Moshe stood before him, dressed in, of all things, a kimono. "Come in, Hakira! You certainly took your time!"

"We set our appointment by the calendar, not the clock."

"Whenever you arrive is a good time. I merely noted that my security system showed you taking the grand tour on the way."

"Manhattan. A sad place, like a sweet dream you can never return to."

"A poet's soul, that's what you have."

"I've never been accused of that, before."

"Only because you're Japanese," said Moshe.

They sat down before an open fire that seemed real, but gave off no smoke. Heat it had, however, so that Hakira felt a little scorched when he leaned forward. "There are Japanese poets."

"I know. But is that what anyone thinks of, when they think of the wandering Japanese?"

Hakira smiled. "But you *do* have money."

"Not from money-changing," said Moshe. "And what I don't have, which you also don't have, is a home."

Hakira looked around at the luxurious parlor. "I suppose that technically this *is* a cave."

"A homeland," said Moshe. "For nine and a half centuries, my friend, your people have been able to go almost anywhere in the world but one, an archipelago of islands once called Honshu, Hokkaido, Kyushu—"

Hakira, suddenly overcome by emotion, raised his hand to stop the cruel list. "I know that your people, too, have been driven from their homeland—"

"Repeatedly," said Moshe.

"I hope you will forgive me, sir, but it is impossible to imagine yearning for a desert beside a dead sea the way one yearns for the lush islands strangled for nearly a thousand years by the Chinese dragon."

"Dry or wet, flat or mountainous, the home to which you are forbidden to return is beautiful in dreams."

"Who has the soul of a poet now?"

"Your organization will fail, you know."

"I know nothing of the kind, sir."

"It will fail. China will never relent, because to do so would be to admit wrongdoing, and that they cannot do. To them you are the interlopers. The toothless Peace Council can issue as many edicts as it likes, but the Chinese will continue to bar those of known Japanese ancestry from even visiting the islands. And they will use as their excuse the perfectly valid argument that if you want so much to see Japan, you have only to bend yourself to a different slant. There is bound to be some angle where your tourist dollars will be welcome."

"No," said Hakira. "Those other angles are not *this* world."

"And yet they are."

"And yet they are not."

"Well, now, there is our dilemma. Either we will do business or we will not, and it all hinges on that question. What is it about that archipelago that you want. Is it the land itself? You can already visit that very land—and we are told that because of inanimate incoherency it *is* the same land, no matter what angle *you* dwell in. Or is your desire really not simply to go there, but to go there in defiance of the Chinese? Is it hate, then, that drives you?"

"No, I reject both interpretations," said Hakira. "I care nothing for the Chinese. And now that you put the question in these terms, I realize that I myself have not thought clearly enough, for while I speak of the beautiful land of the rising sun, in fact what I yearn for is the Japanese nation, on those islands, unmolested by any other, governing ourselves as we have from the beginning of our existence as a people."

"Ah," said Moshe. "Now I see that we perhaps *can* do business. For it may be possible to grant you your heart's desire."

"Me and all the people of the Kotoshi."

"Ah, the eternally optimistic Kotoshi. It means 'this year,' doesn't it? As in, 'this year we return'?"

"As your people say, 'Next year in Jerusalem.'"

"A Japan where only the Japanese have ruled for all these past thousand years. In a world where the Japanese are not rootless wanderers, legendary toymakers-for-hire, but rather are a nation among the nations of the world, and one of the greatest of them. Is *that* not the home you wish to return to?"

"Yes," said Hakira.

"But that Japan does not exist in this world, not even now, when the Chinese no longer need even half the land of the original Han China. So you do not want the Japan of this world at all, do you? The Japan you want is a fantasy, a dream."

"A hope."

"A wish."

"A *plan*."

"And it hasn't occurred to you that in all the angles of the world, there might not be such a Japan?"

"It isn't like the huge library in that story, where it is believed that among all the books containing all the combinations of all the letters that could fit in all those pages, there is bound to be a book that tells the true history of all the world. There are many angles, yes, but our ability to differentiate them is not infinite, and in many of them life never evolved and so the air is not breathable. It is an experiment not lightly undertaken."

"Oh, of course. To find a world so nearly like our own that a nation called Japan—or, I suppose, Nippon—exists at all, where a language like Japanese is even spoken— you do speak Japanese yourself, don't you?"

"My parents spoke nothing else at home until I was five and had to enter school."

"Yes, well, to find such a world would be a miracle."

"And to search for it would be a fool's errand."

"And yet it *has* been searched for."

Hakira waited. Moshe did not go on.

"Has it been found?"

"What would it be worth to you, if it had?"

2024—ANGLE 1

"You're a scientist," said Leonard. "This is beneath you."

"I have continuous video," said Bêto. "With a mechanical clock in it, so you can see the flow of time. The chair moves."

"There is nothing you can do that hasn't been faked by somebody, sometime."

"But why would I fake it? To publish this is the end of my career."

"Exactly my point, Bêto. You are a geologist, of all things. Geologists don't have poltergeists."

"Stay with me, Leonard. Watch this."

"How long?"

"I don't know. Sometimes it's immediate. Sometimes it takes days."

"I don't have days."

"Play cards with me. As we used to in Faculdade. Look at the chair first, though. Nothing attached to it. A normal chair in every way."

"You sound like a magician on the stage."

"But it *is* normal."

"So it seems."

"Seem? All right, don't trust me. *You* move it. Put it where you want."

"All right. Upside down?"

"It doesn't matter."

"On top of the door?"

"I don't care."

"And we play cards?"

"You deal."

2090

It is the problem of memory. We have mapped the entire brain. We can track the activity of every neuron, of every synapse. We have analyzed the chemical contents of the cells. We can find, in the living brain, without surgery, exactly where each muscle is controlled, where perceptions are rooted. We can even stimulate the brain to track and recall memory. But that is all. We cannot account for how memory is stored, and we cannot find where.

I know that in your textbooks in secondary school and perhaps in your early undergraduate classes you have read that memory was the first problem solved, but that was a misunderstanding. We discovered that after mapping a particular memory, if that exact portion of the brain was destroyed—and this was in the early days, with clumsy equipment that killed thousands of cells at a time, an incredibly wasteful procedure and potentially devastating to the subject—if that exact spot was destroyed, the memory was not lost. It could resurface somewhere else.

So for many years we believed that memory was stored holographically, small portions in many places, so that losing a bit of a memory here or there did not cause the entire sequence to be lost. This, however, was chimerical, for as our research became more and more precise, we discovered that the brain is not infinite, and such a wasteful system of memory storage would use up the entire brain before a child reached the age of three. Because, you see *no memory is lost*. Some memories are hard to recover, and people often lose *track* of their memories, but it is not a problem of storage, it is a problem of retrieval.

Portions of the network break down, so tracks cannot be followed. Or the routing is such that you cannot link from memory A to memory X without passing through memories of such power that you are distracted from the attempt to retrieve. But, given time—or hyperstimulation of related memory tracks—all memories can be retrieved. All. Every moment of your life.

We cannot recover more than your perceptions and

the sense you made of them at the time, but that does not change the fact that we *can* recover every moment of your childhood, every moment of this class. And we can recover every conscious thought, though not the unconscious streaming thought behind it. It is all stored ... somewhere. The brain is merely the retrieval mechanism.

This has led some observers to conclude that there is, in fact, a mind, or even a soul—a nonphysical portion of the human being, existing outside of measurable space. But if that is so, it is beyond the reach of science. I, however, am a scientist, and with my colleagues—some of whom once sat in the very chairs where you are sitting—I have labored long and hard to find an explanation that is, in fact, physical. Some have criticized this effort because it shows that my faith in the nonexistence of the immaterial is so blind that I refuse to believe even the material evidence of immateriality. Don't laugh, it is a valid question. But my answer is that we cannot validly prove the immateriality of the mind by the sheer fact of our inability to detect the material of which it is made.

I am happy to tell you that we have received word that the journal *Mind*—and we would not have settled for anything less than the premiere journal in the field—has accepted our article dealing with our findings. By no means does this constitute an answer. But it moves the field of inquiry and reopens the possibility, at least, of a material answer to the question of memory. For we have found that when neurons are accessed for memory, there are many kinds of activity in the cell. The biochemical, of course, has been very hard to decode, but other researchers have accounted for all the chemical reactions within the cell, and we have found nothing new in that area. Nor is memory electrochemical, for that is merely how raw commands of the coarsest sort are passed from neuron to neuron—rather like the difference between using a spray can as opposed to painting with a monofilament brush.

Our research, of course, began in the submolecular realm, trying to find out if in some way the brain cells were able to make changes in the atom, in the arrangement of protons and neutrons, or some information somehow encoded in the behavior of electrons. This proved, alas, to be a dead end as well.

But the invention of the muonoscope has changed everything for us. Because at last we had a nondestructive means of scanning the exact state of muons through infinitesimal passages of time, we were able to find some astonishing correlations between memory and the barely detectable muon states of slant and yaw. Yaw, as you know, is the constant—the yaw of a muon cannot change during the existence of the muon. Slant also seemed to be a constant, and in the materials which had previously been examined by physicists, that was indeed the case.

However, in our studies of brain activity during forced memory retrieval, we have found a consistent pattern of slant alteration within the nuclei of atoms in individual brain cells. Because the head must be held utterly still for the muonoscope to function, we could only work with terminally ill patients who volunteered for the study and were willing to die in the laboratory instead of with their families, spending the last moments of their lives with their heads opened up and their brains partially disassembled. It was painless but nevertheless emotionally disturbing to contemplate, and so I must salute the courage and sacrifice of our subjects, whose names are all listed in our article as co-authors of the study. And I believe that our study has now taken us as far as biology can go, given the present equipment. The next move is in the hands of physicists.

Ah, yes. What we found. You see? I became side-tracked by my thought of our brave collaborators, because I remembered their memories which meant remembering who they were and what it cost them to ... and I am being distracted again. What we found was: During the moment of memory retrieval, when the neuron was stimulated and went into the standard memory-retrieval state, there is a moment—a moment so brief that until fifteen years ago we had no computer that could have detected it, let alone measured its duration—when all the muons in all the protons of all the atoms in all the memory-specific RNA molecules in the nucleus of the one neuron—and no others!—change their slant.

More specifically, they seem, according to the muono-scope, to wink out of existence for that brief moment, and then return to existence with a new pattern of slants—yes, varying slants, impossible as we have been told that was—which exist for a period of time perhaps a thousand times longer than the temporary indetectability, though this is still a span of time briefer than a millionth of a pico-second, and during the brief existence of this anomalous slant-state, which we call the "angle," the neuron goes through the spasm of activity that causes the entire brain to respond in all the ways that we have long recognized as the recovery of memory.

In short, it seems that the pertinent muons change their slant to a new angle, and in that angle they are en-coded with a snapshot of the brain-state that will cause the subject to remember. They return to detectability in the process of rebounding to their original slant, but for the brief period before they have completed that rebound, the pattern of memory is reported, via biochemical and then electrochemical changes, to the brain as a whole.

There are those who will resent this discovery because it seems to turn the mind or soul into a mere physical phenomenon, but this is not so. In fact, if anything our discovery enhances our knowledge of the utterly unique majesty of life. For as far as we know, it is only in the living brain of organisms that the very slant of the muons within atoms can be changed. The brain thus opens tiny doorways into other universes, stores memories there, and retrieves them at will.

Yes, I mean other universes. The first thing that the muonoscope showed us was the utter emptiness of muons. There are even theorists who believe that there are no particles, only attributes of regions of space, and theoretically there is no reason why the same point in space cannot be occupied by an infinite number of muons, as long as they have different slants and, perhaps, yaws. For theoretical reasons that I do not have the mathematics to understand, I am told that while coterminous muons of the same yaw but different slants could impinge upon and influence each other, coterminous muons of different yaw could never have any causal relationship. And there could also be an infinite series of infinite series of universes whose muons are not coterminous with the muons of our universe, and they, too, are permanently undetectable and incapable of influencing our universe.

But if the theory is correct—and I believe our research proves that it is—it is possible to pass information from one slant of this physical universe to another. And since, by this same theory, all material reality is, in fact, merely information, it is even possible that we might be able to pass objects from one such universe to another. But now we are in the realm of fantasy, and I have spent as much time on this happy announcement as I dare. You are, after all, students, and my job is to pass certain information from my brain to yours, which does not, I'm afraid, involve mere millionths of a pico-second.

2024—ANGLE M

"I can't stand it, I can't. I won't live here another day, another hour."

"But it never harms us, and we can't afford to move."

"The chair is on top of the door, it could fall, it could hurt one of the children. Why is it doing this to us? What have we done to offend it?"

"We haven't done *anything*, it's just *malicious*, it's just *enjoying itself!*"

"No, don't make it angry!"

"I'm fed up! Stop this! Go away! Leave us alone!"

"What good is it to break the chair and smash the room!"

"No good. Nothing does any good. Go, get the children, take them out into the garden. I'll call a taxi. We'll go to your sister's house."

"They don't have room."

"For tonight they have room. Not another night in this evil place."

ANGLES

3000

Hakira examined the contract, and it seemed simple enough. Passage for the entire membership of Kotoshi, if they assembled at their own expense. Free return for up to ten days, but only only at the end of the ten days, as a single group. There would be no refund for those who returned. But all that seemed fair enough, especially since the price was not exorbitant.

"Of course this contract isn't binding anyway," said Hakira. "How could it be enforced? This whole passage is illegal."

"Not in the target world, it isn't," said Moshe. "And that's where it would have to be enforced, nu?"

"It's not as if I can find a lawyer from that world to represent my interests now."

"It makes no sense for me to have dissatisfied customers."

"How do I know you won't just strand us there?" said Hakira. "It might not even be a world with a breathable atmosphere—a lot of angles are still mostly hydrocarbon gas, with no free oxygen at all."

"Didn't I tell you? I go with you. In fact, I have to—I'm the one who brings you through."

"Brings us? Don't you just put us in a bender and—"

"Bender!" Moshe laughed. "Those primitive machines? No wonder the near worlds are never found—benders can't make the fine distinctions that *we* make. No, I take you through. We go together."

"What, we all join hands and . . . you're serious. Why are you wasting my time with mumbo jumbo like this!"

"If it's mumbo jumbo, then we'll all hold hands and

nothing will happen, and you'll get your money back. Right?" Moshe spread his hands. "What do you have to lose!"

"It feels like a scam."

"Then leave. You came to me, remember?"

"Because you got that group of Zionists through."

"Exactly my point," said Moshe. "I took them through. I came back, they didn't—because they were absolutely satisfied. They're in a world where Israel was never conquered by the surrounding Arab states so Jews still have their own Hebrew-speaking state. The same world, I might add, where Japan is still populated by self-governing Japanese."

"What's the catch?"

"No catch. Except that we use a different mechanism that is not approved by the government and so we have to do it under the table."

"But why does the *other* world allow it?" asked Hakira. "Why do they let you bring people in?"

"This is a rescue," said Moshe. "They bring you in as refugees from an unbearable reality. They bring you *home*. The government of Israel in that reality, as a matter of policy, declares that Jews have a right to return—even Jews from a different angle. And the government of Japan recently decided to offer the same privilege to you."

"It's still so hard to believe that anyone found a populated world that has Japanese at all."

"Well, isn't it obvious?" said Moshe. "Nobody *found* that world."

"What do you mean?"

"That world found *us*."

Hakira thought about it for a moment. "That's why

they don't use benders, they have their own technology for re-slanting from angle to angle."

"Exactly right, except for your use of the word 'they.'"

And now Hakira understood. "Not they. You. You're not from this world. You're one of them."

"When we discovered your tragic world, I was sent to bring Jews home to Israel. And when we realized that the Japanese suffered a similar tragic loss, the decision was made to extend the offer to you. Hakira, bring your people home."

2024—ANGLE 1

"I told them I didn't want to see you."

"I know."

"I was sitting there playing cards and suddenly I'm almost killed!"

"It never happened that way before. The chair usually just . . . slid. Or sometimes floated."

"It was smashed to bits! I had a concussion, it's taken ten stitches, I'll have this scar on my face for the rest of my life!"

"But I didn't do it, I didn't know it would happen that way. How could I? There were no wires, you know that. You *saw*."

"Nossa. Yes. I saw. But it's not a ghost."

"I never said it was. I don't believe in ghosts."

"What, then?"

"I don't know. Everything else I think of sounds like fantasy. But then, telephones and satellite tv and movies and submarines once sounded like fantasy to anyone who thought of such ideas. And in this case, there've been stories of ghosts and hauntings and poltergeists since . . . since the beginning of time, I imagine. Only they're rare. So rare that they don't often happen to scientists."

"In the history of the world, real scientists are rarer than poltergeists."

"And if such things *did* happen to a scientist, how many of them might have done as you urged me to do—ignore it. Pretend it was a hallucination. Move to another place where such things don't happen. And the scientists who refuse to blind their eyes to the evidence before them—what happens to them? I'll tell you what happens, because I've found seven of them in the past two hundred years—which isn't a lot, but these are the ones who published what happened to them. And in every case, they were immediately discredited as scientists. No one listened to them any more. Their careers were over. The ones who taught lost tenure at their universities. Three of them were committed to mental institutions. And *not once* did anyone else seriously investigate their claims. Except, of course, the people who are already considered to be completely bobo, the paranormalists, the regular batch of fakers and hucksters."

"And the same thing will happen to you."

"No. Because I have you as a witness."

"What kind of witness am I? I was *hit in the head*. Do you understand? I was in the hospital, delirious, concussive, and I have the scar on my face to prove it. No one will believe me either. Some will even wonder if you didn't beat me into agreeing to testify for you!"

"Ah, Leonard. God help me, but you're right."

"Call an exorcist."

"I'm a scientist! I don't want it to go away! I want to understand it!"

"So, Bêto, scientist, explain it to me. If it isn't a ghost to be exorcised, what is it?"

"A parallel world. No, listen, listen to me! Maybe in the empty spaces between atoms, or even the empty spaces within atoms, there are other atoms we can't detect most of the time. An infinite number of them, some very close to ours, some very far. And suppose that when you enclose a space, and somebody in one of those infinite parallel universes encloses the *same* space, it can cause just the slightest bit of material overlap."

"You mean there's something magic about boxes? Come on."

"You asked for possibilities! But if the landforms are similar, then the places where towns are built would be similar, too. The confluence of rivers. Harbors. Good farmland. People in many universes would be building towns in the same places. Houses. All it takes is one room that overlaps, and suddenly you get echoes between worlds. You get a single chair that exists in both worlds at once."

"What, somebody in our world goes and buys a chair and somebody in the other world happens to go and buy the same one on the same day?"

"No. I moved into the house, that chair was already there. Haunted houses are always old, aren't they? Old furniture. It's been there long enough, undisturbed, for the chair to have spilled a little and exist in both worlds. So . . . you take the chair and put it on top of the door, and the people in the other world come home and find the chair has been moved—maybe they even *saw* it move—and he's fed up, he's furious, he *smashes the chair*."

"Ludicrous."

"Well, *something* happened, and you have the scar to prove it."

"And you have the chair fragments."

"Well, no."

"What! You threw them out?"

"My best guess is that *they* threw them out. Or else, I don't know, when the chair lost its structure, the echo faded. Anyway, the pieces are gone."

"No evidence. That clinches it. If you publish this I'll deny it, Bêto."

"No you won't."

"I will. I've already had my face damaged. I'm not going to let you shatter my career as well. Bêto, drop it!"

"I can't! This is too important! Science can't continue to refuse to look at this and find out what's really going on!"

"Yes it can! Scientists regularly refuse to look at all kinds of things because it would be bad for their careers to see them! You know it's true!"

"Yes. I know it's true. Scientists can be blind. But *not me*. And not you either, Leonard. When I publish this, I know you'll tell the truth."

"If you publish this, I'll know you're crazy. So when people ask me, I'll tell them the truth—that you're crazy. The chair is gone now anyway. Chances are this will never happen again. In five years you'll come to think of it as a weird hallucination."

"A weird hallucination that left you scarred for life."

"Go away, Bêto. Leave me alone."

2186

"I call it the Angler, and using it is called Angling."

"It looks expensive."

"It is."

"Too expensive to sell it as a toy."

"It's not for children anyway. Look, it's expensive because it's really high-tech, but that's a plus, and the more popular it becomes, the more the per-unit cost will drop. We've studied the price point and we think we're right on this."

"OK, fine, what does it do."

"I'll show you. Put on this cap and—"

"I certainly will *not!* Not until you tell me what it does."

"Sure, I understand, no problem. What it does is, it puts you into someone else's head."

"Oh, it's just a Dreamer, those have been around for years, they had their vogue but—"

"No, not a Dreamer. True, we do use the old Dreamer technology as the playback system, because why reinvent the wheel? We were able to license it for a song, so why not? But the thing that makes this special is this—the recording system."

"Recording?"

"You know about slantspace, right?"

"That's all theoretical games."

"Not really just theoretical. I mean, it's well known that our brains store memory in slantspace, right?"

"Sure, yeah. I knew that."

"Well, see, here's the thing. There's an infinite number of different universes that have a lot of their matter coterminous with ours—"

"Here it comes, engineer talk, we can't sell engineering babble."

"There are people in these other worlds. Like ghosts. They wander around, and *their* memories are stored in *our* world."

"Where?"

"Just sitting there in the air. Just a collection of angles. Wherever their head is, in our world and a lot of other parallel worlds, they have their memories stored as a pattern of slants. Haven't you had the experience of walking into a room and then suddenly you can't remember why you came in?"

"I'm seventy years old, it happens all the time."

"It has nothing to do with being seventy. It happened when you were young, too. Only you're more susceptible now, because your own brain has so much memory stored that it's constantly accessing other slants. And sometimes, your head space passes through the head space of someone else in another world, and poof, your thoughts are confused—jammed, really—by theirs."

"My head just happens to pass through the space where the other guy's head just *happens* to be?"

"In an infinite series of universes, there are a lot of them where people about your height might be walking around. What makes it so rare is that most of them are using patterns of slants so different that they barely impinge on ours at all. And you have to be accessing memory right at that moment, too. Anyway, that's not what matters—that *is* coincidence. But you set up this recorder here at about the height of a human being and turn it on, and as long as you don't put it, say, on the thirtieth floor or the bottom of a lake or something, within a day you'll have this thing filled up."

"With what?"

"Up to twenty separate memory states. We could build it to hold a lot more, but it's so easy to erase and replace that we figured twenty was enough and if people want more, we can sell peripherals, right? Anyway, you get these transitory brain states. Memories. And it's the whole package, the complete mental state of another human being for one moment in time. Not a dream. Not *fictionalized*, you know? Those dreams, they were sketchy, haphazard, pretty meaningless. I mean, it's boring to hear other people *tell* their dreams, how cool is it to actually have to sit through them? But with the Angler, you catch the whole fish. You've got to put it on, though, to know why it's going to sell."

"And it's nothing permanent."

"Well, it's permanent in the sense that you'll remember it, and it'll be a pretty strong memory. But you know, you'll *want* to remember it so that's a good thing. It doesn't damage anything, though, and that's all that matters. I can try it on one of your employees first, though, if you want. Or I'll put it on myself."

"No, I'll do it. I'll have to do it in the end before I'll make the decision, so I might as well do it from the start. Put on the cap. And no, it's not a toupee, if I were going to get a rug I'd choose a better one than this."

"All right, a snug fit, but that's why we made it elastic."

"How long does it take?"

"Objective time, only a fraction of a second. Subjectively, of course, well, you tell *us*. Ready?"

"Sure. Give me a one, two, three, all right?"

"I'll do one, two, three, and then flip it like four. OK?"

"Yeah yeah. Do it."

"One. Two. Three."

"Ah . . . aaah. Oh."

"Give it a few seconds. Just relax. It's pretty strong."

"You didn't . . . how could this . . . I . . ."

"It's all right to cry. Don't worry. First time, most people do."

"I was just . . . She's just . . . I was a *woman*."

"Fifty-fifty chance."

"I never knew how it felt to . . . This should be illegal."

"Technically, it falls under the same laws as the Dreamer, so, you know, not for children and all that."

"I don't know if I'd ever want to use it again. It's so strong."

"Give yourself a few days to sort it out, and you'll want it. You know you will."

"Yes. No, don't try to push any paperwork on me right now, I'm not an idiot. I'm not signing anything while my head's so . . . but . . . tomorrow. Come back tomorrow. Let me sleep on it."

"Of course. We couldn't ask for anything more than that."

"Have you shown this to anyone else?"

"You're the biggest and the best. We came to you first."

"We're talking exclusive, right?"

"Well, as exclusive as our patents allow."

"What do you mean?"

"We've patented every method we've thought of, but we think there are a lot of ways to record in slantspace. In fact, the real trouble is, the hardest thing is to design a record that doesn't bend space on the other side. I mean, people's heads won't go through the recording field if the recorder itself is visible in their space! What I'm saying is, we'll be exclusive until somebody finds another way to do it without infringing our patent. That'll take years, of course, but ..."

"How many years?"

"No faster than three, and probably longer. And we can tie them up in court longer still."

"Look at me, I'm still shaking. Can you play me the same memory?"

"We could build a machine that would do that, but you won't want to. The first time with each one is the best. Doing the same person twice can leave you a little ... confused."

"Bring me the paperwork tomorrow for an exclusive for five years. We'll launch with enough product to drop that price point from the start."

3001

It took a month for the members of Kotoshi to assemble. Only a few decided not to go, and they took a vow of silence to protect those who were leaving. They gathered at the southern tip of Manhattan, in the parlor of Moshe's house. They had no belongings with them.

"It's one of the unfortunate side effects of the technology we use," Moshe explained. "Nothing that is not organically connected to your bodies can make the transition to the new slant. As when you were born, you will be naked when you arrive. That's why wholesale colonization using this technology is impractical—no tools. Nor can you transfer any kind of wealth or art. You come empty-handed."

"Is it cold there?"

"The climate is different," said Moshe. "You'll arrive on the southern tip of Manhattan, and it will be winter but there are no glaciers closer than Greenland. Anyway you'll arrive indoors. I live in this house and use it for transition because there is a coterminous room in the other angle. Nothing to fret about."

Hakira looked for the technology that would transfer them. Moshe had spoken of this room. Perhaps it was much larger than bender technology, and had been embedded in the walls of the room.

Yet if they could not bring anything with them that wasn't part of their bodies, Moshe's people must have built their machinery here instead of importing it. Yet if they hadn't brought wealth, how had Moshe obtained the money to buy this house, let alone manufacture their slant-changing machinery? Interesting puzzles.

Of course, there were two obvious solutions. The first would be a disappointment, but it was the most predictable—that it was all fakery and Moshe would try to abscond with their money without having taken them anywhere at all. There was always the danger that part of the scam was killing those who were supposed to be transported so that there'd be no one left to complain. Foreseeing that, Hakira and the others were alert and prepared.

The other possibility, though, was the one that made Hakira's spine tingle. Theoretically, since slant-shifting had first been discovered as a natural function of the human brain, there was always the chance of nonmechanical transfer between angles. One of the main objections to this idea had always been that if it were possible, all the worlds should be getting constant visits from any that had learned how to transfer by mental

412

wer alone. The common answer to that was, How do
u know they *aren't* constantly visiting? Some even
eculated that sightings of ghosts might well be of peo-
e coming or going. But Moshe's warning about arriving
de would explain quite nicely why there hadn't been
ore visits. It's hard to be subtle about being nude in
ost human cultures.

"Do any of you," asked Moshe, "have any embedded
etal or plastic in your bodies? This includes fillings in
ur teeth, but would also include metal plates or silicon
int replacements, heart pacemakers, non-tissue breast
plants, and, of course, eyeglasses. I can assure you that
quickly as possible, all these items will be replaced, ex-
pt for pacemakers, of course, if you have a pacemaker
u're simply not going."

"What happens if we *do* have some kind of implant?"
ked one of the men.

"Nothing painful. No wound. It simple doesn't go with
u. It remains here. The effect on you is as if it simply
sappeared. And, of course, the objects would remain
re, hanging in the air, and then fall to the ground—or
e chair, since most of you will be sitting. But to tell the
uth, that's the least of my problems—part of your fee
es to cleaning up this room, since the contents of your
wels also remain behind."

Several people grimaced.

"As I said, *you'll* never notice, except you might feel a
t lighter and more vigorous. It's like having the perfect
ema. And, no matter how nervous you are, you won't
ed to urinate for some time. Well now, are we ready?
nyone want to step outside after all?"

No one left.

"Well, this couldn't be simpler. You must join hands,

413

bare hands, skin to skin. Connect tightly, the whole circl
no one left out."

Hakira couldn't help but chuckle.

"Hakira is laughing," said Moshe, "because he mock
ingly suggested that maybe our method of transfer wa
some kind of mumbo jumbo involving all joining hand
Well, he was right. Only this happens to be mumb
jumbo that works."

We'll see, won't we? thought Hakira.

In moments, all their hands were joined.

"Hold your hands up, so I can see," said Moshe. "Goo
good. All right. Absolute silence, please."

"A moment first," said Hakira. To the others, he sai
softly, "Nippon, this year."

With fierce smiles or no expression at all, the othe
murmured in reply, "Fujiyama kotoshi."

It was done. Hakira turned to Moshe and nodded.

They bowed their heads and made no sound, beyon
the unavoidable sound of breathing. And an occasion
sniffle—they *had* just come in from the cold.

One man coughed. Several people glared at him. Othe
simply closed their eyes, meditating their way to silence.

Hakira never took his eyes from Moshe, watching fo
some kind of signal to a hidden confederate, or perhap
for him to activate some machinery that might fill th
room with poison gas. But . . . nothing.

Two minutes. Three. Four.

And then the room disappeared and a cold wind ble
across forty naked bodies. They were in the open air in
side a high fence, and around them in a circle stood me
with swords.

Swords.

Everything was clear now.

"Well," said Moshe cheerfully, letting go and stepping back to join the armed men. One of them had a long coat for him, which he put on and wrapped around himself. "The transfer worked just as I told you it would—you're naked, there was no machinery involved, and don't you feel vigorous?"

Neither Hakira nor any of the people of Kotoshi said a thing.

"I did lie about a few things," said Moshe. "You see, we stumbled upon what you call 'slanting' at a much more primitive stage in our technological development than you. And wherever we went that wasn't downright fatal, and that wasn't already fully inhabited, there you were! Already overpopulating every world we could find! We had come upon the technique too late. So, we've come recruiting. If we're to have a chance at defeating you and your kind so we have a decent chance of finding worlds to expand into, we need to learn how to use your technology. How to use your weapons, how to disable your power system, how to make your ordinary citizens helpless. Since our technology is far behind yours, and we couldn't carry technology from world to world anyway, the way you can, this was our only choice."

Still no one answered him.

"You are taking this very calmly—good. The previous group was full of complainers, arguing with us and complaining about the weather even though it's *much* colder this time. That first group was very valuable—we've learned many medical breakthroughs from them, for instance, and many people are learning how to drive cars and how to use credit and even the theory behind computer programming. But you—well, I know it's a racial stereotype, but not only are you Japanese every bit as educated as the Jews from the previous group, you tend to be educated in mathematics and technology instead of medicine, law, and scripture. So from you we hope to learn many valuable things that will prepare us to take over one of your colonies and use it as a springboard to future conquest. Isn't it nice to know how valuable and important you are?"

One of the swordsmen let rip a string of sounds from another language. Moshe answered in the same language. "My friend comments that you seem to be taking this news extremely well."

"Only a few points of clarification are needed," said Hakira. "You are, in fact, planning to keep us as slaves?"

"Allies," said Moshe. "Helpers. Teachers."

"Not slaves. We are free to go, then? To return home if we wish?"

"No, I regret not."

"Are we free not to cooperate with you?"

"You will find your lives are much more comfortable if you cooperate."

"Will we be taught this mental method of transferring from angle to angle?"

Moshe laughed. "Please, you are too humorous."

"Is this a global policy on your world, or are you representing only one government or perhaps a small group not responsible to any government?"

"There is one government on this world, and we represent its policy," said Moshe. "It is only in the area of technology that we are not as advanced as you. We gave up tribes and nations thousands of years ago."

Hakira looked around at the others in his group. "Any other questions? Have we settled everything?"

Of course it was just a legal formality. He knew perfectly well that they were now free to act. This was, in fact, almost the worst-case scenario. No clothing, no weapons, cold weather, surrounded. But that was why they trained for the worst case. At least there were no guns, and they were outdoors.

"Moshe, I arrest you and all the armed persons present in this compound and charge you with wrongful imprisonment, slavery, fraud, and—"

Moshe shook his head and gave a brief command to the swordsmen. At once they raised their weapons and advanced on Hakira's group.

It took only moments for the nude Japanese to sidestep the swords, disarm the swordsmen, and leave them prostrate on the ground, their own swords now pointed at their throats. The Japanese who were not involved in that task quickly scoured the compound for more weapons and located the clumsy old-fashioned keys that would open the gate. Within moments they had run down and captured those guards who had been outside the gates. Not one got away. Only two had even attempted to fight. They were, as a result, dead.

To Moshe, Hakira said, "I now add the charge of assault and attempted murder."

"You'll never get back to your own world," said Moshe.

"We each have the complete knowledge necessary to make our own bender out of whatever materials we find here. We are also quite prepared to take on any military force you send against us, or to flee, if necessary. Even if we have to travel, we have *you*. The real question is whether we will learn the secret of mental reslanting from you before or after we build a bender for ourselves. I can promise you considerable lenience from the courts if you cooperate."

"Never."

"Oh, well. Someone else will."

"How did you know?" demanded Moshe.

"There is no world but ours with Japanese in it. Or Jews. None of the inhabited worlds have had cultures or languages or civilizations or histories that resembled each other in any way. We knew you were a con man, but we also knew the Zionists were gone without a trace. We also knew that someday we'd have to face people from another angle who had learned how to reslant themselves. We trained very carefully, and we followed you home."

"Like stray mongrels," said Moshe.

"Oh, and we do have to be told where the previous batch of slaves are being kept—the Zionists you kidnaped before."

"They'll all be killed," said Moshe nastily.

"That would be such a shame for you," said Hakira. He beckoned to one of his men, now armed with a sharp sword. In Japanese, he told his comrade that unfortunately, Moshe needed a demonstration of their relentless determination.

At once the sword flicked out and the tip of Moshe's nose dropped to the ground. The sword flicked again, and now Moshe lost the tip of the longest finger of the hand that he had been raising to touch his maimed nose.

Hakira bent over and scooped up the nose and the fingertip. "I'd say that if we get back to our world within about three hours, surgeons will be able to put these back on with only the tiniest scar and very little loss of function. Or shall we delay longer, and sever more protruding body parts?"

"This is inhuman!" said Moshe.

"On the contrary," said Hakira. "This is about as human as it gets."

"Are the people of your angle so determined to control every world you find?"

"Not at all," said Hakira. "We never interfered with any world that already had human life. You're the ones who decided on war. And I must say I'm relieved that the general level of your technology turns out to be so low. And that wherever you go, you arrive naked."

Moshe said nothing. His eyes glazed over.

Hakira murmured to his friend with the sword. The point of it quickly rested against the tender flesh just under Moshe's jaw.

Moshe's eyes grew quite alert.

"Don't even think of slanting away from us," said Hakira.

"I am the only one who speaks your language," said Moshe. "You have to sleep sometime. *I* have to sleep sometime. How will you know whether I'm really asleep, or merely meditating before I transfer?"

"Take a thumb," said Hakira. "And this time, let's make him swallow it."

Moshe gulped. "What sort of vengeance will you take against my people?"

"Apart from fair trials for the perpetrators of this conspiracy, we'll establish an irresistible presence here, watch you very carefully, and conduct such trade as we think appropriate. You yourself will be judged according to your cooperation now. Come on, Moshe, save some time. Take me back to my world. A bender is already being set up at your house—the troops moved in the moment we disappeared. You know that it's just a matter of time before they identify this angle and arrive in force no matter what you do."

"I could take you anywhere," said Moshe.

"And no doubt you're threatening to take me to some world with unbreathable air because you're willing to die for your cause. I understand that, I'm willing to die for mine. But if I'm not back here in ten minutes, my men will slaughter yours and begin the systematic destruction of your world. It's our only defense, if you don't cooperate. Believe me, the best way to save your world is by doing what I say."

"Maybe I hate you more than I love my people," said Moshe.

"What you love is our technology, Moshe, every bit of it. Come with me now and you'll be the hero who brings all those wonderful toys home."

"You'll put my finger and nose back on?"

"In my world the year is 3001," said Hakira. "We'll put them on you wherever you want them, and give you spares just in case."

"Let's go," said Moshe.

He took Hakira's hand and closed his eyes.